Praise for

Penned
The Fourth Kate Turner, DVM Mystery

"Animal lovers won't mind that the mystery solving takes a back seat to a wealth of fascinating pet lore, including how to clip a cockatoo's toenails and the proper method for tick removal."

—*Publishers Weekly*

"Veterinarian Brady imbues this page-turner with authentic details about a vet and the critters she treats."

—*Kirkus Reviews*

"The fourth book in the veterinary sleuth series by Eileen Brady, *Penned,* is a nice mix of cozy and semi-hardboiled elements, which is one of my favorite kinds of books to read. I am happy to say I was completely wrong about the killer's identity. *Penned* was a very enjoyable read on every level."

—*Mystery Scene Magazine*

Chained
The Third Kate Turner, DVM Mystery

"The discovery of the remains of Flynn Keegan, who everyone in Oak Falls, NY, assumed left for Hollywood after graduating from high school a decade earlier, propels Brady's well-crafted third Kate Turner mystery…

As Kate's digging turns up more secrets and long-buried lies, she has too many suspects and too little evidence. But when a high school classmate of Flynn's is murdered, Kate knows she's both perilously close to the truth and in grave danger. Brady keeps the suspense high through the surprising ending."

—*Publishers Weekly*

"A client's chance encounter with a bone involves veterinarian Kate Turner in yet another murder case in the beautiful but apparently not so peaceful Hudson Valley town of Oak Falls... Brady's years of experience as a veterinarian supply plenty of amusing stories and helpful hints for animal owners while her complicated heroine investigates a tricky case."

—*Kirkus Reviews*

Unleashed
The Second Kate Turner, DVM Mystery

"Brady's sophomore effort is an appealing mix of murder and medicine. Kate is an amiable heroine with lots of spunk. Not willing to leave well enough alone, she joins the list of cozy amateur sleuths such as Laura Childs's Theodosia Browning and Jane Cleland's Josie Prescott."

—*Library Journal*

"In Brady's amusing, well-plotted second Kate Turner mystery, the Oak Falls, NY, veterinarian investigates the death of Claire Birnham, whose Cairn terrier was treated at the local veterinary hospital. Claire appears to have committed suicide, but it begins to look like a case of foul play after various pet owners reveal details about the woman's life... Turner treats a pot-bellied pig and a smelly cocker spaniel, besides getting chased by a flock of geese. Readers will eagerly look forward to Kate's further adventures."

—*Publishers Weekly*

"Now that curiosity has killed the cat, will it kill the veterinarian... Kate's second is a treat for animal lovers. The plethora of suspects keeps you guessing."

—*Kirkus Reviews*

Muzzled
The First Kate Turner, DVM Mystery

"Here is a novel written with exacting authority, along with a frolicking sense of humor about life, animals, and the lengths to which someone will go to right a wrong, all while still maintaining a solid sense of tension and suspense. I look forward to future mysteries featuring the charismatic Dr. Kate Turner...and I'm sure you will, too!"

—James Rollins, *New York Times* bestselling author

"*Muzzled* is an enjoyable read for both the light mystery fan and the dog lover, and if they are one and the same, it's a double delight."

—*New York Journal of Books*

"Readers will want to see more of the likable Kate, who, as she snoops and doctors, provides an inside look at quirky pet owners and the oft-satirized dog show set (shoe polish shines a nose!). She even imparts wisdom on such matters as clipping parrot toenails and the importance of doggie weight loss diets."

—*Publishers Weekly*

"Kate's debut has plenty to offer pet lovers and mystery mavens alike."

—*Kirkus Reviews*

"A delightful and lively mystery that introduces Kate Turner, a veterinarian with heart, humor, and a new penchant for solving murders. A promising first novel that will leave readers begging for more."

—Earlene Fowler, Agatha Award–winning author of the Benni Harper series

Also by Eileen Brady

Penned
Chained
Unleashed
Muzzled

Saddled *with* MURDER

Saddled *with* MURDER

A DR. KATE VET MYSTERY

EILEEN BRADY

Poisoned Pen
PRESS

Copyright © 2020 by Eileen Brady
Cover and internal design © 2020 by Sourcebooks
Cover design by Heather Morris/Sourcebooks
Cover illustration by Brandon Dorman/Peter Lott & Associates

Sourcebooks, Poisoned Pen Press, and the colophon
are registered trademarks of Sourcebooks.

All rights reserved. No part of this book may be reproduced in
any form or by any electronic or mechanical means including
information storage and retrieval systems—except in the case of
brief quotations embodied in critical articles or reviews—without
permission in writing from its publisher, Sourcebooks.

The characters and events portrayed in this book are fictitious or are used
fictitiously. Apart from well-known historical figures, any similarity to real
persons, living or dead, is purely coincidental and not intended by the author.

Published by Poisoned Pen Press, an imprint of Sourcebooks
P.O. Box 4410, Naperville, Illinois 60567-4410
(630) 961-3900
sourcebooks.com

Library of Congress Cataloging-in-Publication Data
Names: Brady, Eileen (Veterinarian), author.
Title: Saddled with murder / Eileen Brady.
Description: Naperville, Illinois : Poisoned Pen Press, [2020] | Series: A
    Dr. Kate vet mystery ; 5
Identifiers: LCCN 2020003606 | (paperback)
Subjects: GSAFD: Mystery fiction.
Classification: LCC PS3602.R34294 S23 2020 | DDC 813/.6--dc23
LC record available at https://lccn.loc.gov/2020003606

Printed and bound in Canada.
MBP 10 9 8 7 6 5 4 3 2 1

To our beautiful Emily. Keep dancing on those tables—
no matter what they tell you.

"Whoever said a horse was dumb, was dumb."
　　　　　　　　　　　　　　　　—Will Rogers

"No matter how much cats fight, there always seem to be plenty of kittens."
　　　　　　　　　　　　　　　　—Abraham Lincoln

Prologue

A WISH CAN BE MANY THINGS: OPTIMISTIC, GREEDY, OR a simple request for a favor from the vast unknown. We look up to the heavens when we wish.

Some of us look down.

Three wishes made in jest might bring three presents to Dr. Kate Turner, a bit of cheer during the holiday season. Of course, you can't wrap dead bodies in red and gold Christmas paper and shove them under the tree—but it's the thought that counts.

A simple card would have to do.

Gossip will run rampant if the wishes come true. So easy to drop a hint here, a confusing lie there—sprinkling suspicion in the streets of Oak Falls like dirty snowflakes.

Always show the world a normal face, but under the surface something dark lurked, tightly tied and bound by societal expectations. Kept in check.

Time to set it free.

Chapter One

"WHO WANTS A SLICE OF LITTER BOX CAKE?"

With that provocative question the Oak Falls Animal Hospital Christmas party shifted into overdrive. It was Friday afternoon, the weekend awaited, and bonuses were being given out along with presents from a Secret Santa. The staff laughed and noisily lined up for a taste of this ever-popular veterinary and/or Halloween treat.

Only weeks before Christmas, and outside the Hudson Valley glimmered with a soft layer of snow. The blue-gray mountains, their dark green pine trees dusted in white, resembled greeting cards, and the village of Oak Falls took advantage of it. Lushly festive decorations evoked a storybook feeling meant to entice tourists to enter the stores and buy buy buy. It was impossible to escape the relentless cheeriness.

This time of the year I morphed from Dr. Kate Turner, friendly veterinarian, to grumpy Dr. Kate Scrooge. The music, the decorations brought back difficult memories. Just before Christmas, the year I turned fifteen, my mom and brother, Jimmy, were killed in a hit-and-run accident. My father and I didn't deal well with our tragedy. I embraced anger, and he embraced another woman. The Christmas tree stayed in the house, all the presents wrapped but untouched, until February, the following year, when Gramps came and took it down.

"Come on, Dr. Kate," my cheery office manager/

receptionist Cindy said, waving a red paper plate. "Dig in. You know you're dying to try it."

Putting away my own thoughts and knowing that tasting this mess was inevitable, I plastered a smile on my face and stood up. The treatment room, the hub of the animal hospital, glittered and glowed with twinkling Christmas lights shaped like dogs and cats. A silver garland composed of hundreds of tiny reindeers draped over the IV stands and hung pushpinned around the windows. Jolly holly Christmas music poured out of the hospital sound system inviting all to sing along.

The infamous litter box cake rested on a Santa-and-his-elves-themed tablecloth, which covered our stainless-steel table, making it as festive as stainless steel can be. The baker, my technician, Mari, had strived for realism—succeeding beyond her wildest nightmares. Tootsie Rolls and Baby Ruth bars starred as the cat poop, while some kind of granular sugar/graham cracker mix stood in for the litter. A partially melted piece of chocolate artistically draped over the side of the litter box represented the kitty that—"oops"—had missed the mark.

And, yes, she had transferred the "cake" into a real litter box, complete with plastic liner, uncomfortably close to the ones we actually used.

"You've outdone yourself," I told Mari. "Now, if only you had buried a tiny Santa Claus surprise in the middle of this…masterpiece."

Cindy raised a carefully enhanced eyebrow while she thought about that comment but proceeded to cut the cake to the delight of the group and present me with the first piece. "To your first Christmas in Oak Falls, Dr. Kate. Ice cream?"

"Why not?" I slid the red paper plate with my generous portion toward her. "What flavors do you have?"

"Only one. I made it myself in our ice cream machine."

When she paused I knew something was up.

Wondering how you top a litter box cake, I asked, "What flavor did you make?"

"Reindeer Crunch."

Score one for Cindy. Medical humor across the board is pretty strange to outsiders, but it helps defuse what can often be a stressful job. "I hope no reindeer were injured in the making of this ice cream."

Mari, busy capturing the fun with her phone, said, "All reindeer are present and accounted for. It's a blend of milk chocolate, which stands for their coats, with vanilla-and-dark-chocolate-covered wafers mixed in to resemble their hooves. Oh, and a couple of Red Hots. They help blast you to the North Pole."

"They sure do," chimed in our kennel helper Tony, always ready with a comment.

"Are the Red Hots an homage to Rudolph's nose?"

"You've got it, Doc."

As soon as I returned to my seat, I tasted an overloaded forkful of litter box cake topped with melted Tootsie Rolls and Reindeer Crunch.

It was delicious.

Thirty minutes later with everyone well fed, the party started winding down. Cindy updated me on two angry clients, one of whom refused to pay his bill. Mari and Greta, the shy intern, were comparing notes while Tony explained something, complete with hand gestures, to the new kennel worker. At the back of the room next to a bank of cages sat our next-door neighbor and snow-plow guy, Pinky Anderson. Pinky had brought his senior citizen dog Princess in to see me several times, but today he'd come in to talk about the holiday plowing schedule. Cindy insisted he stay for the party. Our hospital cat, Mr. Cat, meanwhile, managed to dislodge the red bow scotch-taped to his collar. No attempt to dress him up withstood the power of his claws. Terribly annoyed, he parked him-self under an IV stand festooned with a loop of sparkly garland and vigorously began to groom his fluffy tail.

I jumped up and stashed the bow in my pocket just as Cindy announced it was Secret Santa time.

Blond-haired, blue-eyed Cindy had been a cheer-leader in high school, and you could tell. Her genuine upbeat attitude made her popular with both clients and staff. Today she wore what she called her traditional ugly Christmas sweater, an explosion of badly knit reindeer and lumpy trees with an unintentionally evil-looking Santa suggestively nestled over her chest.

Almost all the staff were here, including our perennial student, Tony Papadapolis, along with a new part-time kennel helper, Aaron Keenan, and college intern, Greta Weber.

Mari scrambled up to the front to help clear the

empty pizza boxes, jingling as she walked, thanks to the two dog collars she'd woven around her neck. She shot an evil eye at her personal nemesis, Tony, who merely turned his back.

I'd forgotten what they were feuding about at the moment.

Before exchanging the presents, Cindy insisted on playing a holiday game. "Well, it's not exactly a game," she said, qualifying her statement. "There's no prize." She clapped her hands to get our attention. "Everyone has to reveal their secret selfish holiday wish." Mari raised her hand with the inevitable question that went ignored.

"And no peace on earth or anything like that. Your wish has to be down and dirty, and it has to involve the animal hospital."

"What if you don't have one?" asked the somewhat shy Greta, sounding worried she might offend someone.

Cindy smoothed down the front of her sweater, inadvertently rubbing Santa the wrong way. "Just try. It will be fun."

"We all have selfish wishes," good-looking Tony piped up. "I'll go first if you want."

Dead silence confirmed that no one else wanted to start.

"Okay. I wish that all the dogs in the kennel," he paused dramatically, confident in front of the group, "took self-cleaning poops that smelled like roses."

A round of cheers greeted his statement, since everyone knew how often he complained about his cleaning duties.

"Good one," acknowledged Mari. "Next? Cindy? Come on, you started this."

Cindy immediately accepted the challenge. "I know it's selfish, but I wish the parking space next to the front door had my name on it." With that she covered her face with her hands, embarrassed.

"Maybe we can arrange that," I announced and stood up. "Presto." I waved a pretend magic wand. "The first space to the left along the sidewalk will be reserved for Cindy."

Everyone clapped.

"What about you, Dr. Turner?" our pre-vet student asked.

"Yeah," seconded Tony.

"Wait a minute. Let me record this for posterity." My assistant stood up and began to scan the room with her phone.

"Well," I began, definitely feeling on a sugar high, between the cake and the ice cream. "Since I have my magic wand out already," I lifted my finger in the air, "I wish that two dissatisfied clients of mine...who will remain anonymous..."

Mari loudly interrupted by shouting out, "Frank Martindale and Eloise Rieven."

"And Raeleen Lassitor," added a voice from the back of the room.

I should have stopped there, but I didn't. Instead, with arm raised and magic index finger pointed, I continued. "I wish that my Secret Selfish Santa would make them all...disappear." With that I drew a few circles in the air and cried, "Abracadabra, poof. They're gone."

Cindy clapped her hands, and Mari called out loud to me, "Well, we can all dream, can't we?"

―――――――――

Party over, Mari and I stayed to clean up and do treatments on Goober, a diabetic dog, and Fluffernutter, a rabbit whose nails and teeth we'd trimmed. Both were being discharged in the next half hour, leaving me with an empty hospital. After checking Goober's blood sugar, we fed him an early dinner, then administered his adjusted insulin dose.

"You surprised me today," Mari confessed as she cleaned the gray laminate countertops.

"What do you mean?" I was busy entering Goober's latest values into his chart and writing up instructions for his owners.

"Your wish."

My fingers paused over the keyboard. "I surprised myself, and not in a good way. Honestly, I don't know what or who possessed me. Maybe I should wish that wish would go away."

"It was a joke," Mari said. "Everyone knew it. You almost never complain about clients, so the universe owes you one."

"Two. Make that three, thanks to Pinky. What exactly was he doing here, do you know?"

She put the plastic covers over the microscopes. "He dropped by to talk about plowing schedules and some hole in the parking lot. Cindy felt sorry for him and invited him to stay for pizza and the cake. I mean he lives right next door."

"True."

"You know, Doc Anderson used to complain every week that his clients were driving him crazy."

"That's probably why he hired me and went on a round-the-world cruise." I finished up my notes and logged out.

"Well," Mari said. "I'm glad he did. If he hadn't, we wouldn't have met you."

"Ahhh. That's so nice. Thank you." A tiny piece of that icy grumpiness I secretly carried around started to melt. "Okay." I stood up next to the computer station. "That does it." Raising my hand, I enthusiastically swirled it around in the air then pointed my finger at my tech. "Abracadabra. I wish everything would go back to normal. There. My magic wand is hereby officially retired."

Chapter Two

ON MY WAY TO THE RECEPTION DESK THE NEXT DAY I heard the familiar voice of Frank Martindale complaining about his bill, his annoyed tone clashing with the sleigh bell music.

"I didn't authorize this test." The words grew even louder.

Hidden from sight in the pharmacy, I listened in.

"Frank," my receptionist, Cindy, replied patiently, "it's right here in the treatment estimate, like I told you before."

"Well, estimate doesn't mean you actually do it."

"That's exactly what it does mean. See, you signed it, giving us permission."

"No. I signed the estimate for the permission," he answered triumphantly.

The scope of that statement baffled me. When I'd first started treating Frank's cat weeks ago Cindy had warned me about him.

"Everyone in town knows good old Frank Martindale," she'd explained. "Half the town won't do business with him, they're so fed up. I can't tell you how many people he's taken to small claims court. He's always playing some kind of angle or get rich scheme. Listen, my older brother went to high school with him. Frank was a pain in the ass then, and he's a bigger pain in the ass now."

Safe in my pharmacy cubbyhole, I waited for Cindy's

response to that last convoluted statement but heard nothing. Instead, my phone vibrated with a text message. H E L P.

After a deep, cleansing breath, I strolled into reception. Cindy looked like steam might escape out of the top of her head. I deliberately headed toward her, the reception desk separating both of us from Frank. He had a tendency to spit out his words when he got worked up.

"Anything I can do to help?" I crossed my fingers and hoped he hadn't heard about the Secret Selfish Santa wish.

Dark, angry eyes punctuated by thick eyebrows stared into mine. In his late forties and about seventy pounds overweight, he vainly tried to disguise his receding hairline with a grayish-brown comb-over that seemed to have a weird life of its own.

"You charged me way too much, Doc," he said. "I never told you to do half of this stuff."

Both of us backed off a bit when Frank emphatically sprayed the word "stuff" at us.

"Mr. Martindale," I began, "all the tests I ran were necessary to diagnose your cat, Teddy. He has feline infectious anemia, a somewhat rare and complicated disease caused by a specific group of mycoplasma bacteria. Did you read the information I gave you?" My medical explanation fell on deaf ears.

"He just needs some red meat to build up his blood." Frank spoke with authority, although he was completely wrong.

"No. Your cat needs antibiotics to kill the parasites

in his blood, or he might die. Also, he needs to be kept indoors and away from other cats until he recovers, because his blood is contagious." This detail was important for Frank to understand. "Teddy probably was infected by an outdoor cat in your neighborhood."

He slammed his hand down on the countertop, his breathing heavy. "See, that's where you're wrong. I never let him go outside except to go to the bathroom." Frank wiggled a meaty finger at me, not seeing how illogical that statement was.

A glance over at Cindy, normally calm and able to handle any problem, made me suspect she'd like to bop him over the head with her copy of his bill.

Tired of arguing, I told Frank that Cindy and I would go over his charges, but he had to make sure to give his cat the prescribed medications. What I didn't say was that my sweet patient, Teddy, deserved a more compliant owner.

Of course, he wasn't finished yelling at us.

"I'm still angry," he reiterated, his face a blotchy red, "and I don't care who knows it. Old Doc Anderson sure never charged me like this." With that he stormed out and slammed the hospital entrance door behind him. The other people in the waiting room diplomatically looked down at their phones.

"That's because Doc Anderson made him pay cash," whispered Cindy. "I'm sure he's going to complain about us to everyone he can, and I'll bet those people in the waiting room are on Facebook as we speak. Two dissatisfied clients in two weeks, Kate. Merry Christmas."

"Please, don't remind me again," I pleaded.

"Where's your magic wand now?" Cindy added, getting in the last whispered word.

━━━━━━

That evening, as I sat in my cramped converted garage apartment attached to the hospital, I felt sorry for myself. Objectively, I went over both cases that had gone sour. Frank Martindale I dismissed, since his concern centered on money, not quality of care. The other, bulldog breeder Eloise Rieven, was another story.

Most people don't understand how unique bulldogs are. Although comically adorable, they have a wealth of physical problems, including difficulty mating and giving birth. Their physiology, the way they are built with huge heads, tiny nostrils, and short stubby legs can lead to breathing problems, heart disease, and other medical emergencies.

Artificial insemination is the norm for many female bulldogs. Knowing when to do it can be tricky. One of my old professors used to say the only one who knows when a bulldog is ready is an unaltered male dog. Not having access to the real thing, we were relying on the frozen one, and Eloise was convinced she knew more than I did. External signs and mucus smears would help me pinpoint when her dog was most fertile, but Eloise preferred to count from when Queenie went into heat. Since my employer, Doc Anderson, currently in some exotic locale enjoying himself, always did it her way, my back was up against the wall.

Headed for a showdown, the odds were stacked against me. Eloise had purchased only enough frozen sperm for two tries. Queenie, her prize bitch, had already produced three litters and was at pregnancy retirement age, in my opinion. Eloise felt Queenie was in her prime.

Although I tried once more to dissuade her, Mari and I were overruled by an increasingly irate Eloise, who insisted that her counting-days system was accurate. Even though my smears showed the dog wasn't ready, we were forced to go ahead. Queenie didn't conceive, and I had one mad customer on my hands.

That was two months ago. At day forty post-insemination, an ultrasound proved there were no puppies and instead indicated an enlarged liver. I strongly urged a medical work-up, but that further infuriated Eloise and she stormed out of our building—well, stormed out as fast as you can with a bulldog at your side. Cindy had received two nasty phone calls from her since then.

"Don't let those two crabapples get to you," Mari had told me. "Everyone else loves you."

Somehow that didn't make it feel any better.

———

The howling wind briefly woke me at two in the morning, before I fell back to sleep. A look out the window while drinking my first cup of coffee the next day showed at least three new inches of snow. Our parking lot, however, had been neatly plowed, thanks to our next-door neighbor, Pinky.

He always seemed to be looking after me.

Chapter Three

"READY," MARI SAID, HER CURLY DARK HAIR ESCAPING from a fuzzy hat. We'd just finished packing up our equipment in the hospital Ford 150 truck, preparing for a new day of house calls.

Before I went out to the parking lot, Cindy came in. "Great, you haven't left yet. Can you do me a favor?" our receptionist asked.

"Sure." In her hand was a small paper bag. "Is that for a patient?"

"Yes. You're going to drive right past his place, so if you can drop it off, it will save him a trip. He left it on the counter last time he was here."

Mari took it from her hand. "Do we need to go over how to dispense it?"

"Don't think so. The name and the address are on the bag."

"No problem. Anything else?" I took my stethoscope off the cabinet pull, where I'd left it, and checked my pockets to make sure I had my phone.

By then Cindy had started back toward reception, her heels clicking on the tile floor. "Drive safe, guys. I'll text you if the schedule changes."

Even on the day of their appointment, some people canceled, which disrupted the entire day. One thing our office manager excelled at was juggling last-minute schedule changes to maximize everyone's time instead of letting us sit around complaining. The many hats she wore—manager, receptionist, accountant—assured a smooth-running office.

With the roads pretty clear and our leaving a little early, I anticipated a good day. Getting out during the week on house calls gave us a much-needed break. Through the windshield the pastures on both sides of the road glistened with newly fallen snow. Here and there a valiant maple clung to a few red and gold leaves until the next storm blew them away.

"Where do we drop those meds off?" I asked Mari, trying to plot out the drive. A four-way stop forced us to slow down.

"Let's see," she said. There was a pause then a huge sigh.

"What?"

"Cindy pulled a fast one on us. She's got us dropping this off at Frank Martindale's place."

"Oh, no." Someone behind me honked. Mari's news stopped me as well as the truck. The last time I'd seen Frank, he was yelling at Cindy and me about his bill. I could only hope he hadn't heard about my antics at the Christmas party—basically wishing he would disappear. Dropping in on him today felt very awkward. Maybe we might be able to take a pass?

When I shared my feelings with Mari, she told me no. "If I know Cindy, she called him to say we were on our way."

I drove a few more minutes before coming to terms with the inevitable. "Alright. Let's get this over with. Where is his place again?"

She shifted in her seat and stared out the side window. "About a mile up the road on the left. A stone house with green shutters." Mari opened our office laptop and typed something in. "I'm recording this stop in our log."

"Put his address into the GPS or let me know when to slow down." Although highly used, the road had only two lanes. In anticipation of seeing Frank, I did a quick mental review of his cat Teddy's medical issue. I planned to make sure Teddy was doing well, then leave as soon as possible. When I ran that past Mari, she agreed. "By the way," I asked, "how come you know where he lives?"

"That's easy. My mom warned me never to cross his property to take a shortcut to the road. He kept a shotgun full of buckshot next to the front door and liked shooting at teenagers—mostly to scare us—and he succeeded. Believe me, all the locals know where Frank Martindale lives."

"Perfect," I said.

A few minutes later Mari cautioned me to slow down. "It's the next driveway on the left, with the metal mailbox. Number 185."

I was happy to see his driveway was newly plowed, because I wouldn't have wanted to navigate it in deep snow. A few feet in from the main road, it dipped into a gully, then rose at an angle to above road height. Safely through, we approached the stone house. I noticed an SUV parked under a covered carport attached to the house. "At least he's home," I told her.

We pulled up the driveway and parked next to the front steps. "Do you have Teddy's medication?"

"Here it is." Mari handed it to me.

I handed it back to her.

"Please. I don't want to go in there by myself," Mari pleaded. "If he starts yelling at me, I don't know…"

"Okay." Since I knew exactly how she felt, I turned the truck engine off. "We do this together. Maybe we'll be lucky and he'll meet us at the door. Since he likes you better, you do the talking. Tell him to call Cindy with any questions."

She didn't look convinced, but I smiled and said, "Come on. I'll race you."

Of course it was no contest. Neither one of us wanted to be first.

I rang the doorbell and waited, then rang it again. No answer.

"He's a little hard of hearing," Mari reminded me. "I noticed he wore hearing aids in both ears during his last office visit. Maybe he took them out. That what my uncle does when he gets home. Drives everyone crazy."

That created a dilemma. I couldn't leave his medication on the front porch in the freezing cold. I rang the doorbell again and this time added a couple of fist pounds.

"Try the handle," Mari suggested. When I hesitated, she said, "Here. I'll do it." She took hold of the handle, and sure enough, the unlocked door opened. We immediately heard a television blaring somewhere in the house.

"Boy, is that loud," I said. "No wonder he didn't hear us." A movement in the hallway caught my eye. It was

Frank's cat, Teddy, staring wide-eyed at the two of us. When we moved toward him, he darted away.

Mari walked further into the hallway and beckoned me along. "I see the top of his head. He's watching television. Come on."

Hoping we wouldn't get shot, I shouted, "Mr. Martindale. It's Dr. Turner and Mari from the animal hospital. Cindy asked us to drop off your medication." As we walked toward the noise, I hoped this would be easy, but I prepared for the worst.

"There he is." Mari stopped and glanced around. In front of us was a living room stuffed with old-fashioned furniture and piles of cardboard boxes. A gigantic television with extra speakers on the floor took up most of the far wall. Stationed directly in front of the screen sat two lounge chairs separated by a small table.

I made my way to the side of the television, prepared to be yelled at.

But Frank Martindale wasn't going to be yelling at anyone. His unseeing eyes were glazed over, mouth open and slack. Even the colorful reflected images from his high-resolution screen didn't alter the grayish color of his skin.

Checking for a pulse was a formality, his skin cool even in the warm room. Down at my feet Teddy rubbed against my leg, then leapt into his owner's lap, big yellow eyes staring at us.

"Mari." I took a step back. "Call 911."

We waited outside, Teddy safely tucked into his cat carrier inside the warm truck. Within fifteen minutes the police, an ambulance, and the fire department were all milling around. Chief Garcia ordered everyone to stay outside so the scene could be secured.

What little I'd seen pointed to a heart attack or an accidental overdose. On the side table next to him lay an empty bottle of whiskey along with a few empty beer cans and some prescription medication bottles. An old-fashioned wooden desk, its writing surface covered with papers, sat at the far corner of the room.

A glimpse into the other rooms showed numerous cardboard boxes stacked three or four high plus an inordinate amount of furniture, wardrobes, and chairs crammed against each other. The place smacked of hoarding.

The only other odd thing I'd noticed before Mari and I left was a round daily pillbox, made of copper, the kind you put in a pocket, which had fallen on the rug, scattering pills at his feet. Was Frank in the process of taking something, but dropped it? I didn't see a cell phone but then, I hadn't lingered.

Mari, it turned out, also had given the room a good look while I approached the body. We compared notes sitting in the truck. "No sign of robbery, but that's hard to tell with the clutter," she said. "Wonder why the front door was unlocked?"

"No idea," I answered. "Maybe he forgot?"

"I'm afraid he took that information to the grave." Her gloomy voice matched our feelings. We were trying to keep our spirits up, but it was hard to walk in on a death scene.

The first responders who came after us pinned our truck in. No one updated us, even though they'd taken our statements earlier. I'd texted Cindy to ask her if I should tell the chief we needed to leave and was waiting for an answer.

"Do you think it was suicide?" Mari asked me. Teddy gave a forlorn meow from the back seat.

"No, I don't. But we'll all know when the toxicology report comes in. Last I checked you're not supposed to wash your medications down with boilermakers."

Sitting in the truck, I started to get antsy. Mari and I had given our statements at least an hour ago, and I know Cindy confirmed the story we were dropping off the cat's medication. I rolled down the window to take a breath of cold air. Someone needed to tell us how long they anticipated us sitting here.

"Wait a minute. That's weird." Mari's voice sounded strange.

"What are you talking about? What's weird?"

Her voice now insistent, she explained. "That wish. The one you made at the Christmas party. You wished Frank would disappear."

"So? Not my finest moment."

"Yes. But you're the one who wished for all of them to disappear with your magic wand."

I corrected her. "Magic finger."

She didn't smile at my joke. "Kate, don't you get it? Your wish came true. Frank disappeared. He's dead."

The rest of the day was a bit of a blur. Chief Garcia, his bushy brows drawn into a permanent frown, freed us to finish our appointments with the admonition to remain available if needed. Cindy sent our intern, Greta, to pick up Teddy the cat, and we were on our way.

Before we left I asked the chief if he thought Frank died from a heart attack or possibly a suicide, but he wouldn't commit to either. I don't even know why I asked.

Mari's phone kept ringing again and again until she turned off the ring and put it on vibrate. The only person she contacted was her mother to tell her we were both fine and going back to work.

And work we did. Because of our delay, Cindy had to move our appointments around, shunting some clients to six o'clock, way past our normal hours. Mari and I didn't mind. We were both going on autopilot. I, for one, was happy to be busy and not reliving the moment I discovered Frank's corpse. I'd have plenty of time tonight, alone in my apartment, to replay every last frame of Frank Martindale's death scene.

I hoped he'd gone quickly with no pain.

"Kate, I've got to tell you something."

We were in the truck on our way back to the animal hospital, and I was bone-tired. "Sure. Things can't get much worse."

The uncomfortable silence that followed made me suspect it could.

"You know how I'm always posting on Facebook and Twitter."

This wasn't going to go well.

Mari continued. "I'm sorry. I posted the litter box cake video from the Christmas party and didn't realize it included your wish."

When I glanced over at her, tears glittered in her eyes. "I'm so, so sorry. It was late. I didn't really notice."

My Gramps always said don't yell at the person who forgot to close the barn door. They feel bad enough already. Just find the darn horse.

"Don't worry. I'm sure no one's looked at it."

She opened her phone and scrolled to a saved page. "Five hundred and twenty-two hits so far."

"What?" My surprise almost caused me to drive off the road. "You need to take it down."

"The chief said I couldn't. Not now." She turned off the phone and stuffed it in her coat pocket.

More and more surprises. "Why not?" I turned the heat setting lower, the windshield clouding up along the wipers.

"Something to do with Frank's death, I suppose."

"That makes no sense." I turned into the vacant hospital parking lot, Cindy long gone. Only Mari's black SUV was left, windshield nice and dry.

I parked the truck alongside her. "Your windshield's dry," I noted, climbing out of the truck. "It's been blowing snow all day. How is that possible?"

Mari stared at it in astonishment.

A thought occurred to me. I looked at the front window of the house next door. Pinky stood behind the heavy living room curtains, visible only for a moment, then vanished into the dark room.

Chapter Four

THAT NIGHT MY FRAME OF MIND WORSENED AFTER I finished a solitary dinner and had nothing to do. My large studio apartment, converted from the hospital garage by Doc Anderson, was adequate at best, with no commute or rent being the best perks. Six months into a one-year contract, I hadn't done much as far as decorating to make it my own. Every dime went to pay off my student loans, which amounted to over a hundred and fifty thousand dollars. Everything in my life felt temporary except my rescue dog, Buddy.

The squishy old sofa I sat on was as comfortable as my bed. When I leaned back, eyes closed, what Mari said about the selfish wish being online went round and round in my head, dragging Frank's body along for the ride. For some reason I felt guilty. Two glasses of white wine, my limit, didn't help. I gave up and called Gramps.

"What if I killed him with my wish?" Said out loud, it sounded preposterous, so why did I feel so upset?

"Katie," he said, "if wishes could kill, half the people I know would be dead."

I'm sure he had a grin on his face when he said it, but I found it hard to enjoy the humor of the situation.

"You aren't seriously thinking there's even a morsel of truth to this, are you?" His voice indignant, he continued. "That's not even an option."

"I'm not, really. At least I don't think I am. This has been a horrible day, Gramps. My brain is muddled, and

I'm exhausted." I lifted my legs and stretched them out over a throw pillow.

"After what you've been through, I don't blame you. Just watch out for the leprechauns."

I sat up on the sofa. "What do you mean?"

"When I'm down in the dumps and had a few too many whiskeys, I'm sure the leprechauns have been moving the furniture around. That's why I keep bumping into the sofa arm."

"Sure, blame it on the leprechauns." Now that Gramps and I were talking about the Irish wee ones, my wish did sound like fantasy or science fiction.

A throaty cough rattled the receiver. Periodically his COPD from working as a firefighter in NYC was aggravated when he caught a cold.

"Feeling okay?"

"Yeah. I'm on the downside of some virus."

Reality cleared my head when arguments couldn't. "Christmas Eve can't come soon enough," I told him. We planned on spending Christmas Eve together at his place in Brooklyn and enjoying a homemade turkey dinner with all the fixings.

"Looking forward to it." He coughed again then said, "Sometimes it's easy to go for a simple explanation when bad things happen—like blaming a silly wish meant to be a joke." His voice steady, he added, "Any explanation is better than the truth—that there simply is no explaining life. Bad things happen for no reason. Or maybe it's the luck of the Irish, as your great-grandmother would have said."

After we hung up, I thought about his comment. So many things in life we can't predict, like a lucrative roll of the dice or a random coin toss. Three heads up in a row. Was it luck or practice or sleight of hand?

Buddy yawned, ready for his final walk of the night. I pulled my coat on and stood at the doorway, encouraging him to be quick. He had a few favorite spots on the small strip of lawn and shrubs between the building and the parking lot. Patches of snow remained, along with a few packed mounds from the snowplow, enough places for him to sniff and paw at. A light went on next door, which meant someone was home. Pinky usually plowed at night, but this evening the stars shone clearly in the black sky.

Up until lately I hadn't paid much attention to my only neighbor. He kept to himself in his big house, working odd hours, always alone. That changed when his elderly dog needed my medical treatment. Now Pinky popped up quite regularly.

Finished doing his business, Buddy sniffed the air and stared at the trees along the property line.

"Come on," I called out. "It's cold." The wind gusts picked up as they often did in the evening. I'd left my gloves and hat inside, assuming we wouldn't be out long.

After a final look, Buddy turned, wagged his tail, and followed me in. I threw the double bolt, then made sure my curtains were tightly drawn before I turned the alarm back on.

That night I dreamed of wizard wands and fairy dust that swirled and danced in the wind.

Chapter Five

"DON'T PUT THE WHAMMY ON ME, DOC." TONY RAISED his arms up from his mop as if to ward off evil from beyond the grave. He'd been cleaning up an accident in the animal hospital hallway from a nervous dog. His easy charm caught Greta the intern's attention and my assistant's ire.

"Knock it off," Mari said, quick to put an end to Tony's notorious pranks.

I appreciated my friend's trying to come to the rescue, but I'd already heard two variations on the same theme this morning from clients. The video of my little magic spell Mari had posted on YouTube seemed to be on Oak Falls's top ten list. So far it had 1,802 hits. So much for my privacy. Sadly, no one appeared terribly upset at Frank's passing but instead focused on the dark humor of the timing.

"Alright. Everyone back to work."

Raising his mop in a final salute, Tony wheeled the yellow bucket toward the dog kennels, where Cindy had him and Aaron doing a deep clean. With the weather outside particularly cold and blustery, most clients stayed at home—which made the number of house call requests go up while in-clinic appointments declined. This lull in hospital cases created an excellent opportunity for cleaning and touching up paint, all jobs that our kennel worker, Tony, excelled at and Cindy excelled in dishing out.

Meanwhile, Mari and I labored to load up the truck for a busy afternoon of appointments, trying to anticipate everything we might possibly need.

Our first afternoon appointment was scheduled for one thirty, which meant we needed to leave in fifteen minutes. I'd stuck my head in the fridge to search for something to eat when Mari came around the corner.

"That guy drives me crazy sometimes," she said as she rooted around in her locker.

I didn't need to ask who "that guy" was. Tony and Mari grated on each other, with Tony deliberately provoking the more emotional Mari.

Pushed to the back of the refrigerator was a chicken Caesar salad I'd bought a few days ago. That and a piece of fruit would tide me over for the afternoon. Mari, on the other hand, had brought a wide assortment of chips, cookies, and crackers along with a homemade sandwich. Her appetite never added a pound to her athletic frame, while my love of pie and chocolate constantly forced me to loosen the ties on my scrubs.

Before leaving, we checked in with Cindy at the reception desk for any last-minute changes that hadn't gotten into the computer.

"You'll probably be out until five or five thirty tonight," she advised us, tucking her blond streaked hair behind her ears. "Sorry about that. Just keep me posted if you can."

Her using the words "if you can" referred to some of the notorious areas nearby with poor cell reception, due to the mountains and terrain of the Hudson Valley.

Everyone complained about the odd spots of uneven mobile coverage depending on your carrier. Hard to believe that the financial hub of the United States, the New York Stock Exchange with its sophisticated high-speed internet connections, was only a little over two hours away.

Sometimes the countryside around Oak Falls felt as isolated as a frozen moon.

———

Our tires squeaked on the crispy snow as the F-150 dug in and climbed up the steep driveway of Maple Grove Farm, a small farm owned by a retired couple from Manhattan. More and more of the properties in the Valley were being sold by longtime residents whose families had worked the land since the Dutch had settled here long ago. Mari said the previous owner, a widow, had gladly packed up her stuff and moved to a condo in Florida. None of her children were interested in the family farm, and the upkeep had proven too much for her.

To our left stood a large pasture with an adjacent corral and barn. A woman wearing a bright-blue coat waved a greeting to us while herding an assortment of animals toward an open gate. Most willingly moved along. The sole holdout was a handsomely sturdy pinto who effortlessly outmaneuvered her, dark hooves digging up brown clumps in the frozen field.

"Need some help?" I called out from the driver's side window.

"Sure. Maybe between the three of us we can convince him to follow us."

Ashley Kaminsky was half of the high-powered couple that had turned the Maple Grove Farm into a refuge for rescued animals. I'd been called out to tend to their cats and dogs, but this horse was a new addition to their family.

We jumped out of the truck and walked over to the fence. "Who is this good-looking guy?" I asked her. His thick winter coat guaranteed he was warmer than we were. An unexpected burst of icy wind reminded me to wrap my muffler more firmly around my neck.

"This is Lobo, a mustang adopted from the Bureau of Land Management. I'm afraid he doesn't trust me much."

"Was he an adult when they rounded him up?" Wild horses still ran free in a few states, but their habitats were shrinking due to encroachment by their biggest enemy—humans.

"I'm pretty sure he was."

I studied the horse standing about twenty feet away. His head swung around, tossing a blond mane to one side. Startling blue eyes in a dark chestnut face stared back at me. His ancestors had flourished in a wild country that no longer existed. No wonder he was wary of us.

"What are you trying to do?" asked Mari, securing the top button of her coat before thrusting her hands in her pockets.

Ashley motioned with her rope lead. Immediately Lobo bolted away. "He's so skittish," she said. "I'm just trying to get them all into the barn before the weather gets any worse."

To my mind, Lobo had shown real horse smarts. Attaching a lead to his halter might mean anything, and he wasn't taking any chances.

"Do you have any apples?" I asked. "Also, which horse is he friendliest with?"

"He prefers the mare, Sweet Potato." We looked back into the field, where she pointed out a small bay horse.

"Alright, Mari, can you help Ashley move everyone in except the mare and the mustang? Anyone have any horse treats?"

Ashley pulled out a handful of apple biscuits and handed me her rope lead.

The owner gratefully made a beeline for the barn. A couple of burros, one big mule with a silvered muzzle, some assorted goats, and a lone sheep immediately followed her aided by Mari, who encouraged them to move along. I stepped up to Sweet Potato and clipped the lead to the ring on her halter. True to her name, she stood still, nuzzling my hand searching for food. Soft dark eyes calmly watched the others leave.

"We'll be going in a minute, girl," I told her, rubbing under her forelock then under her ebony mane. I studiously ignored Lobo, who huffed and tossed his head a few feet away.

Sweet Potato lifted her nose, accidently knocking off my hat, making it wet and mucky on one side. I turned it inside out and shoved it into my pocket.

Twitching ears warned me someone was coming.

"Got the apples and a leather lead," Mari told me, handing over a canvas feed bag. "Ashley is getting the rest of the crew in their stalls." Very familiar with horses, my technician kept her movements slow and steady. "What do you want me to do?"

For a moment I put myself in mind of Lobo's point of view. "Let's not outnumber him. Why don't you stay behind the fence until we move from this pasture into the corral? After we're inside, shut the gate behind us. From there I'll use Sweet Potato to lure him into the barn."

"Okay." She slipped through the metal and wood fencing and turned her back to us. The horses gave her a quick glance before ignoring her for the smell of the apples. In a soft sweet voice, I talked nonsense to the bay, walked her about ten feet, and rewarded her with an apple. Lobo stared at us.

Clucking my tongue, I turned and began to lead the mare into the corral. By the time we got halfway in, I heard the sound of hooves trailing behind us. I fed Sweet Potato an apple on the ground. She picked it up and started chewing. "Come on, girl," I said. After a few minutes I tossed another apple behind us. When we moved away, Lobo came in for his treat.

Mari silently closed the pasture gate after Lobo passed through.

The barn doors stood open to the corral, and the smells of fresh hay, goats, and donkeys hung in the cold air.

Mari came over and took Sweet Potato. I slowly approached Lobo, speaking softly all the time, an apple flat in the palm of my hand. Resigned and hungry, he allowed me to attach his halter lead, and the two of us followed Mari, eight hooves clacking on the concrete floor. A few stall doors at the end stood open. Sweet Potato knew which one was hers and went right in. With only a minimum of fussiness, Lobo stepped into the adjacent stall.

The mustang shook his head back and forth and whinnied, but his ears stayed up and his body language showed no aggression toward me. Very slowly, I unhooked the lead, speaking softly all the while and gently blowing my warm breath on his muzzle, a trick taught to me by a savvy old horse vet.

As soon as the stall gate shut, he moved toward the feeder.

His owner came out of the tack room and gave me a thumbs-up. "I wish he was more trusting," Ashley said, hay clinging to her coat. "We've had him for three weeks now."

Lobo stopped eating at the sound of our voices, again on the alert.

"Let's let them eat in peace," I suggested. Ashley led the way to the main house, our boots picking up more snow mixed with mud along the way.

"I'm sure your large animal vet can give you gentling hints," I began, trying to dodge the piles of muck, "and there are some great websites and blogs on the internet from other mustang owners. Whatever you do, don't take his attitude personally."

"It's hard not to," she answered truthfully.

The old farmhouse on the property had been restored and updated with taste and a lot of money. Ashley stomped her feet on the doormat outside the mudroom entrance, then opened the door. After she slipped off her boots, we followed suit, mindful not to track gunk into her home.

"Sorry, I didn't mean to rope you into helping with Lobo." As we moved through the main house a bevy of dogs, one with three legs, greeted us. A few sharp barks were followed by unanimously wagging tails.

A very shaggy shepherd mix with one ear up and one ear down caught my attention. "Come here, Tommy," Ashley called. "Dr. Kate, this is your patient. I think he has an ear infection."

Mari and I looked at each other. We both smelled the problem immediately.

"When did you notice the odor?" I asked her.

"Oh, a week or so ago. It doesn't smell as much now," she commented, "but I still wanted you to check it out."

The reason the owner didn't smell the infected ear was that her olfactory system had been overloaded. Her nose, in protest, had given up.

"Believe me," Mari said, "it stinks."

Truer words were never spoken. The poor dog had tried rubbing the ear with his paw, transferring the odor not only to his feet but also his mouth and from there to the rest of his fur. Once he licked you, you were done for.

I took out the otoscope but suspected looking into his

ear was a lost cause. With all the goop inside it, I doubted I could see anything. Poor Tommy winced as I gently slid the disposable cone into the ear canal. Sure enough, debris blocked my view.

"Ashley, can you drop him off at the hospital tomorrow morning?" I asked. Mari held a plastic ziplock bag, and I inserted the dirty scope into it. "I'll need to tranquilize Tommy so I can clean the ear out. Because only one ear is involved, I'm worried he might have a polyp or a tumor obstructing the ear canal. That often leads to a ruptured eardrum."

A look of horror passed over her face.

We sat down at the kitchen table to drink some excellent coffee while I explained my treatment plan to her. "If he keeps rubbing and scratching that ear, he can rupture a blood vessel under the skin and cause a hematoma." Hematomas, which are like huge blood blisters trapped in the delicate ear tissue, were messy, deforming, and slow to heal. Quick treatment of the underlying cause of his ear problem might help us bypass that additional worry. "I'll have Cindy call you and arrange everything," I added.

Mari looked at her watch, a signal that we needed to get going. After working together for many months, we could practically read each other's mind.

"Well," I continued, standing up and slipping on my coat, "I'll see you and Tommy soon. I'm going to try and culture what's at the tip of the scope to find out what's growing in there. Meanwhile, no food or water after midnight, please."

"Thanks so much, Dr. Kate," Ashley said as she and

the dogs let us out. "And thanks for helping with Lobo. He seems to like you."

"Maybe I remind him of someone he knew," I suggested. "Horses recognize people."

"You do resemble a young Meryl Streep, sort of," Cheryl noted. "But I don't think Lobo's been spending much time watching movies."

Once we were outside, my client stood on her front porch, surrounded by her rescue pooches, and waved until we turned the corner and vanished from her view.

"Boy, was that guy stinky," Mari said, sniffing at her hands. "Even though we wore gloves and I scrubbed my hands twice, the memory lingers on."

I downshifted the truck and looked out into the darkening sky. The individual trees around us disappeared with the fading light.

The memory lingers on.

Deep in Lobo's brain lived a memory of running free with his herd, grazing where and when they wanted, and feeling the rain and wind sweep across his back.

Then the people came.

And his memory told him that people meant trouble.

Sheer curiosity made me quickly glance at the selfish wish YouTube video on my phone that night. The number of viewings had increased to 1,914.

Like Lobo, I figured all those people meant trouble.

Chapter Six

I'M NOT A GREAT SLEEPER IN THE BEST OF TIMES. ADD stress and a dead body to the mix, and you create a restless night full of vague feelings of foreboding. At seven the next morning, I had to drag myself out of bed to go to work. Between lack of sleep and profound guilt over my selfish Christmas wish, I wanted to crawl back into bed and throw the covers over my head.

But discipline had gotten me through vet school, so I ran a cold shower and got ready. Too late, I saw that Cindy texted me we didn't start until nine thirty, so after reading an article on methods of anesthetizing invertebrates, I checked my email messages. One unexpected name caught my eye.

Gramps had sent me an email, with an attachment. Usually he picked up the phone and called me. Puzzled, I opened it.

And my long morning got even worse.

———

"Hey, Katie," he said, answering on the second ring.

My Gramps was the only person left on the planet who called me Katie.

"So, when did this happen?" There was no point in circling the issue. His email warned me that my father, who I hadn't spoken to in twelve years, had invited both of us to Christmas dinner to meet his new, much younger family.

"I forwarded his invite to you as soon as I got it." Gramps sounded suspiciously noncommittal, as if this sort of thing happened all the time.

"Well, he can bloody well forget about it." The anger in my voice made my Buddy stop chewing on his dental bone, his regal King Charles spaniel face puzzled.

"Okay, I hear you."

"I'm not kidding, Gramps, so don't try and talk me into going." I settled back into the sofa and tried to calm down.

On the other end of the phone his breathing sounded a little ragged.

"You feeling those Christmas blues again, sweetie?"

"Not too bad," I lied.

"You've had a rough couple of months," he reminded me. "You work all the time, and then the split with Jeremy. After being friends for so long. Maybe you should talk to someone again."

Frustrated, I sat up straight. "I talked to a therapist once a week for six years, Gramps. I'm talked out." As for Jeremy, sharing my love life woes was not going to happen.

We connected in uncomfortable silence. "Alright. I'll wait a few days until I message your father back—give you a chance to think about it. But maybe it's time to meet your half brother and sister."

Those last words pierced my heart. Anger toward my father was all I had left. Anger helped me remember my mom and brother, Jimmy. If I let go of my rage, would I be letting go of them, too?

My head started to pound. "Sorry, but I don't want to think about it right now, Gramps. Let's talk later." I used my free hand to massage the back of my head, trying to ward off the pain.

"Sure, honey." He hesitated before saying in a gentle voice, "Remember, your mom was my daughter, our only child, and Jimmy—Jimmy was my grandson. You need to forgive your father, Katie. I forgave him a long, long time ago."

———

Buddy followed me into the animal hospital when I went to work. He probably sensed I needed some moral support because he was sworn enemies with our hospital cat, Mr. Cat. With no one around, I poured a big cup of coffee and snuck into my office. Immediately, Buddy moved toward his plush dog bed in the corner. Mari poked her head in and said, "Take your time. We don't start for a while."

My focus soon shifted to all the incoming lab results, clinical updates, and emails. Daily routine conquered anxiety until Cindy texted me that I had a phone call on line one. Her brother-in-law, otherwise known as the Oak Falls Chief of Police, wanted to talk to me.

"Hello," I said, trying to get comfortable in my office chair. "What can I do for you today, Chief Garcia?" I hoped getting to the point would make our conversation brief.

"You're working all day today?" he asked, with no preliminaries.

With a quick move of my mouse I opened the appointment schedule. "Let me look. I start in twenty minutes, have appointments on and off until five, with a half-hour break for lunch. Do you need me to come down to the station?"

"No. That's not necessary, yet." He cleared his throat. "Dr. Turner, are you aware of a video that has been posted on YouTube, taken at your animal hospital Christmas party?"

Now I cleared my throat. "I just found out about it. Cindy's seen it. It's quite…embarrassing."

I thought I heard a chuckle from him. "No alcohol was involved, was there?"

"No alcohol. I really have no excuse. Just a spontaneous dumb thing to do."

I pictured him writing "dumb" in his notes, then underlining it.

"Why was Pinky there?"

Since the chief's sister-in-law worked here and had arranged for Pinky to visit that day, I assumed he knew all about it but for some reason had to hear it from me. I dutifully told him that there was some discussion of plowing schedules and a hole in the parking lot, and that when he visited, Cindy had asked if he wanted some of our pizza and litter box cake. Why the normally shy Pinky had yelled out that third name is anyone's guess. It simply reminded me that everyone is capable of making a stupid mistake.

"By the way," Chief Garcia asked, "do you know who posted the video?"

"Found that out, too. My best friend, Mari." I closed down the computer and put it in sleep mode.

"Something like that might strain a friendship," he said before he disconnected the call.

Chapter Seven

WHEN MARI HEARD ABOUT THE CHIEF'S CALL, SHE apologized all over again. She kept apologizing until I stopped her.

But she also felt the need to explain again. "I thought the litter box cake turned out great, so I went ahead and recorded you getting the first slice, and then Cindy started the games. Honestly, I forgot that the wish was on there when I posted it. Remember, I'm the one who called out our clients' names. I'm feeling just as guilty, believe me."

Despite our innocent intentions, we both had stepped in it. As a reminder, I pointed to our pending stool samples. "We're deep into that."

The treatment room, where the party had taken place, appeared to be back to normal except for some fake mistletoe taped above the X-ray door. Those few hours of the party now barely registered with me. "Mari, neither one of us is guilty of anything except bad taste."

"I know," she said. "We'll weather this storm together in the same leaky lifeboat." The imagery was meant to be funny. Instead it made me queasy.

She snuck in one more update before we went back to work. "This morning I tried to take the video off YouTube again, but the chief blocked it somehow. Something about it being evidence, I suppose."

Bureaucracy. With a shrug I assumed a few people

would call attention to the link between my silly game and a sad accident. So what if five or ten more locals knew about the wish?

"By the way," Mari interrupted my train of thought, "we've got 2,733 views now."

"What? How did that happen?"

"No idea. Kind of creepy, when you think about it." My assistant picked up a pen and put it in a pocket in her scrubs. "I read a few of the comments. Most everyone loved the cake. A bunch of people mentioned something about wish fulfillment, and one woman said you were secretly a witch, not a veterinarian, who put a curse on everyone in the room." She brushed some fur off her pants and looked up. "No worries. By tomorrow it will be old news and forgotten."

———

The morning zipped smoothly by, with mostly routine exams and rechecks. I was glad to keep busy after our traumatic house call. Frank's neighbor telephoned to make sure Teddy was okay and mentioned she wanted to adopt the friendly cat, if possible. When Frank had had a hernia repair, Ann-Marie Gilderman was Teddy's designated caregiver and his emergency contact. We all were glad Teddy had a new home.

As we were leaving the exam room, one client sheepishly joked he was happy I hadn't wished him dead too. I joined in the laughter, although the humor was at my expense.

When the last morning client left, Mari and I quickly

cleaned and organized the treatment area. Cindy let us know that Chief Garcia approved Frank's neighbor taking Teddy for now.

"What is he, some kind of cat eyewitness?" I joked.

"The Fifth Amendment kind," Mari commented as we started to get ready for late-afternoon appointments. "I'm glad today is almost half over. Did the chief ever call you back, Kate?"

"No." I took the opportunity to sit down and check the list of today's lab tests, making sure the many samples were logged in properly. The lab pickup was promptly at seven tonight.

"Well, he called me back," my assistant admitted. "He made me feel guilty about recording at the party, like I was confessing to some kind of crime. All I did was post a video."

Not wanting to go down that rabbit hole again, I stood back up. "That's it. I'm officially on lunch."

Footsteps clicking down the hall signaled Cindy was on her way. Mari went to the employee refrigerator and removed an iced tea.

"Great work keeping appointments on time, both of you," she said. "Sorry not to give you any time off after… you found Frank. I wish I could have."

"No more wishes, please," I pleaded.

"I'd rather be working," Mari said before taking a gulp of her Raspberry Mist Tea.

"Speaking of Frank, any news about cause of death?" A sudden picture of him sitting in the recliner came and went at lightning speed.

Cindy glanced at her cell phone screen before putting it in her pocket. "The preliminary findings point to a heart attack complicated by an accidental overdose of prescription drugs, but you didn't hear it from me."

What she said sounded about right. I'd recognized some of the pills scattered on the rug near Frank's body as blood pressure and cardiac medications. He'd huffed and puffed walking out to his SUV the last day I'd seen him alive.

"Almost done in here," Mari announced.

"There is one thing," Cindy volunteered to us after retrieving her lunch from the refrigerator. "Something the chief doesn't like," she explained, "is that open door."

"Unlocked. It wasn't left open."

"Whatever," Cindy said. "It complicates everything."

Mari didn't seem fazed at all by that statement. "Half the people I know up here don't lock their doors. What's the chief getting in an uproar about?"

Although she didn't answer out of respect for her brother-in-law, Cindy seemed to be on Mari's page. True to her sense of the dramatic, she'd saved the worst for last.

"Guess who called today?"

"Queen Elizabeth," I joked. "She wants to bring the corgis in."

Cindy rolled her eyes. "I wish. No, it was Eloise Rieven, or as she referred to herself, victim number two on our hit list."

"Crap." That jolted me out of my British royal humor frame of mind. "What else did she say?"

"Actually, it wasn't that bad." Cindy stopped to take

a bite of salad. "She's annoyed and wanted the video removed from YouTube. I told her we tried, but the chief wouldn't let us take it down yet."

She watched Mari's and my reaction, with amusement. "That shifted the blame off of us, temporarily. Next, she wanted to know who was responsible for posting it. I had to tell her it was you, Mari."

My assistant slumped in her chair and covered her eyes.

"But get this," Cindy's voice cheered up. "She likes you. When I told her how sorry you were and it was all a mistake, Eloise said at least she was still alive to talk about it. We had a little chat and it was very civilized." She paused to let that sink in. "Then Eloise told me to tell you, Mari, that you owe her a grooming. Do you know what that means?"

"Thankfully, I do." Mari's face appeared relieved. "I've groomed her bulldogs a bunch of times for her when she was showing, and then recently I groomed Queenie for Thanksgiving. That came out great. There's nothing like a fresh-smelling bulldog. Hey, maybe I got off easy."

"Did she say anything about me?" I asked.

"Yes," Cindy confessed. "Eloise said she expected you, Dr. Kate, to be much more professional and she's still going to sue you."

———

We were all waiting for our last appointment who called to say they were running late, when Cindy handed me some mail. "Looks like you have a few Christmas cards. Don't forget to give them back to me to hang up on the tree."

"Well, then you open them," I suggested. My receptionist liked to run a tight holiday ship. All thank-you notes and greeting cards were put on display in reception. Yesterday, I'd watched Cindy hanging up Christmas cards from clients by punching a hole through the open card and stringing them up with red and green ribbon. Clients and staff love it.

"No can do. These are addressed to you, not me."

"Open them," Mari said to me as she walked by on her way to the refrigerator. This kind of stuff was right up her alley.

I started with the biggest envelope. It turned out to be a thank-you from Daffy and Little Man with an illustration showing Chihuahuas instead of reindeer pulling Santa's sled.

"So cute," commented Mari as I passed it around.

The next two were photos of pets wearing Santa hats and reindeer antlers standing with their grateful owners wishing the entire staff a Merry Christmas.

"Love these too. Why didn't I invent holiday costumes for animals? Think of all the money I'd be making." My assistant periodically threatened to quit and enter the pet accessory field.

Cindy gathered everything together and watched me open the last envelope. Outlined in gold, the pretty card depicted a cat and dog, both with gold collars, watching Santa and his sled through a window. I opened it and read the personalized greeting out loud. "Congratulations, Dr. Kate. Your first Christmas wish came true." It was signed Frank Martindale.

Mari gasped. I picked up the envelope and looked at the postmark. It had been mailed the day after Frank's body was found.

Who had sent it?

One of us reacted immediately. "Those little creeps," Cindy said, taking the card from my hand. "I hate teenagers. I'll bet it's the kid who keeps calling and hanging up on me."

Upset by this nasty prank, I opened one of the cabinets and retrieved a bag we put lab samples in. Trying not to touch anything, I asked Cindy to slide both the envelope and card into the plastic ziplock bag. "We've got to call the chief about this."

I rubbed my face with my hands, noticing the beginnings of another headache. If this was someone's idea of a joke, they had very bad taste.

When Cindy called her brother-in-law, he didn't sound that concerned. In fact, she told us, it sounded like he expected something like this. We were instructed to lock up the card and envelope in Cindy's desk drawer and a police officer would swing by to get it later today or tomorrow.

Definitely by the end of the week.

Chapter Eight

SNOW FELL ONCE AGAIN THAT NIGHT. IN THE morning the windows were frosted with an icy crystalline glaze. Poor Buddy hated walking on the new snow, cracking through the crusted surface with each step. Banging on the ground with a stiff broom helped break it down for him. It was hard to believe we had months more of this in store for us.

At least I could look forward to my morning meal. A client had dropped off some bagels and gourmet cream cheese for the staff late yesterday, so I scurried over to the hospital early in anticipation of a delicious breakfast. Mari showed up as I opened the bagel box.

Five minutes later, bagels in hand, we stood in front of the refrigerator debating the relative virtues of each cream cheese spread when Cindy came into the employee lounge, an odd look on her face.

"Want to vote on which flavor tastes the best?" I said.

Her mouth remained tightly closed.

"Something wrong?" Mari asked, a smear of cream cheese on her lips.

"This is very strange," our receptionist began. Normally upbeat, she slumped in a chair like a deflated balloon.

Mari and I looked at each other.

"It's probably a coincidence…but Eloise Rieven… your bulldog breeder…"

My mind still focused on the "everything" bagel nestled in my hand, I interrupted and said, "What does she want now?"

"Kate. She's dead."

———

I had about fifteen minutes to digest this disturbing news before my first appointment. While we had been talking about bagels, Cindy had been on the phone with her sister. Pinky had discovered the body when he went to her home in the early hours to plow.

The story was sad, but her death appeared to be an accident, the kind that happens too often in rural areas.

Between clients Mari filled me in with the details Cindy had learned. "Eloise went outside to get more wood for the woodstove and must have tripped or passed out. She died of hypothermia out there in the cold. Why she went out in a snowstorm, no one knows." She shook her head but then added. "Come to think of it, I did the same thing the other night."

"But you're a good fifty years younger, Mari," I answered, trying to talk and read triage notes at the same time.

"That's true," she admitted. "But just because you get old doesn't mean you act that way. My mom hauls all her own wood at sixty-three and says she still feels like she's thirty. The shock comes when she looks in the mirror."

"Gramps is like that too."

"Hey, things to look forward to," Mari joked, although none of us were amused.

I tried to put my client's death in perspective. Accidents happen all the time. Eloise was in her late seventies hauling wood in a snowstorm. One of those accidents that happen in or near the house to seniors all the time.

What my technician said resonated with me since I'd heard Gramps say the same sort of thing plenty of times. His brain felt young even if his body didn't. He'd done dangerous things all his life and even now took risks. Anytime the phone rang at weird hours of the night I worried it was bad news about my Gramps. Hearing a story like the death of Eloise Rieven reminded me we all needed to be more careful.

Suddenly I remembered the YouTube video. I wondered how many people had viewed that stupid thing now?

———

I'd managed to get through my morning appointments and was writing up notes when Cindy asked for a favor. Someone had to take care of Queenie, the bulldog, until Eloise's son, Joe, could pick her up. Since she had an enlarged liver the chief wondered if we could board her, with Joe's permission, instead of them sending her to animal control down in Kingston.

And could we pick her up now?

———

Only fifteen minutes from the Oak Falls Animal Hospital, Eloise Rieven's farmhouse had been sitting in the same place, in various states of repair, for over one hundred years. Sure, some of the many layers of paint had peeled off, and one end of the porch looked a bit skewed, but it still was a grand old dame of a home.

"Slow down," Mari said.

We could see the reflections of the police cruiser lights ahead. I downshifted and stared out the driver's side window as we approached the turn-in. My eyes followed a beautifully restored stone wall that met up with another, older, more tumbled down version that marked the beginning of Eloise's property.

"She wouldn't repair that wall," Mari said, noticing me looking at it. "Bragged that her place was the only homestead still in original condition in this entire region."

If original meant difficult to drive, then the rutted road that led to the house was extremely original. The holes were so large we slowed down to a crawl and still bumped hard enough for Mari's head to hit the ceiling.

The chief himself sat waiting for us in his car, most likely under orders from his wife and sister-in-law. When we finally parked, he got out and stretched his shoulders. From the tire marks everywhere, it looked like we must have just missed the crowd of emergency vehicles.

"Hey, Mari. Dr. Turner. Thanks for helping us out with this." A known animal lover, Chief of Police Garcia was very solicitous of animals involved in crime scenes or abandoned due to circumstances beyond the owner's control.

In the background I heard a hoarse "ruff," which repeated every minute or so. "That sounds like Queenie."

"Yep." We started to move toward the house. "That's another reason I called. She won't let anyone get near her, and she hasn't stopped barking this whole time."

Mari followed close behind him. We were heading toward the back of the house walking through snow covered in footprints. While they kept chatting, I kept looking.

A large tarp-covered cord or two of wood loomed around the corner. Painted on the snow butting up against it, a fluorescent outline marked the position of the body. Caution tape attached to thin metal poles cordoned off the area.

"Is that where...?" Mari pointed to the image in the snow.

"Yes." Another "ruff" from Queenie spurred Mari and the chief along toward the back stairs.

I stared at the outline while soft snowflakes began to fall. I hoped it would cover everything so Joe Rieven wouldn't come back and find his mother's body outlined on the ground. I hadn't been so fortunate.

As soon as they told me my mom and brother had died in a car accident two blocks from our house, I ran out the front door. My neighbor yelled for me to stop, but I kept running. Most of the crowd had dissipated, but the remnants of caution tape, shattered windshield glass, and the red-and-yellow investigator marks were still visible in the road. Twelve hours later there was no trace. Rush hour traffic swept by as it always did, oblivious that my life had changed forever at that intersection.

I stood there until my Gramps found me, still holding the flowers I'd brought. There was no place to put them.

The distressed "ruffs" got louder. A gray handicap ramp lay on top of one side of Eloise's back stairs. Covered with rubberized ridges to prevent bulldogs and people from slipping, that must have been how she walked Queenie. While Mari scurried up the ramp, the chief and I chose the regular stairs.

Mari waited at the top. "Last time I was here she'd set up a step-in shower in the mudroom that was perfect for washing the bulldogs. That's where I put my grooming table."

The chief nodded. It wasn't new information. He opened the door before stepping aside to let us through.

Although the lights were on, the inside of the house stayed dim. Rough walls made of stone outlined the mudroom. A long, narrow hallway, made even narrower by the number of oil paintings and photos hanging on both sides, loomed ahead.

I heard Mari speaking to Queenie and listened to the doggy yips of joy at seeing someone she knew. Following their voices, I exited the hallway into an airy sitting room. Two walls were lined with built-in bookcases packed with faded leather-bound volumes. Gold brocaded chairs flanked the fireplace, where Mari sat on the floor in front of cold embers. Queenie leaned against her, fiercely wagging her stump of a tail. My appearance also rated an excited yip.

"Well, that's more like it," the chief commented. "Her harness and leash are on the chair. Do you want to get the bed and her bowls, too?"

"Definitely," said Mari, now packing up. "And Squeaky. Don't forget Squeaky."

The ratty yellow duck, the bulldog's favorite toy, was carefully packed up in a carryall marked "Queenie," and then we all walked slowly back the same way we had entered and out the mudroom door. The ramp proved invaluable as the bulldog headed right toward it, relieving herself only a few feet from the bottom.

Queenie hesitated as we approached the woodpile, anxiously whining and looking up at Mari.

"Come on, honey," Mari coaxed her along. "Want to go for a ride?"

The dog looked dubious, obviously knowing her owner was missing and not sure why.

"Let's go." My assistant gave a quick short tug on the leash and Queenie obeyed, like the good dog she was.

Once at the hospital, Queenie settled in, especially with some extra spoiling from the three of us. Cindy asked all kinds of questions, with Mari and me supplying the answers for a change. After getting an oversized kennel ready with her bed and Squeaky and food and water, the bulldog surprised us by climbing in and lying down.

"It's been a long day for her," Mari noted.

A bulldog snore gently lifted everyone's spirits.

"Same here." Taking a break, I drank some water and shared a bagel with Cindy. "Glad we could help the chief out today. Seeing that woodpile was tough."

Cindy sighed and said, "You two have been through a lot."

"I still can't believe Eloise passed like that."

"I'm stunned, too." Echoing my thoughts, Mari sat in one of the lab chairs, rubbing her arm. "I met her when she was seriously involved in showing her dogs. Must have been in my teens. Very demanding, but very kind to me. That's when she hung out with that Rhinebeck crowd of millionaires."

"Eloise?" I asked.

"Eloise. She was a member of the Historical Society, the Hudson Valley Gardening Club, and the American Kennel Club. I remember because she tried to get me to sign up as a junior member."

"Doc Anderson's mother had some kind of designation on her house from the Historical Society," Cindy said. "He used to say, 'I'd like to have a dollar for every house George Washington supposedly slept in up here.' More likely it was Benedict Arnold, running for his life."

Our receptionist's attempt to cheer us up failed.

"Well," Cindy said, checking the time, "we'll all be in the history books if we don't keep moving. Kate, you've got a couple of call-backs before the next appointment, and Mari, can you make sure all the morning labs are recorded?"

Even in the wake of a tragedy like Eloise Rieven's untimely death, the everyday world doesn't stop for long. Especially when you have a Cindy to keep you on track and on time.

As we hurried off to our chores, the bulldog snored and dreamed.

Chapter Nine

AFTER THE HOSPITAL CLOSED FOR THE NIGHT AND THE world turned still, I sat down in my apartment with Buddy and decided it was time. Like it or not, I needed to watch the Secret Selfish Santa Wish party video. Call it a compulsion. Before she left, Mari had let slip that the litter box cake, Frank's death, and the Christmas wish had been mentioned online by several bloggers and even someone's Facebook page. She apologized once more.

I had no idea what would happen when the online community discovered Eloise also had died.

By the time I pulled YouTube up on my phone, the hits had more than doubled. We were now at 5,637.

Considering the amateur quality of the video, the first part actually was pretty funny and showed a bit of skill. Mari used a movie-shooting-style clapboard app to start, then cut away to pictures of real litter boxes before zooming in on her uncomfortably realistic litter box cake.

We certainly sounded like we were having fun that day. Whoops of laughter greeted the big reveal. Mari took full advantage of her camera's features. She also frequently cut away to show a brief panorama of the treatment room and its occupants.

Snippets of conversation could be heard from the "audience" along with Mari's periodic narration. Then you heard Cindy introducing the game. It was only after several more shots of individuals chowing down on litter box cake that the phone swung back up to the front of the room. The film caught Cindy and me as she asked for my Secret Selfish Santa wish. I appeared decidedly uncomfortable. Encouraged by the crowd, I vaguely heard myself say "dissatisfied clients," but the names Frank and Eloise were supplied by Mari. The last one added by Pinky—which was something Lassitor—I didn't recognize.

If I had stopped right there, my life now would be much simpler. Instead I smiled, waved my magic finger wand, and dramatically wished them to all "disappear." The video ended with a rush of inaudible chatter and a few hands clapping.

The whole scene lasted only a few minutes. As it turned out, those were a few minutes too many.

———

My delicious homemade dinner that night consisted of a packaged frozen meal followed by a tablespoon of peanut butter and jelly as dessert. The apartment felt messy and disorganized, the same as me. Dragging myself off toward the sofa, I started to clean up.

Cleaning slowed down when Luke called. My hunky friend on whom I'd had a crush for the last few months had just arrived back in town on Christmas break from his law school studies. A former Oak Falls police officer currently on a leave of absence, Luke, I was certain, had been filled in by someone from town on all the graphic details of my two clients' deaths.

"Can't keep out of trouble, can you?" he said when I answered the phone.

"Thanks. That's just what I need to hear," I answered, annoyed at his lack of sympathy. But then Luke always came right to the point.

"Sorry. I thought I'd lighten things up a little, but obviously that approach fell flat." He stopped to regroup. "How are you holding up?"

I took a pair of dirty scrubs and threw them in the laundry basket. "Okay. How much do you know?"

While I waited for his answer, I continued straightening up.

"Well, let's see," he began. "Crazy Christmas party video, Frank's unlocked door, and you and Mari discovering his body. Eloise frozen. Miss anything?"

Seeing a stray sock under the bed, I bent down to retrieve it then tossed it toward the laundry basket. It bounced off the rim and fell back on the floor.

Distracted, I said, "That about covers it."

"How do you get yourself..." His voice tapered off. "Forget it."

"How do I get myself in these messes? Is that what you were going to say, Luke?"

He lowered his voice and apologized, but this time it sounded as though he meant it.

Scooping up the sock, I searched for its mate then put both in with the other dirty clothes. If I had to describe my relationship with Luke, it resembled my laundry situation—hit or miss. Lately, with him being away in school and the unwelcome presence of ex-girlfriend

Dina, his high school sweetheart, lurking in the background, I'd say it was more miss than hit.

Tired of explaining, I stretched out on the sofa, glad that the year was finally coming to an end. Luke echoed my thoughts.

"All this nonsense is going to blow over soon," he predicted. "Someday you'll think back on it and find it hilarious. Except for the deaths part."

"You know," I answered, putting my feet up, "I feel sorry for them both, but at least Eloise had her son and friends to mourn her. Frank died alone. His behavior alienated a lot of people, but perhaps there was a reason behind it that none of us knew about. Some kind of deep emotional trauma?"

"You're too nice," he countered. "Frank was a grumpy old man. Period."

"You don't become that person overnight," I argued. "Besides, there was someone who liked him."

"Who's that?"

"His cat."

"I'm sure the cat will move on," he predicted.

That was Luke, optimism with a side of sarcasm.

———

"Queenie's being picked up today by Joe Rieven, Eloise's son," Cindy said when I went into the reception area to check on a record. "Sorry to see her go. She's such a sweetie."

"Glad we could help out," I told her, "especially given the circumstances. I hope he isn't upset about the video."

My receptionist pointed her index finger at me, like a kindergarten teacher. "Stop blaming yourself. This has nothing to do with our party."

I pointed right back to her and said, "Death wish video. That's what they're calling it online. How can I prove it's impossible to wish someone to death?"

"I'll have to think about that."

A "ruff" from the treatment room meant our guest was feeling ignored. Bulldogs take a lot of care, which started me wondering about Queenie's new home. "How well do you know Joe Rieven?" I asked Cindy. A native of Oak Falls and proud of it, she knew just about everyone in town.

"Pretty well. He's quiet, keeps mostly to himself now that he got divorced," she explained. "I see him at church every Sunday. He'd bring Eloise to the ten o'clock service, then she and her friends went out for brunch. A good son."

That dovetailed with the little I'd heard about him, which was, "Joe was a good son to his mom."

The basic facts of his life sounded pretty simple. Graduated from high school then joined the Marines. Came back to town and started doing construction. Met a girl from Maine, got married, and moved to Bangor. Being married didn't last long—no children—got divorced, and eventually moved back to Kingston where he got a job at a lumber mill.

"Someone told me Joe's a very good fly fisherman," Cindy added when I pressed her for more details. "I think he's won some contests. Most of his friends are fishermen, too. My hubby said he knows a bunch of them. They went on some fancy trip to Alaska last year."

I'd seen pictures of those fishing and nature tours. Alaska looked spectacular. "Was he catching salmon?"

"Probably. You can ask him yourself, though." The phone rang as Cindy retrieved some papers from the printer.

"What do you mean? I've never met him." I tried to get Cindy's attention while she listened to the caller.

Using a Sharpie, my ever-resourceful receptionist wrote Queenie Rieven on a manila envelope with our logo printed on a label at the top. She covered the speaker with her hand and whispered, "He's picking up her exam and shot records in about twenty minutes."

———————

I was busy looking up a new protocol for osteoarthritis when she texted me:

JOE'S HERE

Hurrying to catch him before he left, I walked out into the reception area hoping I wouldn't have to guess who he was. I didn't. Cindy was having a conversation with a man holding the manila envelope. Queenie sat next to him on a leash.

"Oh, Dr. Kate," she said as if my entrance was a surprise, "I'd like you to meet Joe Rieven."

About my height, five foot ten, with a neatly trimmed brown beard and calm brown eyes, Joe wore a ski jacket with his Fly Fishing USA baseball cap.

I held out my hand. "So sorry for your loss," I told him.

"Your mother loved her bulldogs, especially Queenie." I bent down to give the dog a hug.

Joe said, "Thank you."

"Are you keeping her?" I was curious if the older bulldog needed a new home.

"No, I wish I could. I'm in a second-floor apartment with no elevator. Queenie's going to live with Julie, one of my mom's best friends," he explained. "Julie's got Queenie's sister and a house with a fenced yard. She's known her since she was born. I'm sure Mom would approve."

It sounded like a perfect arrangement. Joe looked to be in his late forties, early fifties, with a prominent beer belly. I'd hate to think of him carrying a sixty-pound bulldog up and down the stairs three times a day. "Is Julie close by?"

He glanced out the window into the parking lot before answering. "No, Julie moved to New Jersey a few years ago to be closer to her grandkids." Once again his eyes drifted toward the window. "Well, got to go. Nice meeting you all." Joe offered us a quick nod of the head and started to leave; however, he stopped when another man came in.

"Don't forget, she has an enlarged liver," I added. "Tell Julie to schedule a recheck with her vet."

"Will do." His head swiveled toward the man walking toward the reception desk. "Hey, Tank. I thought that was you that pulled up. How are you doing?" Joe's voice suddenly became animated. He smiled and fist-bumped the older man.

"Great. Doing a little ice fishing this weekend up north. You should come with us."

"Maybe. Thanks for the invite."

I noticed that Tank also wore a fishing-themed base-ball hat.

"Well," Joe told him, "got to run, but I'll call you later." With another fist bump he left, holding the door open for the bulldog. Through the window I saw him lift Queenie into the back of a Jeep in the parking lot.

"Great guy," the man called Tank said. "Watching him drop a line in a river is a beautiful sight. Too bad about his mom."

"Yes," Cindy agreed, "but she lived a good life."

My receptionist always knew the right thing to say.

"You fellows must be fly fishermen. My Gramps always envied you guys." I moved behind the desk next to Cindy and picked up some papers as an excuse to hang around. "Isn't there a television show about fly fishing now?"

He warmed to the subject after telling Cindy that his wife had sent him to pick up their dog's medicine. "Doc, it's amazing how many contests and styles of fishing they show you on cable now. When I was a kid it was a line, a float, and a worm if you were lucky. Now some guys earn a living doing the contest circuit and endorsing products. Wouldn't that be the life?"

Tank conveniently forgot about the wife and dog.

"My hubby treats himself once a year to some kind of fishing outing. Last year it was a catch-and-release giant carp trip," Cindy said, handing him the medicine in a paper dispensing bag.

Tank made some kind of whooping sound. "I did one of those three years ago. Never had so much fun in my life. Joe was supposed to go, but he had to cancel. Couldn't get the time off from work. Darn shame. Guess how big my best catch was."

"Thirty pounds?" I'd seen some of these contests with my Gramps, and the sizes of the carp were unbelievable.

"Fifty-one pounds. There's some places overseas where they grow to over one hundred pounds, even bigger."

His face turned red and flushed. I thought he was going to have a heart attack over his fish story.

Cindy intervened. "Now, Tank, if your wife has any questions, tell her to call me so you don't get into trouble."

The two of them shared a chuckle.

"Will do. Thanks, Cindy. See you, Doc." He shoved the small package into the pocket of his coat and left.

"So, did you learn anything?" Cindy asked as soon as we were alone.

"Not really," I answered, my voice echoing in the empty room. "Joe is pretty quiet, although he did get worked up when he talked about fishing."

My receptionist agreed. "Did you know you can spend thousands of dollars on equipment? The hubby and I had to have a little talk about that."

"I'm always amazed at how you can spend your money," I said.

A triumphant grin spread across my receptionist's face. "Well, all this fishing talk reminds me of something odd I heard from one of the bridge ladies."

"Give."

"This is really strange. Did you know we now have a local chapter of a group called LARN, Legalize Animal Rights Now? One of the women, who is a retired lawyer, says they're searching for test cases to present to the courts. One of the test cases has to do with salmon fishing."

"I'm not following you," I said.

"They want to stop wild salmon run fishing. The contention is that legally, all fish have a right to reproduce. Fly fishermen are taking away that right."

"Even catch and release?"

"Even catch and release. If it ever passed, it would put a multimillion-dollar industry out of business."

———

Meeting Joe Rieven sparked my curiosity about Eloise, so I decided to bribe Mari with one of her favorite things. I'd purchased a bag of bite-sized brownies from one of the specialty stores in town. Baked by our local Biker Baker, they were so addictive she limited herself to one bag every month. This holiday bag with little Santa hats had December all over it.

Mari was friends with many of the doggie set in the area, having shown her Rottweillers in both traditional dog shows and agility trials, as well as doing Schutzhund training when she was younger. Because she was a life-time resident of Oak Falls with a wide range of relatives scattered throughout the Hudson Valley, I was counting on her to help uncover details of Eloise's life.

After three or four of the rich chocolate tidbits, my assistant was more than happy to oblige.

"My mom always said that Eloise was a beautiful woman when she was younger. She came from money, brought up in Rhinebeck. Went to some kind of fancy boarding school, if I remember right."

After a quick chocolate break, she continued. "Eloise had her pick of guys but chose Andy Rieven, the youngest son of a bank president. Very handsome, but not particularly ambitious. The two honeymooned in Europe, and when they got back, he went to work in his dad's bank. She started raising and showing dogs. They had two kids, but one died in her teens. The daughter's death affected Eloise terribly," Mari said. "After that, things became worse."

"What do you mean?" I asked her.

"Well, they had, I guess, some financial ups and downs in one of the stock market crashes. The bank went under and Andy lost his job. They sold their big house in Rhinebeck and moved into her family's farmhouse in Oak Falls. Joe went to school here, but just as things started looking up, his father, Andy, committed suicide. Seems he owed money everywhere. Eloise didn't know that he was a secret gambler. Luckily, he couldn't gamble away the house here in the village because her family trust put it in her name. Life's been hard for her ever since then."

Everyone has a story, my Gramps always reminded me. I'd been quick to be annoyed at Eloise, but her bulldog puppies probably represented extra income.

"That's why she was so adamant about the artificial insemination."

"Do you remember any of her puppy sales going bad?" I asked. "Maybe someone who held a grudge against her?"

"I didn't, but my mom did. She sold some newlyweds a puppy with a heart problem."

That confounded me. "If there was a heart murmur or arrhythmia, that's usually picked up during the puppy exam." Most puppies and kittens had their first veterinary exams around six to eight weeks old.

After a quick sip of water, Mari continued. "Eloise didn't take them to a vet. She decided to save money and do everything herself."

That, unfortunately, is an all-too-common problem.

"Let me guess," I said. "The couple buy the puppy, take it to their vet for shots, and their vet has to give them the bad news. When they confront the breeder, Eloise tells them no refund unless they give her back the puppy."

"Sounds like you've heard this before."

Sadly, I had. Now the new owners are in a terrible position, of giving their baby puppy that they love back to the breeder, who may or may not get it proper medical care. Or worse yet, sell the puppy again and let another couple deal with the problem. I'd heard about every version of this basic story you could think of.

"Did they resolve it?" I asked.

Mari shook her head. "They were weekenders, and I think they brought the puppy for heart surgery in New

York City. Doc Anderson was pretty annoyed about the whole thing, though. He and Eloise had been friends."

One more reason the owner of Oak Falls Animal Hospital was on a round-the-world cruise and I was filling in for him.

A last question remained. "Why did she decide not to have puppy exams?" It might have cost her fifty-five or sixty dollars a puppy, and she sold them for one thousand dollars each. Of all the dogs to take a risk on, bulldogs were right up at the top of the most medical problems list.

Mari threw up her hands. "Money. Isn't it always about money?"

After a few phone calls, I had a basic understanding, thanks to Mari and her mother, of Eloise's life before she died. Living on Social Security, she owned her house outright and lived frugally. A proud woman, she wouldn't ask her own family for help. Little by little she'd sold off land when her children were young, keeping about fifty acres. All that was left on the acreage was the farmhouse—not a beautiful historic building full of antiques, just a worn old house in need of repair—and a broken-down garage.

Her will gave her entire estate to her only living child, Joe Rieven. The evidence was mounting up that this was simply a tragic accident.

So why did some people blame me?

I decided not to check how many more people logged on to YouTube to see the wish.

Chapter Ten

WINTER DAYS NOW FELL INTO A PATTERN, USUALLY predicated by the weather. On bad days my only trips outside were to walk the dog. Frank's and Eloise's deaths dampened my desire to socialize. I started skipping social media entirely. The amount of interest in my Christmas magic "death" wish, as people referred to it, escalated, I was told. Almost every other client we saw chided Mari and me about the video. Cindy reported receiving more crank phone calls, probably from teenagers, asking if they could add a few more people to our list.

Since there was no such thing as a secret in Oak Falls, the Christmas card we received from a dead guy bumped up the gossip.

It was less of a surprise when the second card arrived signed by Eloise, also deceased.

No one envied our office manager/receptionist Cindy having to slog through the mail each day with vendor bills, endless solicitations from brokers, and training seminars promising to whip your staff into shape over a weekend. That's why the square Christmas card envelopes stuck out from the rest. With a certain resignation on her face, she stopped me in the pharmacy. "These two are for you."

A glance at the first envelope set off no bells. It contained a return address. I opened it up to find a rambling note imploring me to use my "special" powers to get rid of someone. At first I thought it was another prank, someone pulling an elaborate joke on me...but the more I read the tangled and twisted pleas of the writer—who sincerely believed I might wish someone dead on his behalf—the more disturbing it became.

The second card presented a whole different problem. This familiar ivory envelope, of very good quality with a hallmark on the lip, looked identical to the previous card from Frank. Dreading, but needing to confirm who sent it, I slipped on a pair of exam gloves and very carefully opened the flap.

Cindy stood next to me, watching.

Inside rested a card with the same gilded edging, the same dog and cat in golden collars looking out the window at Santa Claus. It was signed Eloise and congratulated me on having my second wish come true.

"Things are getting out of hand," I told Cindy. We preserved both pieces of correspondence in separate bags and added them to Chief Garcia's items for pickup.

My receptionist locked the new evidence in her desk and said, "It always gets worse before it gets better."

"Should we tell the chief to put a bodyguard on that third person? The one Pinky added?"

From Cindy's expression I suspected she was tired of my worrying. "I'll say it again, Kate. Frank and Eloise died from accidents. Accidents. I know the whole thing seems weird, but weird things happen all the time in this world. These cards are from someone with a sick sense of humor."

She could repeat it a million times, but that didn't get rid of the feeling in my stomach that something was off.

Weird things. We all read bizarre stories about something or other all the time. In line at the drug store I'd read about sisters separated at birth only to end up twenty years later living next door to each other. A woman finding her lost wedding ring inside a potato. There even was an entire tabloid dedicated to paranormal stories of ghosts and aliens. Strange stories fascinated people. My story would probably show up in the Christmas issue.

———

Resigned to my current fate I tried to make the best of it. As Gramps said when he'd called to check up on me, "Everybody messes up. It's only a matter of time. Learn your lesson and forge ahead."

So forge ahead I did. Soon the jokes fell off, and some folks expressed concern that I was being harassed. Conversations in the hospital turned back to Christmas vacation and shopping and endless stuffing recipes. Talking about the weather rose to topic number one, with the YouTube video coming in a distant fourth.

My tension headaches lingered, though, especially at night after a demanding shift. Tired after a long day, I'd finally gotten rid of a lingering low-level throbbing at the base of my neck. Snuggled up with my happy dog after a glass of wine and an entire pint of fudge ripple ice cream, I was sleepily watching HGTV when the cell phone rang.

"Hey, Cindy. Anything wrong?" Caller ID had warned me my receptionist was calling. I just hoped she had no new disaster to report.

She laughed. "We're fine, but the night is young. I called to say don't you dare drive anywhere tonight. The roads are a mess, and this storm is way worse than anyone thought it would be. The ice is bringing down power lines."

As if on cue I heard the wind howl around the corner of the building. A tree limb pounded on the kitchen window. "Don't worry, I'm in for the night. The hospital is empty, and the emergency clinic has been on since we closed."

"Good. Let me know if Pinky comes by to plow."

"Sure thing."

Next to Pinky's house stood a modern garage, where he seemed to spend most of his time and stored snow blowers, riding tractors, at least two huge trucks, and all kinds of equipment.

"Don't forget, if the electric goes off, the generator should automatically kick in."

"Fine."

Cindy was the mother hen to everyone at the animal hospital, whether they needed a mother hen or not.

"Alright. If you want anything just call us. Stay warm."

"You too."

After another hour of mindless television, my eyes started to droop, but I needed to find out which home the couple from Phoenix chose, in a rerun of *House Hunters*.

They chose house number three. A big mistake, in my opinion.

That night a pounding on the door accompanied by barking from Buddy woke me from a sound sleep. The backup alarm clock on the nightstand said 1:15 in the morning.

"Dr. Kate, Dr. Kate!" The pounding continued. "Wake up. It's an emergency."

As the sleepiness cleared, I realized I recognized that voice.

"It's Pinky, Dr. Kate. My dog, Princess…" Garbled sounds followed, lost in all the noise.

I'd fallen asleep on the sofa. Despite being in wrinkled old sweats, I hushed Buddy and quickly opened the door.

There he stood, a massive three hundred plus pounds, clutching his toy poodle, Princess, to his chest. Snowflakes covered his hat and shoulders.

"Come with me," I said and led him through my place and into the hospital treatment area. Gently, I took Princess from him and grabbed my stethoscope.

"What's happening?" Before he could answer, the tiny dog started hacking, the dry cough echoing in the empty treatment room. I'd seen her before, a beautifully groomed senior dog much beloved and in good health. Now she lay in front of me struggling for breath.

Pinky stared at his pet, tears streaming down his face. "I took a break from plowing and found her on the floor, just like that."

While I listened to her heart and lungs and palpated her slightly swollen belly, my mind ran through a list of possible problems, from kennel cough to heart disease to cancer. First, we needed to help her breathe, so I placed her in an oxygen cage, inserted an IV, and pulled some bloods. That was enough stress until her breaths came easier.

"How long has her belly been swollen?" I asked while preparing to take an X-ray.

Pinky fixed me with a blank stare. "Swollen? I thought she was getting plump, like me. Princess eats what I eat. Always has, since she was a puppy."

Each time I heard that high voice coming out of Pinky, it caught me off guard. Physically imposing and completely bald, his round pink head looked welded to his body, with no neck to speak of. The odd high school nickname came from a propensity to flush dark pink when embarrassed or nervous.

I checked my patient, relieved to see her gums had gone from a muddy bluish color to slightly red, a very good sign.

"Why don't you sit down?" I told him. His breathing sounded labored to me. I didn't need to have him take a nosedive onto the floor.

I'd never be able to get him up.

———

About twenty minutes later I had some preliminary results for him. Meanwhile, both Pinky and Princess looked much better.

"Once she's stabilized, I'd like to transfer her to the emergency clinic."

"No," his voice thundered at me. "I want you to take

care of her." He was agitated now, and his round face deepened further into shades of dark rose.

In this state it was useless to argue with him.

"I don't want to leave her." Pinky stood up then, towering over me. Alone with him in the hospital, for a second I felt threatened, but with my insistence he quickly sat back down in one of the lab chairs. It creaked under his weight. When he looked back at me the tears started again.

"Well, I've got some more tests to run, so if you don't mind waiting here…" I broke off my sentence, not sure what else to say.

"Thank you, Dr. Kate. You're an angel." He wiped his eyes with a massive hand and rolled the chair closer to his pet. "This way she'll see me."

I pulled a white lab coat over my sweatshirt and got down to work. About ten minutes later the hospital quiet was shattered by a loud snore. Pinky had fallen into an exhausted sleep, one hand on the cage, the other across his belly.

Most of what I knew about our snowplowing neighbor came from our receptionist.

Cindy had described Pinky, whom she'd known for over twenty years, as a gigantic toddler. She avoided any clinical terms like autistic or on the spectrum. Those descriptions were kept only for family to use in some of these rural areas. The toy poodle had been his and his mother's pride and joy for the past thirteen years. It had fallen to Pinky, an only child and unmarried, to live with his failing mom and take care of her until she passed away a year ago. Since then, he'd only had his beloved dog for company.

Just Pinky and his Princess.

―――――

While he slept, I called the emergency clinic, which revealed some bad news. Their power had gone out due to a fallen tree, and the backup generator had failed to kick in. With no electricity or heat, they were closed and in the process of transferring their remaining patients even farther away from us.

By now it was seven a.m. and I'd heard the snowplows rumbling since early morning light. With no emergency clinic to pick up the slack, I did the next best thing. I called Mari.

When the phone picked up, all I heard was barking. Her pregnant Rottweiller, Lucy, had decided the phone was evil. "Just a minute," she yelled into the receiver. Muffled sounds followed until all was quiet. "Alright, is that better?"

"Hey, I hate to ask you…"

"What's the emergency?" she interrupted. "This better be good."

"It's Pinky."

"Princess? Oh, no. He must be a wreck."

That was one of the many things I liked about Mari, her big warm heart for pets and their people.

"Probable congestive heart failure, maybe complicated by kennel cough. She was groomed recently, so that's a possibility. Can't transfer her because the emergency clinic had to close. Power failure."

"Of course I'll help. When do you need me?" Bad weather never bothered her. Her gigantic four-wheel drive with oversized snow tires came complete with chains.

"How about later today, so I can get some sleep? The roads should be clear by then."

"Where's Pinky?"

"Asleep in the treatment room. Can't you hear him?" I held my phone up and sure enough, he rewarded us with a gigantic snore.

"See?" Mari laughed. "And you thought you'd be all alone this weekend."

———————

True to her word, Mari spelled me off, providing great care to our only patient. Pinky left early Sunday morning to finish plowing out his customers but came back every two or three hours, never empty-handed. He must have stopped in every store that was open, because I received an odd assortment of gifts, from a hula-girl keychain to a Halloween-size bag of Snickers bars.

Each time he visited, Princess stood up and wagged her tail, already feeling better. Of course she turned her nose up at the special dog food for cardiac patients, preferring to eat the roasted rotisserie chicken Pinky brought with him. We showed him how to mix the prescription food with a little bit of people food so Princess would eat it. He was under orders to then slowly increase the heart diet food and decrease the people food.

"You're a miracle worker, Dr. Kate. She's hardly coughing at all."

His enthusiasm needed to be tempered with some facts. "Pinky, Princess has a very common problem we find in older dogs." The more I talked about enlarged hearts putting stress on the lungs and the need for special diets and medication, the more his eyes glazed over. It would take time to process all this. The folder of information Mari prepared for him to read lay unopened on the counter.

"I'd like Princess to have a cardiology consultation and ultrasound," I said.

"Pinky, I'll help you make the appointment, if you like. Your schedule must be crazy right now." Mari patted her friend on his arm. "And thanks for plowing me out."

"You're welcome, Mari."

I gave Mari a thumbs-up for her suggestion. Poor Pinky looked exhausted and overwhelmed. "The veterinarian I'm sending you to in Kingston is board-certified in cardiology, and their office isn't that far away," I said.

"Okay, I'll get their info. Be right back," Mari told him. She left for the reception area, whistling in the hallway.

Pinky watched her leave.

"I've included a diet you can cook for her at home, too, if you want." The jolt from too many chocolate bars gobbled up to stay awake had started to fade. Maybe I could squeeze in a nap, since I'd be up most of the night checking on Princess. Over my shoulder I heard Mari coming back. "Alright, Mari will take it from here. I'm going to take a nap." I'd almost made it out of the treatment area when I heard Pinky's high-pitched voice.

"Dr. Kate, if there's anything I can do for you… anything…let me know. I've always known you were a wonderful person, an angel, and…I'd kill anyone who's mean to you or hurts you."

Chapter Eleven

THE ALARM ON THE NIGHTSTAND JOLTED ME AWAKE. Not quite recovered from my long night, I sleepily entered the hospital break room, lured by the welcome fragrance of freshly brewed coffee. Cindy constantly surprised us with premium blends, and this morning's eye-opener smelled of hazelnuts. My unaccustomed gift of free time from the snowstorm was over. I'd been warned we were completely booked.

With Princess stabilized and the weather improved, things quickly got back to normal. Ever-efficient Cindy had secured a cardiology appointment for a reluctant Pinky, with Mari serving as his wing man.

By the second cup of coffee my eyes sprang wide open. Another client had gifted us with a tin of homemade granola, which I ate with some fresh apple slices provided by health-conscious Cindy. The caffeine and the brown-sugared cereal did their jobs. Full of temporary energy, I'd already run through my morning email and checked lab results when Cindy knocked on the door of my office.

"Compliments on your coffee choice this morning," I told her. "It's my favorite so far."

The usually chatty Cindy appeared subdued. "I heard Pinky's been saying some odd things."

"Not really." It was too early in the morning to go there. Soon, I'd be so involved in medical cases I wouldn't have time to think about anything else. With a mental push I shoved everything related to Frank and Eloise and holiday selfish wishes and Pinky killing my enemies into that already-crowded problems drawer in my brain.

"Let's talk later. We've got a full day ahead of us."

She didn't look pleased.

"Oh, listen," I said to distract her. "'Deck the Halls.' My favorite."

With a phony smile on my face, I walked over to exam room one, knocked, then entered to see my first client of the day.

The problem was that the mental drawer kept popping open unexpectedly throughout the day, and all the unanswered questions inside insisted on waving their little hands at me.

Finished with morning appointments, safe in my office, I took a bite of my turkey sandwich on rye, finally enjoying a moment of down time, when Mari interrupted me.

"You busy?" Her head poked in first before the rest followed.

"That depends." My mouth continued its trajectory toward the sandwich target. Usually when people ask me if I'm busy it means they've got something they want me to do. Immediately.

I'd been looking forward to this sandwich since our lunch order arrived and, short of a medical emergency, these thirty minutes allotted for eating were all mine. When I looked up, she was still there.

"Someone in the parking lot needs to see you."

"Ahhh, no. An emergency? Do we need a stretcher?" I stood up, rammed the last bit of sandwich in my mouth, and washed it down with coffee.

"Sit down," Mari said. "It's nothing like that." She closed the half-open office door. "I'm not sure you're going to like…"

A million horrible scenarios ran in and out of my head. "Will you please tell me what's going on?"

"Jeremy is here."

"Jeremy?" That was the one scenario that hadn't occurred to me. "What does he want?" My old college buddy, turned boyfriend, turned cheating boyfriend, had been persona non grata to me for the last month, despite his several apologies and imaginative excuses for his bad behavior. I'd blocked him from my phone, social media, and everywhere I could.

My assistant paced back and forth before gingerly taking a seat. I wondered how long she'd chatted with him in the parking lot and how high he'd turned up the old charm.

"He's got a Christmas present for you."

"Well, you know what he can do with it." To stop our discussion, I poured more coffee and began entering some notes on the computer. If I thought that would end the matter, I was wrong.

"Actually, he has presents for all of us." Her voice perked up, a willing victim of Jeremy's bribes. "Godiva chocolates and all sorts of delicious things."

It was nice to know how little it took to win the staff over.

When that didn't work, she rationalized, "Hey, you have to face him sometime. We start in fifteen minutes or so, and the first two appointments are in the waiting room staring at your old boyfriend and his Mercedes in the parking lot. Please, can we just get this over with?"

Despite feeling waylaid, I saw her point. He'd been a big part of my life and I missed him. I'd been thinking of calling him up and wishing him a happy holiday season—testing to see if we might revert back to just being friends.

"Alright." I logged out of the computer. "But I'm going out through my apartment. No need to let the whole town know." As if that wouldn't happen.

Her head nodded in agreement. "Smart idea. Good luck."

Good luck. I certainly could use some, but it wasn't in the cards.

———

Throwing my warmest coat on and raising the woolly hood over my head, I left the apartment and snuck around the side of the hospital toward the main parking lot. Sure enough, Jeremy lounged against the hood of his Mercedes holding a box with a glittery gold bow. A professor of anthropology, he had an Indiana Jones thing going that he cultivated to the max. I tried to surreptitiously gesture him to come over to me, but instead he saw me and waved.

"Kate, thanks for coming out here." His voice exuded warmth. "I'm really glad to see you."

"You could have texted me first, instead of surprising the whole staff." My tone of voice sounded anything but friendly. Glancing over to the hospital entrance, I noticed a mob of people staring out the picture window at us.

"Did you forget you blocked me?" He followed my glance. "Hey, we've got an audience." Then to my horror he waved at everyone, a great big wave.

For some reason that wave pushed my buttons. Angry, I whirled around, amazed he had no respect for my privacy.

"Okay, I admit, this might have been a bad idea." Jeremy circled around to head me off. "At least take my present." With a sad puppy-dog look on his face, he held the red-and-gold wrapped gift out to me. I hated that face.

On impulse I grabbed the gift, walked over to the dumpster and threw it in. The metal top slammed down as I said, "Happy Holidays."

The audience at the window had horrified looks on their faces.

Fueled by my emotions, I stomped off, shooing away his outstretched hand. Jeremy appeared astonished at my actions. Still annoyed, I pulled open the apartment door, and just as I was about to slam it for effect, I noticed Pinky standing in his driveway, staring at us. Embarrassed, I gave him a little wave and silently shut the door.

"Don't say anything," I admonished Cindy and Mari, who rushed into the treatment room after watching our argument through the reception picture window along with everyone else.

"You should take this weekend to relax. Maybe get a massage." Cindy busied herself with straightening up while catching sideways looks at me. "I'm afraid this will be a hot topic in town tonight."

"So what else is new? Just pile it onto everything else."

Mari handed me my stethoscope, and both my friends took off.

Ready to start afternoon appointments, I caught a glimpse of myself in the employee lounge mirror. My straight blond hair was sticking up, electrified from being under the wool hood of the coat. I plastered it down with a little water. Anxious eyes stared back at me, my supposed resemblance to Meryl Streep barely noticeable. The lip gloss in my pocket, worn down to the nub, broke off while applying it. When I threw the remainder in the garbage can, it rattled around in protest.

After a few more breaths I'd started to calm down, when the speakers came to life with a loud and lively chorus of "On the First Day of Christmas." I replaced their words with my own.

Two dead clients, one ex-boyfriend, and a present dumped in the trash.

———

The ringing noise started at three a.m. and woke me up. Was it Pinky again? Then I realized no one was at the door. I fished around for the cell phone.

"Hello?" My brain still felt mushy with sleep.

"Is this Dr. Kate Turner?" asked an unfamiliar voice.

I bolted straight up in bed. "Has something happened to my grandfather?" I'd been dreading this kind of call in the middle of the night. "Did he fall?"

"This is Kingston Hospital admitting. We have a Jeremy Engels here, who has asked us to call you."

"Jeremy?" The clouds lifted as I switched into emergency mode. "Was he in a car accident? How is he?" My studio apartment felt claustrophobic.

Hesitation on the line. Why were they hesitating? Visions of mangled arms and legs made me leap out of bed and reach for my scrubs.

A voice came back on the line. "Just checking that he signed a release for medical information to you. HIPAA rules."

I knew all about the HIPAA rules. "Is he okay?"

"He's got a head injury and contusions on his arms where he fought off his attacker."

"His attacker?" Now I was completely confused.

Again, there was a muffled silence, before the voice explained, "I'm sorry. That's all the information I can give you at the moment. You are free to visit him."

"What room is he in?" I pulled on my boots and searched for my purse and backpack, trying to figure out what I needed.

"You'll have to check at the information desk." Then, just before she hung up, she added an incongruous "Have a nice day."

Taking Buddy out before I left reminded me of the

freezing temperatures and to get some warm gloves. I had no idea about the parking situation at the Kingston Hospital.

Our automatic motion detector light flipped on when I opened the door, casting a yellowish light on the animal hospital parking lot, which to my surprise had been newly plowed by Pinky. He'd even brushed the snow from the windshield of the hospital's old F-150 truck.

Grateful for his kindness, my thoughts focused on my injured friend.

It wasn't until later that I questioned Pinky's intentions.

Chapter Twelve

THE KINGSTON HOSPITAL PARKING LOT SURPRISED ME by being half full at 4:15 in the morning. I walked through the crowded emergency room only to have to wait in line to ask a question.

Once more I was grateful to be a veterinarian instead of a human medical doctor. Sick children cuddled limply in their parents' arms. Scattered among the crowd were the injured, with stark white bandages wrapped around various body parts, a few speckled with blood. As I scanned the people waiting, my eye first passed, then went back to a middle-aged man sitting alone in the corner. Beads of sweat were visible on his forehead, and his right hand pressed tightly against his chest. Overweight and pale, he looked to me like a heart attack waiting to happen.

By then I'd reached the top of the line.

"I'm Dr. Kate Turner," I said. "I'd like the room number of Jeremy Engels, please."

"Certainly, Doctor," the woman said, taking a quick look at my scrubs underneath my coat.

"Oh, and you might send the triage nurse to look at that gentleman in the corner in the blue shirt," I said, turning toward him. The man had closed his eyes, a look of discomfort on his face.

She quickly followed my glance, then picked up the phone.

Jeremy looked better than I'd imagined when I opened the door to his room.

"Hi, Kate," he said cheerily. "Sorry to get you up in the middle of the night."

"You always were dramatic," I told him before reaching for his hand, careful to avoid the intravenous line taped to the inside of his arm.

"Didn't see him at all," he confided, sipping from his glass of water. "He jumped me when I was opening the car door."

I brushed a lock of brown hair from his forehead. Against the white pillow his skin appeared bruised and swollen, peppered with small bloody scrapes. "Have you spoken to the police? Can you identify your assailant?"

A confused look crossed his face. "No and no. I think the noise of people coming around the corner scared him off. By then I was down on the ground, my nose in the gravel."

That accounted for the multiple abrasions on his face. I hoped Jeremy hadn't looked at himself in the mirror. A puffy bruise over his right eye and forehead was in the process of turning multiple shades of blue and purple.

Knowing it was important to write things down as soon as possible, I asked, "Do you have any memories of what he was wearing, or a distinctive smell or anything?" I knew victims sometimes remembered strange things.

He thought for a moment. "I heard footsteps behind me, and then I got knocked down. I've got a big bump on the top of my head." His hand involuntarily went to the spot. "The EMTs thought I hit the curb." His former bravura had been replaced by a forlorn expression reminiscent of a three-year-old with a booboo.

We sat together holding hands, while a nurse came in to check his vitals. Idly, I noticed our animal hospital had the same brand of IV stand as they did. A doctor checked in for a brief exam and updated us. With a normal CT scan and everything else stable, the plan was to keep him overnight, then release him in the morning.

"Do you want me to call your parents?" Since Jeremy and I had a long history from college, I knew his parents and he knew Gramps.

He shifted his position on the bed. "Ouch. Not right now. Dad got diagnosed with atrial fibrillation last week, and my mom is a wreck. I'll tell them later."

"Well then, you're staying with me," I told him. "No way you're driving a car or doing anything until we're sure you aren't bleeding into your brain from the concussion."

His eyes dilated at the thought.

"Too much information?" I asked.

"Yeah, especially the bleeding brain part." Jeremy leaned back into his pillow. "But I'll take you up on your offer. Thanks."

"You're welcome, buddy."

"Buddies again?" He managed a wan smile.

Recent events melted away. Instead, I saw the skinny guy who pulled all-nighters with me, shared pizza and school gossip, and always had time to listen to my crazy family stories. All I saw was my old college friend again.

"Buddies."

Chapter Thirteen

WE BOTH DOZED OFF, UNMINDFUL OF THE BUZZING overhead fluorescent panel and the steady beep of his vitals. A loud knock on the door woke us up.

Two police officers strode into the room. "Jeremy Engels?"

Sleepily, Jeremy answered, "Yes?"

They looked like Mutt and Jeff, one tall and skinny and the other round and short. The short one pulled out a small notebook from his pocket. "I'm Detective Muldorf, and this is Detective Murphy."

Punchy from lack of sleep, I stifled a laugh at the idea of M & M, the humor being completely unintentional.

I got an odd look from Officer Muldorf and a raised eyebrow.

Feeling a necessity to identify myself, I said, "I'm Dr. Kate Turner, a friend of the victim." Even to my ears my statement sounded like it was written for a television show.

However, it only elicited a nod.

"Were you with him when the attack occurred?" This time Officer Murphy asked the question.

"No," I began, suddenly very formal. "I wasn't."

Their attention immediately shifted to Jeremy, who sipped some water from his cup. Now awake, he reached for my hand for support. I doubted he'd ever been interviewed by the police, while I, unfortunately, was quite an expert.

"Can you describe the incident to us?"

As Jeremy recited the circumstances, I realized no one at the animal hospital knew where I was, and I had several texts to illustrate the point. I'd put my cell on mute, as requested by the nurse, and forgotten about it.

While I texted a quick update to Cindy and Mari, the interview swirled around me. From what I gathered the police felt this was a mugging, with the perpetrator targeting Jeremy and his expensive Mercedes parked amid the pickup trucks and beat-up minivans. When several noisy patrons from a local bar rounded the corner, the attacker fled, leaving Jeremy's wallet and identification intact in his inside pocket. Jeremy owed his life to those party animals.

My buddy had been drinking his sorrows away at his hotel bar in Kingston and only made a quick run to his car to retrieve his forgotten overnight case.

From their discussion it sounded as though the police felt Jeremy was the victim of a quick grab-and-run. In his expensive leather jacket, sporting a Rolex watch and a wallet full of money, they suspected he'd been targeted in the hotel bar. The cameras in the parking lot were iced over, but one provided a blurry picture of someone in a bulky dark coat and black knit hat coming up behind him.

"Robberies always increase around the holidays," Officer Muldorf stated stoically.

"I guess criminals need money to go holiday shopping too," I muttered under my breath. "Merry Christmas."

Except for a quick run back to my apartment to straighten up and take a shower, I spent the next twelve hours in the hospital room with Jeremy. I'd brought journals to read and my laptop but found it hard to work scrunched up in the visitor's chair.

His hospital room looked like all hospital rooms—a crowded, uncomfortable place that made you want to run away and never come back. Although the nurses and staff were great, they didn't have much time to spend with an obviously improved patient. Sicker people and new arrivals commanded their attention.

We didn't blame them, but it made us itchy to leave. However, if Jeremy thought getting sprung out of there would be easy, he didn't know hospital procedure. Over a period of three hours we waited for first one release paper, and then another, then one more order to be signed, until finally, suddenly—we were free to go. With Mari's help I had already coordinated the check-out at his hotel, driving the F-150 back to my place.

"Now," I said, as I loaded him and his possessions into the Mercedes, "feel free to stay as long as you want."

Yet another pronouncement I'd live to regret.

Chapter Fourteen

Two days later Jeremy seemed a little too happy being ensconced in my apartment.

"Kate, we need to decorate this place," he announced as we sat down to breakfast. "Don't forget, it's almost Christmas."

How could I forget? That's why I hadn't decorated—to create a sanctuary of quiet.

"Believe me," I answered, "I know it's almost Christmas. No one lets me forget it."

I'd laid down strict rules for him while he was recovering from his injuries. No alcohol, no stress, no driving, and no late nights. I'd given him my bed and was camping out on the sofa, although he frequently invited me to share with him.

"And no sex," I added.

While I went to work, he played with Buddy, did some paperwork, worked on projects from the university website, and corresponded with other anthropologists all over the world. His amorously inclined but married Italian colleague, who'd gotten him into trouble with me, was conspicuously absent in the conversations.

When I summoned up enough nerve to question what she was up to, he replied that she and her husband, also an anthropologist, had a very…sophisticated relationship…and both currently had "intimate" friends. I left it at that.

After a quick glance at the time, I left him lounging in his pajamas and went to work.

———————

Mari and I were in the Ford F-150 headed for a recheck of our stinky-eared dog when she broached a topic I'd been avoiding. Jeremy.

"I'm sorry to bring this up," she started while eating potato chips, "but Cindy and I were talking…"

Oh no, never a good start to a sentence. The bare trees guarding the side of the roads loomed ominously closer.

"And we wondered if Jeremy getting, you know, beat up had anything to do with your…you know, evil Selfish Santa wish?" She nervously looked down at the computer in her lap, avoiding my stare.

Concentrating on the road, I pretended to ignore what she was talking about.

"You know," Mari persisted, "that argument in the parking lot. Maybe someone wanted to teach him a lesson."

"Highly doubtful," I commented. "You and Cindy have been watching too much television."

I stared out the windshield. We'd had a temporary increase in temperature with some sunny days, so the formerly pristine white fields around us now were a muddy, grayish mess. Anything that the snow had concealed now lay revealed. Broken tree limbs littered the ground. Jagged pieces of wood stuck out of the slush.

At the turn to our appointment I slowed down, snow

tires digging into the exposed gravel on the driveway. "We're here."

Mari began to gather up our supplies and closed down the hospital laptop.

Sun broke out from behind some clouds, filtering bright light through the treetops. In the field to our right I spotted Ashley's flashy mustang, Lobo. The horse looked like he'd bolt any second.

I slowed the truck down and practically crawled the rest of the way, careful to stay in the middle of the plowed driveway. About two feet of compacted slush guided us along.

"I wonder if Ashley's having any more luck getting him to settle down?" Mari buttoned her coat and finished the bag of chips.

"No idea. I hope so," I commented as we passed the field, the house in sight. But while the other horses and donkeys stood peacefully munching near the hay mound, Lobo's body language showed an animal on high alert.

Ready to run.

———

Happily, our dog patient no longer smelled since I'd removed the benign polyp in his ear. With a good cleaning and diligent medication program to address the several types of bacteria and yeast we'd cultured out, he'd had a remarkable recovery.

After a quick cup of coffee we made our way out to the mudroom, stopping to put on our boots.

"Thanks for coming to the house," Ashley said. "I've got about four more weeks in this brace." The large Velcro and plastic device snapped on her left knee was hard to miss.

"What happened?" Mari asked her.

"Slipped in the pasture. It's a long story, but I've had to put Lobo's training off for a bit. I can't stand for very long," she explained. Her fingertips touched the side of her leg next to the brace, and she winced.

"How's that going?" Mari asked, leaning against the tack room wall.

"Not as well as I hoped," confessed Lobo's owner. "And now, with this setback…"

I impulsively volunteered to work with him, trying to ignore Mari's raised eyebrow.

"Dr. Turner," she interrupted me, "did you forget…?"

"It's alright. I can periodically drop in and work a bit with Lobo. I drive past here all the time." In fact, I found the prospect exciting. After graduating, I focused on helping small animals but really missed interacting with the big guys. And it would provide a challenge, trying to help him adjust to his new reality. Dealing with a horse always puts problems in perspective. Your mind can't wander when you're standing next to twelve hundred pounds of unpredictable muscle and bone towering over you. Secretly, I sympathized with the mustang.

In a way I was being forced to adjust to a new family, too.

"Are you crazy?" Mari started in on me as soon as we got in the truck. "I see how tired you are all the time. You're already juggling a full workload, and now with Jeremy recuperating and Luke finishing his semester and who knows what else…" Her voice spluttered to a stop as she ran out of steam.

As usual my friend was watching out for me. Maneuvering down the driveway, I gathered my thoughts. They were complicated, both personal and professional. She knew all about some, and nothing about the most important one. No one but Gramps really knew. "Mari, there's something…" I hesitated. Did I really want to go into this with her?

"Don't tell me your father finally contacted you?"

How did she figure that out from three words? At the bottom of the driveway, a car then a truck whizzed by. I waited for a chance to pull onto the main road. Mari came from a very happy family situation. Would she understand how I felt?

Sometimes I didn't understand it myself.

"Never mind," I told her, decision made. A lull in the traffic provided the perfect diversion. "I'll tell you later."

———

By the time we finished our last appointment it was five thirty, and we were at least a half hour away from the animal hospital. Cindy called to tell us she was closing up. The remaining staff had cleaned and finished treatments, so we were off the hook for the rest of the night.

"Shoot," I said. "When we go back I've got to go to the grocery store. Jeremy texted me a list."

"We're going to pass one on the way back," Mari reminded me. "Why don't we stop now? I've got to pick up a few things, too."

"Good idea. Once I pull these boots off, I'm not putting them back on."

The market appeared on our right, its parking lot well plowed and practically dry. As soon as we found an empty space over by the dumpsters, we both made for the entrance, anticipating a quick in and out.

This wasn't my usual grocery store, so it took longer to find everything, but soon I headed toward the front to meet my assistant.

Standing in line at the checkout, Mari and I chatted about our evening plans. With Jeremy still recuperating for the next few days, it was probably a choice between TV programs or a movie. Mari, on the other hand, was having a few friends over to play video games, which explained the pile of chips, dips, peanuts, and snacks in her basket.

My chaste veggies and roasted chicken looked incredibly healthy, if you didn't count the ice cream and doughnuts.

A blond woman in her late twenties busy bagging Mari's groceries suddenly looked up and obviously recognized her. "Mari?" she asked.

"Rae?" The greeting my technician returned sounded a bit forced. "How's it going?"

"What do you think?" came the angry response. "I'm

bagging groceries for a living, thanks to you and her." She pointed her index finger at me.

I'd never seen this person in my life. Baffled, I said, "What?"

My response opened a big can of slithering worms.

"When I applied for another vet tech position," Rae said, angrily tossing first some chips then two bottles of salsa into a plastic bag, "someone told me Dr. Turner, here, got involved and personally badmouthed me to every vet in town."

"I'm sorry," I said, "but I don't even know you."

"Yes, you do. I worked with you after Doc Anderson left."

I remained baffled. The first few weeks I worked at the practice, six months ago, were a blur. She didn't look familiar. Did she confuse me with someone else?

Mari waited near the door, ready to leave. The cashier quickly scanned my chicken and started on the other items, a resigned look on her face. I'm sure she just wanted us out of there.

Before Rae could hurl the chicken at me, I placed it in my canvas shopping bag.

"I don't blame you, Mari, that much," Rae explained, turning toward her. "But I do blame Dr. Smart Ass here."

The Dr. Smart Ass remark came with a rude gesture. "You should mind your own business and butt out," she continued.

It felt like forever until my credit card was accepted. The strangely calm cashier handed me my receipt as if nothing had happened. Clutching the rest of my order,

I almost escaped before Rae called out a threat loud enough for each customer in the store to hear.

"Everyone thinks you're so nice. But I know the truth." Her pretty face contorted with rage while groceries from the next customer piled up at the end of the conveyor belt.

When I opened the door, Rae yelled one last thing. "You better watch your back, Kate Turner."

———

"What the heck was that about?" Our tires screeched as the truck sped out of the parking lot and back onto the main road. Our groceries in the back seat took a nosedive.

"Is it a full moon tonight?" Mari asked, twisting around to put her salsa back in her bag. "People are acting nuts."

"Except most of it is directed at me."

"Well, I have no idea what she's talking about. You had nothing to do with her being let go. Cindy hired Rae part-time for thirty hours a week but realized we only needed to fill in for about twenty, because Tony changed his mind and kept his extra shifts."

Staffing at a veterinary hospital always presented a juggling act. "Did you offer her fewer hours?"

Mari shrugged her shoulders. "Of course, but she needed more money than that. There had been some kind of emergency, and if I remember, she'd been fighting with her boyfriend and mentioned moving out."

"Where do I fit in to this story?" Her anger toward me had been disconcerting.

"No idea."

At the welcome sight of our animal hospital sign, I made a sharp turn into the parking lot before pulling up next to Mari's truck parked in front of my apartment.

"Sorry that happened to you." As we got out my assistant added, "If she should be mad at anyone it would be Cindy, not you. But hey, people do strange things around Christmas."

I had to agree. And things were about to get even stranger.

Chapter Fifteen

DESPITE MARI'S REASSURANCES, MY STOMACH FELT like I'd swallowed a lead weight. I'd never regretted stopping to pick up groceries more. How could something so simple end up complicating your life? After saying goodnight to Mari, I stared at my sad garage apartment, wishing I had somewhere else to go. Unable to put it off any longer, I hoisted up my groceries and started toward the door.

Buddy greeted me, barking at the large canvas bag of groceries balanced in my hands. Jeremy looked up from his computer. "Hi. Need some help?"

"No, I'm fine," I said, fully expecting him to jump up and help anyway. He didn't.

"How are you feeling?"

"Perfect. No headaches. No dizziness." With a smile he went back to Facebook, or whatever he was doing. I lugged everything into the kitchen, beginning to realize how much time Jeremy logged in on different websites.

"What's for dinner?"

Despite the question, he didn't even look up from the screen. This was not how I envisioned helping him recuperate. It was now almost three days after the mugging, and he had no headache, no memory problems—just a voracious appetite and ability to sleep through my morning wake-up alarm. A recheck this morning through the ER doctor gave him the all-clear to resume his life.

Suddenly an overwhelming urge to get out of the apartment blasted me into action.

"You know, I've got an idea. We haven't been to the diner in a while," I said while carefully putting away my haphazardly packed groceries. "Why don't you get dressed and we'll celebrate your recovery? Your treat."

He quickly got my drift.

"My treat? Absolutely. The doctor said I'm alright—so I'll even drive you."

"Perfect." I forced a smile on my face to match his.

On the way out to the car, the tape recorder in my brain replayed the supermarket worker's voice yelling over and over at me.

"You're quiet," my friend noticed as he spotted the diner's big sign.

"A little tired," I said. "But let's try to have some fun for a change."

Winner of numerous awards, the Oak Falls Diner routinely made the top ten lists of best diners on the East Coast. Family owned, they used locally sourced food as much as possible and were famous for their desserts—especially their pies. Which made me a slavish devotee.

I had a thing for homemade pie.

In fact, if someone asked me what I would choose for my last meal on earth, pie would be front and center, with fruit or berry pie under a lattice crust definitely topping the list.

Jeremy and I found a table relatively quickly and both ordered the nightly special, pasta with a homemade meat sauce spiked with wild mushrooms. The place was warm and noisy and had that delicious diner smell to it. Periodic bursts of laughter lifted the spirit of the room and our spirits as well.

We wasted no time digging in. As usual, the food tasted delicious, and authentically Italian, thanks to Luke's grandmother's family recipes.

"Isn't this owned by the Gianetti family?" Jeremy conveniently stuffed his mouth with a piece of homemade bread, between forkfuls of pasta. "Haven't seen much of Luke since I've been here."

"Mmmmm."

"Is that a yes?" he asked.

"Yes." There was no way I wanted to discuss relationships or lack of one with Jeremy, so I desperately thought of some other topic. "Hey, something odd happened earlier today, with Mari and me at the grocery store," I said, sprinkling my pasta with grated Parmigiano cheese. "This woman yelled at me."

"Did you smash into her cart?"

"No."

"All the members of my dig team used to get yelled at by the locals. And spit on, especially in some parts of Africa. The natives thought we were stealing their ancient ancestors."

My fork halted midway to my mouth as I asked, "Well, weren't you, in a way?"

He frowned. "We only worked with approval of the local government. But I can see your point."

Immediately, he honed in on my lame story. I suppose he

was starved for entertainment. "Let's get back to the supermarket. Why would anyone yell at you? You're so sweet."

Accepting the compliment, I explained about the strange encounter at the checkout line. "Mari and I have no idea why she'd be annoyed at me. And she was *really* pissed." I pushed my empty plate away, hunger satisfied. "Oh, my gosh." I rested both hands on my stomach. "I'm so full."

"Too full for pie?" he raised his eyebrows with a cocky grin.

"You've got to be kidding." This time I pointed to my abdomen. "There's always room for pie in there."

———

Jeremy suggested a pie contest, so after a leisurely orgy of multiple desserts we lingered over coffee—decaf for me but high test for him. The day's escapades faded into a hazy mist.

"So, getting back to this strange argument."

Oh, no. My friend never could let a topic go until it was discussed to death.

"Maybe later?" I looked at my watch. Almost nine o'clock.

Our waitress returned with our receipt and several take-out boxes with leftover slices of pie and cake.

"Just one question. Did this person tell you why she was so mad?" Knowing Jeremy, he was taking notes in his head.

I thought back to the encounter, the woman's image seared into my brain. Sun-streaked blond hair, big blue eyes, more like a small-town beauty queen than a super-market store bagger. A vicious look on her pageant-worthy face, there had to be more to her story than getting fired from Oak Falls Animal Hospital.

Discussing the incident felt wrong. "Let's forget it."

"No. It's obviously bothering you," he said. "Spit it out, Kate."

I scratched the side of my mouth even though it wasn't itchy. "Alright. What I don't get is she accused me of spreading lies or something." Again I thought back to her words. "Wait. That's not quite right. She accused me of telling other veterinarians nearby not to hire her. Which, of course, is ridiculous."

Jeremy didn't see anything funny. "The meeting was simply a coincidence, right?"

"Right. After our last house call, Mari and I decided to pick up a few things at the supermarket, since we were driving right past it. The stop was supposed to save us both some time."

"So, no premeditation on her side? No deliberately trying to get you into trouble?"

What an odd question. "Of course not. How could there be?"

"Then you have to consider the other possibility, Kate." His tone of voice turned serious.

I still didn't get it.

He reached over and took my hand. "People spread rumors for a lot of reasons. Anthropologically speaking, it is fascinating. You might have to consider…that maybe she was telling you the truth."

Chapter Sixteen

HIS WORDS KEPT ME UP THAT NIGHT. LONG AFTER Jeremy started to snore away in blissful sleep, I tossed around on the sofa. The blanket was too tight. Then the pillow needed to be fluffed up. All the while Rae yelled "Watch your back" over and over.

How could her statement be true—that I told all the local veterinarians not to hire her?

Someone must be lying to her.

———

I fell into a fitful sleep only to awaken at one a.m., eyes wide open.

My eyes weren't the only ones alert in the dark. My dog was sniffing around the apartment front door that opened to the parking lot.

No growling, which was a good sign, but it couldn't be a coincidence we both woke up at the same time.

"Buddy," I whispered. The room was dark except for a night-light in the bathroom. Jeremy's rhythmic snoring punctuated the stillness. No headlights glowed outside. I peeked out the window. There was nothing, just a light dusting of snow on the windshields of my truck and Jeremy's Mercedes. Buddy stood on his back legs and nosed under the blinds. Reluctantly, he whimpered and moved away toward me.

We sat together on the sofa, ears alert, until finally Buddy licked my hand good night, jumped down, and curled up in his own bed.

———

"Wake up, sleepyhead," Jeremy whispered.

I stretched and yawned and almost slid off the sofa. "What time is it?"

He looked down at me, a Christmas-tree-covered apron protecting his clothes. "Nine o'clock on a Saturday morning and you are off the entire day. Finally!" His enthusiasm outpaced mine by a mile. All I wanted was a cup of coffee. Then we could celebrate.

My guest had given me an early Christmas/thank-you gift. The new addition to the tiny kitchen was an expensive combination coffee/espresso machine. Jeremy drank espresso and called it a necessity of life. I liked whichever one I could pour quicker.

"Ready for Jeremy's internationally famous egg and cheese on a muffin?"

That made me laugh. It was about the only thing Jeremy could cook other than microwave popcorn. We'd lived on both of them while studying for finals at school.

I dressed and answered a few animal-hospital-related emails and texts while he made breakfast. Soon we were sitting down at the kitchen table chatting about pranks we pulled in the dorm—me being a reluctant participant most of the time.

"Let's do something different today," he urged. "What about a trip to Rhinebeck or New Paltz?"

"What about Paris instead?" I joked, then remembered my vow to visit Lobo, the mustang, for the next few Saturdays. "Sorry, I've got a date with a horse."

Jeremy frowned. "That's a new one."

"You're welcome to come along. It should be interesting." I took another sip of coffee, my second delicious cup of the morning.

"Why is that interesting?" Jeremy knew a little bit about horses. His older sister trained as an equestrian jumper for many years, and her little brother had taken a few lessons.

"Lobo is a wild mustang, or rather, he grew up wild. My client, Ashley, adopted him through the Bureau of Land Management." I stood up and brought the dishes to the sink. "He went through their program but still needs more gentling around people."

"So who doesn't?" he commented. "I'm up for that. Then we can drive over to Rhinebeck and wander around or do whatever you want to do. It's all fine with me."

Together we made short work of the breakfast dishes. I advised him to wear his waterproof boots, since the pasture and stalls were bound to be muddy and mucky. As always, I picked up my emergency backpack and flung it over my shoulder.

"You still carry the Swiss Army Knife Gramps gave you in that thing?" Jeremy asked.

"Sure do," I admitted. "Did I tell you for high school graduation my best friend received a necklace with a solid gold locket from her family? I got a Swiss Army Knife. Perfect gift."

"He always worried about you. I did too." Jeremy used to walk me back to my dorm at night after our marathon study sessions.

"That's because Gramps heard all these horror stories from his buddies on the police force about women getting assaulted. Every Saturday until I left for school, he made me take self-defense lessons and then karate. I've got the black belt to prove it." Just for fun I swung my leg sideways and delivered a roundhouse kick in his direction.

"Not much need for it up here," my friend said, looking out the window at the quiet winter landscape surrounding us.

———

We drove down the road, the F-150 truck quite a bit bouncier than his Mercedes. The morning stayed cold and clear for our entire trip, a bonus when working with large animals out in a field. We stopped for gas and loaded up on real apples to supplement the horse treats Mari had stashed in the back seat. With food bribes in place, I looked forward to another encounter with Lobo. I'd texted Ashley before we left so she was expecting us. Sure enough, the security gate at the base of the driveway opened quickly after the truck rolled in front of the sensor.

As soon as the herd appeared, Jeremy tried unsuccessfully to spot Lobo. I didn't see him either, although

I knew Ashley had turned him out into the main pasture. "Look for a mid-size bay mare. That's his buddy, Sweet Potato."

"Cute name," he said. "Lobo is a pinto, right?"

"Right. Very flashy with a blond mane, dark face, and blue eyes." Having almost nicked one of the snow shoulders with the right tire, I refocused my attention to the road. "I'll pull up closer to the barn and park."

"Wait. He's off in the corner with another horse in front, throwing a block." Jeremy pointed to a cluster of trees on the far side of the field.

Sure enough, on close inspection what looked like one horse was really two, as if Lobo deliberately chose to hide behind his friend, Sweet Potato.

By pulling over we stirred the curiosity of the diverse animal herd in the field. Thinking we might be carrying something tasty on us, they ambled over for some nose scratching and treats. Sweet Potato made a leisurely break from Lobo to see what all the fuss was about.

"Shoot," I said. "We still need to cut him out of the crowd." Before I could finish, a donkey head butted me, probably annoyed I wasn't faster with his apple. They all smelled the various treats I had hidden in the bag and in my pockets.

"Love this," Jeremy said with a smile as he stroked Sweet Potato's velvety nose.

My phone buzzed with a text from Ashley:

If you want to work with lobo by himself, we can bring everyone in a little early. Another storm is

moving in, so actually, you would be doing me a
favor

I slipped under the fence and tossed Jeremy the truck
keys. "Valet parking, please. I'll meet you in front of the
barn."

He grinned and made a request: "Can I curry-comb
Sweet Potato when we put them in the stall?"

"She'll love it."

When the truck left I strode out into the field making
a clucking noise with my tongue. Two horses, a donkey,
one mule, a mixed crew of pygmy goats, and a sheep
tagged along. All except the pinto mustang, wary and
watching from under the trees.

I looked directly at him and said, "Come on, Lobo."

Without waiting for a response, I walked toward the
barn, with the impatient donkey still giving me some
nudges in my back to hurry me along. Sweet Potato
looked up and whinnied for Lobo, which prompted the
first bit of movement I'd seen from him.

Now he had a choice. Stay out alone or join his friends
inside.

The herd instinct won out. From the corner of my eye
I watched him plod along on a trajectory toward the bay
mare.

"Good work, Sweet Potato." I dug into my pocket and
slipped her an extra horse treat.

Ashley limped into the barn in her knee brace and directed the animals to their own stalls. The smell of hay reminded me of early morning large animal rounds in vet school. Sure enough we'd just turned a straggling goat in when I noticed dark clouds outside and a drop in temperature. So much for our plans to walk around Rhinebeck.

That didn't seem to matter much to Jeremy, who'd gone to the tack room and loaded up on combs, curry brushes, and a hoof pick.

"I'm impressed," I said, after introducing him to my client.

"Well," he admitted, "my older sister used to give me a dollar for grooming her horse. When you're ten, that's a lot of money. Especially when you didn't get an allowance."

Ashley laughed. "Go ahead and groom as many as you want. I'll match your sister's prices."

———————

With Jeremy busy we concentrated on Lobo. Ashley sat down outside the stall and nursed her bad knee, while I opened the stall door and stood there, waiting for him to make the next move. His twitching ears indicated he was deciding something.

"Will he let you groom him?" I asked her, still not engaging him.

"Yes, but he's very nervous and doesn't enjoy it. Stomps his feet and makes a big fuss the whole time."

I held my hand out flat then showed him the quartered apple.

Again, he appeared to be deciding something.

Clucking my tongue, I said, "Come here, Lobo."

The love of food won. He took the few steps that separated us and slowly lowered his head toward my hand. Soft lips nibbled cautiously before each piece disappeared.

After making friends, I put a rope lead on the mustang, cross-tied him in the grooming area, and gave him a gentle rubdown with a medium soft brush. I spent a lot of time on his head, neck, and ears until he stopped shuddering every time I touched him.

———

"He likes you," Ashley told me later over a cup of tea at the kitchen table. Jeremy, smelling distinctly of horse, enthusiastically chomped on a slice of banana bread.

"Maybe I remind him of someone. Horses can recognize people and remember them for a long time." Sitting opposite a large picture window that looked out over the front pasture and orchard, I envisioned it filled with blossoming trees in the springtime. Her renovations took advantage of the beautiful views.

Our hostess squinted her eyes and gave me the once-over. "Come to think of it, you resemble one of the horse wranglers who worked with him. About your height and coloring."

"So you were sort of familiar?" Jeremy asked us. "Can horses process that kind of recognition?"

"Oh, I'm sure they can," Ashley replied. "My dad had a horse for twenty-some years, a mixed Thoroughbred. He bought her before he married my mom and rode her every day. When we moved to the city, he retired the horse to a farm not far from here. A couple of times a year he'd go visit Buttercup and I'd tag along. Dad would stand by the fence and whistle for her—and she'd come running to him. She was twenty-seven years old at the time and greeted him like it was yesterday. Then they'd stroll around the pasture talking to each other. At least that's what he told me."

"Your father sounds like a devoted horse lover."

"He was, even more so after my mom died." Ashley's voice sounded thoughtful. "My little Buttercup, he called her, even though she stood almost seventeen hands high. As soon as we bought this place, Dad moved into the guesthouse and I trailered Buttercup up here. If the weather was good, Dad would sit on that bench." She pointed out the window toward a cluster of seats by the pasture fencing. "Buttercup would stand next to him, leaning on the railing, sort of dozing by his side."

Ashley continued to stare out the window then said, "They both passed within a few weeks of each other, but sometimes I swear I see them walking around in the pasture together…chatting away."

Chapter Seventeen

THE STORM ASHLEY PREDICTED ROLLED IN SOON after we left, so we opted for an early dinner at the old and very expensive Patriot's Revenge Inn, a converted historic roadhouse just outside of Rhinebeck. Its massive blazing fire quickly warmed us up, and the exposed brickwork and dark overhead wooden beams made the large space feel cozy and comforting. Best Inn awards and reviews filled an entire wall. Too bad we were underdressed and smelled like horse.

To his credit, when the very proper waiter came to take our drink order, his nostrils and eyebrows only went up for a second.

"We've been horsing around," Jeremy told him with a straight face.

"Indubitably, sir," he countered before leaving to get our drinks.

"That deserves a big tip," I said with a laugh. We'd washed up as best we could at Ashley's, but short of a shower and complete change of clothes, this was the best we could do.

Of course with his Rolex and designer clothes, even impregnated with horse as they were, Jeremy fit in better than I did. Target designed the clothes I wore.

My companion busied himself with his phone for a minute before passing it over to me. The text he sent read:

Groomed a horse today. Thought of you. XXXXX

I handed it back. "Your sister?"

"Yeah. Funny how listening to Ashley reminisce today and the smell of horses made so many memories come to life, like seeing my sister, Kim, dressed in her riding habit. The day we French-braided her horse's tail with ribbons to match her own French braid. I'm glad I decided to stay with her and the kids for a while, before we join our parents for Christmas." He put the phone away when our drinks arrived. Jeremy ordered a whiskey sour while I kept to a single glass of white wine.

We started talking about Christmas plans, and I let slip my predicament. I didn't have to explain anything to him. He knew that my dad, the big-shot surgeon, had remarried only a few months after my mom died. And when I discovered the new bride worked with him in the OR and was pregnant, I lost it. At fifteen I didn't handle that sort of thing very well. After months of out-and-out war between my dad and me, Gramps stepped in. By that time my father was overjoyed to get me off his hands.

Since then I hadn't spoken to him, accepted any money from him, or met his new family. The day I graduated from vet school, Gramps threw a big party for me—rented out our favorite Italian restaurant in Brooklyn and invited the whole neighborhood. My father sent a card and a check.

I tore that check up into little pieces.

The smell of apple wood burning lent a faint smoky perfume to the air in the inn. Our dinner ranked up there among the best, a bit formal, but nice for a change. "Today has been a lot of fun," Jeremy admitted to me. "Working outside made me miss my own fieldwork."

His African dig had been abruptly canceled due to political unrest, his team now scattered around the world. Taking advantage of his unexpected free time, Jeremy enrolled in a few post-grad courses at the University of Pennsylvania, concentrating on the DNA recovery/ genome aspects of modern anthropology. As much as he enjoyed his classes, I knew he missed being in the field.

"Do you think you might go back?" I asked him. We sat relaxed in front of the fire, both lingering over espresso. Jeremy held an after-dinner liqueur in his hand, a treat for his horse grooming, he joked. I agreed but insisted we trade driving duties.

He shifted in his chair. "It doesn't look like we'll be welcomed back. Unfortunately, it's the emerging pattern we deal with. My entire profession is scrambling to adjust to DNA advances, site-mapping drones, random attacks, and kidnappings—and a general sense of distrust of science and scientists that is spreading in undeveloped countries. The new reality."

The new reality—wild animals also had come face-to-face with the new reality, from highland gorillas to migrating monarch butterflies.

"You just met a fellow casualty of that reality, Ashley's

mustang, Lobo. He's lucky to have a loving, safe home. We've got several states here in the USA with wild horses and different styles of management. Herd population is a huge issue. Control means anything from rounding up individuals for auctions to administering birth control. Horse advocates and veterinarians are also getting into the discussion, and it's anyone's guess if they can all agree to a realistic and humane answer."

Jeremy took my hand. "Stuck with problems we can only chip away at."

"If you chip away long enough…"

"Your arm gets tired."

I squeezed his hand tight then let go. "Don't spoil it."

"Since you're already a little worked up, let's discuss another touchy topic—your father. Maybe it is time to let go," Jeremy advised, his eyes sympathetic. Inside the expensive exterior was the same sweet guy I met the first day of my first class—the guy who always saved a seat in the lecture hall for me.

I stared at the fire, the orange flames licking the fire-box. "That's what Gramps says, too."

"Gramps is a wise man. You know he's right—you're just too stubborn to admit it, Kate."

Too stubborn to admit it.

That personality trait fit the mustang, too. Lobo knew he'd been captured, but he was too stubborn to admit it.

Both of us needed to change.

A familiar SUV waited for us in the animal hospital parking lot. As soon as I pulled into the driveway, Luke hopped out of his car.

Then he saw Jeremy in the passenger seat.

"Hey, Luke," Jeremy said, very friendly after a whiskey sour and a Rémy Martin under his belt after days of no alcohol. "How's our budding lawyer?"

"On the final stretch." Luke glanced toward me then Jeremy, then back again. "Kate. Hope I'm not disturbing you two," he said, awkwardly kissing my cheek.

The cheek kiss from an on-and-off boyfriend is bad news.

I, for one, didn't feel like standing in the parking lot, wind blowing in my face, staring at each other. The motion detection light flicked on. "Guys, it's cold out here. Let's go inside."

Locking the truck with the remote, I opened my apartment door to be greeted by Buddy, who gave a bark of joy at seeing Luke. Luke had earned undying love from my dog by surreptitiously feeding him people food under the table during almost every one of his visits.

The guys followed me in, chatting about antifreeze and snow tires.

Great. Cooped up with an ex-boyfriend and possibly a soon-to-be ex-boyfriend, while pretending everything was normal. "I'm making some tea," I announced. "Anyone interested?"

"I'll have a cup," Jeremy chimed in, then added, "First Buddy and I are going for a quick walk."

By now comfortable in his friend status, Jeremy

diplomatically removed himself so Luke and I could talk. I hadn't seen Luke in person for a while, and his calls and texts had dwindled in the last weeks. Ours had been an on-and-off relationship of sorts for quite a while. His high school girlfriend, Dina, kept jumping in and out of the picture, breaking up with him and then begging him to forgive her. Dina was another former high school cheerleader, like Cindy, but she was the kind who'd trip you in the middle of a cheer and laugh when you fell down.

She'd been living in Albany after breaking up for good with Luke. At least, that was the latest rumor. I wondered if things had changed.

"How's school going?"

The kettle whistled, calling me into the kitchen.

He started to take his coat off, then hesitated. "Very good. I should be eligible to take the law boards next year."

Muffler in hand, Luke remained in the living room. I ignored his rather obvious indecision whether to stay or leave. "That's great." Placing a few decaf tea bags in my blue china pot, I poured the boiling water in. Steam rushed up and bathed my face.

"Kate," he began, "we need to…"

The back door burst open, and a barking Buddy stormed into the room. Jeremy followed, his cheeks red from the cold.

"I'm ready for that hot tea…" His sentence petered off after catching a glimpse at the two of us.

"Tea's ready. Take off your coat and come get it." I opened the pantry searching for some cookies or biscuits to put out, but no such luck. Jeremy had eaten his way through everything.

Reaching up to hang his heavy coat on the hook, Jeremy winced. "Ouch," he said then rubbed his shoulder and wrist. "Still a little sore. Guess I shouldn't have groomed that second horse."

His grimace caught Luke's attention. "Something wrong?"

It finally occurred to me that Luke might not be up to date with the town gossip so didn't know why his former rival was here.

"Jeremy is recovering from an assault." Before I could complete my explanation, the patient took over.

He poured some tea while enthusiastically telling Luke all about the attempted robbery and hospitalization. "Kate was nice enough to take me in while I recovered," he ended, giving me a hug. "But the best news is we made up after I was such a jerk."

"Friends only now," I reminded him. "No benefits. It works much better for us that way."

"So, that's why you're here?" Luke asked, looking at me and then at Jeremy. "You haven't gotten back together?"

"You got it." Jeremy took another sip of tea as the color in his cheeks settled back to normal. "It's been almost five days with no symptoms, thanks to a smooth recovery courtesy of Dr. Kate. Just got the okay from my doctor, so I'll soon be off to spend the holidays with my family. What about you?"

"I'll be here most of the break." Luke reached down to pet Buddy, a bit reluctant to leave us. "Well, I hope you continue to recover quickly." His brow furrowed. "I'm curious. Did this assault happen at the university campus?"

"No."

Still puzzled, Luke asked, "Then where?"

"Here in your beautiful Hudson Valley, in the parking lot behind the Eden Glenn Inn near downtown Kingston—that's where."

Luke stared at me then made his decision. "On second thought, I think I will have a cup of tea."

"So, let me see if I have this right," Luke began, his long legs tucked underneath the kitchen table. "Two disgruntled clients of Kate's have died, Jeremy's been beaten up, and a stranger screamed at you in the supermarket. You also have a video on YouTube from the staff Christmas party in which you wish those same two clients would disappear—using your finger as a magic wand. All in the last twelve days?"

"The twelve days of Christmas with a slight rewrite."

Silence was his reaction.

I thought that line was funny, but it didn't get me a laugh. "At least the third person Pinky mentioned is alive and well."

"Cheers," added my slightly inebriated friend.

"When were you going to update me on this?" Luke didn't disguise the annoyance in his voice.

Jeremy rose to my defense. "She's been busy. You didn't exactly announce your visit tonight either."

"Touché."

Building on the attack, I added, "We haven't been in very close contact lately, in case you haven't noticed."

Our angry glares at each other made Jeremy snicker. He was known for having a warped sense of humor.

"Calm down, you two. Luke, the detectives from Kingston and the Oak Falls police agree—Kate's clients were two accidental deaths, and as for me, I was in the wrong place at the wrong time." With that Jeremy felt everything had been satisfactorily explained but added, "Bad idea to flash your cash in a strange bar while getting loaded."

Luke thought for a moment then stated, "I don't like coincidences. Kate, what about this person who yelled at you?"

Now it was my turn to explain. "Her name is Rye or Rae, I think, and she worked at Oak Falls Animal Hospital for a short time. Cindy had to cut back her hours and she quit. This happened my first week on the job. Somehow she's gotten the idea I'm responsible."

"Are you?"

Now I vented my frustration. "Absolutely not. I didn't even know who she was. Mari had to tell me."

"This Rae. Did she threaten you?"

That made me uncomfortable. "Ah, maybe a little threat."

"You didn't tell me that," piped up Jeremy.

"I didn't take it seriously. We were in the supermarket checkout line, for goodness' sake." As if that made any difference.

Luke persisted, concern in his voice. "What exactly did she say?"

With reluctance I thought back to that evening at the supermarket. I saw the woman's face contorted with anger. "'Everyone thinks you're so nice,'" I recited. "'But I know the truth.'" Then I remembered what she yelled at me as I was leaving. "You better watch your back, Kate Turner."

"Holy moly," Jeremy said.

Luke shook his head. "I second that."

———

I had finally convinced the guys not to worry about a supermarket bagger's crazy threat when someone knocked on the back door. Hard.

Buddy started barking.

"Who's that?" Jeremy asked. "Another gentleman caller, perhaps? I suppose we can squeeze another in at the table."

"I'm not expecting anyone." My clock read 8:15. I had no idea who it might be. A client? Maybe Pinky?

When I opened the door, my stomach dropped.

———

The chief of police didn't usually make house calls, especially this late in the evening. But since Cindy, my receptionist, was his wife's sister, he made an exception.

Now all four of us sat at the crowded kitchen table. I

didn't know why Chief Garcia was here, because he and Luke started comparing notes as soon as they greeted each other. When they paused, I interrupted.

"Excuse me for asking, but I'm curious. What are you doing here? Is this a social call?"

The chief stopped, tapped his fingers on the table, and said, "A woman was murdered behind the supermarket off Route 10 sometime between midnight and noon today. Name was Lassitor, Raeleen Lassitor, but most people knew her by her nickname, Rae."

I felt a thud in my chest.

"Her name was the last one on your wish list, Dr. Turner."

"Rae?" Luke recognized the name and twisted his head toward me. His eyes darted over to mine, then as quickly settled back on the chief.

"Kate's been with me the whole time," Jeremy volunteered. "Dinner together last night at the diner. Went right home. Breakfast here. Then we went to see one of her clients. Got there around eleven, I think. You can check with Ashley, the mustang owner." Unfortunately, Jeremy then burped, which undermined his credibility. Ignoring the eructation, he continued. "We then had an early dinner at somebody's Revenge, near Rhinebeck. Go ahead. Check our phones and my credit card if you don't believe me. Check the hospital cameras." His tone turned belligerent, asking for a fight.

The chief poured another cup of tea for himself. "Oh, I believe you, but I'd still like to ask Dr. Turner a few questions."

"Sure." Stunned that the Raeleen Lassitor on the video was the Rae from the supermarket, I felt flushed, my face warm.

Luke got up and casually brought me a large glass of ice water.

"This must be about Racleen's tirade in the supermarket, because it's the only recent interaction I've had with her."

"So," he began, "you were on the supermarket checkout line…"

"With Mari."

"With Mari. Then tell me in your own words what happened."

As he took notes, I repeated the same story I'd told earlier, ending with Raeleen's threat as I tried to escape out the door.

We all sat quietly while he scribbled away.

Too anxious to hold still any longer, I said, "You can check this out with Mari and the cashier. I'm sure they remember. It caused enough of a disturbance."

"Kate," Luke said gently, trying to ease my worries, "the chief isn't a rookie at this."

"Do you need my statement?" Jeremy tried again to deflect the tension building in the room.

Smoothly changing the subject, Chief Garcia suggested that since it was so late, Jeremy should go down to the station in the morning and be interviewed.

"Cool." That made my friend sound way too excited, like he was going to appear on *Law & Order* or something.

"And let us know if you have any travel plans," Chief

Garcia added in a bland voice. "By the way," he asked Jeremy, "I understand you were the victim of an assault last weekend?"

"Yes, I was. In Kingston, behind my hotel."

Luke stared at me and subtly shook his head. The police had tied all these incidents together, just as he had done.

From the sudden tightness around the chief's mouth, I was pretty sure that Luke's slick shaking-his-head maneuver didn't pass unnoticed by his former boss.

Chief Garcia leaned forward and looked at his notebook. "Dr. Jeremy Engels, I believe. I've changed my mind. Maybe you can tell me about your assault now…in your own words." He purposefully excluded Luke and me.

———

"That was fun," I said after Chief Garcia left. "What's going on, Luke?"

From his expression I wasn't sure I wanted to know. "I would take his visit tonight as a gentle warning."

"Warning?" Jeremy shouted. "I've been beaten up, she's been vilified and screamed at, and he's warning us?"

"Calm down," Luke said, smiling his crooked smile— the one that made his eyes crinkle. "The police are at the beginning of a murder investigation and the chief is casting his net out as wide as he can. When he pulled it in, you popped up."

At first it sounded like a reasonable explanation, until I thought more about it.

"How did the chief know? Mari and I certainly didn't discuss it." Even as I mentioned it, I figured it out. My receptionist, Cindy, was the wild card: Mari to Cindy to the chief's wife to the chief—the perfect example of the children's game of Telephone.

Everyone stayed quiet until Luke voiced what had been on my mind.

"All these deaths have a connection to you, Kate," he began. "What if a person who saw the video—I'll call him your nasty Santa—is giving you some early Christmas presents?"

"What presents?" Jeremy expressed complete bewilderment.

Luke focused his gaze on me, brown eyes questioning. "This really does have me worried. You want to explain it to him, Kate?"

"Bodies," I said. "My Christmas presents are dead bodies."

———

Long after Luke had left and Jeremy had begun to snore, I remained awake. The idea of someone "killing" my enemies sounded preposterous, like something out of a thriller novel. My annoyance at having a prolonged houseguest vanished. At this moment I felt grateful for the company. Contemplating someone out there spying on me, perhaps taking notes or photos, made my skin itch.

Luke hypothesized that the killer was fixated on me,

thought of me as perfect, and resented anyone who intimated that I wasn't. Channeling some of his police profiler courses, he expected the person responsible was a white male, twenty to forty years old and isolated from the community around him. Our point of contact might be the animal hospital.

Did I know of anyone who fit that description?

Only one face surfaced.

Flushed cheeks, round, bald head, physically imposing—someone who vowed to kill anyone who hurt me.

Pinky.

Chapter Eighteen

THE SOUND OF HOWLING WIND AND THE KITCHEN window softly rattling woke me up. I didn't even remember falling asleep. Lying on the sofa, I pulled the covers over my head. My blanket smelled of fabric softener and dog. A wet nose nudging my hand signaled that trying to go back to sleep was futile. Any movement and Buddy assumed it was morning and time for his walk. With only twenty minutes to go until my alarm rang, I got up.

Blowing snow and wind greeted Buddy and me on his abbreviated bathroom break. Tired and cold, I grasped my coat tighter around me, jamming my hood over my ears. Every so often I'd steal a glance next door, but the house was dark and quiet. Snow meant plowing. I wondered if Pinky had heard the news about Raeleen Lassitor's murder, isolated as he was.

Unless he knew before anyone else did.

Unless he'd killed her for me.

———

Sneaking out and leaving Jeremy sound asleep, I took refuge in my office in back of the hospital armed with a cup of caramel-flavored coffee already brewed by Mari, whose eyes were puffy and red. With plenty of paperwork to catch up on, I was thankful the appointments on the schedule looked light this morning. Doing paperwork meant not thinking about murder for a while.

Unsure what to do, I kept my suspicions about Pinky to myself. If I spoke to Cindy, it would put her in a terrible position of revealing or keeping secrets from her brother-in-law, the chief. Did I have any proof of any crime? No. Only a distraught statement from a grateful client that at any other time would be dismissed as "sweet."

After the chief and Luke had left the previous night, Jeremy and I had talked. Now that Jeremy's obvious bruises had faded, he could leave and go visit his sister and her family in Connecticut a little earlier than planned. A big family party was in the works.

But he didn't want to leave me with this mess.

I should have won an Academy Award for the show of carefree confidence I put on, and a wish for him to see his family. Don't worry, I told him. I have Luke.

Having Luke was debatable, but Jeremy's privileged life was not. Thanks to the family trust fund set up by his grandfather, all of his close relatives were well off, well educated, and living an American dream most could only speculate about. That difference in our situations always bothered me, not him.

It must be nice not to worry about money. My student loan debt loomed high as a mountain that I had to climb every month. Work meant everything to me. Massive debt made a steady job a necessity, which was one reason that after I quit my job on Long Island, I grabbed at the first position that came up—babysitting an entire hospital for a year for the globe-trotting Dr. Anderson.

As I worked, I speculated about Pinky. Was Pinky a murderer? I didn't think so, but I'd been wrong about men in the past. Neither could I suggest the possibility to anyone. A misplaced suspicion or accusation by a careless resident might damage Pinky's ability to make a living. He'd end up being a victim too.

Between clients, I snuck a look at the number of hits on YouTube. We were over twelve thousand.

For now, I'd wait and see if the police announced a suspect in Raeleen's murder. Mari had heard there was a person of interest, a boyfriend, she thought. All I'd found out was that Rae had been shot.

———

Cindy pulled me aside just before lunch. "Kate, I need to tell you something. You've got a fan."

"That's nice," I said, not really listening. My mind was occupied with reviewing the latest protocol for canine osteosarcoma, a cancer of the bone. A veterinary vaccine was being tested for use after surgery to prevent reccurrence, and I had a call in to an oncologist classmate of mine to discuss the case I was referring to her.

She leaned over and whispered, "If he comes in, try to pretend it's a complete surprise."

"What?" Trying to do two things at once wasn't

working for me today. Gathering up my notes, I started to relocate to my office, but Cindy stopped me.

"Remember. It's a surprise." Then she held her finger up to her lips and pretend-zipped them. "I told him you might be embarrassed by his generosity."

"Sorry, Cindy," I said. "I must have missed something. Who are you talking about?"

Shaking her head as if annoyed, she answered, "Pinky. Who else?"

———

By the end of the day I had ferreted the whole story out of her. Since his mother had died last year, Cindy had become Pinky's go-to woman for advice. Cindy's mom and Pinky's mom had been longtime friends and often let their children play together. The big guy felt comfortable with his old playmate, while most other people made him anxious.

In the beginning of December, before all this wish stuff, Pinky had asked my receptionist what kind of gift to get me for Christmas, in appreciation for taking care of Princess. Of course, Cindy encouraged him to buy something for the hospital—like food—but he specifically wanted to get me something more personal.

Horrified that my awkward fan would focus on jewelry or intimate items of clothing, she convinced him to get me a gift card. Cindy wanted to tip me off because she didn't know the amount. If it was too much, she suggested, we could creatively give it back with veterinary services. If it was too little, well, it was the thought that counted.

Given the odd assortment of gifts and trinkets I'd received from Pinky already, most bought at the drugstore or supermarket, I was glad to be forewarned.

"Cindy," I said, trying to phrase my question carefully, "do you think I need to be worried about Pinky's...interest in me?" Interest sounded better than obsession.

Smart and thoughtful, she immediately replied, "No, I don't." Her focus shifted to a spill on the countertop, which she immediately wiped up.

"So, there's nothing to worry about? Because I'd rather you talk to him if he's got some idea in his head about the two of us..." I rambled then stopped, waiting for her to continue.

"No. It's like you're the teacher and he's the schoolboy. Harmless."

I waited for more.

"Well, he does have a bit of a temper." She went on to tell a story about a client of his who shorted him his plowing money, so Pinky piled all the snow back on the guy's driveway in the middle of the night, blocking him in.

"Ah, I guess I understand that." Great, a schoolboy three times bigger than me nursing a serious crush. A schoolboy with a temper.

Our receptionist revisited her opinion about the situation and repeated, "I'm sure he's harmless," more to herself than to me.

I'd learned from experience that getting even physically took you in the wrong direction, even if it felt good at the time. "So, you don't think he was the one who beat up Jeremy?"

"Kate," Cindy commented in a sarcastic manner, "if Pinky had beaten Jeremy up, we'd be attending his memorial service."

She had a point.

―――――――

Later after work I had an opportunity to rethink my suspicions when I decided to take Buddy for a walk before going out to dinner. I'd left Jeremy singing off-key in the shower.

Buddy began to bark immediately when I opened the door and got a shock. A human mountain stood in my path.

The mountain bent down to gently pet my dog.

"Hi, Pinky," I said, watching Buddy break away to sniff around every bush and tree. "Everything okay? You're here late."

He whipped his ski hat with ear warmers off his head and clutched it in his meaty hands. "Yes, Dr. Kate. I just wanted to ask if you will be here on Christmas...so I know if I have to plow you out?"

The request sounded reasonable, but I didn't want this hopefully gentle giant to know my holiday plans, so I improvised. "I'm pretty sure Cindy wants the parking lot plowed every day. You know, in case of an emergency."

A smile broke across his face burying his pale-blue eyes. "Sure. That's what I figured." Question answered, he didn't seem to be in a hurry to leave. Meanwhile, Buddy had created several small piles of yellow snow and now sat on my left foot, tail slowly wagging.

"How is Princess doing?" Although his senior dog came in regularly to be weighed, Mari usually took care of that. The few minutes we spent listening to her heart and lungs and recording her progress in the medical record were more to calm Pinky's anxiety.

"She's good. Up to her old tricks now."

Which probably meant copious treats from her devoted dad.

"Alright, I'm freezing," I motioned for Buddy who appeared more than ready to go inside. "If you need anything, let me know."

"Thanks, Dr. Kate," he replied, jamming his hat over his head. "Ah, it's nice not to have Eloise and Frank complaining all the time, don't you think?" The earnest expression on his face belied his words. "I'll bet you're glad they really did disappear, just like you wished for. Happy Holidays."

Caught off guard and horrified, I waved goodbye and went inside.

———

Jeremy stood in the living room drying his hair with a towel. He wore a thick mahogany-colored robe, which made him the only man I ever knew who traveled with a monogrammed bathrobe and slippers.

"Well, you missed an odd conversation with a

potential murderer," I said, removing my coat and hanging it on the coat rack.

"Explain," he muttered, vigorously rubbing his hair.

"Gladly," I told him, walking into the kitchen to get a glass of water. "Let me know if I'm getting paranoid or not."

"We're all getting paranoid," he said with a grin. "It's an insane world out there."

Not sure how to begin, I paced into the living room then back to the kitchen, water glass in my hand.

"Sit still," he said. "Or do you want me to follow you around?"

"I'm feeling agitated." Was Pinky's earnest face hiding something horrible, or was I letting my imagination get the best of me? "A moment ago, Pinky asked me if I was happy my two clients were dead."

"What? When did he do that?" Jeremy took a quick look around the room. "Was he here when I was in the shower?"

"No. Worse. Standing outside on the walkway when I let Buddy out."

My friend sat down. "Don't tell me he's stalking you? Was he waiting for you outside your door? There's no way I'm leaving if that's what you're up against."

Much as I enjoyed Jeremy's company, I longed for my privacy again. One large room is a bit cramped for two people and a dog.

"I don't think so," I said. "His truck was still running, parked behind my truck. I'm pretty sure he'd just pulled in, because I saw Buddy react as we went outside."

Jeremy visibly relaxed. "Alright. What did he want?"

"To check if I needed plowing on Christmas Day." After I told him, I realized how stupid it sounded to be concerned about a valid question. What followed got me spooked, I explained.

"Hmmm." Jeremy leaned back in his chair. "Not sure how to take that. Was he creepy when he said that?"

Creepy? That's hard to judge, I thought. "Not particularly. He's kind of a sweet, gawky guy."

"Maybe he has a crush on you. God knows I did, and I definitely was a sweet gawky guy in school. Everything I said came out wrong."

"Well, not everything. You had me going for a while," I reminded him.

Jeremy reacted by putting the towel completely over his head, hiding. "Yep, then I messed it all up. I guess I cleared the way for Luke."

Not quite. That path came with a few roadblocks. But, after seeing him again, they were roadblocks I hoped Luke and I would be able to conquer.

———

As promised, Jeremy and I went to the Oak Falls Diner again, this time for his farewell dinner. Rosie, one of my favorite servers and Luke's cousin, took our food orders.

"Who's this you've got with you?" Rosie asked.

"I think you've met him before," I answered smoothly. "This is Jeremy. We went to college together. He's leaving tomorrow to spend the holidays with his family." Pretty sure that I'd hit all her unasked questions, I asked, "What kind of pies do you have tonight?"

Our server smiled, her rosy cheeks shining. "One of your all-time favorites. Dark chocolate topped with hazelnuts and pecans. Also, we have a cranberry-orange pie with a streusel crust and," she glanced down at her list, "a few pieces of the Boston cream pie."

Jeremy went for the Boston cream pie then turned the dessert order to me.

"Let's get a slice of each of the other pies," I proposed. "We can always take it home if we're too full."

No one was fooled by my pious statement. Those slices of pie were never going out the diner door.

As we chatted, I kept finding excuses to turn around or twist my head each time the door opened. My non-chalant attitude didn't cut it.

"He's not here," Jeremy said, taking a piece of home-baked bread from the basket. "I can see the whole restaurant including the counter."

Caught red-handed, so to speak, I protested. "I wasn't... Alright, it was very awkward between us when he left last night, so I wanted to...be prepared."

"Girl Scout night tonight?"

Jeremy always knew how to rile me up. I decided to ignore him and concentrate on the food. It didn't help that several of the servers were related to Luke and knew we'd been dating. Maybe they knew more than I did at this point.

I'd just buttered a large piece of bread and shoved it in my mouth when someone walked past us in the identical brown coat I'd seen last night.

"Luke," Jeremy said and popped up out of the booth. "Would you like to join us?"

When he turned and faced us, Luke didn't appear happy to see us.

"No, thanks. You two enjoy yourselves. I'm picking up my takeout order."

Rosie strolled by with a carafe of coffee. "Hey, cousin," she said, "how's it going?"

He gave her a quick peck on the cheek. "Good."

"You must be on winter break."

Luke nodded. He seemed agitated, eager to leave. "Well, good night, Jeremy. Kate."

"Don't forget your takeout," Rosie called after him. "You know how Dina hates having her dinner get cold."

Jeremy was gentleman enough not to comment, but he knew that name as well as I did. So, Dina, Luke's high school sweetheart, was back in town and sharing takeout with him. And after I'd hoped things were warming up again between Luke and me.

I didn't see that coming.

Didn't see that at all.

Chapter Nineteen

FAREWELLS ARE TIMES OF MIXED EMOTIONS. STANDING side by side in the parking lot, Jeremy and I said our goodbyes the next morning. I felt a pang of regret for everything we'd put ourselves through but thankful my friend and I had emerged on the other side. Why had we complicated our friendship with a romance that had become such a burden at the end? I'm sure loneliness on both our parts had played a role in it. Without a deep emotional commitment to being a couple, mounting frustration made us drift apart. Why did we need a disaster, like Jeremy being injured, to bring us back together?

Too often our feelings are as much a mystery to ourselves as to others.

His Mercedes pulled out of the parking lot, turned right onto the road, and quickly accelerated away. Jeremy would be at his sister's place in Connecticut in two, maybe three hours, surrounded by family. I stood outside in the cold, watching cars and trucks pass by. The gray road bleached from the winter salt stretched off in both directions under the bare tree branches.

Movement to my far right made me turn my head.

Pinky stood at his front door watching, Princess in his arms. His gaze had been focused on the back of Jeremy's car. After I noticed him, he put the elderly dog down on the cleared sidewalk. How long had he been standing there?

I put my hands in my coat pockets and walked back into the animal hospital feeling more upset and confused than I thought I would.

———

Mari was busy in exam room two setting up my next appointment. I took the opportunity to ask our volunteer if she'd like to help me. She'd been shadowing us for about three weeks, as part of a work-study program. Greta jumped at the chance to help rather than take notes.

We were doing a quick recheck on a case previously in the hospital for diarrhea. Duke, the dog, wagged his tail on seeing us, his owner trying unsuccessfully to get him to sit.

"So," I asked, "how's he doing?" His shaggy coat and broad face defied fitting into any known breed.

"Doing great."

"Excuse me, Dr. Kate," Greta said. "Do you want him on the table?"

I looked at the diminutive girl and at Duke sitting on the floor. The dog almost outweighed her.

"No, we should be fine, thanks." I performed a basic exam on the floor while asking the owner about any other symptoms.

Our office had run a fecal panel, which checked for many types of bacterial DNA, such as salmonella and e coli variants. We'd hit the jackpot on cryptosporidium, a particularly nasty bug that can also affect people. Duke had been on the approved medication for dogs and was much better. The problem was to figure out where he'd gotten it from to prevent re-infection.

"Would Duke have any access to livestock, or rodents?" I asked, getting up off the floor.

"No," his owner told me. "We don't live on a farm, and we certainly don't have mice in the house." She sounded a bit indignant that I might even suggest it.

Taking a medical history is like spotting clues in a murder mystery, one of my veterinary professors used to say. Ask questions, and then ask some more.

"What about your neighbors?"

"We have fields on either side of us, but no close neighbors."

"That sounds nice," said Greta. She nervously looked back and forth between the two of us, not sure what to do.

"It's very nice," Duke's mom agreed. "Some days I can look out and only see cows grazing with the mountains in the background. Quite a different view than the one from my apartment in the city, that's for sure."

Cows grazing. My first clue.

"I bet Duke likes to look at the cows, too," I said.

"He does," she agreed enthusiastically. "He'll slip under the fence and walk around with cows, but he doesn't chase them. Duke's too much of a gentleman."

Duke wagged his tail when he heard his name. I was sure this big dog was doing more than walking around with the cows. Nothing is more tantalizing to a dog than a pasture full of cow pies.

"One last question. Are you on well water?" The mystery was close to being solved.

"Yes, we are. The best water ever." Getting restless with all my questions, Duke's owner snuck a look at her watch.

Greta's forehead wrinkled in thought.

"Can I ask you when you last had your well water tested?"

Now my client appeared puzzled. "You test well water? Why? It's pure, one hundred percent natural, I mean, right from the ground."

Sometimes ignorance can be bliss. Unfortunately, I intended to rock that bliss boat.

"I'm going to recommend you have your well tested, to make sure you aren't getting contamination from the farm next to you. There's a chance that if they are on a higher elevation than you, their...waste products can... contaminate the aquifer below. The same aquifer your well draws its water from."

"AGHhhh." Her sound of disgust was unmistakable.

"And Duke here," I patted his head again, "is probably sampling some of the dried cow turds."

"YUCKkkkk."

The dog licked his chops and smiled.

"Welcome to life in the country."

"That was fantastic," Greta said after we finished the appointment. "How did you figure that out?"

"Just a sec. I'll be right with you." I needed to finish a text message for Cindy and note my recommendations on Duke's record. My receptionist also had a handout of state contacts for clients with possible public health water issues, and poisonous plant questions. I'd have her add another handy list with the closest licensed animal rehabilitators for injured or orphaned wild animals and birds.

"Okay," I smiled at Greta. "Now to answer your question."

I explained that Duke's source of infection was most likely direct from the cows, but checking the well was a prudent step for the well-being of everyone. Understanding the most common sources of parasites and bacteria helps the doctor, patient, and the client.

"Don't worry," I reassured her. "You'll get the hang of it. When do you apply to vet school?"

Her answer surprised me. "I'm still not sure about what medical field I want to go into. That's why I signed up for this internship. I'm also going to shadow a chiropractor, an orthopedic surgeon, and a dentist."

I compared how she felt to my own experience. There never was any doubt in my mind I would study veterinary medicine. I'd always been drawn to and loved animals. Veterinary medicine fascinated me. Still does. But that passion for your work didn't happen to everyone.

"Your school program sounds like a good one. Without some real-life experience, students don't know what to expect." I turned the microscope off and swung my chair in her direction. Greta had a very professional business-like appearance: crisp new scrubs, shiny closed-toe shoes, and a stylish modern haircut completed her image. In fact, looking down at myself wearing a white jacket decorated with a light covering of brown dog hair and slip-on knockoff Crocs, she looked more professional than I did.

Silently vowing to go shoe shopping, I gave her some additional advice.

"Pre-med can lead to many very different professions. Explore your options. Find a career that excites you. I know a human doctor who didn't realize he hated the sight of blood until his second year of med school."

Greta seemed horrified. "What did he do?"

"Became a psychiatrist."

———

When the mail arrived, we took the sight of another square Christmas card in an ivory envelope for granted. No return address, as usual.

This time I didn't open it, simply handed it back to Cindy.

"From Raeleen?" she asked.

"That would be my guess. Go ahead and put it in a lab bag and store it with the others," I cautioned her.

Whoever mailed these Christmas cards to me could stop.

Frank, Eloise, and Raeleen were all dead. Vanished from this earth.

All the wishes had come true.

Chapter Twenty

THE FOLLOWING DAY CINDY TOOK ME ASIDE AND herded me into reception. "Sit," she demanded and handed me an evaluation form I had to fill out from Greta's school.

"Really? I've barely had a chance to talk to her. Same for Aaron, the new kennel help." Yesterday had been particularly crazy. Mari and I had waved to both of them as we dashed past.

Cindy rubbed her hand over her face. "I feel the same way. We're supposed to be getting a new intern in a few days because we signed up for some kind of rotation schedule. It's only for three months, so we'll see how it works out."

I reserved my judgment for now. Each intern came with a list of things they had to accomplish, as well as specific tasks the school required them to master. Greta came close to failing the surgical part of her rotation because of a queasy stomach. With some accommodations she eventually made it through the experience.

"Right. Meanwhile, I guess we need to check with Mari for feedback." I leaned back and said, "If there's anything I hate doing it's this kind of paperwork."

"Me, too." Uncharacteristically Cindy plopped down in her desk chair. "I didn't get much sleep last night— sorry if I'm grumpy."

I scooted over to her. "You aren't grumpy. Everything okay?"

"Oh, there's just so much to do and so little time to do it. And Raeleen's murder has me wondering…" She didn't have to finish the statement. We both knew what she meant.

"It has me wondering, too."

Now she resembled a cheerleader whose team lost the big game.

"Trouble seems to follow you, Kate." Her eyes met mine. Was there a hint of blame?

"Yeah," I admitted. "I've noticed that."

The ring of the bell chime on the front door made us look up. A well-dressed woman in her seventies strode into the room then zeroed in on us.

"Excuse me," she began, her blond pageboy partially hidden by a shearling hat that matched her coat. "I'd like to speak with your manager about Queenie, a bulldog previously owned by Eloise Rieven."

Cindy and I exchanged glances. This woman meant business.

"I'm Dr. Turner. Can I help you Ms…?"

"Babs." She thrust her hand forward. "Babs Vanderbilt-Hayes. I was a dear friend of Eloise, and I want to know who killed her."

———

We escorted Babs into my office/conference room for privacy. I started by giving her my condolences, but she waved them away. Her presence hijacked the room.

"Those idiots at the police station wouldn't talk to

me," she began, gracefully sitting in the chair opposite my desk, "so I came here to at least find out about Queenie. Joe hasn't been that forthcoming." Babs conveyed what she thought of her friend's son with a discreet sniff.

A force of nature like this woman could be handled in many ways, but I figured I'd expedite it for everyone. I laced my hands in front of me and said, "What would you like to know?"

Her narrowed eyes took my measure. "First, Queenie—is she in good hands?"

"Yes. Eloise's son has decided to give Queenie to a family friend, their former neighbor, Patty Whiffenwood. Joe currently lives in a second-floor condo walk-up, and it's hard for him to get Queenie up and down the stairs. I believe he already took her to New Jersey to her new home."

"Hummp. Where there's a will, there's a way. Just saying." Her hand loosened some buttons on her coat. "I know Patty. She'll take good care of her. One problem solved."

This time I asked a question. "When did you learn about Eloise's death?"

"Smart." Those clever eyes squinted at me again. "Nice way of asking why are you bringing all this up now? Well, I've been in the city, hospitalized at New York Presbyterian Hospital with double pneumonia, for the past two weeks. When I called Eloise, her phone was disconnected. Joe said she'd died. They'd already had a private memorial service and cremated her. Like that." She snapped her fingers. "No trace of my LouLou left."

Behind the bravura I saw pain.

"LouLou, that was my nickname for Eloise. Anyway, she and I went to boarding school together. We were friends for over fifty years. I can't believe she fell down and froze to death. That's just not acceptable. Getting wood at her age." Anger flashed in her eyes. "Being hounded by those anti-bulldog people didn't make her life easier either. My poor LouLou." Babs's rigid posture wilted for a brief second.

I'd encountered many cases of people denying circumstances surrounding the death of their pet, or a family member, and recognized it as a stage of grief.

"This has been a shock, I'm sure," I reiterated to Babs. "Is there anything I can do for you?"

"Not unless you can bring her back."

She rose and slid her Gucci purse over her shoulder. "I've hired a lawyer to review the radiologist's and pathologist's findings. We're getting a second opinion. It's the least I can do for my oldest friend. What about her house?"

The abrupt change of subject took me aback. "I assume the house went to her son, Joe. You'll have to see if the will has been filed."

"This is very disturbing. She loved that farmhouse, felt it should be a museum, an historical treasure. Never got the heat fully installed because of that. A bit of a mess, really, but I kept that opinion to myself. Keep things authentic, she'd tell me. I told her to stop burning wood, much too dangerous at her age, but LouLou was as stubborn as I am. We're both tough old birds." With that announcement Babs swept out of my office and, exhibiting a keenly honed sense of direction, headed straight for reception. She graciously thanked Cindy for her time and then was safely ushered into a large Bentley by a chauffeur. This woman had serious money.

"What was that all about?" Cindy asked.

"Mourning a loved one. And a hint of guilt, I think."

Despite privacy laws, I expected her to bulldoze through any obstacles set in her way and get her second opinion. I hoped it would give her some comfort.

———

With Greta's official evaluation form from her school program finished, I still had our new employee assessment to fill out. That reminded me. I wanted to make an effort to get to know Aaron better. I ventured over to the dog kennels, being deep-cleaned in time for the pre-Christmas boarders. Our new kennel helper had no idea I was behind him due to the bright white earbuds in both ears. For some reason I thought he was about nineteen or so but realized he was a bit older, maybe twenty-two or twenty-three.

Both his body and the mop jerked comically to a decidedly hip-hop beat.

Since I didn't want to scare him, I slowly walked along the closest kennel so the movement would catch his eye. My plan didn't work because his eyes were fixed on the long scrub mop cleaning the cement and floor drains. All the rubberized matting and beds were clean, elevated, and arranged in stacks to be placed down after everything dried. The air smelled of cleaning products.

Trying to get his attention, I stuck my foot out, only to have it mopped with a saturated lemony-smelling liquid.

"Oops." Aaron's inquiring look became one of terror when he saw me. "Sorry." A quick pull dislodged the earbuds but didn't stop the beat that kept pounding away. Darting glances searched for someone to help him.

Thinking I would smooth things over with a joke, I said, "There's no one here to save you, Aaron."

My smile froze when I saw his reaction. He trembled, pupils dilated. The skinny kennel worker looked like he might faint. What the heck was going on here?

"Continue what you're doing," I told him. "Cindy sent me over to meet you officially." A slight relaxation of his shoulder encouraged me to continue. "Good work. Keep it up."

"Okay." He directed his word to the wet floor.

With one shoe and the bottom of my pants leg sopping wet, I detoured into my apartment to change. Our encounter hadn't gone as planned. Why was he so scared of me?

After changing into clean scrubs, I stopped to check the Christmas wish YouTube video—15,106 viewings.

Since I was online already, I decided to learn a little more about Aaron and why I frightened him so much. The answer came in an unlikely place—Aaron's

Facebook page. Up popped a link to the YouTube video from the staff Christmas party that showed Mari's litter box cake and me, forever stuck in my fateful wish. On his board were reposted some troubling conspiracy theories, as well as more links—one to a wishful thinking site and the other a rant about a breakup.

Once again I had underestimated social media.

———————

Raeleen Lassitor's story became more complicated later that day. As usual, Cindy and her sources beat the local news by at least twelve hours. Normally I'd have heard everything directly, but this time I became updated simply by accident.

I'd been scrambling to finish Aaron's paperwork as well as reviewing the next intern's resumé with Cindy. Instead of jamming it into my pocket, I'd been ordered to put everything in the appropriate folder, labeled either "Intern Program" or "Employee Files," which she kept in a locked drawer in the reception area. Since we were closed for lunch, I decided now was a good time to get everything done.

That's when I overheard Cindy on the phone say, "Raeleen? Are you sure?"

Pretty sure my friend wasn't conversing with the dead, I waited until she hung up before questioning her.

"Do you have a minute? I want to go over those forms with you," I added to cover my interest in listening to gossip.

We sat at her desk side by side. While glancing through the mostly completed forms about the number of hours Aaron spent in the hospital, Cindy said, "That phone call doesn't have anything to do with you, Kate. I'm only telling you because I know you're upset. It's about Rae."

"Oh."

"There's a boyfriend. The chief has declared him a person of interest in her death."

"Of course there is." The number of boyfriends and husbands in the news lately who had killed their partners was disconcerting, to say the least. One of the risk factors of falling in love or being pregnant in America shouldn't be murder.

We finished Aaron's evaluation and went on to the next person on the intern list, due to start on Monday. To my surprise I recognized the name.

Juliet Bradsher. At my old job on Long Island I'd worked with a very skilled licensed technician with the same name. What was she doing in upstate New York?

"Unusual name," Cindy commented. "That would be nice if it was your friend. Let's hope she's your Juliet."

"Does that make me her Romeo?"

Cindy cracked up. "You made a joke, Kate. Things are finally looking up."

I wasn't sure about that, but hearing that Raeleen's murder probably had nothing to do with any of us was more of a relief than I realized.

Mari decided to add to our Christmas decorations because we weren't "cheery" enough. While we were in the middle of hanging more lights, the chief and a deputy swung by to pick up the Christmas cards sent on behalf of three dead persons.

"You be nice to Kate," Cindy scolded her brother-in-law. "The whole stupid game was my suggestion. Kate didn't even want to play, but I forced her into it. If I could take it back I would."

"I know, I know." His voice conciliatory, he gathered up the envelopes sealed in plastic, holding them up to the light. "Just you two handled them, right?"

"Once they got to the hospital, yes." She looked around as though confirming the statement.

"Well, I'll tell you one thing," he said, holding up the bag with the first card we opened signed Frank Martindale. "This isn't Frank's signature. I've got plenty of complaints at the office signed by the deceased. Obviously, someone else wrote this. And it wasn't no ghost."

"A prankster?" Cindy volunteered.

"If you call this a prank. All three deaths and they used the same card. Someone wants us to focus attention on that wish, or on you, Dr. Turner."

His last words made me freeze.

"Alright, then." He looked around for his deputy, who stood on a ladder helping Mari string the lights. From the laughing and body language their exchange looked quite friendly. "Come on, Phil," the chief said, keeping his visit brief.

We followed the officers out the door and into the parking lot. After whumping the siren twice, they drove up to the main road and took off.

The three of us stared at the disappearing patrol car before hurrying inside. "What do you think they'll do with the cards?"

Cindy answered. "The chief said this sort of thing happens all the time. Some federal agency will investigate because the Postal Service is involved, but there's been no threat, no extortion. No nothing."

With not much at stake, I doubted any sophisticated or costly tests would be run. The cards warranted only a minimal investigation. I made my way into the treatment area and began packing supplies to take out to the truck. Then I checked for my personal backpack, sort of a mini emergency kit I'd been carrying since vet school. Ever since going on a hike and encountering a dog suffering from heat stroke, I'd kept that backpack nearby.

———

With two house calls scheduled this afternoon, I glanced out the big picture window in the reception area to check on traffic. From the number of cars and trucks speeding by, I guessed the latest snowfall hadn't slowed anyone down.

Our own parking lot, most of it in direct sunlight, was perfectly dry thanks to Pinky's plowing and Cindy's salting the walkways.

"I'm saddled up and ready to go, Mari," I yelled out to

my technician. Greta was busy running some lab tests, the manual open on the countertop next to her. "Do you have any questions?" I asked her.

"So far, so good," she said. "Mari set up some fecal tests and bloods to run with extra samples you had. That way I can compare my results to yours." Given the fact she was surrounded by ziplock bags full of organic matter, she had a cheerful smile on her face.

A text message from Cindy said Mari would meet me at the truck. Glad we could teach this departing intern something new, I said goodbye, threw my backpack over my shoulder, and hustled out the door.

Once we reached the edge of town I relaxed as the scenery changed to fields, farms, and mountains. Getting out into nature and away from the white walls and fluorescent lights of the clinic usually afforded me a much-needed mental break.

However, before that happened, I had to battle wits with our most frequent house call client and her ferocious Chihuahua.

Daphne Davidsen had been given the nickname Daffy by family members, and she strived to live up to it. She was an eccentric retired teacher and former librarian, and her chief pleasure in life was her tiny dog, Little Man. The daffy part centered on her enjoyment of dressing them both in matching homemade costumes.

Now her Chihuahua wasn't a dainty little female with

melting dark eyes. No. Her male looked like a thug, a muscular no-nonsense sort of guy. Dressing him up was like dressing up a gangster in a bonnet. Which made it all the more fun.

Once in Daffy's home, Mari and I prepared for the main event. Directly across from me disguised as a Christmas tree, weighing in at seven pounds, two ounces, was Little Man.

Cloaked in my magical white coat as returning champion Dr. Kate Turner, I wasn't required to give my exact weight. My veterinary disguise didn't fool anyone. Armed for battle with a pair of toenail clippers, we faced off for round one.

While I distracted the growling dog with Christmas carols and jazz hands, Mari circled behind and slipped a custom gauze muzzle around his pointed snout.

After appropriate high-fives all around, she held while I clipped.

Under his breath and between snarls, Little Man told us what he would do to us if he ever got sprung. Most of it was a big act for his mom, Daffy, also dressed as a Christmas tree, but her costume was topped with a glowing star. Our client circled around us, making conciliatory promises to her pet for this terrible invasion of his privacy. "Be good, Baby," she'd implore him to no avail. With teeth bared he continued to protest. I'd been clipping his nails every three to four weeks for months, but Little Man never gave it up without the semblance of a fight.

Once finished we reversed our choreography. Mari slipped the muzzle free then escaped as I captured the angry Chihuahua's attention. His big bat ears glowed translucent from the reflected starlight on his mom's head.

Once in her arms, he dialed it down to a half-hearted snarl.

Every visit she insisted on feeding us a little something, often related to whatever they were celebrating. That held true today as iced Christmas cookies and sliced fruitcake appeared on the kitchen table.

Mari eyed the fruitcake, trepidation in her glance.

"Doing anything for the holidays?" I asked our host. Some shortbread with ribbons of chocolate caught my attention.

"Of course, dear. I need to finish decorating the house before Little Man and I have Christmas Eve dinner with the family."

For the life of me I couldn't see one single surface not festooned with something. There were figurines on handmade doilies, artificial pine boughs woven in and out of the stair rails and draped over every door and window. A large nativity scene took up the middle of the dining room table, and I counted three Christmas trees of various colors and styles.

Daffy's enthusiasm was evident, so I simply said her home looked lovely.

"Thank you, Doctor," Daffy said. "This holiday must be a bit stressful for the two of you."

It had begun. The second inquisition from Oak Falls's Queen of Gossip. Although she rarely left her home, she knew everything.

"How do you mean?" I pretended innocence.

Her tree shook with laughter, the star tilting to one side. "Whatever possessed you two? What a pickle to be in."

Mari lightened the mood by asking if we were dill pickles or bread and butter slices, but it only briefly deterred Daffy.

"So much gossip about this wish of yours. I wonder who's behind it?"

That sparked my interest. "You think the gossip is deliberate?"

Daffy and her dog both stared at me, sympathy in one set of eyes. "Don't you?"

Averting my face from her keen scrutiny, I muttered, "I have no idea."

We almost escaped when she asked how the investigation of Raeleen's murder was going.

Mari helped me out by implying that the general consensus was that her death resulted from domestic violence and left it at that.

"The ex-boyfriend or someone new?"

Since anything I said would lead to another question, I remained silent. My assistant, on the other hand, had no problems speculating about murder with our client.

"Now don't quote me," Mari began. "But I think the focus is on Devin, her ex. They say he has an alibi. But I didn't hear that from any official source."

She may as well have posted it on Facebook. It felt incongruous to be talking about murder under a sprig of mistletoe.

"A lovely girl, Raeleen, dedicated and uncompromising. Devoted to her animals and yet unsophisticated in the ways of the world—completely oblivious to the messes she created." Daffy stroked the smooth fur of her Chihuahua. "Mark my words, being impulsive and naive is what got her murdered."

Mari got up from the table, an extra cookie in her hand, and said, "Sorry to cut things short, but we need to get going. Want to start the truck, Dr. Kate, while I pack up?"

Although glad Mari had thrown me a life preserver, I had to admit I was curious about our conversation. After wishing happy holidays to all, I took off for the safety of the truck.

⸻

About ten minutes later Mari opened the passenger door and climbed in, a small wrapped box in her hands.

"What took you so long?" I asked as she buckled up.

"Oh, Daffy and I had a little talk. She also gave us this to munch on." Mari pointed to the package.

"I believe that was a new world's record for clipping his toenails," I said with a laugh. With the GPS set for our next appointment, I settled in for an uneventful ride. I was contemplating the ins and outs of Christmas with Gramps at my Dad's house when Mari interrupted my thoughts.

"That's odd," she said.

I automatically slowed down. "What's odd?"

"Pinky. He's plowing out Frank Martindale's place."

"So?" I'd read in the paper that my former client's estate might go into probate. His closest relative was rumored to be a second cousin, located somewhere on the West Coast. Searches were being ordered by the court to find any other relatives.

Mari scratched her head and turned down the heat. "Pinky plowed out two of the people who died: Frank Martindale and Eloise Rieven. He's also the one who added Raeleen's name that day at the party, and now she's dead. Don't you think that's a little odd?"

I did think it was odd, but for now I wanted to give Pinky the benefit of the doubt. "Doesn't he plow out most everyone on this side of town?" I asked her.

"I guess so," she answered tentatively. "You're probably right."

The traffic light at the next intersection turned yellow, so I eased my boot onto the brake. How many people in the vicinity were in the business of plowing out driveways, I wondered?

Waiting at the intersection, I recalled an emotional Pinky telling me that he'd kill anyone who hurt me. The light turned green, and I hit the gas.

"Don't worry about it, Mari. It's just a coincidence."

Another coincidence.

Our afternoon of house calls continued uneventfully, the roads slushy but drivable. Since Cindy had put us on a tight schedule, Mari and I ended up snacking on cookies in the truck. We checked each other for stray crumbs before our next appointment.

Situated in a natural glade, the home was a modern-build log cabin, with soaring ceilings and exposed beams, a far cry from Daffy's modest ranch. Our delightful client was a stay-at-home artist mom and her three children under four. Their cat and dog stoically rose above the chaos, barely waking up for their exams. Child gates separated the rambunctious kids from the woodstove and potential trouble.

Although the temperature outside was in the thirties, we'd both peeled off all our outer clothing and Mari had quietly threatened to strip down to her underwear. Like many folks in the country, the family had their wood stove functioning at full blast with the inside temperature hovering around seventy-four. The babies comfortably ran around dressed only in their diapers. We didn't have that luxury.

Mrs. Haber noticed the pile of clothing on her living room chair and apologized. "We like it nice and toasty," she said, dressed in a light t-shirt and shorts in December. "But I confess I overloaded it a little this afternoon. With the woodstove going we can have all the heat we want and a low electric bill."

We both nodded, the sweat trickling down our backs.

"It also makes my paintings dry faster." She shifted a small sleeping child to her other hip and pointed to several large canvases painted in a dramatic modern style. The splashes of color and changes in texture in the paintings looked pleasing and very professional.

Mari recognized the technique. "Didn't you have a show at one of the galleries in town last year?"

"Mommy," interrupted a small boy with red hair, "Jason hit me."

"Say you're sorry to your brother," she answered in an absentminded way. "Let's see, I was pregnant with Pearl at the time, so that must have been the spring before last."

"Sounds about right." Mari tried to put down our cooler with the vaccines in it but thought better when she noticed both boys eying it.

"Haber is my married name," she explained. "I exhibit under my maiden name, Lark Moreux."

Even I recognized that name. Luke had introduced me to her paintings. She was a local celebrity and as unassuming as could be. Her work sold in the tens of thousands of dollars.

After I got over my shock, I tackled the pet exams and booster shots. Both went smoothly, each animal being pleasantly plump and agreeable. The only recommendation was a dentistry for their middle-aged Cornish Rex cat.

"Did I give her the wrong food?" Lark asked.

"A different diet might have helped, along with brushing, but some breeds like Rex, Siamese, and exotic shorthairs are notorious for having dental issues. As it is, she has a loose canine that might have to come out."

"Oh, no. I didn't notice anything, but honestly with the kids now, I don't devote as much time to her as I should. She was my first baby." Lark gave her somewhat hairless cat a pet. Immediately the yellow-eyed kitty's motor started purring.

"I am going to recommend a dental diet, though. Plus, we'll show you how to easily clean her teeth with either wipes or a product you slip over your finger. But for you," I pointed my finger at the mixed-breed dog, "we might have to use the dreaded doggie toothbrush."

Lark promised to do her best.

"How do you manage all these kids plus a career?" Mari asked. "I can barely juggle two dogs."

Our client gave us a surprising answer.

"My husband is a graphic designer and writer for several magazines and needs his own space, so one day we sat down and decided to organize our week; otherwise we'd go mad. We use Alexa a lot here." As if on cue the smart device on the kitchen counter glowed blue. "She keeps us on schedule and reminds all the kids what chores they have that day. We turned off her spy mode though."

Noticing the blue light, the toddler said, "Can I play a song, Mom?"

"Sure. Go tell Alexa what you want to hear."

We moved toward the dining room table as "The Wheels on the Bus" began to play.

"My husband, Philip, has the studio in the afternoon to work, and I have it in the morning to paint. Nighttime and bedtime are a free-for-all."

From the racket of the kids dancing around the room pretending to be buses and then crashing into one another—I believed it.

"My parents live close by for babysitting, so we have a pretty good support team." The child in Lark's arms slept blissfully through the music and noise and general bedlam. She smoothly transferred the little one to a crib tucked in the corner. "We've got about twenty-six acres, but this sweet local guy helps us," she added. "He delivers the wood in the spring so it can dry all summer, and then before the cold weather arrives, he stacks a few piles on the porch so I don't have to go to the woodpile. Such a nice fellow." She smiled, adding, "He also cuts the grass in the summer and plows our driveway in the winter."

Mari glanced over at me.

"Do you remember his name?"

"Pinky. His name is Pinky. Silly name for a big guy, isn't it, but I quite like it."

Before I could respond Alexa blasted another chorus of "Wheels" to the delight of the boys, who now pretended to be trucks that crashed into each other. Lark appeared delighted as well as she swayed to the music.

―――――――――

"So Pinky strikes again," Mari said after we'd climbed into the truck on our way to the main road.

"Afraid so," I noted, thinking back to Eloise Rieven's porch. "When we picked up Queenie did you notice any wood stacked against the house or up on the porch?"

"No," she quickly answered, "and I'd remember, since I use a woodstove at home. Her hearth only had one or two small split logs and some twigs left in the kindling box."

Too bad Pinky hadn't stacked extra wood on Eloise's deck. Perhaps her death might have been avoided. I shared my thoughts as we turned up Bates Lane.

"Pinky probably charges extra for hauling wood onto the porch. Between her pocketbook and her pride, I bet Eloise wouldn't admit she needed some help." Mari opened the laptop and made notes on my recommendations to Lark.

Small decisions sometimes had big consequences.

We drove along in silence for a while, our thoughts kept to ourselves. A few flakes of snow flittered across the windshield.

Mari closed the laptop then made a startling statement. "Guess what I'm doing? Daffy told me about an amazing psychic, so I'm getting a reading,"

Jolted out of my thoughts I asked why.

"The big reason," she confessed, "is Daffy gave me a fifteen percent off coupon. But another friend of mine had a reading and said it was very revealing, in a good way."

My Gramps had worked as an arson inspector and a fireman in New York City most of his career, and he had some experience with the many storefronts that opened up overnight advertising readings and fortune-telling. His advice to me when I asked him about psychics was to enjoy a reading as though it was entertainment, because most of them were cons.

Despite my warning, Mari stayed enthusiastic. "I'll ask her if she has any messages from Frank and Eloise."

When I turned to give her the evil eye, she beat it with an evil grin.

"Hey, it's on my bucket list," she added.

When Mari said we were going back to Daffy's place I thought there had been a mistake. "We were just there," I said. "Even Chihuahua toenails can't grow that fast."

With her eyes focused on the computer screen Mari simply grunted a no. After pulling up a computerized Post-it note from Cindy, she explained. "She forgot to tell us. Little Man has a tick."

"Can't you talk her through it?" Tick removal wasn't difficult, but you wanted to make sure the entire body and mouthpiece were intact when you took it off.

"That's what I told Cindy, but I guess Daffy's too squeamish when it comes to her baby,"

"Alright," I said, "but let's make it quick."

Mari closed the laptop and agreed. "I'll take my cookies to go."

The tick turned out to be a gray skin tag impersonating a tick. I went through some options with Daffy for removal, but for now she was content to leave it.

As we picked up our things, Daffy said, "Mari, I meant to tell you. Your litter box cake was very...inventive."

Coming from our hostess, that was a glowing recommendation, but it also signaled to me that our client had something on her mind.

"Thanks," my assistant said. "That cake is always good for a laugh."

"Someone is not laughing," she said primly. "Your video and the unfortunate deaths that took place after your wish, Doctor, have stirred up some controversy in the psychic community. An unfortunate display that should never have been shown to the public."

Our costumed client prized decorum above all while secretly relishing gossip of any sort. Mari jumped in to explain. "We were all joking around. If you listen carefully, Dr. Kate doesn't even name any names."

"No, my dear. She had you for that."

My assistant and I debated about what Daffy was talking about until we were all talked out. Since there was nothing left to say, I stared out the window.

With only two more clients to see, we headed toward a more rural area, about thirty minutes away from home. The scenic road, normally busy in season, was nearly empty.

"It sure is beautiful up here," Mari commented.

I had to agree.

The mountains glowed purple on the horizon as we climbed a long hill. A glorious panoramic view revealed itself. Stands of tall pines bristling with spiky green needles stood out among the stark trunks and branches of leafless trees. Each season brought its own visual reward. Maybe that's why so many artists were drawn to the Hudson Valley.

Spring was all about the flowers, summer gave us fruits and vegetables, autumn produced foliage, but winter—winter stripped the land down to bare bones.

Chapter Twenty-One

OUR LAST APPOINTMENT OVER, MARI AND I STARTED to wind our way back to the animal hospital. When we approached Eloise Rieven's home, I asked, "Do you mind a quick detour?"

"No problem. I'd hate to have you explore this place all alone at night."

We drove slowly up the well-plowed driveway. Someone, most likely Joe Rieven, had smoothed over the ruts and filled them temporarily with crushed gravel. We parked in front of the front steps. I walked up and rang the doorbell, but no one answered.

"Why don't you stay here?" I suggested to Mari. "Keep the truck running. I'm going to check the porch and backyard." What I was looking for I hadn't a clue, but Babs had stirred my curiosity. Maybe something odd might catch my attention.

There was no evidence of any logs ever being stacked on the porch, and it appeared from the lack of smoke in the chimney that Eloise's son wasn't using the woodstove. The woodpile, covered with a plastic tarp, was located near the side of the house. It stood unused, the bottom of the tarp held down by individual logs with several inches of undisturbed snow on top.

Again I noticed how flat the well-worn pathway from the back stairs of the house to the woodpile was. What did Eloise trip on? The winter weather had faded the spray-painted outline of her body, but I could still make out the shape of her outstretched arm, hand splayed out as if reaching for something. Maybe my bulldog client enjoyed an evening nightcap and that had contributed to her fall. It wouldn't be the first time alcohol played a deadly trick on someone. I made a mental note to see if the coroner's report showed results of a drug and alcohol screening.

"Pretty sad."

Mari stood slightly behind me, probably bored from sitting in the truck. She stared at the outline in the snow.

"Yes. Sad to die from a needless accident." I didn't add the irony of freezing to death only a few steps away from warmth and shelter. A gust of wind whipped around the house making the dark tarp shudder. I noticed a motion detector light like mine over the back door.

It stayed dark and still like the house.

Mari remained quiet, lost in her thoughts.

As I slid into the driver's seat, I envied the sense of place, the sense of history some people had. Mari and Eloise both appreciated and felt protective of Oak Falls. The last few years I more or less lived out of suitcases, and the only sense of place I felt were destinations explored on the Travel Channel.

Ever so slowly I backed up and turned around, leaving the farmhouse behind. Even after we turned back onto the road, the image of that outstretched hand stayed with me.

So did a question: How did she intend to carry the wood?

I peppered Mari with that question on the way back. My assistant said she personally used a canvas sling to carry logs from her woodshed. Some of her friends had little rolling iron carts. Very rarely did she heft a log with her hands, and then always with gloves; otherwise you get bark and splinters all over your hands and clothes. A vague recollection told her Eloise used a canvas sling bag, too.

But what if something else had been in her outstretched hand? A flashlight? A gun?

Maybe she'd gone out to the woodpile for a different reason.

When we got back, Mari and I complained a bit about our long day. I think Cindy felt sorry for both of us, so she invited us on a shopping trip in town. With her husband busy playing cards with his buddies tonight, she suggested an impromptu girls' night out—finishing with drinks and dinner at the Red Lion Pub. Being a bit more enthusiastic about Christmas, thanks to Gramps, I realized I needed to buy some presents. A hostess gift, at least, and something for my new siblings—my half brother, John, and my half sister, Jennifer.

I didn't even know what they looked like.

That was going to have to change.

Once the three of us loosened up we had a blast. At first, all we talked about was work, but as we walked around the village of Oak Falls, darting in and out of specialty stores, art galleries, and a popular emporium down by the river, we started getting silly.

Cindy made us laugh recounting domestic household struggles with her teenagers. No wonder she bossed us all around at the animal hospital. She had plenty of practice. I think she considered us all just an extension of her family, except we weren't sneaking out at night and driving her crazy.

Mari's dog stories and pet pictures on her phone looked unbearably cute, embellished with funny captions and filters. Our junk-food-eating athlete confessed a secret desire to compete in one more Iron Man. We both encouraged her to start training the first of the New Year.

As I listened to their stories and laughter, I realized how private and withdrawn I'd become. My perception that everyone was interested in my love life, though, was true, said Cindy. For my entertainment they started listing the highs and lows of my dating life from the staff's point of view. Not only was it hilarious, but strangely freeing.

We ended up at the pub relaxed and hungry.

"Hello, ladies," the waitress greeted us. "Girls' night out?"

"You bet," Cindy answered. "I got almost all my Christmas shopping done, too."

We had snagged a corner booth large enough for

the three of us and our coats. Mari's puffy jacket almost needed a booth of its own.

Soon we were enjoying food we didn't have to cook and talking about our favorite subjects, including the ongoing murder investigation of Raeleen Lassitor. After we begged Cindy for any new information, she whispered that Chief Garcia was taking a closer look at Devin's alibi, which involved a lady friend, and the FBI was actively following up on a death threat lead.

"I thought there was a problem with his alibi?" I asked.

Cindy explained that a close look at certain electronic devices on the night of Raeleen's murder might put ex-boyfriend Devin back in the running for prime suspect.

At the corner of the bar a young man stared at us then turned away.

"Is that Aaron?" Mari asked.

A waiter passed with a platter of burgers, blocking my view. When I looked all I saw were some strangers leaning on the bar drinking beer. "I don't think so," I told her.

We chatted some more. I tried to dodge Cindy's questions about Luke.

Taking pity on me, she touched my forehead and asked, "What's really going on up there, Kate? Anything Mari and I can do to help?"

Put on the spot, I blurted out the truth. "I started out wanting to prove the wish had nothing to do with those deaths, but now I'm tired of it all. The jokes from clients, all the views on YouTube... I only want it to end."

"I was hoping you'd say that," Mari said. "I've never been involved in something so confusing in my entire life. These three deaths remind me of a magic show I once saw. Everything in the show that looked real turned out to be an illusion—a way of getting you distracted so you'd miss what was really going on."

———

You'd miss what was really going on.

Mari's magic show story still rumbled around in my brain the next day. That visit to Eloise's house brought up some questions. As I did chores and indulged in a long hot shower, I played with the idea of a noise or disturbance bringing Eloise out of her house in the midst of a storm. Without any proof, I let my imagination fly everywhere, as scattered as a shotgun blast. Babs and her questions about Eloise's death had gotten under my skin. Gramps told me I was the most stubborn and tenacious person he'd ever met, and I was about to prove it.

I sat down at the desk chair, Mr. Cat in my lap, and attempted to clear my thoughts. The world kept demanding too much. My neurons hadn't adjusted. Here in the quiet, only one noise sounded. Purring. Purring would be my calming mantra for now.

With my eyes closed I focused on the purr and used it as a focus of my meditation. Gradually, I noticed the tension ease down a notch.

As always, when I tried to meditate, random ideas interrupted my concentration. The phrases Daffy had used to describe Raeleen bobbed to the surface like bubbles. Impulsive and naive, an orchestrator of her own disastrous end—descriptive words but no real help in finding the person who shot and killed her.

The police were focused on Devin, her ex-boyfriend and former fiancé, Cindy said. Constantly fighting then reuniting, Raeleen nevertheless loved and confided in him. FBI agents took a different approach. As the vice president of Legalize Animal Rights Now (LARN), she was opposed to a wide range of animal abuse that put her in direct conflict with various food industries who preferred to keep their handling of animals a secret. Raeleen's ability to make people mad drew constant attention—the wrong kind of attention.

The purring became louder as I stroked Mr. Cat's neck and head, his throat vibrating under my hand. What had Luke said? Most people don't know what they are capable of.

A familiar ring tone put an end to our session. Mr. Cat showed his disapproval by jumping off my lap, his back claws digging into my skin.

"Hello," I said.

"Don't forget we have a date," Gramps said. "They want us there at two, with dinner around three."

"How could I forget?" Especially since he'd reminded me at least three times and texted me twice. "It's practically tattooed on my forehead."

His raspy voice sighed. "Yeah, I've overdone it a bit," he admitted. "I think I'm more nervous than I thought I would be."

I reacted to that confession with disbelief. "You? Nervous? Funny, I never thought about that. Gramps, you handled everything so much better than I did. Even when I came to live with you, I heard you talking on the phone to my dad. Mostly at night, when you thought I was asleep."

"Not so much anymore, Katie. It became too hard for me…and truthfully…maybe hard on your father, too."

Whatever short-term peace I'd enjoyed shattered. I didn't want to admit that my father might have some redeeming qualities. As far as I was concerned, he'd moved on and forgotten my mother and brother, just as he'd forgotten about me. Thinking his heart might also have been broken gave me too much pain.

———

With the hospital closed and Jeremy safe at his sister's place, I found myself getting more and more restless. Gramps uncovered a nerve in that phone call. Even my dog, Buddy, became tired of my pacing around and retired to his bed for a well-deserved nap.

When I'd gone shopping with Cindy and Mari in the village, I had an ulterior motive. I wanted to get each of them a Christmas present but wasn't sure what they liked. In a gift shop chocked full of specialty items Cindy had lingered over a silver letter opener.

"Look. Isn't this pretty?" she asked us. Her fingers slid over the raised sunflower design on the handle.

"Do you think someone would use that?" Mari, ever practical, held up a pair of potholders depicting a snowy woods scene.

"Haven't you ever broken a nail opening up an envelope?"

"Yes," my assistant said, "but the world is going paperless. Right?"

With regret Cindy put it down. "I suppose so. Then what about one of these journals, or a sketch pad?"

"You keep an electronic journal on your computer and graphic tools on your…"

"I know. On your computer. You're no fun to go shopping with," Cindy said and strode away through the cinnamon-stick-scented air.

Mari shrugged. "I like to find something, buy it, then go home."

"The antithesis of the shopping mentality." Feeling a little bad for Cindy, I asked, "Do you see anything in here you'd love to have but don't really need?"

Her answer told me a lot. "Yeah. This." Mari picked up a geode on a stand. In the center of the rock was a cluster of amethyst crystals. "I had one as a kid, but we lost it somehow during one of our moves. I always meant to get another one, but now…" She placed it back down. "This will have to move to the back of a very long line."

I decided to go into town and buy the anti-technology letter opener and the geode loved by a young Mari.

———

Armed with knowledge of what caught their fancy, I set out to purchase gifts for my friends, beautiful things they didn't need. The entire town was lit with twinkling

golden lights. Rich velvet ribbons and fantastic cornuco-
pias of frosted glass and pine cones decorated the gazebo
in the town square. Once I found a parking spot, I strolled
toward the gift shop, pausing to admire several decorated store windows. One of my favorites had turned the
curved glass front window into a miniature child's room.
Above the bed tiny fairies danced and played with sugar-
frosted plums. Above a headful of sleepy curls another
fairy hovered to bestow a sugary kiss.

The town bustled with visitors, happy to wander
around such a picturesque village. All the locals contributed to keeping it that way, since the season was always a
profitable one for everyone. Spoiling the beauty momen-
tarily, a gray-paneled van veered close to the curb, lightly
splashing the busy sidewalk.

I held open the Gift Shoppe door as a young couple,
loaded down with packages, inched past me and offered
a thank-you and a Merry Christmas. The bell on the door
tinkled with each coming and going, creating a nonstop
melody. A steady flow of customers came and went while
I was there, all with smiles on their faces.

First, I needed to find the two gifts I was after. The
stock was down to a final silver letter opener, so I immediately grabbed it. Thank goodness I hadn't waited. I
could see Cindy skillfully opening mail with the opener,
now nestled in a plush-lined box. Mari's geode turned
out to be a bit harder to find. The store had restocked
and moved many items around. I wanted to get her the
same one, which meant opening at least ten cardboard
boxes and sliding wrapped geodes out of them. When I

came to the last box, her amethyst rock popped out. A salesperson explained they rotated them throughout the store to spark new interest.

Happy and relieved with my purchases, I took out my credit card. The young girl behind the counter with a gold eyebrow piercing stared at the name and expiration date and then said, "You're the one, aren't you, the one with the death wish on YouTube? Was that for real, or did you stage it?" Her face lit up with excitement and an enthusiastic manner that belied the ending of three lives.

Was this some kind of trap? A quick look around confirmed no one with a camera lurking nearby, only fellow shoppers.

Eager to pay and leave, I confessed. "That's me, and no one staged anything. Just a stupid moment in my life forever playing on YouTube."

The girl agreed vigorously, her holiday earrings swaying and jingling. "You are sooooo lucky," she said, printing up a receipt. "Maybe you'll go viral. Like that would be sooooo slick." Christmas-inspired red, green, and polka-dotted fingernails on a graceful hand gave me back my credit card.

For some unknown reason I felt a need to explain. "You don't understand. I don't want to be on YouTube. It's embarrassing."

An incredulous look came my way. "No, it's you that doesn't understand. It's the medium you focus on, not the message. This is your fifteen minutes of fame, like my professor always says."

Not wanting to be quoted or lectured, I started to leave.

"Thanks for coming in," she said as I began moving toward the door. "Loved the litter box cake. You should post the recipe."

My first reaction of annoyance from having no privacy gave way to a revelation. This salesperson had a point. The only one likely to feel embarrassment about that video was me. How did the average person react? Most likely with laughter, very happy it wasn't them on the video doing something stupid. Then it was on to the next video of a cat knocking things off the countertop, or person trying to parallel-park an RV or some goofy moment in someone else's life.

I recognized how for some people it was all about the medium. The more people who clicked on your website the better. It didn't matter why. Sheer numbers and keeping your name out there became paramount to staying successful in this new type of society.

Even Aaron, a kennel worker, provided a link on his Facebook page to the video—ultimately shared with how many others?

You might look at it as a certain kind of power.

As I passed the bookstore I paused, then ducked in. I realized I didn't know much about wishful thinking and decided to pick up a book about it. Once inside, I noticed the self-help area packed with books on mind over matter, make your own future, and inspirational memoirs.

By wishing out loud, one book suggested, I might have released an energy whose only purpose was to make the wish come true.

I put that one back on the shelf.

I was tired of being blamed for the consequences of my wish.

———

Hands now stiff with cold from wandering through town, I deserved a break. Most of my presents were bought, except something for Jeremy. It was impossible to shop for someone who had everything. I talked myself out of a one-of-a-kind hand-forged silver tie clip, went back to buy it, but it had sold. Tired, I decided to get a late dinner and made a beeline for my favorite spot in town, Judy's Place. It was packed with shoppers. I spotted an empty space at the counter and gladly rushed over, put my packages down, and got off my feet.

Judy's was a hangout for local residents as well as tourists. Normally closed at five, it stayed open late during the holiday season, along with most of the shops on Main Street. Her homemade soups and sandwiches were deservedly popular for being delicious and easy on the wallet.

"Coffee, Doc?" I looked up to see Judy herself waiting on customers. Seasonal help came and went with surprising regularity in Oak Falls.

"No thanks, Judy. I've been drinking that stuff all day. Can I get decaf tea instead?"

"Sure thing." She slid the one-page menu over to me and handed the fellow on the next stool his party's bill. I'd arrived just as things were winding down, so one by one the crowd began to thin out.

I ordered a soup and rye toast. While I waited, I checked my hospital email.

"You can move to a table if you like," Judy said. She held my bowl of mushroom barley soup. "There's one open by the window."

"No thanks," I replied. "It's just me tonight. This is fine."

She nodded and walked back toward the open kitchen.

I tucked into my soup. The thick, warm broth felt great going down after being outside in the cold.

"Surprised seeing you here so late. How's it going?" Judy had returned with her own cup of coffee. She leaned against the countertop, arms pressed to the wood, and took a sip.

"It's been better." I bit into the crunchy toast. "What about yourself?"

She laughed. "Way less stressful thanks to your magic wand wish. Don't you love Facebook and YouTube?"

"Yes and no."

"I know what you mean. Those Yelp and Tripadvisor reviews can make or break us."

I took another spoonful of soup. "It's tough being critiqued every day of the week. Did Frank post something about the restaurant?"

"Frank had two nuisance lawsuits running against me," Judy explained. "First, he fell at lunchtime getting up from one of my chairs, claimed the seat was greasy because I didn't clean it—and refused to pay his bill. A week later he came in during the lunch rush and claimed I refused to serve him. Crazy thing is, I wasn't even working that day. The whole thing was just bull."

"Sounds familiar."

"Who ratted you out, by the way?" Judy asked.

"Mari, sorry to say. She took a video at our Christmas party of the litter box cake, and my stupid wish got captured at the end of the recording."

A couple leaving wished us happy holidays and vanished into the night. That's when I noticed the blessed quiet. "No Christmas music," I noted, completely surprised. "You're not playing any music?"

"Nope," she admitted. "There's enough of that everywhere else in town. I need a break this time of year. Heck, they start putting up Christmas decorations right after Halloween. No one even waits until after Thanksgiving anymore. I've got one wreath on the front door and we update the community billboard over there with holiday stuff—and that's it."

"Thank you," I said. "A little decorating goes a long way."

"I agree."

Done for the night, I asked for the bill. But Judy wasn't finished with her questions.

"Did you know Raeleen very well?" she asked me.

An odd question I thought, but I answered, "Not at all. How about you?"

"She picked up some part-time work waitressing this summer," Judy confessed. "Not the best server but not the worst. Smart girl but for some reason she had a big chip on her shoulder. Her fiancé kept trying to get her to go back to school. Or maybe he was her ex-fiancé by then—it was hard to keep up. Fight and make up, fight and make up all the time. Exhausting to watch."

Asking a direct question usually pays off. "What can you tell me about her boyfriend?"

"Devin Popovitch? A very good-looking guy. He's a student at the community college and works part-time at Mr. Fix-it's Auto Repair out past the supermarket on Route 10. He's got an alibi for the murder, though, I hear, if that's what you're thinking."

Ashamed of being so obvious, I handed her my credit card and the bill. Only two other customers remained, both finishing their coffee and getting ready to go. I decided to take a chance and asked, "Who do you think killed Raeleen, Judy?"

A deep chuckle escaped. "Well, here in town, we all think you did it."

"Me?" The breath stuck in my throat.

"Just kidding," she said and handed me back my receipt. "Merry Christmas, Doc."

———————

After putting my coat and hat back on and organizing my packages, I opened the café's front door and braved the cold. Wind whipped around the corner, carrying tiny shards of ice. I'd parked in front of the jewelry store on Main Street, now closed for the night. One or two shops stayed open, trying to catch the last-minute stragglers, their lights blending with the Christmas lights twinkling on the storefronts and streetlights. As I walked I heard Judy bid someone good night then pull down her security shutter. The sound of grating metal hitting the ground clattered behind me.

Only a few people, mostly couples, strolled along Main Street. Bustling with packages, I made my way to the truck, thinking about my conversation with Judy. Her description of Devin and Raeleen's relationship echoed their other friends' impressions.

With all the presents securely stowed, I thought of how domestic violence cut a swath among so many couples. When I first started dating, Gramps told me there was never any excuse for a man to hit me. That's not love, he said. That's bullying.

When the truck hesitated on starting up, an idea hatched. I'd stop at Mr. Fix-it's Auto Repair sometime tomorrow and meet Raeleen's ex-fiancé, Devin Popovitch, face to face.

Question is, would his handsome face be the face of a killer?

Chapter Twenty-Two

MARI AND I WERE DRIVING BACK TO THE ANIMAL hospital after a long day when she sprung it on me.

"So, that's settled. We're both going tonight, around eight thirty."

Dragged back from my daydreaming, I said, "What do you mean 'we'?"

"You said you'd come along," she protested. "To the reading."

"Your appointment with the psychic? Is that tonight? I've got things to do." My voice sort of spluttered in frustration.

Mari didn't answer but instead opened up our laptop and began to update the day's computer record. We drove in silence, the frozen landscape gliding past the truck window, ice crystals glistening in the headlights.

I hated to upset Mari. This posed a dilemma. I wanted to go with her, but I'd planned on researching the psychic, Delphina, a bit before meeting her. When I explained that to Mari, she called me on it.

"You research everything. Why don't you just go with your gut instinct this time?"

It sounded like a challenge, but the more I thought about it the more I realized she was right. I did research everything. Google had me wrapped around its search engine. Maybe I should walk in blind and concentrate on the experience, without any preconceived ideas.

Mari's fingers clicked angrily on the keyboard.

"Okay," I agreed. "Are you going to prepare a list of questions at the least?"

"There you go again," she pointed out. "No. I'm going to wing it. Just go with the flow."

Our turnoff approaching, I said, "Excuse me. Did we just enter a time warp? You're the second person this week who quoted the sixties to me."

My friend rose to the bait. "That's right. Tune in, turn off, drop out."

———

As I made the turn into the parking lot, the truck acted up a little as if on cue, giving me the perfect excuse to check with a mechanic.

"That doesn't sound good," Mari said. "Maybe you have gunk in your fuel line. Cindy's husband can take a look at it for you. He's always complaining about bad gas with his tow truck."

I kept quiet about my plan to meet Raeleen's ex-fiancé, using the F-150 as bait.

Luckily, Cindy had already left when we arrived. As soon as we parked, Mari took off to run home and take care of her dogs.

"Don't forget I'm picking you up at eight thirty," she reminded me. "We've got a date with a psychic."

"Looking forward to it," I yelled back to her.

Once her SUV was out of sight I backed up and drove in the opposite direction toward Mr. Fix-it's

Unlike the employees at the big-name car dealerships, the two fellows laboring on cars at Mr. Fix-it's were streaked with grease and oil. Nor did they wear matching overalls with their names embroidered on the pocket. I doubted things had changed much here since the late sixties, which seemed to be the year of the vintage pin-up calendar on the wall.

Although the time approached five thirty, the little garage was still open. As soon as I pulled in, someone without a coat walked out of the office.

The man heading toward me could have graced one of those ripped-guys-at-work calendars. Tall, with broad cheekbones, thick black hair, and a build that kept on giving. I believed I'd stumbled on Raeleen's ex-fiancé.

"Can I help you?" His voice betrayed a trace of an accent.

This must be Devin Popovitch. Just to be sure I asked. "Are you Devin?"

"Yes." This time he seemed a bit wary.

I quickly started telling him all about the F-150, and how I needed it for work. After I described the engine hesitation, he pulled on work gloves and asked me to pop the hood.

For the life of me I couldn't figure out how to segue into questions about a deceased loved one from discussing car problems. Then he surprised me.

"Do you work at the animal hospital?"

I'd forgotten the prominent magnetic signs displayed

on both front doors. After I told him I did he explained that his girlfriend had died and left him with all her animals.

"The oldest one isn't eating, and she's having accidents. I need to make an appointment with the doctor."

Was he the only one in town who hadn't seen that YouTube video? Since he looked directly at me with no sign of recognition, I guessed he hadn't. "No problem. Call our receptionist, Cindy, in the morning and she'll book you in."

Devin took a picture of our logo and phone number with his phone before shoving it back into his pocket. "So," he said, wiping his hands on a towel, "you probably have a clogged fuel line from a delivery of crappy gas. We've got some additive I can put in now, or you can buy some. Your choice."

"If you could do it now, that will save me a trip."

He disappeared into the small office attached to the garage area. Meanwhile, another mechanic under a car remained oblivious to my no-appointment transaction. I wondered how he stayed warm until I saw two heaters glowing red, suspended from the ceiling. A devious thought came into my brain. What was to stop Devin from pocketing my money?

The answer turned out to be an extremely old-fashioned numbered paper receipt that also produced a yellow copy, which he left in the pad.

When I glanced at the bill, I was surprised at how reasonable it was. By the look of the many cars waiting for service, Mr. Fix-it's had a good business here. Part of me wanted to ask Devin if there really was a Mr. Fix-it.

The other part wondered who had supplied him with his alibi for murder.

———————

All the way back I thought about Devin and how shaky his alibi might be. What exactly did it mean to be a "person of interest"? I heard this phrase more and more, and it didn't always lead to an arrest. Perhaps law enforcement used it to get the media off their backs or lull a criminal into thinking they'd gotten away with something.

By the time I'd finished walking and feeding Buddy and changed out of my scrubs, Mari arrived—a little early, as usual. Our big night had begun.

Mari's SUV drove much more comfortably than the work truck, the interior luxuriously appointed with plush leather seats and plenty of cup holders. She'd acquired it used, well-maintained, but with quite a bit of mileage on the odometer. So far, the older-model vehicle had performed perfectly. Of course it helped when the owner took excellent care and garaged it. Our poor F-150 sat outside in all kinds of weather, scratched up and dented, but a real workhorse.

A gray-paneled van pulled in behind us from a side road.

"That guy should turn his lights down," Mari complained.

———————

I hadn't paid much attention as she drove, so when the GPS told us we had arrived, I was a little surprised.

"Are you sure this is the right address?" I asked Mari for the second time. I was glad we hadn't gone in my truck with the animal hospital signs on the doors. There was no way I wanted a picture of us parked in front of a Psychic Readings sign linked to that YouTube video.

She double-checked her coupon. "This is it. Not much to look at."

Understatement of the year. This dirty white trailer set off from the road had seen much better days. There was no evidence of any attempt to landscape the property, nor was there any garage space. Like me, these residents had to clear off their car after every snowstorm and ice storm and hailstorm or any other winter storm thrown at them by Mother Nature.

"You'd think a psychic would make enough money to get a better place," Mari said, unbuckling her seat belt and buttoning up her coat. "I mean, they're psychic, right? Can't they figure out what the stock market is going to do?"

"I don't think it works that way," I answered. "At least that's what one of the mediums told someone on television."

Before we opened the SUV doors, an outdoor light clicked on, illuminating the entrance, which consisted of a sloped wooden handicap ramp.

"Here goes nothing," my assistant said, her former enthusiasm gone.

The brightly lit front made the trailer look even

worse. "You wanted an adventure. You got an adventure. Hold on tight."

━━━━━━━

The woman who answered the door appeared to be a normal housewife, no veils, no bangles or flashy gold jewelry—quite the opposite. She wore a flowered apron with a spaghetti sauce stain over a housedress. The modest interior smelled like cabbage and sausages.

In the kitchen a man in a t-shirt with broad shoulders and curly black hair sat hunched over with his back to us, finishing his dinner. A bottle of red wine with two glasses, one empty and one half-full, sat in front of him.

"I'm sorry. Did we interrupt your dinner?" Mari asked.

"We're finished," she stated with a raspy smoker's voice. "I'm Delphina. You must be Daffy's friend, Mari. Come this way."

Together we followed her down a dim hallway toward a pale blue curtain embroidered with sparkly golden stars. She pushed the curtain aside to reveal a dimly lit room and a round wooden table with four chairs.

"Tonight's session is sixty-five dollars. Payment is due before we begin."

"Of course." Mari fished around in her purse for a few bills from her wallet. The psychic made no attempt to give her a receipt. "Oh, I have a fifteen percent off coupon."

"That is the fifteen percent off price. Now sit, sit." Delphina took her place in the only armchair and positioned a red tasseled pillow behind her back. Mari sat opposite while I moved one of the chairs against the wall.

The psychic never asked who I was.

Once we all were seated, soothing New Age music mixed with nature sounds flooded the room. Chimes and bells combined with flowing water, the surround-sound speakers giving us three hundred and sixty degrees of melody. Sonorous temple gongs resonated in the background. The lights faded further while a rosy glow rose up, bathing the room in a warm pink.

"Take my hands."

After a slight hesitation, Mari placed her hands in the psychic's grasp.

Since my chair faced Delphina, I got a good long look at her.

Her silver-white hair was pulled into a tight bun, but curly strands escaped here and there. Wispy tendrils framed her flushed face. She was an obvious beauty, blessed with high cheekbones and a strong broad nose, but time hadn't been kind to her. Multiple deep wrinkles around her mouth and brow spoke of a life of hard living, but her eyes were something else. Pale blue with large black pupils, their intensity mesmerized me, even though her attention had completely fixed on Mari.

"Relax your body. Free your spirit," Delphina began. "Let your mind drift to a safe, joyous place."

Without thinking I leaned back in the chair and closed my eyes. A soft, spicy scent of incense made the air taste exotic and delicious.

"Wrap yourself in a warm cosmic blanket. Take your tensions from your neck and shoulders and drop them to the ground. Let them slide away. Feel how freeing that is."

Her raspy voice now sounded like honey pouring over pebbles. The voice made it so easy to release yourself and float away.

Then my scientific mind clicked into sharp focus. This was a subtle type of hypnosis. The lighting, the music, her suggestions, all guaranteed to induce a state of tranquility and a more suggestive frame of mind.

Instead of listening to Delphina, I silently recited the anatomy of the kidney and stared at specific items in the room. Although the lights had been dimmed, I noticed the chair legs looked old and nicked by use—and needed a good cleaning. The hem of the starry curtain was creased, one corner torn and frayed.

The oldest part of my brain, what my neurology professor called our lizard brain, gave me a sudden warning. With a slight turn of my head I locked eyes with Delphina, staring at me. Her black pupils dilated even further as she realized I'd slipped away from her self-inducing hypnotic state, no longer a participant but an observer. Our eyes held only a few seconds, then she shifted back to Mari, her honeyed words thick and flowing over everything in its path—like sweet lava.

"Tell me what you wish to know," she asked Mari.

My assistant asked questions about her future. Delphina replied with predictions of travel, a relationship that wasn't to be but would lead to another, more fulfilling destiny.

Then she lurched forward, eyes closed and said, "Katherine, remember to take your enemy's hand." The tone of her voice changed, the honey gone.

She'd used my given name, not Mari's.

After a few seconds Delphina's eyes opened, and she spoke of a possible illness for a loved one and future good fortune.

As I listened, her words ran together, bits and pieces designed to make you feel good. With so many predictions, some of them were bound to be right.

I sensed a subtle change in the lighting as Delphina murmured something about healing grace and being mindful of your third eye. Slowly, the lights brightened as the session came to an end. Mari stood up, smiling broadly, and thanked the psychic, promising to make another appointment soon. Our hostess explained in a much more business-like tone that for a limited time she offered a value pack of ten sessions for the price of eight, good for one year.

I trekked behind them retracing our steps through the hallway into the kitchen. Still at the table, the man began to pour two more glasses of wine. Mari gushed about how wonderful the session was and started down the ramp. As I walked past Delphina on the way out, she turned toward me and firmly grasped my hands in hers. A zap of electricity shot through my fingertips.

"You, Dr. Katherine Turner. You possess a power you do not understand. Be careful."

I started to protest, but she shushed me.

"Listen to those who come, or you will bear the

consequences." Her eyes widened and then I found myself outside her door, standing in the cold wind.

———

Driving back to my apartment at the animal hospital, Mari went on and on about how uplifting and relaxing her experience felt. Although short on specific details that Delphina revealed, she waxed blissful on how much she enjoyed the evening, the stress of the last few days erased.

"She said something to me, did you hear it?" I asked.

"The Katherine thing? I've got a cousin named Katherine."

I let it slide. Delphina had put on a nice show.

To be stress-free right now would be nice, I thought. My problem was that stress gave me an edge, an edge that sharpened my brain like a couple of cups of strong coffee. I liked the feeling more than I disliked it. Until the stress levels went overboard.

"There's nothing like a one-on-one session," Mari insisted. "It was very personal."

In the comfort of the SUV away from that raspy silken voice, I had to agree. In person, on the radio, watching television or experiencing a movie, each type of experience produces different results in our brains. Marshall McLuhan was right. The medium is the message.

Was this hypnotic pseudo-science message one that my assistant wanted to pursue?

"Of course not," replied Mari. "It was fun. I've never done anything like that before."

"So you aren't going to buy ten sessions from her?" I tried to keep the relief out of my voice.

"Are you crazy, Kate? I've got a bucket list of things I want to do like skydiving or learning to rappel down the side of a cliff." She put the turn signal on and waited for a panel van to pass before maneuvering into our parking lot. "What's on yours?"

"My what?" The gravel crunched under her big tires while my eyes searched for signs of life at Pinky's house. Only the porch light shone above the front door. The other rooms stood quiet and dark.

"Have you even been listening?" she chided me. "Your bucket list. What's on your bucket list?"

I was embarrassed to confess I didn't have one.

The last thing I did before turning off the light was to check the latest number of viewings on the YouTube video. It had jumped to 18,996.

When I closed my eyes Delphina's words slipped into my consciousness. "Remember to take your enemy's hand," her melodic voice whispered over and over. "Remember to take your enemy's hand."

Chapter Twenty-Three

WHEN I DRESSED FOR WORK THE NEXT MORNING AND reached for my scrubs, I realized how much science and logic were my refuge. The reading with Delphina had put that into perspective. Not for me were vague predictions of future adventures.

As for having a special power, everyone had a special power—they only needed to look deep inside themselves to find it.

The best thing that came out of that night? I started thinking about my bucket list.

———

Even Cindy's rigid scheduling didn't help during morning appointments as I tried unsuccessfully to keep on time. One of our patients needed much more time than usual, so each appointment after them ran a little late. Mari worked at breakneck speed, trying to catch up with the increased lab work, zipping past me toward the treatment room. That's why it surprised me to get a non-business-related text from Cindy.

WHATS YOUR DATING STATUS?

I shook my head in astonishment. Another topic to bring up in our staff meetings. Inappropriate texting. Trying to put an end to speculation, I texted back.

OPEN TO INTERPRETATION

She answered back with a smiley-face emoji.

Finally caught up, I was halfway down the hallway to my next appointment when Mari waylaid me.

"Why don't you go comb your hair, or put a little lipstick on," she suggested. In the six months I'd been working at the Oak Falls Animal Hospital, this was the first time anyone suggested a makeover between clients. Something strange was brewing.

"Mari," I hissed, "what are you up to?"

Had they stashed Luke somewhere in the building hoping for a Christmas engagement? Or somehow pulled Jeremy back in the picture for a good old college try?

My technician put her finger to her lips, indicating there was someone waiting in the exam room right next to us.

I took the chart out of her hand, knocked on the door, and walked in, sure I was being set up. No such luck. The astonishment on Devin Popovitch's face probably reflected mine.

"You're the F-150 with the clogged fuel line, right?" he said.

His eyes tracked down to my doctor's white jacket embroidered with my name. I watched his lips move as he sounded out the letters.

"And you're the old dog whose owner died and now is having accidents in the house?"

We both laughed. "Well, the truck is working a lot better."

"The dog isn't." He lifted an elderly gray terrier mix onto the exam table. "I saved some of her pee." With a flourish a ziplock bag half full of a familiar yellow liquid emerged from his leather messenger bag.

I considered him very brave to lug that around with him. Or very foolhardy.

As if reading my mind, he said, "I double-bagged it."

———

While completing my exam on the dog, it registered again what an attractive man Devin appeared to be both physically and personally. Given his lightly quiet, unassuming but confident demeanor, I could see why Raeleen had stuck around Oak Falls to be with him. But why did he stick with her?

Questions I couldn't and wouldn't ask while examining their dog.

"Do you think Rae's death has something to do with Muffin getting sick?" he asked after we admitted the dog for X-rays.

That was a hard question to answer. "There are many documented cases of dogs mourning the loss of someone close to them—human or even another animal. Muffin may have reacted by not drinking or eating as much, which leads to dehydration. The dehydration could have precipitated her urine issue. Or it might be a coincidence. That's the medical answer."

I smiled at him. "The non-medical answer is every pet

owner knows in their heart that their pets love them and miss them."

He leaned against the table. "Well, Muffin loved her, that's for sure."

"It's obvious she did." It also was obvious Devin loved her, but I doubted he'd given himself enough time to grieve.

"You know, Rae was feisty and super smart, but I liked that about her. We must have broken up and got back together a dozen times over the last two years. Always jealous, though, or pissed at someone. After a while I didn't want to listen to that anymore. I told her to keep the engagement ring, but we were done." He picked up his leather bag and shifted it back and forth. "I still don't know all the details of what happened. The police don't say much."

I felt the same about the assault on Jeremy. The M & M detective team from Kingston assigned to his case hadn't contacted him again.

"Did you know she dropped out of law school? On full scholarship? Rae told me she got fed up with everyone wanting to make money. She wanted to make a difference."

"That's very idealistic and admirable," I told him. Raeleen must have felt like she was fighting at windmills, and I was one of them.

Devin pointed to the messenger bag over his shoulder. "She gave me this. It cost her a week's pay," his voice cracked. "Nobody's telling us what happened to her."

"I'm sure Chief Garcia is doing his best," I said, trying

to distract him. "Anyway, Cindy will go over the treatment plan again with you, and I'll try to get Muffin back home tonight. I don't think your little girl needs any more surprises in her life." We walked toward reception and I handed him off to Cindy, who had freshened up her makeup since the last time I'd seen her. "Take good care of Mr. Popovitch," I told her.

"Devin, please," he said. "Thanks, Doc. Thanks for everything."

―――――――

"That hunk was Raeleen's boyfriend?" Mari asked in disbelief. Morning appointments finished, we started working up our sick patients.

"Ex-fiancé." I picked Muffin up and brought her into X-ray.

"Even worse. He was engaged to her?" she commented. "He seemed so nice and she seemed so…"

"Not nice?" I suggested.

"I was going to say something else."

"Well, he's pretty broken up about it." We laid Muffin down to measure and position her for the X-ray. Unlike most dogs, she stayed still. "Mari, I'd like to see if we can do this without any tranquilization. She's being very good."

We got Muffin ready to take the X-ray and darned if the little girl stayed still for us. Mari brought her back to the cage while I wrote up the labs and began the urine analysis. Muffin could have anything from a urinary tract infection right up to bladder or kidney stones, or worse. She didn't like the special kidney diet, of course, when we tried to feed her, but after spiking it with a teaspoon of canned kidney diet cat food, she ate almost the whole serving.

Devin needed to stay strong if he was going to take care of a menagerie of Raeleen's rescues.

━━━━━━

Around lunchtime Mari tapped on my office door where I sat multitasking in front of the computer. Reviewing my clinic notes competed with eating a pear, so between the juicy half-eaten fruit in my left hand and typing with one finger of the right hand—well, let's say it didn't look too attractive.

"You're dripping on your keyboard," Mari said.

"Ahhhh." A quick backward slide with the desk chair simply left a dappled pattern of drips on the floor.

As I cleaned, Mari talked. "Meeting Devin and Muffin today made me remember Raeleen as a person who had a lot of problems but a good heart. We've concentrated so much on Eloise and Frank because of that dumb video, I started to wonder why Rae was murdered and who did it."

"In case you were wondering I didn't kill her, so that's a million suspects left, minus one." With the floor cleaned up, I used hand sanitizer on my sticky fingers before I stood and stretched.

"The murderer can't be Devin. He's too nice to be a killer."

"A classic killer move."

My assistant tried to see the good in everyone, not always successfully.

Ignoring me, she continued. "Well, we know Rae didn't shy away from speaking her mind. That I can swear to." I hadn't noticed, but Mari was also multitasking, a Post-it note in one hand and a giant bag of corn chips tucked under her arm.

I snuck a chip from her before going back and sitting down. "Other than being shot, I don't remember reading much about the circumstances or anything else."

Mari's face grew thoughtful. "Come to think of it, I'm sort of foggy on what happened the night she died, too. You know what that means?"

We both smiled and said in unison, "Ask Cindy."

———————

Annoyed slightly at being called away from her desk, Cindy took one look at the two of us munching chips and said, "What are you guys up to?"

"We're a little curious about what happened to Raeleen, especially after meeting Devin," I began, "and wondered if you knew anything about the case?"

Cindy folded her arms in front of her. "What's it worth to you?"

That, I didn't expect.

Mari picked up the challenge seamlessly. "What do you need?"

"Oh, I'll think of something."

Cindy always won.

Mari usually put up more of a fight, but she must have succumbed to the holiday spirit. As the "Little Drummer Boy" kept a slow steady background beat, Cindy spilled the story.

"At eleven Raeleen got off work at the supermarket. Only a few employees work that late shift. She walked to her car alone, before saying good night to everyone, as usual. The last one to leave said when he looked in his rearview mirror, she was standing with her clicker in her hand pointing at the car lock. A video from the supermarket security camera confirms that. Then for some reason she looks over toward the dumpsters. After a moment Raeleen leaves the car, walks into the trees, and disappears."

"Was she alone in the parking lot by then?"

"Yes, as far as they know."

Mari and I looked at each other. We knew that parking lot. In fact, we'd parked near the dumpsters the night of our encounter with Raeleen.

Cindy continued. "Someone tried to jump her, they think, in the trees. She struggled. Rae's hands and face showed multiple defensive wounds. There's some confusion as to the gun. Forensics hypothesizes there was a struggle and she got shot at point-blank range in the abdomen. The second wound was to the head after she'd collapsed on the ground. Rae's hands also showed gunshot residue."

I shuddered. Someone really wanted Raeleen to die.

"Where did it happen again?"

"That's the weird thing. Not next to her car. Whoever killed her hid in the trees behind the dumpsters in the employee parking area. It's tucked over to the side near the building."

It was obvious that detail puzzled our receptionist, and probably the police.

After my initial reaction, I asked, "What about the parking lot cameras? Did they show anything? Did they check her cell phone messages for any threats?"

Cindy rolled her eyes. "Of course. Oak Falls may be small, but our detectives still have access to the latest technology. The video footage shows Raeleen about to get into her car when she stops, looks up, then starts walking toward the woods."

"No strange vehicles or people in the parking lot?"

This time Cindy didn't even bother to answer.

"The chief thinks someone hiding in the trees may have called her name, lured her into the woods, then ambushed her. The gun wasn't recovered."

After a moment Mari replied, "What voice would make her walk into the woods that late at night?"

I put myself in her place. A voice, perhaps familiar, unexpectedly calls her name. Why did she go? The ambient temperature must have been around freezing then, no time to be outdoors. Unafraid, Raeleen walked into a death trap.

The sound of my assistant's voice chased the images away. "That had to be one persuasive voice."

"Maybe it was," I answered. "Maybe it was someone she loved."

Chapter Twenty-Four

THE SMALL MEMORIAL SERVICE FOR RAELEEN LASSITOR started at seven p.m. Mari felt too upset to go, but I went and sat in the middle of the room, head slightly bent, trying to blend into the crowd. All the front rows were packed with people, and a few service dogs. I noticed Pinky sitting as far away as he could, in the opposite corner. A large professional portrait of the deceased smiled at the mourners as calm, nature-themed music played softly in the background.

Dressed in a somber black suit, a portly man with a white beard and mustache began the celebration of life services. Unfortunately for the occasion, if he'd worn a red suit instead of a black one, he'd be a ringer for Santa Claus. With a surreptitious look at his watch and a nod to his associate standing by the door, at the dot of seven he began the service.

"We are here tonight to remember Raeleen Scarlett Lassitor, taken from us much too soon."

The first few rows erupted with sobs. One woman threw her hands up in the air. From the family resemblance I guessed Raeleen had a few sisters who shared her exuberant nature. In the second row, tall and stoic among the family, sat Devin Popovitch. Eyes focused straight ahead, he appeared to be the calm eye of a swirling storm. Pausing for the sobs to cease, the funeral director invited the audience to share memories with the gathered.

Her look-alike mother told of a sensitive loving child with few filters, who grew up to be a scholarship winner— only to turn her back on academia to help animals. Admitting that they often quarreled, she noted that after every fight they made up, secure in the knowledge that despite everything, their love for each other and family was strong.

———————

Person after person described a Raeleen I hadn't met. Most of her friends also worked with animals. A number of employees from the local rescue group recounted how dedicated the deceased had been in helping care for feral and abandoned animals. It seemed she regularly fostered dogs and cats, as well as rabbits and hamsters, and frequently reported the owners of abused or neglected pets. The president of the local chapter of the Legalize Animal Rights Now movement announced an internship in the name of their vice president, Raeleen Lassitor. He recounted how her drive and enthusiasm tripled their membership in the last six months and her grant-writing skills brought multiple donations to their cause.

The only animals she didn't get along with, it seems, were humans.

———————

Hustling across the dimly lit parking lot after the ceremony, a middle-aged woman in a green wool coat approached me.

"Dr. Turner, isn't it?" She reached out her gloved hand to me.

"Yes," I admitted.

"I'm Nancy Tolberg. I knew and worked with Rae for many years," she added. "I heard about your encounter at the supermarket. Please don't dwell too much on that final conversation with her. She sometimes let her emotions get out of hand."

Not sure what to say, I made a noncommittal sound of agreement.

"She meant well," Nancy reiterated, "but…"

"Would you like a cup of coffee, or a tea?" I asked, increasingly aware of the cold wind and the disappearing cars around us.

"Sounds wonderful. Meet you at Judy's Place, in town, if that's alright?"

"Perfect," I said. Judy was going to start getting tired of seeing me. On the way to the truck a sudden gust of wind almost blew me off my feet.

━━━━

Warmed up by a decaf coffee for me, and a luscious-looking hot chocolate with whipped cream for her, Nancy quickly began telling stories about her friend.

It seemed they had worked at the same animal rescue center as volunteers, and Nancy soon witnessed the fiery Raeleen in action.

"For a smart person, she jumped to conclusions, a lot, without asking questions. That got her into trouble."

Nancy chuckled at the memory. "One time she started to take a cat from a doorstep when the owner saw her." The chuckle became a laugh. "Rae acted first and thought later."

"So she thought the cat was abandoned when it simply was waiting to be let in?" I asked.

"Even worse. A workman had let the cat out by mistake. The owner was coaxing it back inside the house when Rae interfered. She called Animal Control."

"What?"

"The owner showed Rae her phone with dozens of pictures of the cat in her photo albums, but she didn't back down. The two began to fight about it with the owner demanding Rae get off her property. It escalated so much that a worried neighbor called the police. Sure enough, when the cops arrived their siren frightened the cat and it took off."

Nancy started to laugh. "Those ladies went at it full tilt until the police separated them."

This crazy episode stayed in my head as Nancy went on and on. Bottom line: the cat came back, the owner didn't go to jail, but a simple situation had turned into a big emotional mess for everyone.

Story after story illustrated Raeleen's misplaced good intentions. Nancy thought this pattern of impulsive behavior had been one of the reasons her relationship with Devin Popovitch had stalled.

"After this last fight with Devin, she was devastated." Nancy went on to recount multiple times Rae accused women of flirting with her fiancé, being so bold as yelling at them right to their face and embarrassing Devin. After one of those episodes, he broke up with her.

"That's when I suggested counseling to her. Her jealousy had spiraled out of control. To make things worse, the shelter asked her not to volunteer for a while. They said Rae needed some time off to gain perspective. Can you believe it? Being fired from a volunteer job?"

I didn't know what to say.

"But the animals loved her," Nancy reiterated. "They all loved her. Even the feral kittens weren't afraid of Rae. Last time I saw her she was sitting on the floor with a bunch of little kittens in her lap that she'd rescued, just in heaven." The memory prompted a smile from Raeleen's old friend. "I'd like to think of her that way."

A fitting epitaph. Maybe somewhere in those stories was a clue that might lead to her killer.

———

It was about nine thirty by the time I arrived back home. Two trucks were waiting outside my apartment. One sported a shiny snowplow. The other looked suspiciously like the police.

Chief Garcia climbed out of his patrol car first and walked over to the driver's side of my truck. I rolled the window down to check if Pinky could hear us over his engine.

On the same wavelength, the chief blocked Pinky's view, leaned in, and said, "I'm only here because you and Cindy are close. But you really screwed things up by showing up at Raeleen's funeral tonight. Make sure you had a good reason to be there, because a certain agency that we both know and love may be stopping by to interview you. The FBI likes to see who shows up at the funeral of a case they're interested in."

"What?" I turned off the engine.

"Her murder is now being viewed as a hate crime. Raeleen Lassitor was the vice president of a militant animal rights group, Legalize Animal Rights Now. That organization wants the FBI to investigate. They've had several threats recently, one that specifically targeted Raeleen." He looked over his shoulder at the snowplow. "You okay if I leave?"

"Sure," I said, even though the tiniest bit of doubt lurked in my brain.

"Don't linger, now. Send him on his way. Good night, then." On the way back to his squad car he made a point to wave at the driver of the snowplow and slap the hood of his vehicle twice.

That left me alone in the dark with Pinky.

━━━━━

Despite the chief's advice, I invited Pinky in. He sat in my apartment on my sofa, Princess cradled in his arms, his bulk creating a valley in the cushions. I could barely understand him between the sobs. The shirt he had on smelled faintly of roses.

As far as I could make out, he'd had an encounter with Raeleen before her murder and felt guilty about it, which is why he attended her memorial service.

"Pinky," I interrupted for about the third time, "take a deep breath and calm down. I don't understand what you're saying."

A big wad of Kleenex appeared from deep within his pocket. He used it to dry his eyes. Sliding his thick winter coat off revealed massive shoulders, bulging deltoids, and the kind of neck you see on bodybuilders loaded up with steroids. Tiny alarms went off on the back of my neck.

His chest heaved a bit more then settled down, like a boiling pot taken off the stove. "That's better," I told him. "Princess doesn't want to see you upset."

Between the sniffles and soothing his dog, he began to calm down. Pinky reminded me of those goofy pit bull puppies that don't know their own strength. How could I ever have been afraid of this sweet guy?

Then I remembered what Cindy said about his temper.

We sat together for a few minutes. I got him a glass of water and put it within reach. Cozy now, he said, "Thank you, Dr. Kate."

"You're welcome." With a leap, Buddy jumped up and sat opposite our unexpected guests.

I hated to set the waterworks off again, but I was curious about his interaction with Raeleen and why the memorial service had upset him so much. After a little prodding on my part, he explained.

"She said she was going to take my Princess away." His voice wavered but stayed steady. "It happened at the Circle K. I left Princess in the truck while I went to the bathroom. The cab was nice and warm, and she had her pillow and blanket. I was gone for maybe three or four minutes." He placed his hand on his abdomen. "My tummy hurt. One of those gas station burritos, I think."

"You actually ate one of those things?" An image of a congealed mess of beans and cheese sitting under a heat lamp for a couple of hours popped into my head.

"It tasted pretty good, but about a half an hour later…"

"Spare me the details." I'd already watched him break down and cry. That was enough sharing for tonight.

Pinky leaned forward, his face turning red. "She yelled at me so much the manager came out and told her to leave. Then she yelled at him."

Unfortunately, the story had a familiar ring. Nancy's stories sounded more or less the same.

"But Princess is here with you. Why are you still so upset?" I asked, not understanding the problem.

"Because…" his lip started to tremble, "because I killed her."

———

A half hour later I still hadn't convinced Pinky he didn't kill Raeleen. We kept revisiting the same unfortunate encounter between them over and over.

"I was mad at her. She said something mean about you, too. That's when I told her I wished she was dead, and I did what you did with your finger." To my chagrin, he demonstrated with his index finger. "Abracadabra."

"As soon as I said that, she clutched her heart." Pinky

put his hand to his chest and again demonstrated for me. "It scared me, so I drove away."

Picturing the meeting, I realized the distraught Pinky had mistaken a sarcastically dramatic gesture on Raeleen's part for the real thing. How long had this been weighing on his mind?

"But Pinky, she didn't die from a heart attack. She was shot."

His hand still clutched his own chest above his heart, subconsciously mimicking their unfortunate encounter. "Someone said she was shocked. I thought that meant her heart."

"You heard them wrong. They said shot, not shocked. Believe me." I'd forgotten how isolated Pinky kept himself from the world around him. According to Cindy, he never watched the news and never had company. The last time Cindy and her husband saw him without his snow-plow equipment was when they forced him to come to dinner for Thanksgiving. He left early.

"Are you sure?" he asked in his high plaintive way.

"Trust me," I said.

His eyes dropped to the floor. "I am a little hard of hearing in this ear." A huge hand pointed to his left ear, while his body tried to process the news. He placed a kiss on the top of his dog's head. "I trust you, Dr. Kate. With Princess's life and mine."

"Thank you." But my response masked the growing feeling that Pinky had developed an unhealthy attach-ment to me, one that I needed to stop without hurting his feelings. Big and emotionally fragile, he was a unique individual. I liked him but didn't want to be the center of his small universe.

"Do you want a little more water before you go?" I asked, walking into the kitchen. "I need to get some rest so I can do my job tomorrow, and so do you."

He jumped up as if I'd set him on fire. Princess let out a yip at being disturbed.

"No, thank you, Dr. Kate. We'll get going." He slipped on his coat. "That explains why the police didn't come to arrest me. I kept expecting them, so except for plowing, I haven't left the house much."

"Well, now you can. Go to the mall, walk around and look at the decorations." Ironically, it sounded exactly like the advice Cindy and Mari had given to me.

He moved toward the door, bundled Princess under his coat, and waved goodbye. To get through my front door into the parking lot he had to maneuver through the doorframe sideways.

A roar sounded when the snowplow truck started up. The big engine's vibrations rattled the glass. Headlights smoothly curved past, headed up toward the road. Gazing through the window curtains, I watched him immediately turn into his own driveway, which ran parallel along the animal hospital property line. After parking the plow truck outside, Pinky walked up his front stairs at a surprisingly fast pace before he disappeared inside.

Did I feel safer with Pinky so close? My answer used to be maybe.

What was it now?

Chapter Twenty-Five

"Alright. I'll go."

As soon as I made the decision to spend Christmas with my estranged dad, a huge weight lifted off my chronically tensed neck. Commitment sealed. Just not having to worry about making up my mind felt great. Was it the right move? Who knew? But I'd find out.

Mari and Cindy both clapped their hands. They'd been pestering me on our lunch break for the last ten minutes, bombarding me with inspirational stories of friends and estranged families finding each other while sharing homemade pizza. Tired of going it alone, I'd asked for their opinions and gotten them in stereo.

Even Mr. Cat, who rubbed against us looking for a handout, meowed in agreement.

"You need to come to terms with your father if you are going to move on," Cindy said, sounding like one of the television self-help gurus. I diplomatically didn't remind her of the huge fight she'd recently had with one of her aunts. They didn't speak for three weeks until Cindy's mother forced her to make up.

A twelve-year estrangement, like mine, carried a lot of baggage.

Mari had a different take. "Do it for your half sister and brother, as well as for yourself. They are innocents in this. I think developing a relationship with them will benefit you tremendously." In her large extended family, she still socialized with ex-sisters-in-law, ex-brothers-in-law, and assorted relatives, including a pair of elderly twin aunts always feuding with one another. At family gatherings, for the sake of harmony, politics and religion were not topics up for discussion.

"Peace in the family is better for everyone," Mari reminded us all.

Gramps couldn't have said it any better.

———

With about ten minutes to spare before appointments started, I poured a cup of coffee and texted Gramps to accept the invitation for Christmas dinner. My response was an immediate call back.

"I'm proud of you, Katie," he said. "We can spend Christmas Eve together, then head out to your dad's place in the Hamptons on Christmas morning."

"Where exactly in the Hamptons?" That's when I realized Gramps never talked about what my dad was doing. Even with access to social media, his profile was one I avoided. My circle of friends stayed pretty small, deliberately.

Gramps laughed. "I'll send you the address. You've got a lot of catching up to do."

Cindy stuck her head in and signaled to cut the call short. To make sure I got the message, she tapped her watch and raised her eyebrows.

"Sorry, Gramps. Got to go. Cindy is chomping at the bit to start appointments."

"Say hi to her for me."

I waved "hi" and mouthed Gramps.

"Hi, Gramps," she yelled back.

"Tell her to check the joke I posted this morning on Facebook. I'm trying to get fifty likes."

———

After saying goodbye, I put my phone on vibrate and searched for my favorite stethoscope. I'd almost given up finding the darn thing and had reached for another one when I saw it draped over a lab chair. Stethoscopes are like shoes. You always end up with a favorite pair.

I brushed my hair into a high pony and went back to work.

———

About fifty minutes later, Mari approached me in the hallway with the afternoon schedule in her hand. I'd just finished one appointment and was going to the next. "Busy?" I said. "I might need some help."

"Oh, you can handle this one alone," she answered, before disappearing down the hall.

Shoot. That must mean they booked Devin Popovitch…again. The staff loved matchmaking and had cooked up an imaginary holiday romance between me and Raeleen's handsome former fiancé, now back on the market, thanks to her murder. Even Cindy advised me to strike while the iron was hot.

In my experience, that only led to getting burned.

When I opened the door, someone unexpected turned around.

"Luke?" I glanced at the table looking for my patient, his grandmother's cat. A quick look around the room revealed it to be empty, except for him.

He followed my train of thought. "No animals here. I convinced Cindy to sneak me in for a few minutes."

"I'm at work…"

"Just listen for a second. Each time I try to see you we're interrupted."

I sat at the small exam room desk and left him standing. "Maybe if you called ahead of time, you'd have better luck."

Luke leaned against the stainless table and crossed his long legs. "Okay. Are we done arguing yet?"

"Make it quick. I've got another appointment in fifteen minutes." My resolve to not let him rile me up had evaporated.

"So, first let me apologize for not telling you Dina moved back to Oak Falls. That position in Albany didn't work out for her." He watched my face for a reaction.

I kept my expression noncommittal. Luke knew I was not a fan of his ex. What did he want me to say? Poor Dina?

I relented and said, "Poor Dina."

My platitude didn't fool him.

In the short time I'd known her, not only had the self-absorbed Dina made a play for my best friend, Jeremy, but she liked to keep Luke dangling in her orbit. They'd been high school sweethearts, lived together for a few years, and had loads of mutual friends. This meant they shared a huge history. She knew every member of his extensive family and all their stories. I struggled to remember half their names.

"That night at the diner, when I picked up takeout for us, she'd dropped by my place unexpectedly. We weren't on a date."

Right. Luke might think that, but I knew better. Dina was checking up on her old flame and probably trying to fan the fire.

"Thanks for sharing," I said. "Is that all?"

"No, as a matter of fact, but I'll let you digest what I told you." The expression on his face tugged at my heart.

Not sure what I felt, I said nothing.

"Since this is going nowhere, I'll tell you something that will interest you. There's a rumor going around the station that a private pathologist hired by a friend of the family has some questions about Eloise Rieven's death."

"I bet it's the broken arm?" Good for her. Babs must have gotten hold of the radiographs. My attention shifted away from my life to hers.

"Right. They did some calculations, and that degree of fracture could only have happened following a specific impact velocity. Simply falling after tripping wouldn't have done it."

"Didn't she have osteoporosis?" I asked.

"Surprisingly not. With all the farm work and lifting bulldogs, she had great upper body strength. So that means…"

"There's a possibility that someone pushed her."

Technology played a huge part in the reopening of the Eloise Rieven case. Since X-rays and autopsy records are now stored in digital files, it's a simple thing to send them by email—and in the Eloise Rieven case they were sent to a private pathologist and radiologist hired by Babs Vanderbilt-Hayes. Although not conclusive, the new report raised enough doubt for the Oak Falls Police Department to reopen the case and assign a detective to review the evidence.

What had been a simple accidental death now might be a clever case of murder.

"The chief is furious," Luke said.

No surprise there.

"As someone who would benefit from her death," Luke explained, "you may be on the interview list. I came here to give you a heads-up. And don't expect they'll come to your house and have a friendly discussion. This will be by the book and down at the station. And recorded."

"Benefit? Me?"

"She was planning on filing a complaint to the veterinary board and suing you for the value of the lost litter of bulldog puppies in small claims court."

How many suspect lists was I on? Stunned that it had gone so far, I stared back at him.

Luke took a step closer, his eyes concerned. "Kate, I know you. There is no way you contributed to her murder—but do you have an alibi for the time of death?"

My mind blanked. Truthfully, I didn't remember

when or what time the accident—well, what I thought was an accident—happened. My best guess? Sometime in the early evening. Which meant my alibi most likely was a dog, a sofa, and HGTV.

None of whom were talking.

———

After Luke left, the day crawled by. Every free moment I spent thinking about Raeleen's murder and whether my stupid Christmas wish for Eloise and Frank to disappear had given someone a crazy idea. A grateful but disturbed client? A murderer with OCD who needed to finish the list? Or a killer using one death to mask another?

When I took a moment to check my computer, the YouTube video viewing number was up to 27,613. Most people commented on the three deaths following my wish. As usual, conspiracy ideas abounded. Next to be blamed were my avenging guardian angels, followed by devils, sorcery, and black magic. Some were too bizarre to read. The worst one predicted more deaths to follow.

Did the police have access to viewers' info? How do you go about checking alibis for over 27,000 strangers?

Or did a local detective already have a much smaller list of suspects, with Pinky being number one and me standing right behind him?

Chapter Twenty-Six

MUCH TO MY SURPRISE, NO ONE IN LAW ENFORCEMENT wanted to talk to me. Cindy said the statement I gave the chief satisfied them for now. They had other leads to follow.

It felt like the Christmas music had been playing for a year. Someone suggested we should buy a huge count-down sign in the office, keeping track of the number of days left until Christmas. I pointed out that not everyone celebrated the same holidays.

Cindy kept busy juggling holiday hours. Most of the staff planned either to travel to family gatherings or host their relatives at home. Discussions of recipes flew back and forth in the treatment area and during surgery.

Their banter never struck a chord with me. For years it had only been me and Gramps.

Since my Christmas Eve supper and Christmas Day dinners were covered, I listened with half an ear and added little to the conversations. Not that anyone wanted my hints on cooking. Sadly, the microwave was my favor-ite kitchen tool and takeout my go-to recipe.

Mari continued to chatter away about green bean casseroles and whether to add sliced almonds or sliced mushrooms while I performed minor surgery to clean a small abscess. Cindy interrupted us during the stuffing debate. It looked like she'd been crying.

"They might arrest Pinky," she blurted out, obviously distressed. "I can't believe this."

"Slow down," I said, almost finished opening and cleaning the two infected teeth marks located just where the tail met the back. Like many cats I'd treated, this tabby had tried to avoid a fight but hadn't run fast enough.

Our visibly upset receptionist began picking up pens and straightening the cluttered countertop. Cindy's nervous energy usually propelled her into cleaning. She explained as she concentrated on the computer station.

"Some detectives from Kingston have focused in on Pinky because he plowed Eloise Rieven's driveway the night of her death and he discovered her body. Now an eyewitness says they saw him enter Frank's home the night he died. Pinky swears Frank was alive when he left but admitted they argued about his bill and the holiday schedule."

"Poor Pinky," Mari said, checking the level of anesthesia on the kitty as I finished up.

"Eloise's son, Joe, is very upset. What do you think, Kate?"

Her question took me by surprise. "I'm not sure."

I concentrated on my patient. Satisfied with the minor surgery, I gave him a long-acting antibiotic shot so his elderly owners didn't have to struggle with medicating him. With all that finished, I told Mari to let him up from anesthesia and removed his intratracheal breathing tube as soon as he demonstrated a swallow reflex.

"Sorry. You guys are busy," Cindy noted, still aimlessly puttering around. "I'll talk to you about this later." Visibly worried, she went back to her desk in reception.

Mari and I watched the cat begin to wake up. This

classic American tabby cat had survived hopefully to not fight another day. We carried him to his cage cushioned with a soft blanket as he looked around.

"No more arguing with other kitties," I cautioned. "Stay at home and out of trouble."

Being a cat, he took it under advisement.

I wish I could have said the same thing to Pinky.

———

As it turns out, the Anderson family lawyer stepped in and advised Pinky not to speak to anyone or answer any questions. He met with law enforcement and set guidelines on any interviews with his client.

For now, without hard evidence, the detectives backed down. The lawyer assured them Pinky wasn't going anywhere.

The news of him being under suspicion of murder spread rapidly through the town and drastically cut into Pinky's plowing business. Cindy revealed to Mari and me during a break that all day Pinky had gotten calls from his more rural clients abruptly canceling his service.

"Guess they didn't want to take any chances he'd plow first, kill later," Mari said with a grin.

"I assume that's a joke." Cindy was a staunch supporter of Pinky's innocence and resented anyone saying otherwise. My suspicion is she'd brought the family lawyer on board.

"You've known Pinky a long time," I remembered.

Like so many busy people, I found I really knew very little about my neighbors.

"Since forever," she answered. "My mom and his mom were best friends. We played together as kids and went to high school together. Pinky was always big, very shy, and uncomfortable around strangers. I guess that would be called social anxiety today."

"Probably."

She thought for a moment. "When I was in high school an ex-boyfriend used to harass me all the time. One day Pinky saw him say something that made me cry. The next day that bully had a black eye and a bandaged hand. Every day after that Pinky walked me to my house, or my mom's car—he protected me. We never talked about it. You didn't talk about stuff like that when I was growing up. I wish I could do more for him."

"You're doing all you can," I reminded her.

Someone was playing a nasty game of cat and mouse, only the dead weren't mice, but people—people with lives and hopes and dreams. Gone forever.

A predator who carefully chose specific victims.

Who was better equipped to catch a predator than a veterinarian?

Chapter Twenty-Seven

DEEP IN THE STORAGE CLOSET OF THE HOSPITAL I FOUND my trusty dry-erase board. Its surface no longer pristine, it still suited my purpose. I'd used one in school to organize my thoughts. Since I'd done it before, why not try it again? Plus, if nothing comes to mind you can doodle on it. Perched on top of a side table in my apartment, it cried out for someone to draw something. Anything. So I wrote SELFISH CHRISTMAS WISH MURDERS in bold letters.

My next step was to talk to my grandpa.

"What am I going to do with you, Katie?" Gramps had listened to my theory on the three possible murders and wasn't happy with me. "Is Luke going to help? He may be on a leave of absence from the Oak Falls Police Department, but he's still a cop."

Of course I couldn't answer that because I didn't know what to expect from Luke. He always said to leave the investigating to the professionals. I saw his point, but what if they weren't solving the crime?

"Did you hear what I said?"

"Yes, Gramps. I'm just not sure about Luke."

My explanation didn't satisfy him. A sigh was followed by another question. "Did you break up with him?"

"Gramps," I tried to explain, "I'm not sure there was anything left to break."

After promising that, yes, I would be careful and, no, I wouldn't take any chances and maybe I should leave the sleuthing to the detectives, I said good night and hung up. Speaking to my Gramps forced me to think about Luke. We'd always been very casual in our attraction to each other. Had casual morphed into forgotten? Because if it had, then it was best to end any pretense of a relationship right now. Amputate and be done.

I walked into the kitchen to get a glass of wine and passed by the whiteboard. Should I start tonight? Putting it off again, I waited at the kitchen table, glass in hand, and stared at it. Selfish Christmas Wish Murders stared back at me.

"Oh, what the heck," I said out loud and picked up a dry-erase marker.

In no time I had three bodies marked off in different corners, their names in bold red. Frank Martindale, Eloise Rieven, and Raeleen Lassitor.

For aesthetic balance, I added Jeremy in the remaining corner with a forest of question marks surrounding his name. Nothing pointed to his assault being tied to any of the wishes.

The only thing I knew they all had in common was Pinky and me. I took another sip of wine, confirmed that I was not the murderer, and tried again.

I didn't believe a serial killer was working in Oak Falls, but I decided to entertain that ever-popular movie theory. Let's pretend someone wanted one of these victims dead.

Maybe the coincidence of my wish getting such publicity spurred that someone into action. I decided to go by order of death. But first I added X-MAS CARDS in the middle of the board with a couple of question marks, to remind me that someone had posted phony cards from the victims specifically to me.

Frank Martindale was contentious and had many people in town mad at him. They found his body because he didn't show up in court. What was this pending lawsuit about? I wrote LAWSUITS in bold letters underneath his name. Money made a great motive.

Next came Eloise. Babs thought her death was suspicious, but I wasn't so sure. My own experience a few days ago led me on a different path. Did the outside pathologist consider wind gusts? Random powerful wind gusts hit all the time here in the Hudson Valley. I'd been almost blown off my feet by one. A strong gust of wind might very well have initiated her fall, and the combined velocity caused the nasty fracture. As far as motive, I wasn't aware of any—except mine, so I wrote MOTIVE and underlined it twice. Now if someone had killed Frank, Eloise's accidental murder would play into the wish.

Next came Raeleen. I knew from talking to her ex-fiancé that she felt strongly about animal rights, to the point of stepping over the line many times. The FBI was investigating threats made to her and other members of LARN. Her accusation against me, however, needed to be explored. With a purple marker I wrote ANIMAL RIGHTS GROUP and FIANCE under her name. Then

I added GRUDGE and KILL TO MAKE THE WISH COME TRUE.

That left Jeremy. Of course, he was alive and well and might not be part of this at all. Why would anyone attack Jeremy? I personally thought his assault was a robbery attempt, but because he also was tied to me, I wrote ARGUMENT. Then I wondered, how would a murderer find out we'd argued that day in the parking lot? HOSPITAL STAFF with a question mark joined the other notations on the board.

The memory of those clients staring out the animal hospital window at us yelling at each other came back to haunt me. Maybe Jeremy was supposed to be dead.

With that horrible thought in mind, I immediately texted him.

No answer.

An hour later there still was no reply.

I tossed and turned most of the night dreaming of Jeremy running for his life.

During breakfast the next morning I heard back from him. He'd fallen asleep early after playing chase with his toddler nephew.

Glad to hear his voice, I quickly went over my thoughts with him, trying to tie all the deaths together.

"So, what you're saying is I have a big target on my chest?" Jeremy asked.

Oops. It was one thing to hypothesize but quite

another thing when it became reality for someone else. "I'm not really sure. Maybe?" I tried to finish up my maple-flavored instant oatmeal but put it down.

"Maybe? That's comforting." My friend didn't sound particularly friendly.

Time to lay it on the line. "Jeremy, just be careful, please. All these deaths occurred when the victim was alone at night. Please don't let your guard down."

He laughed. "Believe me. I've still got a lump on my head. My guard is at an all-time high at the moment. Thanks for the warning. This is turning out to be an unforgettable holiday season, for all the wrong reasons."

Chapter Twenty-Eight

I'D JUST WALKED OUT OF MY APARTMENT AND INTO the animal hospital when a similarity between all the deaths struck me. Frank took too much medication, Eloise might have been pushed, and Jeremy had been attacked from behind. Only Raeleen put up a fight. Someone tried to ambush her but didn't succeed. Feisty, infuriating Raeleen had multiple contact injuries before a gun silenced her. None of the other incidents required brute strength.

Could the murderer be a woman?

In the middle of morning appointments, Raeleen's fiancé, Devin, showed up for a medication refill for Muffin. By his side stood a familiar figure. Our former intern, Greta, proudly accompanied him, her hand lightly resting on his arm. The look of adoration on her face was unmistakable.

Mari's eyebrows went toward the sky when she saw the new couple.

Cindy interrupted her transaction and waved me over. "Just need you to okay this, Dr. Kate," she said to me.

Determined not to show my own astonishment, I concentrated on the medicine.

"How's your dog doing?" I asked, scrolling through my notes on the portable tablet. "Any problems?"

Greta answered for him, which further surprised the heck out of all of us.

"Muffin's doing great, isn't she, honey?"

A man of a few words, Devin said, "Sure. Much better."

He might as well have been Shakespeare. Greta beamed at his response.

After I approved the refill, I asked, "How do you guys know each other?"

Again, Greta jumped in first. "We're in the same history class at school. I needed an elective this semester, and so did he. Luckily, we ended up in the same class."

"Yeah," he added in a flat voice. "Greta helps me with the homework. They give us way too much homework, by the way."

Greta sagely nodded in agreement, before giggling. "You're so right."

There was a distinct possibility that my former intern had mistaken friendliness and the need for a study partner for romantic interest. Devin's body language didn't show any particular tenderness or interest. I couldn't help but wonder how long they'd been "doing homework" together. And had Raeleen found out about it?

Mari had a question for Greta. "Have you started another internship?"

"Yes," she answered enthusiastically. "A radiologist's office. I love it. No emergencies, no real patients to talk to. So far this matches my needs, perfectly."

"And veterinary medicine?" my assistant persisted. "What did you think?"

She shook her head. "Nope. Too messy, emotional, and frankly—you all work too hard."

With that pronouncement she and Devin bade us goodbye and left. Our shy student had been replaced by a decisive woman in love. Crossing the parking lot, Greta again slipped her hand around his arm.

Cindy waited until the door closed completely to comment. "That's something I didn't predict. She seemed so nice."

"Boy," Mari added. "She pounced on him pretty quick. Anyone know if Greta is his alibi?"

I sagely failed to remind them of their own matchmaking attempts. Instead, I shook my head while Cindy said, "No comment."

My opinion of Greta had changed, too. She'd attended the Christmas party and heard everything. Greta could have used the "death wish" to camouflage the reason behind Raeleen's murder, clearing the way to console a grieving Devin. I decided her name would soon be prominently written on my dry-erase board just below Raeleen. Only next to Greta I'd write—killer?

"He's going to dump her, mark my words," Cindy predicted. "If Gramps was here, we'd bet on it."

———

The final client of the day had a bizarre problem. Her completely lovable kitty who lay purring on the exam table, waiting for her yearly physical, had learned to turn her touch-free faucet on and off and on and off, thereby providing hours of feline paw-dipping pleasure.

"See," she said and held her phone up. We both watched her Siamese, Simba, jump onto the kitchen counter. After staring at the faucet, she held up her paw. When the faucet began to flow, Simba leisurely dipped her paw into the water, then scooped a little up for a drink. This continued for a good three or four minutes.

"Very ingenious," I told the owner. "Now, let's figure out what to do about it."

Simba stood up and gave a loud Siamese meow, inviting a conversation with her owner. "She's very smart," my client commented. "She also opens doors. I had to change all my handles for doorknobs." Despite the inconvenience, Simba and her owner obviously enjoyed a happy relationship—a Siamese queen and her lowly human servant.

"Have you checked this brand for an override command? Maybe it can be set to a two-taps code. Or, you can cover it with an appliance cover when not in use."

None of my ideas appealed to either of them.

"I thought cats hated water," she added, stroking Simba's shiny fur. The blue-eyed cat responded by molding herself into her owner's hand.

That was one of the biggest misconceptions around. "Many house cats enjoy a little water. I've had clients tell me their cats curl up in the bathroom sink, lick the leftover shower water when they're done, or put their heads under running water to lick the droplets. I think Simba is amusing herself while getting a fresh drink using her front paw as a spoon."

We both stared at the cat who disdainfully turned her back and began to groom her naughty paws.

"A barrier of some sort might help," I suggested after finishing my exam. All Simba needed was a booster of her rabies shot, which went smoothly. Rabies was a shot I always recommended, especially here in rural Oak Falls. The story my client shared with us illustrated why.

Simba's owner told me her neighbor had two bats fly in through her chimney this past summer which scared everyone. Another neighbor didn't realize she hosted a bat colony in the eaves of an unfinished basement.

"Bats are wonderful creatures and eat large amounts of insects," I reminded her. "If they become ill or disorientated, a sick bat is easy prey even for a pampered house cat." I draped my stethoscope around my neck. "Now, what are we going to do with you, Simba?"

After discussing some options my client decided to try my tinfoil barrier idea while at the same time providing Simba with an alternative source of water—a cat fountain.

Everyone left happy, which was a great way to end my day.

Too bad it didn't last.

———

In my apartment I must have walked past the dry-erase board a dozen times while cleaning up and doing a load of laundry. Still thinking about where Greta fit into everything, my thoughts were interrupted by a text.

U busy? Want 2 talk?

Having Luke come over would definitely liven up my evening one way or another. Tonight, we'd finally be alone for more than a few minutes. This "talk" was long overdue, but I had a bad feeling. It would be the perfect topper of this stressful holiday season—being officially dumped just before Christmas. I took a deep breath and texted:

Not busy. See you soon?

He replied:

K

His one word response usually meant he was in the neighborhood. I barely had time to brush my hair and change out of my sweats before Buddy started his happy bark. Like most dogs, he knew the sound of familiar car engines—and Luke was his favorite visitor.

———

Usually Luke and I felt comfortable together, but tonight we might as well have been strangers on a bus. The air prickled with tension. Even Buddy's tail wagged in a tentative rhythm.

"I can't stay long," he said, setting the tone of the visit.

"No problem," I answered, gamely keeping up pretenses.

The casual tone hit a snag as soon as he saw the dry-erase board festooned with victims and suspects.

He moved past me, shoulder briefly brushing mine, his dark hair tousled from being temporarily trapped in his hood.

"I see that Frank Martindale's entire family is on your suspect list. Who are they, exactly?" Luke picked up a blue marker and tried it on the board.

His challenging tone wasn't lost on me. "The courts haven't yet identified an heir that I'm aware of. But it's always wise to follow the money."

"Frank didn't have much money. All that's left is his house and a few lawsuits. His estate will most likely go to probate unless a will is found."

"Right." I wasn't about to argue with a law student. "That's just a reminder for me so it doesn't fall through the cracks."

"Plenty of those around." His fingers touched Raeleen's name. "I recognize the boyfriend, Devin, but who is Greta?"

Tired of speaking mostly to his back, I moved closer. "That's the new girlfriend wannabe. Strangely enough, she worked as our intern for the last three weeks, which ties her into the YouTube video. Jealousy might be her motive for murder."

"Are you thinking that Greta wants the fiancé for herself, so she murders Raeleen and throws in a couple of extra bodies for the heck of it? You can do better than that, Kate."

This time his voice had that lilting, teasing quality I knew so well.

"What about Eloise?" he continued.

"Listen, this is a work in progress," I told him. "I'm trying to prove none of these deaths had anything to do with what everyone sees on that YouTube video. Did your pals at the police department tell you anything?"

"Not a lot," he admitted. "After the coroner admitted Eloise might have been pushed, they started looking at Frank's death, too. But so far no one can prove anything. Raeleen is a different ballgame. They've got plenty of physical evidence of a fight, but so far no match on the DNA. If it is the same perpetrator that attacked Jeremy, he covered his or her hair with a hat and wore gloves."

"So why focus on Pinky?"

Luke turned toward me, a frown on his face. "Because he was at each crime scene at the crucial time and he plowed the supermarket parking lot, too. He's lucky that lawyer stepped in to protect him from himself."

"Poor Pinky." On opposite sides of the board we faced each other. "Are you here to tell me to stop?"

We stood our ground, both stubborn as usual.

"Actually," he answered, "I'm here to help."

And just like that, the painful heart-to-heart talk I both wanted and dreaded was deleted from our to-do list, replaced with a whodunit list.

"You've got a good start here," Luke said, picking up the marker. "I can fill in some other details, but the biggest question marks are these." He wrote MOTIVE and SANTA.

Immediately, I said, "You can't call the killer Santa."

"Only joking with you." His smile got to me like it always did.

As I watched him write down where the deaths took place, I had to ask, "Why are you doing this?"

"First of all, this is temporary help. I'm going back to school the week after New Year's. Second, I figure you're going to nose around anyway, which will make me worry—so maybe we should pool our energy."

"It's been a while since we've pooled our energy," I said with a grin.

His ears were the first part to turn red. "I am very— very aware of that."

Luke moved closer, but I slipped under his arm. It wouldn't be that easy to make up with me.

"Are we starting with the premise that these are three murders?" I picked up a green marker and held it ready for battle.

With a blue marker still in his hand he said, "That's a very good question, and I'm not sure of the answer. There's always the possibility that Eloise's or Frank's passing were accidents." With that he began a new heading called QUESTIONS. The first one read *Accident or Murder?* The second question mentioned Kate's wish with a question mark.

"Are you implying that the killer took advantage of my wish to outsmart the police?" Although it originally seemed far-fetched, I'd started to consider it more and more.

"The wish acted like a smoke screen, I would say. But why?" Luke stared at the board then wrote *Love or Hate?* next to my name.

"No idea." I didn't want to be an integral part of this mess.

He turned toward me. "Does the killer love you, killing those who upset you—or does he hate you and is trying to frame you for murder? Or is it both? Or neither?"

A chilling thought either way. "Luke, can we please look at the facts? Only one person of the three was definitely murdered, without a doubt."

"Executed, actually," Luke pointed out.

We both raced to the same conclusion.

It was all about Raeleen.

Chapter Twenty-Nine

THE FOLLOWING DAY ICY SLEET TURNED THE ROADS into skating rinks. Luke and I had agreed to disagree before he left for home. Cindy was kept busy with a number of canceled appointments. I sat in the employee lounge munching on a brownie while reading a veterinary journal with my feet up. Our generous clients had been dropping off homemade goodies for us all week. My larger scrub pants were feeling a bit tight.

Mari strolled in carrying a spray bottle of cleaner, looking for something to do.

"Well, I've cleaned all the exam rooms and pissed Cindy off by spraying the reception room chairs while she was working. A very productive morning." She plopped down and placed the cleaning stuff on the closest counter. "What are you eating? The brownies?"

"A clever diagnosis. Let me get rid of the evidence." I held the remnant up before finishing it off.

"Didn't work," she said, looking at my jacket. "Don't eat chocolate when you're wearing white."

One quick glance confirmed the observation. It doesn't seem to matter how careful I was, I usually dropped food on my clothes.

"Can I get you anything?" I asked my assistant. All I needed was another half cup of coffee to make the universe right.

"A brownie, and one of those squiggly things in that

Christmas box, please. You know we're eating much too much sugar, don't you?"

Putting everything she asked for on a paper plate, I added a few jellybeans for color and more sugar. Mari was a sucker for jellybeans.

"This is so strange," I commented, "the two of us sitting around doing nothing."

Almost immediately Cindy interrupted, holding the hospital portable phone in her hand. "Want to go pick up some donations?" she asked. "A couple of dog beds, some puppy enclosures, a few dog bowls. It's at Eloise Rieven's old place. Her son, Joe, is cleaning out the house."

I sat up, suddenly interested. "Sure." Many of our clients gave us used pet items, which we washed and kept for emergency situations or donated to local rescue groups. It felt good to be able to offer a nice dog or cat bed to a needy pet.

But I had another motive for wanting to visit Eloise's house.

"The weather is pretty bad," Mari said. "Why don't we take my truck?"

I readily agreed. Mari's monster four-wheel-drive with big snow tires and a full set of chains made me feel safer on our slippery roads.

"Guys," Cindy added, "if it keeps up like this we're going to close early. Text me when you're leaving the Rieven place, in case someone books a last-minute appointment?"

"Will do," I told our commander in chief.

Mari drove, an unusual situation for us. I'd thrown my emergency backpack on the second row seat, as well as our medical supplies, just in case. The roads, slick with layers of thin ice, were as bad as described. Busy work crews sanded the main thoroughfares. Eloise Rieven's farmhouse wasn't too far from the animal hospital, but it took us twenty-five minutes going at least ten miles below the speed limit. Sited relatively close to the road, like many older homes, it nestled in a cleared area, with an orchard and gardens in the back of the house.

By the time we turned into the driveway, most of the main road had morphed to dirty slush. The uneven driveway, however, sported some icy patches despite being sanded and plowed.

"If this freezes tonight, I don't want to be anywhere near it," Mari said.

"Second you on that."

We both held on and slid out of the truck, our boots hitting slush and gravel. There were two other cars parked near the stairs. Last time when we picked up her bulldog, we'd used the back stairs. I was curious what the front entrance looked like. Someone had cleared a walking path on the bluestone sidewalk. As soon as we reached the front door, we both got as much ice off our boots as we could. A worn welcome mat didn't help much.

I heard some movement inside before I rang the doorbell.

When the door opened, a woman in overalls and a

coat stared me in the face. She obviously didn't recognize either of us.

Mari spoke up first. "We're from Oak Falls Animal Hospital. Joe Rieven told our receptionist you had some animal items to donate?"

She smiled immediately. "Karen." A firm handshake ushered us both inside. "I'm with Clutterbusters. Thanks for coming on such a horrible day. Everything's in here."

We immediately noticed there was no fire in the wood stove. The radiators in the main room banged a little when the furnace kicked in, but it didn't feel much warmer inside the house than outside.

A woman dressed in business casual with a tape measure, helped by a younger man in a suit and tie, measured the front room.

"Real estate agents," Karen said while walking down the hallway. "Can't sell the house full of stuff. We've been hired to get the place cleaned up, but the weather isn't helping any."

After nodding at the agents who paid no attention to us, we walked down that same dark, narrow hallway crowded with artwork I'd seen before. A quick turn put us into a charming but outdated kitchen.

"I forgot how her kitchen looked. Talk about vintage," Mari said.

Glad to have Mari be the social one, I stared at an avocado-green refrigerator, a matching electric stove with coil burners, and a brand-new stainless-steel countertop microwave. The countertop itself was made of one of those plastic materials best forgotten—with a prominent burn mark from a pan right in the middle.

At the kitchen table a middle-aged woman with a kind but tired face packed an assorted pile of stacked dishes and platters. On the floor around her stood several taped-up boxes marked Goodwill.

"Find anything else?" asked a man with his back to us who seemed in charge.

"Nope. We already packed her good china and silverware for you to keep. This is the everyday stuff. No hidden treasures. Most of it is from the dollar stores." She made a mark in a red notebook before wrapping each plate in newspaper.

When he turned toward us, I realized it was Joe Rieven.

Karen interrupted them. "Here are the people from the animal hospital. Where is the dog stuff?"

"On the covered porch," Joe answered, bending down to try and open a cabinet door that didn't want to open.

"Follow me," Karen said, walking at a quick pace. "Did you bring any bags or anything?"

Mari and I looked at each other.

"There's a bunch of plastic garbage bags out there," the woman who was wrapping plates said. "Let me know if you need more."

In single file we moved through a large attached pantry area to another door that led to the back porch.

"They used to call these summer sleeping porches," Karen mentioned, looking for the light switch.

Maybe thirty boxes stood piled in one corner, all neatly labeled. Some dining room chairs stacked against each other took up the other corner. Pale light filtered in through dirty glass panels. Here and there clusters of spider webs attested to no recent use.

Mari put her hand to her mouth. "Last time I was here she'd just put those glass panels up for the winter. In springtime when the weather turned warm, Eloise would put in the screen ones. One year she hired my cousin to do it for her. This porch is where all the houseplants were kept and where she started the vegetables for the garden. I hate seeing it like this."

"All the plants got thrown out the first day," Karen said. "Anyway, here's the animal stuff." She pointed to a pile of dog beds and collapsible crates. "Take whatever you want. I'll be in the kitchen."

When she left Mari glanced out into the backyard and said, "It used to be beautiful out here with all the flowers blooming and her wicker furniture."

"Well, let's get going and pack these things up."

Joe Rieven popped his head in. "Need any help?" He caught my eye then frowned in recognition. "Dr. Kate? Is that you?"

Bundled up with a fake fur cap jammed on my head, I was surprised he'd noticed. "Yes. Hi there." I thought about shaking his hand but felt too awkward. "Thank you so much for donating to us."

"No problem. Mom always bought the best for her dogs. Of course, once she got down to just Queenie, she didn't need most of this, but she never got rid of anything."

I saw what he meant. There must have been ten good-quality dog beds, barely used, in the pile of stuff.

"We put the leashes and collars and small things in a separate bag. Can you use the dog crates?"

"Absolutely," Mari said, already packing loose items in a plastic garbage bag. "Don't worry. Nothing will go to waste. We regularly bring things down to the shelter, too."

"Good," he commented. "That's what I hoped for."

Since he was here, I decided to take a chance. "Do you know a Babs Vanderbilt-Hayes?"

His mild round face tensed up. "Why do you ask?"

"She came by our office and she was...distressed by your mother's death. Cindy told me she mentioned it to you?"

Joe took a moment to compose his answer. "Babs was an old and very dear friend of my mother. They often met for lunch in Kingston or Rhinebeck."

I nodded and waited to see if he'd volunteer anything more.

"For some reason Babs has gotten it into her head that mom's death is suspicious. She asked for a copy of the medical records. I didn't see any problem at the time with giving them to her." He rubbed his eyes. "Now it's led to an ugly disagreement between pathologists. Mother would have hated having her death become fodder for the public."

"So stressful," Mari agreed, checking for more small items before we tackled the dog beds.

"Yes, it is." He appeared overwhelmed. "You know, I took Mom to church on Sunday and lunch afterward just about every week. She always met me in the front parlor, wouldn't let me in the rest of the house. Said it needed cleaning. I had no idea everything had gone downhill." Joe rubbed his eyes again. "Mom was very proud. Wouldn't take any help. Said she was perfectly capable of living her own life and making her own decisions."

That sounded like the Eloise I knew.

———

We began to ferry the bulky items out to the SUV through that narrow hallway. Trying to maneuver the largest pet bed past everything, I knocked two low-hanging pictures off the wall.

"Shoot." Nothing appeared damaged when I picked them up. I didn't know much about art, but I did realize these oil paintings were incredibly dirty, probably from years of woodstove smoke and general grime. One showed a large-headed woman, hands folded in her lap at an odd angle, staring balefully at the viewer. The other captured a typical Hudson Valley vista along the river, but the film of grease gave it a yellowish muddied look.

"You're holding Great-aunt Harriet," Eloise's son said as he and Mari came toward me, arms full of dog stuff.

I almost dropped the painting.

"Joe here has been reminding me about all the champion bulldogs his mom owned." Mari, an aficionado of dog shows and agility trials, loved to talk dog.

"Let me show you her trophy wall," he said, carefully inching past me.

We all trooped over to a study off the main parlor crammed with old black-and-white pictures of a younger, happier Eloise. Several captured various events at the Westminster Dog Show, the Academy Awards of the dog world.

I suddenly realized I still held Great-aunt Harriet and the dirty landscape in my hands, having abandoned the dog bed in the hall.

"When are you selling the house?" Mari asked him.

"I'm not sure. I asked the local real estate agency to give me an idea of its value. They aren't very optimistic. It needs a lot of work. We found out today that the heat isn't working that well. Part of the house never got hooked up. I had to get a plumber to come in and drain the pipes so they wouldn't freeze."

That wasn't a big surprise. Without gloves on, my hands were cold. "Too bad it's the wrong season for a yard sale."

Joe continued to stare at the photos.

We waited, not wanting to intrude on his memories. After a moment he sighed and turned toward us.

"Already had an auction house come in to appraise the good stuff. I kept most of the personal items, but the rest is being donated or sold. The real estate people recommended Clutterbusters to come in and help." Joe picked up a paperweight and shook it. Snow swirled around in the glass globe. "I'm keeping all her trophies."

"Winning them meant a lot to her," Mari agreed.

We continued out toward the front door, past the real estate agents, when Joe asked me, "Sorry. Did you want to buy those? Great-aunt Harriet isn't for sale, but I can give you that landscape for twenty bucks."

Embarrassed to be standing there with my fingers clutching a family picture, I shrugged my shoulders and said, "Sure."

Joe and Mari headed out to her truck while I hung Great-aunt Harriet's portrait back up. She stared at me, annoyance forever frozen on her face.

―――――――

"Boy that thing is dirty," Mari said, taking a quick look at the painting I put in the back seat. Cushioned between two old dog beds, it looked right at home. "Hey, maybe it's painted by some famous artist and is worth a million dollars."

"Doubtful. Remember, an auction house already checked the entire contents. I imagine those guys look very carefully at paintings."

A more pressing problem was the driveway. Only the width of one car, it didn't leave us with much room.

"Thank goodness Joe didn't mention that video," I said as I buckled up. "That was very nice of him considering I wished his mom would disappear." Out of habit I pulled up YouTube and checked the number of views. "Do you believe we have more than thirty-two thousand views?"

Mari backed out of the driveway then performed a skillful U-turn at the base. "Sorry, Kate. That video is going to haunt us forever. And so will my litter box cake."

―――――――

By the time we got back and unloaded all the donations, the temperature had started dropping. With the phones silent, Cindy decided to close early—great news for all of us. I had a ton of laundry to do and more cleaning than usual, thanks to Jeremy. I'd told him not to do any house-work because of his wrist and shoulder injuries, and he'd done just that. Nothing.

Not sure where to store my new painting, I decided to hang it on the wall. I'd deal with restoring it later. Seen in the light, it had a certain rustic charm. Maybe I would ask Lark, my artist client, for a cleaning recommendation.

Buddy happily followed me around until he realized I wasn't going to give him any extra food. His brown eyes took on a look not unlike Great-aunt Harriet's. Chagrined, I handed him a bone from the pantry, and he retired in ecstasy.

A glance at the dry-erase board reminded me of an abstract painting, a series of brightly colored arrows and names that led the eye to nowhere.

———

With the final load in the dryer, I rewarded myself. Glass of wine in hand, I curled up on the sofa and turned on HGTV. Predictable as my habits might be, they were very comforting. Buddy's head rested on my foot for extra warmth.

A rumbling noise became louder as headlights swept across the window. From the scraping noise, I suspected Pinky had started working on the parking lot. All my lights were out except for the glow of the television. I didn't pay much attention until I realized the noise had stopped but the headlights still glowed.

Pinky remained parked outside my front door.

———————

I held my breath, even though he obviously couldn't hear me. The semicircular glass panel at the top of my front door let in a beam of light. I secretly thanked Jeremy, who had hung new blackout curtains on the big window facing the neighbor's house for privacy, after I'd noticed Pinky watching us when he walked Princess.

My phone lay on the coffee table a foot away. By the time I reached it, the lights had swept past and he had driven away.

Chapter Thirty

"DON'T ALL SINGLE GIRLS SPEND SATURDAY NIGHTS trying to solve murders?" That joke barely rated a smile as Luke and I sat at my kitchen table eating Chinese takeout.

"You and your family know all the gossip going on in town and at the station," I said between bites of mu shu shrimp. "Haven't you unearthed something?"

"Not yet." He munched an egg roll. "I'm still mining my cousins for dirt."

"All thirty-seven million of them?" Come to think of it, Luke and I had most of our conversations over take-out. In a sneak attack, I stole the last remaining pancake, dipped it in hoisin sauce, and bade goodbye to the last of the mu shu.

"You know," he told me, hunting for the duck sauce, "that's one of the things my cousin Rosie likes most about you, your prodigious appetite."

"Thank you," I said with a bow.

Returning the bow, he said, "Hey, a good appetite means everything in a restaurant family. You'll be happy to know that your pie habit also has my grandmother's stamp of approval."

His dumb comment made me inordinately happy.

An hour later we sat frustrated in front of the whiteboard, our brains temporarily tapped out.

"Alright," I said to him, "let's start with the basics."

"More from your fictional murder mystery plots?"

"Based on real life," the sleuth inside me countered. "Except for the surprise ending where an evil twin shows up and confesses."

"Let's agree to rule that one out." Luke chewed on the end of his marker, staring at the ceiling. "Basics. What do you mean by that?"

The furnace kicked in with a low hum, pushing a blast of warm air into the room. Outside the temperature continued to fall with no snow forecast until tomorrow night.

The warm air and background humming made me want to close my eyes, but I fought the urge. With Pinky and Devin both persons of interest and Christmas around the corner, I needed to stop wondering if one or more of my clients were killers.

"Love or money," I blurted out. "Those are the two most common reasons to kill someone, right?"

Luke continued to look up at the ceiling. "Statistically, I believe you're right. That's lumping jealousy, possessiveness, and control freak in under love. It's a warped individual who kills what they love."

"I agree."

Luke jumped up and wrote *Woman or Man?* next to *Killer.* "I agree with you. No particular strength was necessary in any of these deaths. I also think the killer brought the gun with him or her during every assault, just in case it started to go wrong. Something went very wrong with Raeleen."

"Agreed."

"Why would Raeleen walk into a stand of trees behind the dumpster?" He tapped his hand on the chair in frustration.

A lightning bolt hit. Why would anyone walk behind a dumpster? Well, an animal lover would if they heard a cat crying.

"I've got it. The murderer pretended to be a kitten."

His high five caught me off guard. It felt good. "Of course. She walked into the trees to investigate meowing."

"She told her friend about a plan to rescue some feral kittens living by that dumpster."

"Now we're getting someplace."

———————

I got up to pace around the room and sneak a spoonful of ice cream. Buddy followed me around, but I didn't fall for it. Luke had already stuffed him with orange chicken under the kitchen table. Since he had some arthritis from an old injury, I tried to keep his weight stable, but if my pet had his way, he'd be blimp-shaped.

Luke stood at the board with a fistful of markers, making notes. "It's a toss-up who had more people annoyed at them, but Raeleen's confrontations are the ones that became physical. Quite a few reported shoving and screaming, and one complainant is sure that Raeleen keyed his vehicle."

"What?" With sticky hands I headed for the sink.

"She took her car key and scratched the side of some-one's truck. They filed a report about it over a year ago, while I still was on the force."

I had no doubt the impulsive Raeleen was capable of all kinds of mischief.

"It was mostly nuisance stuff, as I recall. Threatening to take their pet…"

"Like she did with Pinky."

"Right." He walked over and sat opposite me. "Accusing people without knowing the facts. One person complained Raeleen screamed at him and his wife for starving their dog—when the dog had cancer and was undergoing chemotherapy."

Those dog owners were probably horrified and resentful. But murderers? I didn't think so. "All these scenarios are interesting, but they don't add up to much, certainly not any suspects as strong as Pinky."

Luke went over the evidence. "Pinky had access to all the crime scenes and can be put in the vicinity of each one. You told me the guy said he'd kill anybody who hurt you—and he had a very public fight with Raeleen over the only thing he loves better than his truck. Princess." Absentmindedly, he arranged the markers in a box shape on the coffee table. "If I were the lead detective on the case, that would be enough for me."

"But Luke," I said, "I know he didn't do it."

This time he stopped fiddling around and stared straight at me. "I have my doubts, too, believe me. But I'm not that sure he's completely innocent."

"Well, I am." There was more bravura than truth to my statement. Did Luke realize that? On the day Pinky cried and told me he killed Raeleen I had tried to comfort him, but afterward, when he talked more calmly about the deceased animal rights activist, his eyes were cold.

Cold enough to murder someone?

We sat staring at the board a few minutes until I suggested, "Why don't we go and ask him?"

The simplicity of the idea was a hit with Luke. Was he afraid of Pinky? Not really. Did he expect a confession? No. What we did expect were some answers to our questions. Since we knew Pinky had been at all the victims' homes or workplace, maybe he saw something?

"Kate, you ask the questions. I'll try and check out his guns."

We took Luke's truck and drove next door. I alerted Cindy in case we ran into trouble. She thought it was a stupid idea but promised to call us in ten minutes.

"Remember, Pinky was brought up by a much older mom, and one of the things she stressed was good manners. You can remind him about manners if he gets out of hand. Call me if you need to."

"Will do."

"Kate, promise me you and Luke will be gentle with him. He's much more fragile than he looks."

Chapter Thirty-One

LUKE'S TRUCK MADE ITS WAY SLOWLY DOWN THE meticulously plowed driveway. I'd texted Pinky to tell him we were stopping by. We'd seen his truck pull into the garage about ten minutes ago, so he couldn't pretend not to be home.

So far no one had returned our text.

The huge modern garage built next to the old farmhouse looked out of place. It stored Pinky's equipment and vehicles—riding mowers and gardening tools for his summer jobs and plows, snowblowers, and a slew of other things for his winter jobs.

"He's got at least two trucks that I know of," Luke told me as we walked along the bluestone pathway to the front stairs. "I saw them multiple times in the parking lot of the diner. He and his mom used to eat there twice a week or so. Now Pinky only does takeout." He gestured to the large flower beds sleeping under the snow. "All the formal landscaping here in front was designed by his mother. She was a well-known amateur gardener who always competed at the county fair in Rhinebeck. Pinky learned a lot from her."

Let's hope he didn't learn to shoot first and ask questions later.

The first thing I noticed when Pinky let us in was the smell—the smell of roses. I once knew a girl in high school who used some kind of rose petal perfume that permeated everything she wore. At first pleasant, it became more cloying the longer you were in contact with it.

"Pinky," I said as we followed him along an open corridor, "I smell roses. Do you grow them inside?"

My answer came when we burst into a small room covered with delicate rose-patterned wallpaper. The Queen herself would have approved. On the mantel stood two glass vases with oil infusion sticks in them.

"Mommy liked the smell of roses, especially in the parlor." He gestured for us to sit in the upholstered armchairs opposite the sofa. Each piece of furniture was encased in plastic. An underlying aroma of furniture polish competed with the floral odor. The room was spotless.

"Ah, we came because Dr. Kate here is worried about the recent deaths in town." Luke gently laid out a stage for questioning that Pinky couldn't object to. "Do you know anything about them you might tell us?"

He didn't appear to be listening to Luke but instead began searching the room.

"She's over here, next to my chair," I said. Princess had risen from her fluffy bed to rest under a side table against my leg.

Obviously relieved, he relaxed his shoulders. "I wondered where she'd gotten to." His face beamed at the sight of the old dog. I scratched her graying muzzle.

Luke knew better than to try and hurry Pinky along. "How old is she now?"

"She just turned thirteen. And she's doing really well with her congestion thanks to Dr. Kate." At the sound of his voice Princess cast me aside and walked over to her owner. He scooped her up in his arms and set her down on his lap.

Leaning forward, Luke continued, "That's why we're here. Dr. Kate wants to know if you can tell us anything about Eloise's or Frank's death? We know the police interviewed you, since you plowed both of their driveways."

The word plowing caught Pinky's attention. "Still do until everything is sorted out. You know," he glanced over at me this time, "Mommy's lawyer said I'm not allowed to talk about murder. But I can talk about plowing, I guess."

"Right. Until the estate has been settled you have to plow. People need to be able to get up the driveway." That made me realize how much access to so many properties Pinky had. Few residents question the guy with the snowplow, especially if he's plowing in the middle of the night.

If Pinky didn't do it, he might have seen who did.

Tucking my hair behind my ear, I carefully crafted a question for him. "Did you see anyone else at Eloise's or Frank's place the night they passed away? Maybe someone you didn't know or were surprised about?" Knowing his angry feelings for Raeleen, I bypassed her murder for now.

Pinky's light blue eyes remained blank.

"Maybe a car or truck on the road that you didn't

expect?" Luke threw out a wide net of possibilities, but Pinky looked confused.

"Ahh, I'm not sure. Please don't be mad at me," the big guy pleaded.

Pinky probably felt like we were ganging up on him. It was important that he not be bullied, especially by me. "Luke and I aren't mad at you, Pinky," I explained. "This is like a puzzle that we're trying to put together. Someone may have harmed Frank or Eloise and if they did, they must be punished."

He nodded emphatically. "Bad deeds should not go unpunished."

"Did your mom tell you that?" Luke quickly glanced over at me, as if signaling something.

"Yes, she did," he answered. In a singsong voice, he continued, "An eye for an eye, and let the Devil have his day."

Things were getting mixed up.

Spurred by memory, Pinky continued. "A bird in the hand is worth two in the bush, especially if it's your neighbor's bush. That was one of her favorites." His head bobbed up and down as Princess slept quietly in his lap. "Mommy believed in angels, too. She was always seeing them, sometimes in the supermarket or gas station. One time at Kmart."

"What about the night you found Mrs. Rieven, Pinky?"

"Miss Eloise was on the ground in the dark. I saw her with my headlights. She looked like she was asleep, but I knew she wasn't because I got out and asked her."

He looked straight at Luke like a schoolboy reciting his lesson.

"Was anyone else around?"

Pinky shook his head no.

"Can you tell us about Frank Martindale now?"

This time Pinky appeared uncomfortable and wiggled in his seat. Princess lifted her head then set it down again on his lap. "Mr. Frank was mean. He didn't want to pay me. I told him I was going to tell Cindy and she would have a talk with him." After the last sentence he visibly relaxed.

Before either of us could ask another question, he surprised us.

"That's why I know you have a guardian angel watching over you, Dr. Kate." Pinky lowered his voice to a whisper. "Because I saw him."

———————

After sifting through some talk about smiting evil, we finally separated out a few facts. Pinky had seen something white moving out of the corner of his eye the night Frank Martindale died. He swore it had wings. That's why he wasn't surprised the next morning to find Frank had passed.

Unfortunately, that's about all we got out of Pinky. That and the lingering smell of roses.

"I didn't realize angels watched YouTube videos," Luke commented while we crept along the driveway.

"Maybe they're looking for angel food cake recipes," I joked.

"So if someone drove up to Frank's place, I wonder where they stashed the car?"

Not being familiar with the area, I didn't have any suggestions.

"Both Eloise's and Frank's properties border on National Forest land," he noted, "like most of the older homesteads around here. The farmers cleared right up to the tree line. They'd hunt game in the woods and build their homes on the flatter land, closer to the road for convenience."

That answered a question I'd had about why so many of my house-call clients had land that backed up to the mountains.

"Plenty of logging roads, hunting trails, and small cabins in those woods," he added. "Quite a few share access lanes."

At the top of Pinky's property Luke abruptly turned the wheel to the right. We slid a bit before coming to a stop. "Want to go look at Frank's place?" he asked.

"Sure. Safety in numbers." My Gramps would approve.

Of course we'd be trespassing a little, but what the heck. As an Oak Falls police officer currently on leave, Luke was the perfect accomplice.

———

"Uh, oh."

Lights shone brightly at Frank Martindale's home, an unwelcome surprise. We parked next to a Mercedes SUV pulled up close to the stairs. If someone was burglarizing the place, they had good taste in vehicles.

"Wait here," Luke said.

"No way," I answered and opened the passenger side door.

We both hurried up the stairs to the front door. I noticed several boards that appeared loose and a rung missing along the railing. All the coming and going were taking a toll on this porch. His typical stone house needed some emergency TLC.

"It used to be nice when Frank's brother, Chuck, lived here," Luke said, ringing the bell. The sound of a television could be heard inside.

Chuck? Who the heck was Chuck?

Someone opened the door and peered out with the chain still engaged. All I could see was half a man's face wearing glasses.

"Sorry to disturb you but…"

"Aren't you Officer Luke Gianetti? Just a second." The door opened to reveal a slim middle-aged man in a suit and glasses. Not typical burglar couture.

"Sorry but I don't recognize you."

"Come inside," he told us, "and shut the door firmly. It sticks." We followed him into a living room crowded with old pieces of furniture haphazardly stored between towers of cardboard boxes. The wooden desk I remembered lay on its side. Someone had scrawled Comic Books on one box with a Sharpie, on another Dolls.

The recliner I'd discovered the body in had been removed. I didn't see the huge television either.

"Frank appeared to have been quite a collector," Luke commented.

"Quite a hoarder was old Frank. I'm the deceased's lawyer, Salvatore Tregari, by the way. One of his many lawyers."

"This is Kate." Luke deliberately offered no more information about me. "Sal Tregari. Yes, I recognize you now," he said. "There was a shoplifting case I testified for. Nice lady with a bad habit."

"That's right." He cleared a space for all of us to sit down. For some reason our showing up out of the blue didn't bother him at all. "What can I do for you?"

"Sorry. We were driving by and saw the lights, and I wondered who was here."

"Got it." Salvatore gestured with his hands at the mess around them. "You probably thought I'd be family. Except no family has come forward. I was arguing a case for Frank the morning of his death so the judge appointed me administrator. I'm hoping we can find a will somewhere."

The lawyer didn't slow down for comments from us. His voice sped up as he continued, "When Frank had hernia surgery, he told the nurse he had a will, and she put it in his notes along with the DNR he signed. We found those hospital papers on his desk but no will. Turned the desk upside down looking for hidden drawers but nothing. What the heck did he do with it? So far there might be a second cousin in California, but we're waiting for birth certificates. Time marches on, so I figured I'd look around again for evidence of a will or a relative. As you can see, that's going to be harder than anyone thought."

Taking advantage of a break in his monologue, Luke

said, "I wish I could help you. Chuck and Frank were the only two siblings. Both parents died quite a while ago, and Chuck died almost seven years ago. Frank moved back into the house when Chuck passed, and I don't think I've been here since."

"Ever hear Frank talk about striking it rich?"

"No."

"What about visiting cousins or other relatives? Maybe from the city or out of state?"

Luke shook his head. "No one comes to mind. I'll ask my grandmother. If she remembers anything, I'll call your office. Do you have a card?"

The lawyer slid a hand into his suit jacket and came out with a silver-plated cardholder. He then handed his business card to Luke. "You can leave a message anytime. If no will is found, the court will appoint an executor and the estate goes into probate." He glanced around the room. "These cases are trying on everyone involved because you don't want assets to go into probate if they rightfully belong to an heir. Everyone blames the lawyer."

"That would be a shame," I agreed.

Salvatore ran his hand through his thinning hair. "Hopefully, we can avoid that. Listen, if you don't mind, I was just leaving. I hoped I might find a wall safe or a floor safe or something like that. Believe me, I didn't expect it would take so much time."

"Me, either," I muttered under my breath. Frank had hoarded all sorts of things and a lot of them. The house served as more of a warehouse than a home. I wondered if he sold items on eBay or supplied antiques for the auctions so popular in the summer. Maybe he bought storage units hoping to strike it rich, as his lawyer suggested? Once in a while those storage people found a rare item, but most people didn't.

What if Frank had found something that got him killed?

———

Salvatore waited until we left to lock up the house. He still hadn't moved by the time we were out of sight.

"Did you get a look out back?" I asked. "Maybe there's a white flag in the garden or a piece of cloth stuck in a tree that Pinky might have thought was an angel."

"Not a bad idea. We'll have to stop back during the day," Luke said. "As for Frank finding something valuable on one of his buying trips, that's doubtful," he said, waiting for a large truck to pass. "Look at the place."

He had a point. I'd snuck a quick peek into some of the other rooms as the two men had been talking. Each space had been packed almost to the ceiling with boxes of stuff, all labeled in Sharpie with Frank's signature scrawling handwriting. Some of the boxes looked new, while others resembled the kind you get from a supermarket dumpster.

"Frank may have been my veterinary client," I said to Luke, "but I didn't know him that well. Would he brag if he'd struck pay dirt?"

Luke's puzzled glance told me he had no idea. "Remember I was friends with his brother more than him. All I remember is Frank always said the government and big business were out to get him. If he struck it rich, I'm not sure if he would gloat about it or stay silent. Wouldn't want to pay taxes on it, though."

"Why all the lawsuits?" The passing landscape suggested Luke was headed back to the animal hospital. For a moment I thought he might suggest someplace else.

"He was obsessed with people cheating him." We slowed down near Payson's Pond before taking a left toward town. Once past the intersection he continued the thought. "It's ironic because he was known as, how can I put this, being someone who dealt cards from the bottom of the deck."

Poor Frank. His life had become a tight little ball of anger toward everyone. Now strangers would catalog his stuff, go through his clothes and tools, and all traces of him would slowly disappear. Had he been murdered or simply overdosed on alcohol and pills? Were his medications deliberately scattered out of reach as he sat helplessly in his armchair, or did they accidentally drop when he passed out? I doubted we'd ever know. In fact, all these unfortunate incidents felt random—except for Raeleen.

I kept coming back to her. Had she been the target all along?

Chapter Thirty-Two

BACK AT MY PLACE, LUKE AND I SAT ON THE SOFA together, the picture of domestic tranquility except for the massive argument that was taking place.

"You didn't think it was important?"

He backed off a little. "Look, it wasn't that important to me. I'm so busy it didn't matter."

We weren't discussing murder, although at the moment, I wanted to murder him.

"Your ex-girlfriend, Dina, your high school sweetheart, is staying at your cabin, and it wasn't that important?"

"Hey, Jeremy was staying here, and you forgot to mention that to me."

"Jeremy had a concussion." Even I realized how ludicrous that sounded, but I said it anyway.

"Well, I had a brain fart, so we're even."

It's hard to continue arguing when you're laughing like fools.

He reached over and took my hand. "I've been renting the cabin out as an Airbnb on weekends when I'm away at school and told Dina she could stay until the next renter comes in, on Christmas Eve. Then she's going to live with her mom until she moves into her new place in Kingston on January first. I'm bunking at my grandmother's place. The whole family knows, and now so do you."

Buddy came over and whined for some attention, breaking the mood.

Luke pet him and scratched his belly. "Dina just started dating some local guy. If you're that concerned, ask my cousin, Rosie, who doesn't like Dina, by the way."

"So the two of you aren't..."

"Just friends. What about you and Jeremy?" His warm hand in mine felt comforting on this cold night.

"Friends without benefits. His Italian anthropologist sweetie went back to her husband, his girlfriend and, I think, her other boyfriend. It's all very sophisticated, very European."

"Like gelato."

My face scrunched up at the thought. "Gelato?"

"It was either that or lasagna." He raised both hands in the air as if seeking divine help.

"I'd go with the gelato."

———————

For the first time in a long time we talked to each other instead of at each other. I confided my fears about meeting my father and new family, while he revealed that he often had second thoughts about law school and where his future was headed.

Then we cozied up together and didn't talk at all.

———————

A bit of romance must have put him in the mood for murder. After getting some relationship details straightened out, Luke took a detour by going back to Raeleen's death.

My eyes were drooping but he was revving up. To prove it he grabbed a marker and paced back and forth. "The feeling at the station is that Raeleen's murder was personal. They're looking at the boyfriend, Devin, and Pinky. So far neither one has a good alibi for the entire time in question."

"What do you mean, 'entire time'?"

He started to write on the murder board. "The supermarket closes at eleven and the staff left by eleven thirty. There were only three employees working in the store. Raeleen was the last one out. The stock boy said he saw her in his rearview mirror as he left, looking at her phone and pointing the clicker at her car door. The supermarket camera video confirms that. But instead of getting into the car she stops and looks up at something or hears something in the direction of the dumpster. Then she leaves the car and walks into the trees. We only have visual, no audio."

Now I thought I understood.

"Then she disappeared."

"Right, so the time in question is somewhere between eleven thirty at night and eleven the following morning. The day shift arrived at five thirty to open the store and didn't think much about her car still being there. They thought it had broken down. I guess it happened once before. Odd, because that boyfriend of hers, Devin, is a mechanic."

"Ex-boyfriend, I believe."

"Anyway, later that morning around eight the supervisor called Rae's cell phone when she missed her shift.

The message went straight to voice mail. Then she called Raeleen's mother, who checked her room. It was the mom who ended up reporting her missing. When the police came by the supermarket after interviewing the mom, they noticed Raeleen's car was unlocked. Normally a missing person doesn't get this much attention in the first twenty-four hours, but Chief Garcia remembered Raeleen Lassitor as the last name in your YouTube video."

I sighed. That video felt like a stone around my neck.

Luke drew a picture of a tree. "After looking at the footage from the parking lot, they started searching the woods. I gather it was a particularly gruesome scene." He made a few more notes on the board under Raeleen's name. "Exact time of death is complicated by exposure to the weather."

Something puzzled me. "Did she leave anything in the car?"

"No."

"Who takes their purse into the woods?" I asked.

"No idea. The ex-boyfriend said he hadn't talked to her for a few days." Luke drew some question marks beside Devin's name. "They'd broken up, he said, this time forever. The detectives are checking his phone records. Good-looking fellow."

"Yes, I know Devin." I also remembered who had stood next to Devin the last time I saw him—our former intern, Greta. From his attitude you'd never guess he'd just lost someone close to him.

As for Greta, she seemed like the cat that caught the canary—and the mouse.

"My money's on the boyfriend." Luke drew a star next to Devin's name.

"It's always the boyfriend, or the husband, or the ex-husband," I added. Then I filled him in on the antics of our former intern. "Greta was at the Christmas party and heard the stupid wish game. Maybe that gave them the idea."

"Are we dealing with a team effort here?"

No idea. We'd brought out some corn chips to help our thought processes. Automatically, my hand scooped a bunch of chips from the bowl. I ate them one by one, carefully thinking. "I thought the FBI was checking into evidence of a hate crime."

Luke tossed a chip in the air and caught it in his mouth. "A well-placed spy says the Bureau has nothing. Nada."

"Is the chief annoyed the Feds are involved in his murder?"

"What do you think?"

Chapter Thirty-Three

BY THE TIME LUKE LEFT THAT EVENING THE DRY-ERASE board had exploded into a complicated mass of arrows and colors, but we had made progress on our personal issues. At the moment work and school pulled us in different directions. That we recognized. What to do about it? Neither of us had a clear answer yet. It's hard to talk in depth about an uncomfortable topic when both parties actively avoid it.

Cleaning up afterward, I decided to call Gramps to weigh in on our Christmas plans. He'd entered an independent living facility, and I worried sometimes about him adjusting to his new life. I needn't have. While I was cleaning, Gramps was partying.

"Hi, sweetheart." The rest of his sentence got lost in the noise.

"What?" The deafening music in the background eliminated all attempts at conversation. Intermixed were bursts of high-pitched laughter.

As he moved to find a quieter space, the music faded. "Is that better?" he asked. "Just a second, I'm going into the hallway."

That made it bearable. "Some party," I said.

"It's about the third pre-Christmas party we've had so far," Gramps told me. "This one's got free draft beer. Two-beer limit."

"Good." The image of inebriated seniors getting their

party on floated by. Hopefully, they weren't drinking and driving their electric scooters into each other. "Don't stay up too late."

"Please. I remember telling you that all the time. Times sure change, don't they?"

I looked around my empty studio apartment. "They sure do, Gramps."

He laughed and confided that he was waiting for his poker game to start. "I'm no dummy. While these guys were feeling no pain, I was drinking the non-alcoholic beer. Guess who's going to win big tonight?"

I'd seen his poker gang in action, and they didn't mess around. One older gentleman whose math skills waned had appointed himself permanent dealer—complete with hat and pulled-up sleeves.

"You're an incorrigible card shark, Gramps. I'm surprised anyone wants to play with you after you beat them the last time." My grandfather had a well-deserved reputation as a skilled poker player, and never missed an opportunity to show it. A kind-hearted guy, though, he only played for low stakes—penny games being the rule.

"Short memories around here," he joked. "That's one good thing about playing with guys who have a touch of dementia. Puts the odds in your favor."

I loved my Gramps. Even after all the deaths and hardships he'd endured, he still maintained a zest for life. That was something I struggled with every day.

"Well, go back to your party. I'll catch up with you later." The noise in the background kicked up a notch as they played "YMCA."

"Alright, sweetie. We'll talk on Sunday. If I think of anything else, I'll text you or shoot you an email."

Very proud of embracing technology, he never missed an opportunity to prove it to me. "Play a couple of rounds of Texas Hold'em for me." Gramps had taught me the popular poker game on one of my holiday breaks from school.

"Love you, kid."

"Back at you, Gramps."

When I hung up, the room became heavy and still.

———

The next morning all our underground theories had to be dragged into the piercing light. Pinky went down to the police station and confessed to the murder of Raeleen Lassitor.

"Have you heard?"

Cindy was the first to call me, followed by Mari and Luke.

Jeremy weighed in a half-hour later.

"How the heck did you hear about this?" I asked him. "Aren't you in Connecticut?"

"There's internet and television in Connecticut, Kate. It's quite civilized up here."

"Very funny."

Jeremy obviously thought so since he was chuckling. "So, what are you going to do about Pinky?"

Still rushing around trying to get ready for work, I didn't answer his question because I had no idea what to say. Or do. "For now, the same Anderson family lawyer is down at the courthouse screaming his head off."

I remembered a distraught Pinky telling me he thought he killed Raeleen when he wished her to disappear outside the gas station. After we talked, he seemed fine, convinced he'd misunderstood the manner of death. But what if he still believed it? And confessed again and again?

———

It turns out that false confessions aren't that unusual, and they're handled in a number of different ways, depending on the circumstances. The chief took Pinky's latest confession with his lawyer present, determined an alibi for a large portion of the time in question, then released him into the family's custody. Although he had no siblings, he had an uncle and cousins willing to help. Because of the lack of evidence, no weapon, and Pinky's clean record, he became one more loose end in Raeleen Lassitor's story.

———

Although Cindy showered Pinky with offers of dinners and movies, the big guy preferred to stay home alone with his Princess. Staying alone had become the most comfortable thing for him. Initiating relationships for someone with social anxiety or shyness often felt like being tortured. But fate intervened in an odd way.

My first client of the day was a woman in her early

thirties, with an older dog suffering from multiple problems, including an enlarged heart.

Mari had taken the history, but the veterinary record stretched back twelve years, since the day Beth Orstead brought a puppy she had named Lady in for her first exam.

Beth had a calmness about her, and her dog reflected that personality. An elderly poodle mix, Lady was fluffy and sweet, her silver muzzle barely showing in her gray coat.

"What brings you here today?" I asked while visually assessing the dog. For her age she looked great.

The owner's hand went to the dog's head and scratched her ear. "She seems to be coughing a little when we go for our walk. I know she has an enlarged heart, so I wanted to have her checked."

A prudent philosophy. "Good idea," I told her. "Any new symptoms in an older dog might be a cause of concern. Has she had an echocardiogram or an ultrasound recently?" I'd scanned her records but hadn't seen one. Sometimes referral records never make it into the chart.

But I didn't have to worry with Beth. She had her own copy of Lady's records and a copy of the cardiologist's report from two years ago. When I complimented her on being so organized, she admitted that as a psychiatric social worker, documenting medical visits was an important part of her job.

Listening with the stethoscope, I heard a mitral valve murmur and slightly raspy lung sounds. "Can Lady stay with us awhile and have some tests run?" I asked. "I'd like to make sure her condition is stable and isn't moving toward congestive heart failure."

Beth nodded, as though she'd expected my reaction.

"You can go home or wait in reception," I suggested. "It shouldn't take more than an hour or so, if that's okay." Mari picked Lady up and had her wave bye-bye with her front paw.

"You know," Beth said, her makeup-free face thoughtful, "I'll wait in reception, if you don't mind. I brought along some paperwork and my knitting." She pointed to a sturdy briefcase. "Being nearby will make me feel more comfortable. She's my baby."

We left exam room two and walked down the hallway toward Cindy and the reception area. To my surprise, Pinky sat in one of the chairs, Princess in his arms.

"Is everything alright with Princess?" I asked.

"She's coughing a little today, Dr. Kate. Cindy told me to speak to you." Pinky's flush started to rise as three women stared at him.

"Mari, can you also bring Princess into the treatment area?" Then something struck me as funny. "Beth, your dog's name is Lady, and Pinky's dog is Princess. Mari, you and I are taking care of royalty."

Both owners took what I said as fact. The only one to crack a smile was Mari before she disappeared with the dogs.

Beth put her heavy briefcase down and pointed to the chair next to Pinky, "May I?" she asked. "I'm Beth." She held her hand out.

"Pinky. I'm pleased to meet you." Although he blushed terribly, he shook Beth's hand.

"I'll be out to talk to each of you as soon as I'm finished," I told them both. "Meanwhile, Cindy, can you give Beth and Pinky the new handout on canine cardiac disease?"

Cindy came around to the front with two pamphlets in her hand. "I've got the heart diet information here, too."

That's when it happened. Beth said, "Lady won't eat that. I've tried so many times."

"Neither will Princess," said Pinky.

Beth turned toward him, a smile on her face. "We shouldn't let them boss us around."

"That's what my mom used to say."

An awkward silence was broken by Beth offering to show Pinky some pictures of Lady on her phone. He reciprocated with his fur baby pictures.

Cindy and I looked at each other. What was going on here?

After watching the two heads sharing photos I said, "Alright. Please make sure both of you go over the information Cindy gave you."

"We will," Beth said. "I'll see to it."

Pinky shifted in his seat and confessed, "Sometimes I don't read these because they scare me."

Beth touched his sleeve. "That's okay. I'll help you."

As Christmas music played away in the background the warm and fuzzy feeling Beth's kindness generated in me lasted until I reached the treatment room door. That's when I remembered my dry-erase board and its doodles of many colors.

Did I just introduce Beth to a murderer?

Murder suspects fell from the skies that day as Devin and Greta showed up with his dog, Muffin, for her recheck. Cindy whispered to me that Devin was still a person of interest as she escorted them both into exam room one.

"I know," I whispered back. After one last look at the remarkable sight of Pinky and Beth chatting in the waiting room while she knitted, I checked my neck for my stethoscope.

As I made my way toward the exam room our entrance door flew open and two figures, neither of whom had an animal with them, strode into the waiting room. Everyone stared at these exotic creatures. I recognized one of them, although she appeared completely transformed. The psychic, Delphina, whom I'd last seen in an apron, was now dramatically made-up. She wore a long black coat over a shimmering silver dress, with several colorful scarves wrapped around her neck. However, it was the younger woman by her side that commanded attention. Long blond hair framed a beautifully sculptured face, the kind you see in magazine ads or old black-and-white movies. Very tall, she had dressed all in black, from her leather boots to her onyx-and-gold necklace.

Mari came up behind me, a lab report in her hand. "Delphina? Is that you?"

"Mari." Delphina acknowledged her greeting but stayed put.

The young woman stepped forward, eyes seeking mine. "May we have a few moments of your time, Dr. Kate?"

I had no idea who this beautiful bird of paradise was or what she wanted. Luckily, Cindy had returned by then and jumped into the fray. Nobody but nobody messes with Cindy's schedule without a good reason.

"I'm sorry, but Dr. Kate is completely booked this afternoon. If you'll follow me, I'll see what I can arrange." Her steely manner dared them to argue with her. "Your next client is ready, Dr. Kate."

Taking advantage of Cindy's maneuver to get me out of there, Mari and I disappeared into the treatment area, leaving the psychic and her sidekick no choice but to negotiate with Cindy for my time. Mari escorted me into exam room two, looking over her shoulder to make sure no one was following.

What did they hope to accomplish with this performance in my waiting room? Obviously meant to impress somehow, it simply put me on guard.

Thankful for my skillful receptionist, I hid my laughter and scurried down the hall.

A somber Devin waited in the exam room, one hand steadying Muffin, who sat happily on the table. Greta stood pressed against him. I noticed she wore much more makeup than when she interned with us. Not particularly flattering.

I also noticed that Greta's face wasn't beaming as before. What had adjusted her high beams down to running lights?

"Morning, Dr. Kate. Muffin's here for a recheck."

Something was definitely odd here. Devin's normally pleasant voice sounded flat. I moved toward the dog, who wagged its tail at me. "She seems happy today. Mari, let's weigh her and check her kidney function with a quick bun and creatinine. Can you two wait here? Be back in five minutes."

Mari scooped up the dog and, excusing myself, I followed into the treatment room. After a quick blood draw, we began the computerized test then put Muffin on our scale. She'd gained a healthy one and a quarter pounds. Our blood-chemistries results also showed improvement all around.

"Did you notice a chill in the air between the lovebirds?" Mari asked.

"Definitely down a few degrees." I finished my notes and gave Muffin a doggy high five.

When we returned to the exam room only Devin was there.

Mari of course blurted out, "Where's Greta?" Muffin stayed in her arms.

"She's in the waiting room. I wanted to speak to Dr. Kate, alone, if you don't mind." Devin stared pointedly at Mari.

More and more puzzling. Even after I gave him the news about Muffin's kidney function tests, Devin only said, "Good."

"Let me take Muffin out to Greta, then," Mari said, getting the point. She quickly disappeared, diplomatically closing the door after her.

I walked over to the desk and sat down. Our exam rooms were a pleasant size, furnished with a small desk and chair for the doctor to use, two client chairs, and a stainless-steel exam table.

"Please, take a seat, Devin, and tell me what's wrong."

No one could have predicted his dilemma.

Devin fidgeted with his hands, then said, "May I tell you something in confidence?"

"Sure. As long as it isn't something illegal."

"No, it's very legal. Too legal. Everyone will find out soon enough. I'm meeting with some lawyers today." He took a breath and continued. "Raeleen left me a million dollars in a life-insurance policy, and I'm pretty sure the police want to arrest me for her murder."

The continued flatness of his voice made me suspect he was in shock.

"Why did she have such a large policy?" I asked without thinking. "She was a young woman."

Devin looked down at his hands. "Most of the LARN board of directors carry insurance policies with the group named as a beneficiary. The board constantly gets death threats. Their larger office in North Carolina was firebombed in the middle of the night last year."

I had no inkling of that level of violence associated with the animal rights movement.

"Rae even talked about getting a gun for protection."

"Why are you telling me?"

In an agitated voice he answered, "If they arrest me, can you make sure all our animals are taken care of?" He dug into his jeans pocket. "Here, I made a list of them and who volunteered to foster them if anything happened to me. But someone needs to supervise." A slightly rumpled piece of paper was thrust into my hand. "Raeleen and I promised each other that the animals came first," he said.

"Of course I'll help." For the first time I felt genuinely sorry for him. "Please believe me, despite what she thought, I never spread any rumors about her. Ever."

Devin's hands clenched and unclenched. "Pretty sure I know who did."

In anticipation I waited for him to reveal the name, but he simply retreated again.

"I've got to do the thinking for both of us now that she's gone." He stood up, still a bit distant in his manner, shell-shocked by the gift Raeleen had left him.

"You'll figure it out, I'm sure."

"Thanks, Doc. The truth is I loved Raeleen. Her and me, we were crazy about each other."

———

When we walked back to the waiting room Greta greeted Devin like he'd been gone for a week, loudly asking him what he'd been talking about with me. Muffin wagged her tail and barked, demanding attention, while Beth and Pinky watched everything going on as if it was a reality television program. I realized Devin said he loved Raeleen but never said he was innocent of her death.

The psychic and the sidekick had vanished as swiftly as they'd appeared.

When Greta and Devin left, Cindy tried to catch my eye. I resisted. I had the feeling that after today Devin's secret wouldn't be a secret for long.

Things were about to change. What could be a better motive for murder than a million dollars in cash?

Chapter Thirty-Four

THE REST OF THE AFTERNOON CINDY AND MARI TRIED to pry loose the secret Devin told me. But he'd trusted me with his news, and I wasn't going to disappoint him. My friends would have to wait until someone else revealed the million-dollar surprise. His newfound riches made me focus on his alibi, rumored to be a woman.

Was he too much of a gentleman to rat out a lady?

———

Toward the end of the day, Cindy handed me a note. "I forgot—Athenina told me she's excited to talk to you," she said in a whisper. My receptionist doesn't normally whisper anything, far from it.

"Who the heck is Athenina?" I asked. "A sales representative, someone who wants me to eliminate their boss with a wish? How about a hint?"

"She's the psychic." My receptionist shook her head in frustration. "Mari told me that Daffy said her friend saw her last week on one of the morning shows and raved about her." Along with the note, Cindy handed me a colorful business card with swirly gray clouds and thin drifts of mist covering the printing.

What I read and heard confused me. "Wasn't the psychic Mari saw named Delphina?"

"You don't understand." She spoke as though I just

crawled out of a haystack. "There are two of them—a mother and a daughter. Delphina, who is the mom, is semi-retired now, gives local readings, but her daughter, Athenina, is very big in New York City. She's more than a psychic; she's a mystic and a life coach, too."

Mari came by and said, "Your next appointment is ready."

"Shoot, I've got to run, too." Cindy took off in the direction of the reception area while my assistant handed me our tablet notebook.

"What were you guys talking about?" Mari asked on the way to exam room one.

"Mind reading."

"Always kidding," she grinned.

———

Being summoned by a pair of psychics was nothing I imagined I'd experience in this lifetime. The similarity of their names I was sure was deliberate, possibly stage-type names? One suggested the Oracle of Delphi while the other, Athenina, sounded like a variation on Athena, goddess of wisdom.

Ordinarily, I would have thrown this invitation away but for one thing: They wanted to talk murder.

———

When an appointment rescheduled, I took the free time and Googled Athenina. To my surprise she had pages of postings, most of them glowing recommendations. Her special interests were Guardian Angels, wish fulfillment, and something called the happiness quest. Now I had an inkling of why she might be eager to speak to me. With my "lethal Christmas wish" video garnering more looks every day, I presented an opportunity to prove the existence of wish fulfillment.

Did that mean more publicity, more unwanted notoriety, just when things around me had started to die down? Should I meet her?

I subscribed to the idea of knowing the worst. My personality type doesn't like surprises. Using the animal hospital landline, I called the number on the card. As the phone rang, I clutched at the last-minute hope that the psychics wanted veterinary advice.

Instead, Delphina had a proposition for me. She invited me to join her and her daughter at a very expensive restaurant for an important "conversation" that might prove very "beneficial" to me. That was all she could discuss over the telephone.

Very hush-hush stuff.

"Tonight at the Tuscan Gardens out by the reservoir?"

"Don't you want to go somewhere closer to town?" The restaurant was a good thirty-five or forty minutes away.

"If I had the energy to drive farther, I would. This is a very small community, Dr. Turner, believe me. Too many nosy neighbors."

Her husky voice came across as soothing and understanding. One more tool in her bag of techniques. If I didn't already know her, I wouldn't have agreed to go. "Alright. I'm coming from work so seven, seven fifteen at the latest."

"And please come alone."

Before I could protest, she hung up.

———

Anticipating an unusual night, I began to get ready after my last appointment. In a hurry as always, I flung a red scarf around my neck, as a fashion statement and camouflage for any pet fur I missed. During the long ride I would have plenty of time to think of questions for both psychics. How did wish fulfillment mesh with the deaths of Frank, Eloise, and Raeleen? Did they know any of the victims? Newly energized, I made my way to the truck.

My hand was on the truck door handle when I saw Pinky and Princess on their porch. A tentative wave from Pinky evoked a similar one from me before they made their way down to the last step, Princess cuddled in his arms. Only when she was safe did he let go of her, allowing her to explore and walk the cleared pathway next to the house.

On guard I slid into the driver's seat. At least twice Pinky had come out of the house at the same time I did. I hoped it was a coincidence, but I didn't think so.

———

Tuscan Gardens blazed with lights that reflected off the vast, icy reservoir far below. It was one of several destination restaurants run by a celebrity chef, and I'd been there just once, with Jeremy.

I almost didn't go in. I felt I was stepping out of my comfort zone. Because of my work schedule I had no time or interest in keeping up with social media or pop culture. Once in a while an item might catch my eye, but for the most part I kept away from non-scientific discussions. Being immersed in the private lives of my staff and friends, whether I wanted to be or not, was exhausting enough. Hollywood gossip and the latest fads lived far off my radar.

But that didn't make me naive. Gramps taught me you don't get something for nothing, and these psychics obviously wanted something from me. Curiosity caught me again with its sharp little claws.

———

The inside of the restaurant glowed softly, the sense of money well spent everywhere, from the tufted leather chairs to the sparkling floral china. Flowers and garden references were scattered throughout, discreetly woven into the carpet and repeated in the artwork on the walls.

"May I help you?" The older gentleman at reception looked like part of the decor.

"Yes. I'm meeting someone here." I'd forgotten Delphina's full name. Embarrassed, I looked up at him, swiftly trying to scan the seated customers. "She's very... dramatic looking."

"Let me guess." He held his fingers to his temple as though in deep concentration. "You seek a psychic."

A tiny smile curved on his lips, just enough to tell me we shared the joke. "Yes."

"Come with me." He held a dinner menu and what appeared to be a drinks list close to his suit jacket and threaded his way to a table at the far end of the room, overlooking a sweeping water and mountain vista.

To my astonishment only Athenina sat at the table. Close up, her radiant smile, glowing skin, and carefully managed theatrical impression appeared more impressive. She wore a beautifully constructed high-end dress, hand-embellished with intricate embroidered crystals.

Athenina must have sensed my puzzlement because she asked, "Expecting someone a bit older? Delphina, sadly, is indisposed." Her hand, decorated with a diamond ring and thin gold bracelets, brushed a stray curl from her face.

I'm not sure what I expected but not this professional, controlled individual. She seemed more at home in a boardroom than behind a psychic's curtain.

"Forgive me, I'm confused. Delphina is your…"

"My mother. We have a tradition in our family of passing similar names down between mother and daughter. I assume you did some research on us? Daffy told me you were very cautious."

The waiter came to take our drink order. Athenina chose a champagne cocktail, but I stuck with water. Between the long ride back and the grilling to come, I needed my wits intact.

"Since I had my mother ask you here tonight, please consider yourself my guest," she began graciously. "I didn't think you'd come simply on my invitation."

"I'm not sure that I would have," I answered honestly.

Not comfortable about this meeting, I pretended to peruse the menu but actually studied the woman opposite me. I noticed men and women alike stared at her. Her toned arms with a ballet dancer's elegance complemented a long, graceful neck. I suspected physical beauty helped in whatever her con was.

"May I call you Athenina—and do you have a last name, too?"

"Silly. Isn't Athenina quite enough?" Her laugh tempted me to laugh along. The lilt reminded me of the bubbles in her drink.

It occurred to me that she glittered like a jewel in a gilded setting, perfectly staged for maximum impact. The sudden appearance of someone very different confirmed my suspicions.

"Sorry, darling, business," said the dark-haired man who kissed Athenina's hand. "Also set the thermostat in the weekend house. " He turned toward me next. My impression was of a sleek sea otter who might slip away at any moment. "J. D. Dowd, and you must be Dr. Kate Turner. Glad you could make it."

He settled into the chair next to Athenina and immediately signaled for a waiter. "Vodka martini, very dry."

"Have you ordered?" Impatient dark eyes focused first on me then our hostess. A gold watch gleamed subtly under his starched white cuff.

Everything about him was slim and slick, from his gelled hair to the subtle sheen of his Italian suit. I wondered what his relationship with Athenina was and why he was here. Once the food had been ordered, he got right into it.

His voice did not soothe. It grated, insistent and pedantic like a sledgehammer. J.D. was her business manager and agent. They'd been working on a pitch with a publisher and wanted to "buy" the rights to my story.

"What story?" I asked, determined not to give in to any demands. If they pressed, I'd blame it on my business advisor, Gramps.

A couple swept by, the man stopping to greet J.D., who turned on the charm by promising to get together soon. Once they left, he went right back to his spiel.

"What story? Your wish, of course, and the aftermath. Haven't you checked your YouTube video lately?"

"Checked it yesterday." I put my phone on the table and opened the screen.

"Don't bother. You're up to almost 230,000 views, thanks to a newscast in China. You're about to go viral."

"Oh, no. I've got to stop that." The thought of all those people watching me made me choke on my appetizer.

J.D. shook his head. "Are you kidding? I could get you a small advertising deal linked up to the video with one phone call. You might make a couple of thousand, or more if you actively promote it."

"Why did you say I could make money from that video?"

"Sales, kiddo, linked with products being pushed to viewers. Data capture can be sold and resold. It's a brave, screwed-up world out there." He buttered a piece of bread and smoothly hailed our waiter for another drink. "You ladies want anything else?"

Athenina said no and pushed away her calamari, not even half-finished.

"Discipline," J.D. said with approval. "She's loaded with it."

"I need to keep myself at a strong and healthy weight," Athenina replied. "Long ago spirits told me that my future depended on discipline and discovery."

Her voice and manner seemed sincere. That made me curious. "Spirits have been talking to you for a long time?"

She sighed, as if explaining was some enormous effort. "The spirits claimed me for their own when I turned twelve. Sometimes they warn me...or help me with a task. They're always nearby, whether I want them or not. As I became older, I learned to harness my energy."

"That's where you come in, Doc," J.D. added. "One of her online classes is about wish fulfillment. What happened to you she thinks is an example of destructive wish power instead of constructive. Athenina just finished a self-help book about channeling your inner power and making your wishes come true. I can negotiate a better deal if I have your story on board."

"You must be confused. I didn't record that video. My friend Mari did." This was fast moving out of control.

With his refreshed martini in hand he explained, "Don't need the video. We need your firsthand account."

Now I got it. "So, you want to tell my story as an example of what not to do?"

"Probably." A look passed between the psychic and the agent.

"Why do you need to buy my story? People are watching it for free."

J.D. explained this too. I suspected he had plenty of explanations in his pocket. "Our proposal is based on controlling access to your story. It's perfect. We've got tons of free publicity, and people are curious about the wish and you. You're a public relations gift. You haven't spoken to a single member of the press, which is unbelievable." He leaned back and eyed me with snake eyes while he sipped his drink. "If we pay you for your story, in your own words, you can't sue us if it's in the book. Her publisher has a bunch of corporate lawyers involved, and they've got pretty strict guidelines for this stuff. So, what's it worth for you to sign it over to us?"

Now, I might only be a veterinarian, but I grew up with a very savvy grandfather who emphasized that salespeople never present their best deal first. Also, get everything in writing and never commit to anything before you read it. Especially don't trust lawyers who pitch deals over drinks.

They stared while I casually sipped my water. Did I sense a hint of panic in the supremely confident J.D.? After a second deliberately long sip, I countered, "Why don't you come up with a package proposal, and I'll have my lawyer take a look at it?" Then I casually speared a leftover sprig of broccoli.

"Hey," he turned to Athenina and said, "I thought you said she'd be an easy mark. Guess your psychic powers were wrong, honey."

"Not at all," her voice purred like a kitten. "Our kind doctor is just too smart to be taken in by you. Get all her info and send her something tonight. And make it worth her while, J.D. I'm sensing there are some huge student loan debts in her background to pay off, isn't that right?" Her eyes sparkled with mirth.

It felt like I'd won. Or maybe that's what they wanted me to feel.

When the waiter came by with the after-dinner drinks and dessert menu, I excused myself, citing having worked a long day. I'd listened to J.D. boast nonstop about his client list for a half hour, at least. His partner in crime, Athenina, sat back in knowing silence, preferring to insert periodic esoteric comments that occasionally made sense.

While their conversation was fresh on my mind, I decided to call Luke and ask for some advice. After all, he was studying to be a lawyer. If he didn't know the answers to my questions, maybe he could steer me to someone who would. Besides, with this news about the video going viral, I wanted to hear his voice.

Driving the truck around toward the back of the restaurant, I put it in park and dialed his number.

After five rings he picked up, music blaring in the background. Why were all my friends at parties when I called?

"Hey, Luke. Bad time?"

"Kate. No. Let me go into the bedroom and get away from the noise."

I vaguely heard a door open and close. "Much better," I told him. "Are you at a party?"

"I'm at my sister's house. A bunch of relatives dropped by and now they're dancing in the living room. You know how it is."

No, I didn't. Not much dancing in my family. "Maybe I should call back."

"Don't be silly. What's on your mind? More suspects? Need more markers?"

"Very funny." I was beginning to regret this call. "Have you ever heard of someone called Athenina?"

"Hmmm. Sounds like someone in the entertainment industry. Only one name." He paused then said, "Never heard of them."

That didn't surprise me. Luke also wasn't big on social media and didn't pay much attention to extravagant behavior. Just a quiet, solid guy.

"What about J. D. Dowd? An entertainment lawyer."

That got more of a reaction. "He sounds familiar. Local?"

"More of a weekender, I believe." The lawyer had mentioned his second home during our conversation. I had the impression it was somewhere close in the Hudson Valley.

Again Luke was silent. "The plot thickens, but I can't quite place him. Why do you want to know?"

"They made me an offer I might not refuse." I explained about the restaurant invitation and the strange offer to buy my wish story.

He laughed. "A little obtuse for me. Are you home now?"

I confessed I was calling from the Tuscan Gardens parking lot.

"Why don't you come over to my sisters' house?" he suggested. "Or I could meet you halfway if you want and we could talk."

This time I hesitated. "Well…"

"I'll make it easy. I'll head over to your place now. As an enticement I'll bring an apple-cranberry pie Rosie brought over from the diner."

"Don't take their food," I protested.

"We've got twenty of them. Someone in the kitchen screwed up and made a double batch. You can eat it tomorrow for breakfast."

"A pie bribe? That's low, Luke."

"Did it work?"

"Sure did. See you soon."

———————

I beat him by fifteen minutes, just enough time to walk Buddy and check to see if Pinky's lights were on. I doubted he had to plow tonight. There'd been no new snow in the last twenty-four hours.

Was he watching, hidden behind the curtains as my dog joyfully barked a welcome to me? Would he continue watching when Luke pulled up at my door?

No doubt about it.

Chapter Thirty-Five

I BREWED A DECAF COFFEE FOR LUKE AND AN HERBAL tea for me as he set up his laptop on the kitchen table. I'd told him everything I remembered about the meeting with Athenina and asked if their proposal might be real.

"This isn't the type of law I'm that familiar with, although we did touch on copyright laws, contracts for intellectual properties, and that sort of thing. First of all, they want to take advantage of your publicity now. And second, it sounds as if they are in a bit of a legal bind with her publisher."

As he spoke, he began typing up searches on legal websites and a law student bulletin board. He also searched Athenina and J. D. Dowd.

His search confirmed mine. Athenina had quite a following. Her workshops drew large crowds, and after a celebrity raved about it in a blog, her private client list tripled. Billed more as a life coach than a psychic, she had a website on her business card that described personal traits such as "empathic" and "deeply aware of the spirits that surround us all."

Her agent, J.D., was another story. Although not accused of any crimes, he'd come close, with at least two disagreements with clients over money settled out of court. Most of the people he represented were hangers-on, reality-type stars, and some social media influencers.

"Influencers?" That description rang a bell. "I've heard of them, but I'm foggy as to what they actually do."

Luke explained. "These are people with a large following on social media. Advertisers pay them to mention their products or to endorse them. You'd be surprised at how much they can make."

"We're in the wrong businesses."

"So many ways to make money these days...and lose it. So, where does this duo fit on your murder suspects list?"

"Good question. I'm not sure if they do." I got up and went over to the messy board, and on an impulse wrote Athenina and J.D. in scrolling pink script. "Maybe they can influence one of our suspects to confess."

"Ha. Ha." Luke took a moment to post our dilemma on a legal site used by many of his fellow students. The responses were not considered legal opinions, simply guidelines.

The consensus among Luke's contacts was to take the money and run—but make sure the contract was detailed and in writing. A disclaimer absolving me of all and any penalties, lawsuits, etc., was vital. Everything had to be classified as "for entertainment purposes only." And, of course, have the contract reviewed by a lawyer. Nonfiction books played by different rules than fiction. There had recently been several scandals involving nonfiction and publishers of personal memoirs that trampled on the truth.

"One of my professors used to work for a big New York City entertainment firm. I'll run this past him. When did J.D. and the psychic say they'd be in touch?"

"My impression was that it would be soon. They both appeared pretty anxious to get it wrapped up."

Luke typed a note on his phone calendar. "Can't do anything until you get the contract."

"Right." But what I could do is a little bit of snooping of my own. Luke forgot I had a big New York City contact too, and his name was Gramps.

———

Luke left soon after, confessing his grandmother had asked him to pick up something from the store for her and preferred him to get in at a reasonable hour.

"It's like high school. Her place, her rules," he muttered. With a long kiss, he reluctantly bid me goodnight. "Don't forget to set the alarm," he reminded me.

There were a few things on my list, too. Buddy needed his last walk of the night, and I had to check to make sure I had a clean pair of scrubs for the morning. After talking to Luke, I debated whether to call Gramps this late and decided to email him instead. That's when I discovered J.D. had sent me a proposal. Stunned by how quickly he acted, I was equally surprised at the offer of fifteen hundred dollars for the rights to my "story."

Fifteen hundred dollars was a drop in the deep bucket of my student loans, but it was fifteen hundred more than I had now. Figuring he'd just left, I called Luke.

"Are you at your grandmother's yet?" I asked, hearing music in the background.

"Nope. Can't live without me for two minutes?"

"Obviously. So, what are you doing that you can talk to me? Not in the car, I hope," I questioned.

"Grocery shopping for Granny."

Ah, one of the few solitary errands that allow you to use your phone while adding items to your cart. It only took a moment for me to explain my surprise email.

"Go ahead and forward that proposal," he told me. "I also included that group query to my contracts professor earlier, and he found it a very interesting teaching case. If you don't mind allowing me to share the situation, suitably disguised of course, I may have a solution for you."

Figuring many heads were better than one, I readily agreed. Also, I liked knowing my odd experience might end up as a teaching exercise for students. At least someone would benefit from it.

"Did that proposal include a confidentiality agreement or nondisclosure attachment?"

I thought for a moment. "I'm not sure. I kind of stopped reading at fifteen hundred bucks. Is that important?"

"It's for both parties, Athenina and company, and you."

Interesting. None of that had occurred to me, and I told Luke.

"See," he said, "lawyers do have a reason to exist."

———

The news of Devin's million-dollar windfall spread like gas on a fire the following day. Law enforcement focused intensely on his alibi for the hours in question.

"So, what do you know about Devin's alibi?" I asked my receptionist.

"About as much as you knew about the million dollars," she answered.

At a stalemate I assumed she couldn't reveal anything just yet. "Okay. I sympathize. Devin made me promise not to tell anyone."

She saw a spot on her desk and scraped it off with her nail. "I'm sort of in the same position."

"Can you tell me anything? I heard he was with a woman."

"You may have heard right." Her fingernail kept worrying that spot.

Mari had already gone home, and Cindy and I were closing up the hospital. "Greta. I bet it was Greta."

My receptionist's blue eyes revealed nothing. Luke rapped on the front door. He waved at us through the big picture window.

"I thought you two had broken up," she asked.

"So did I. It's a long story."

"For being broken up, he visits you a lot." She thought a moment then said, "Here's a hint. It's someone you know, all right? But it isn't Greta." With that, Cindy walked over to the front door and let him in.

"Good evening, ladies," he said, brushing his feet off on the mat.

"I'm on my way home," Cindy explained, slipping into her coat and picking up her large purse. "Lock me out?"

"Sure."

I started flipping lights off and logging out the

computers. Luke followed me, his attention on a text he'd just received. "Come along," I told him.

Mr. Cat jumped down from wherever he'd been napping, in anticipation of an evening snack. Tail fluffed up after seeing Luke, he darted in front of us and disappeared into the treatment room.

"Did I scare him?" Luke slipped off his coat.

"Not really. He'll come out when the cat food can is opened."

Sure enough, as soon as he heard the lid pop, he jumped out onto the treatment table and waited patiently.

"You're a handsome guy." Luke took a moment to pet the big tabby's fur. "Where did he come from?"

I put the empty can in the recycle pail. "He's sort of a rescue cat. One day he showed up at the hospital door, no chip, no collar, and wouldn't go away. Cindy let him in, and he's been here ever since. We put up posters and contacted all the shelters, but no one claimed him. We've tried to adopt him out, but he likes living in the hospital."

"Does he come over to your place?"

"No. He and Buddy don't get along."

Hospital secured, Luke and I went into my place. My dog danced around, happy to see his friend again. "Can't stay long, but I wanted to tell you to ask J.D. and Athenina for a description of the property they are making an offer for."

"So I don't tell them…"

"Right. They tell you."

"Clever." I walked over to the whiteboard with the suspect names crowding each other out. "Okay, what are we going to do with this thing?"

"Erase it." Luke picked up a paper towel and proceeded to wipe the board clean. "Now that the chief has focused his investigation on Devin, I think you can consider the mystery solved. I have it on good authority his alibi didn't hold up. Now he's got a million dollars' worth of motive. All they need is some physical evidence, and they'll charge him with murder. Eloise and Frank died of natural causes, albeit with eerie timing, and Raeleen died from domestic violence. Cases closed. No curse. No fatal wish."

What a relief, was my first reaction. But Devin had seemed truthful and sympathetic. I decided not to tell Luke I still had doubts. "No fatal wish?" I repeated.

"Nope." He pulled me close. "Merry Christmas."

Even without the Christmas music, I felt the joy.

———

Finally relaxed, I was contemplating asking the chief if we could take down the YouTube video, when my phone rang.

"Hey, Mari."

"Kate. I'm glad I caught you. I'm at Redcoats, and I heard something odd."

Redcoats was a popular local bar, close to town. "What was it?" I felt I practically shouted the question at her.

Crackling washed out the beginning of her sentence. I caught it in midstream: "...was telling us about a rumor... you...a month ago."

"What? I can barely hear you."

"...not to hire Rae because of..."

"Mari," I yelled into the receiver, "you're fading in and out. Can you repeat that?"

I caught another sentence fragment: "...it was very odd, so I thought I'd call."

With a temporarily good signal, I asked my veterinary assistant to repeat that story again.

"Hold on. I'll go outside."

After a few minutes, I heard her say, "Thanks. Can you hear me?"

Happy to be able to tell her yes, I listened, shocked, as she relayed her story to me.

At Redcoats while ordering a beer she had met a receptionist from an animal hospital in Kingston who asked about Raeleen's death. Long story short, Rae had applied for a job as an assistant, but someone heard a rumor that she'd been fired from our hospital for mishandling the cash. Dr. Turner had personally been involved in the decision. Of course, they didn't hire her.

The source of the rumor? Our little intern, Greta.

Baffled by such an outrageous lie, I now understood why Raeleen had been so furious with me. Greta targeted her specifically, using my name. Was she trying to drive her out of town? That way she'd have Devin all to herself. Was it cold and calculating, or nasty and personal?

I bet both.

The empty dry-erase board looked a little forlorn. Faint shadows of my arrows and suspect names clung like ghost writing on the now empty space. Was it time to tell Chief Garcia directly what I'd learned? Before I made that phone call, I'd ask Cindy for the latest on the investigation.

Taking advantage of a lull in our appointments just before lunch, I ambushed my receptionist at her desk. No lengthy explanation was necessary as to why I was asking her all these questions. Cindy assumed everyone was curious-bordering-on-nosy about their fellow man and woman.

She unpacked her lunch while we talked. "Pinky is in the clear. He was working the night of Raeleen's death—all verified by clients and credit card receipts for coffee and occasional bathroom breaks. During the six critical hours for Frank Martindale's time of death, Pinky was ten miles away, plowing out multiple homes." With her manicured fingers, nails painted a pleasant plum color, she started on a Caesar salad. "Same for Eloise. The chief plotted out a map of where he was for the whole night up to when he discovered her body."

"I'm so happy," I told her.

Her face turned serious. "It's not good news for Devin. At first he said he was at a bar, but no one remembers him there. Cell phone records show he and Raeleen argued by text around nine thirty that evening, and then his phone went silent for about ten hours."

"While he slept at home."

"That's the problem. He wasn't at home. He was with a lady friend."

That didn't sound far-fetched to me. "And you still can't say?"

"Sorry. But you and someone you know will be very surprised." A conspiratorial look crossed her face, and then she reached for a cheese stick. "Devin says the mystery lady and he were together all night, but they supposedly were sound asleep during part of that period of interest—between midnight and five a.m. He clocked in at Mr. Fix-it's at six in the morning."

Of course—why not add a love triangle complication to this messy situation? But didn't Raeleen refer to herself as Devin's fiancée? When I asked Cindy, she smiled and went back to her salad.

When I got a break, I called Luke. "You were right about retiring our suspect board," I told him. "It looks like none of these deaths have anything to do with me or that dumb wish. We let all that paranormal talk sweep us away."

"Kate…"

"I feel like a fool."

Chapter Thirty-Six

NOW THAT IT LOOKED LIKE RAELEEN'S MURDER WAS solved, the Christmas tunes sounded cheerier, the decorations brighter. With Christmas looming, clients and staff alike were in festive moods.

Whoever came up with the idea of Pinky playing Santa Claus was a genius. He'd been hanging around the hospital, helping out, since he'd had so many cancellations from his plowing customers. I suppose the remote possibility of being plowed out and murdered at the same time scared some of them off. Sort of a deadly two-for-one.

Dressed in the traditional red costume with a fake white beard and a white wig transformed round-faced Pinky into the image of jolly St. Nick. Cindy designed an ad for a free photo of your pet with Santa—and emailed it to all our clients. The number who took her up on the offer was staggering. It was mostly our dog clients, because as everyone knows, cats don't get into the holiday spirit like dogs do. A smattering of guinea pigs, rabbits, and one parrot rounded out the crowd. Since each family had a photo appointment, there had been no glitches so far. Pinky kept out of my hair, and everyone got the photo immediately emailed thanks to Cindy's iPhone.

Our side business threatened to take over the waiting room until Beth Orstead volunteered to assume Cindy's duties, appropriately dressed as Santa's helper—thanks to the help of a little bird who suggested this fun activity…the little bird being Mari and Daffy, who supplied the outfit.

Cindy, Mari, and I had a powwow on how to handle Pinky.

"Why did he want to confess to murdering Raeleen?" Mari had come in late to the conversation, so Cindy brought her up to speed.

"First of all, Pinky is very literal. He doesn't process information like we do," she began.

"Well, you know him best of everyone here," Mari said.

"He really believes that Kate wished Eloise and Frank away, so when he wished Raeleen would die and she did…"

Mari finished the sentence. "He thought he did it. Now I get it."

I continued the theme. "I've told him over and over that's not what happened, but it's stuck in his head now. He's already confessed to me, and to the chief, and probably to his family lawyer. Let's try to keep him from doing it again."

Cindy agreed. "I'd rather Pinky get counseling, not become someone's statistic."

We all understood. The murder of Raeleen Lassitor had produced too many suspects. First the local detectives, then the FBI, investigated Pinky, then Devin, and then every enemy of LARN came under scrutiny. Before the day was over, we heard that new DNA evidence found on the body had turned the investigation in yet another unexpected direction—a direction that once again involved me.

Luke brought the animal hospital the bad news along with takeout from the diner for the staff. With his contacts at the Oak Falls Police Department, he'd heard almost immediately that DNA found on Raeleen's coat and a glove matched someone living in Oak Falls.

The surprise suspect? Ashley Kaminsky, the owner of Maple Grove Farm.

"You've got to be kidding," I said, pushing away my plate. The idea that Ashley, owner of the mustang, Lobo, might be a killer stunned me. "Why is her DNA in the system?"

"Federal database and a genealogy company, my dear. Law enforcement's new best friend." He stacked some papers together on my desk to make room for his paper plate.

"I don't believe it."

Luke picked up an egg roll. "What you believe or don't believe doesn't matter. They're evidence-gathering as we speak."

With my own egg roll I countered his claim. "Have they got a motive?"

"Raeleen opposed the wild horse adoption program and told Ashley she was going to look for evidence of neglect. She threatened to file a complaint against her and send Lobo back."

"The neglect part is bull. I've been to Maple Grove Farm multiple times. Ashley takes wonderful care of her pets. Plus, Lobo is just now beginning to feel comfortable in his new home. To disrupt him again with an uncertain fate in front of him is simply cruel. I thought Raeleen loved animals?"

"That's the sad part. She did. But her activism backfired in some cases. She never learned from her mistakes, always blamed someone else. When I was on the police force, we had a few run-ins with her."

While I ate, I went back over my own run-in with Raeleen and the look of absolute rage on her face. What if Devin was innocent, as he now claimed? I wondered if a disgruntled local decided to take advantage of the "deadly wish" theory and stop her once and for all.

A tempting scenario, but it didn't cover how Ashley's DNA came into the picture. Reluctant to believe my friend was involved, I decided to take a deeper look at Maple Grove Farm and Lobo.

———

I didn't anticipate it, but an opportunity presented itself later that day, when I realized Mari and I were driving right past the farm after one of our house calls. I took a chance and had Mari text Ashley from the base of the driveway. The doors immediately swung open, and as we came up the hill, I saw my client waiting anxiously outside for us. Her normally calm face betrayed her. She appeared worried, very worried.

"The police were just here," she began without any prompting on our part.

I put my hand on her shoulder and guided her inside. Her knee buckled for a moment even with the brace on. "Do you want to talk about it?" I asked, concerned for her privacy.

"You bet I do. They seem to think I have something to do with Raeleen Lassitor's death. Are they crazy? First, I'd never kill anyone. And second, does it look like I'm going anywhere with this brace on?"

We all sat down at the kitchen table, and Mari asked if she'd like her to make some tea.

I got right to it. "When was your injury?" Her menagerie of rescue animals padded into the kitchen, looking for attention and possibly some treats. The older one, Tommy, pushed his nose into her hand.

"Tuesday night," she replied. "I just went through this with the cops. Around nine in the evening the dogs started to bark. I was worried the coyotes were visiting us again, so I went out with my paint gun to scare them off."

"That's a novel idea," Mari observed. Ashley handed us both cups of steaming hot tea.

"Thanks. Anyway, it wasn't coyotes. Someone had sneaked onto the property. I found the barn door open. Lobo was all riled up, snorting and kicking the side of the stall. Anyway, as I was shutting the door a figure ran across the field off to the right and climbed over the fence. When I followed, I slipped in the mud and fell."

"Did you go to the emergency room?"

"No," she confessed. "I limped back home. Took a

shower to get the muck off, downed a few ibuprofens, and put an ice pack on it. Originally, I suspected one of the neighbor kids. I've found the oldest one in there before making out with his girlfriend."

"So you went to the emergency room...?"

"The following day because when I got up in the morning my knee had swollen so much I couldn't bend it. The orthopedist said I have trauma to the joint and a partial tear of my lateral collateral ligament, which should heal if I stop reinjuring it." An expression of pain appeared when one of the dogs accidentally banged into her brace. "Ouch."

Mari distracted the dogs while I created a barrier from two spare chairs. "Leave a thick towel or pillow here by your chair to cushion your knee. Believe me, it will come in handy with all your critters around."

Her story of someone being in the barn interested me. "Were you able to recognize who you saw running away? Could it have been a woman?"

Puzzled, she asked, "Why would a woman be in my barn?"

Why, indeed. Maybe snooping around and checking on Lobo's stall and exercise area. That might account for the hay and Ashley's DNA found on Raeleen. "I notice you have security gates at the base of the driveway. Do you have any cameras?"

"Loads of them. Problem is they shorted out in the last big storm. Honestly, I haven't gotten around to fixing them. The ones in the barn work, though. Separate circuits. The police took all that video as evidence. Actually, it's the dogs that sounded the alarm."

"Best alarms ever." With no other questions to ask, I focused on the other reason I came here. "Do you mind ˋ if I say hello to Lobo?"

"Sure," Ashley said. "If you don't mind, I'm going to stay here." Her hand rubbed the skin above her brace. "Text me when you're ready to leave."

Mari and I headed for the barn, but my assistant stopped halfway there. "You go ahead. I'm going to run back and see if she wants us to do anything else for her. My cell service is bad in the barn."

"If you don't mind," I said.

Alone I continued on to the barn while Mari went back into the house. The door squeaked a bit as I pulled the handle toward me. Familiar farm smells wafted out, odors of animals and hay and earth. A pair of dim lights lit a pathway in front of the stalls. I realized this is what an intruder would see, even more if they had a flashlight. What might they be after?

Were these motion detector lights? Probably not. You wouldn't want them going off all night whenever any of the animals moved. What about the barn camera videos the police took? I made a note to ask her.

Just to the right of the entrance was the tack room/office that Ashley used for her husbandry documents, crop reports, medical records, and supply orders. I'd sat opposite her in that room while generating a rabies certificate for one of her dogs. There were photos of a younger Ashley at an agility trial and with her arm around a calf at the state fair. Nothing of particular interest caught my eye, certainly nothing to implicate anyone in any wrongdoing. High up in the corner was a camera focused on the desk.

A creak of the hinge warned me that Mari most likely had returned.

"I'm in here," I told her. Light flooded the inside of the barn.

"I threw the main switch," she said. "Everyone's been fed and watered. Ashley did want us to check Lobo's left front hoof. He had a stone wedged in it the other night, but today when she turned him out in the field, he appeared perfectly fine. The farrier is coming next week to check his shoe."

"Okay." As always, I approached the mustang slowly. He backed away only to reconsider when I stood still at the front of his stall. Mari came up next to me with a lead, which I snapped onto his halter. A few sugar cubes from my pocket convinced him everything was fine.

We brought him out into the hall so I could check his hoof. From experience I knew what it was like to be pinned against a wall by a thousand-pound horse, so there was no way I would examine him in the stall. With good hoof manners I checked his shoe, even running my finger along the inside for any small pebbles, but nothing seemed amiss.

Sweet Potato next door gave a soft whinny, probably wondering where her sugar cube was. Mari obliged while I brought Lobo back in and rewarded him. We texted Ashley that all was well and then secured the animals for the night.

One final look around revealed nothing. If Raeleen had snuck in, what did she have in mind?

After turning off the overhead lights, and leaving on the nightlights, we walked outside and closed the thick wooden doors. A crescent moon shone its pale light on the red painted barn, which turned pearl gray in the glow. Snow crunched under our boots on our way back to the truck. Ashley texted us to have a safe journey home. The field Raeleen had fled through revealed nothing as we drove by nor did the silent surrounding woods.

Why did I feel I had missed something?

———

Once in my apartment I checked YouTube. The number swam before my eyes. Could it be? Could 315,000 people have viewed it? One comment caught my attention as I scrolled through them. They claimed to have heard another voice after Pinky said Raeleen Lassitor. A ghostly voice.

I didn't think so.

But I was about to find out.

Chapter Thirty-Seven

THAT VIEWER ON YOUTUBE WAS RIGHT. BUT IT WASN'T no ghost.

A frame-by-frame viewing of the video picked up our former intern Greta muttering "Good" after I wished Raeleen Lassitor away.

My eyes stung from staring at the screen. Did this count as evidence that Greta hated the victim? Not sure, I called Luke.

The noise in the background sounded like a store of some kind. "You must have read my mind. I'm at Raeleen's last workplace, buying groceries and asking a bunch of questions." He lowered his voice. "A few days before she died Raeleen told a coworker that she was going to help rehome some of the kittens that hang out at the market's dumpster. It was super hush-hush because she's gotten into trouble with management for feeding them."

"Was she working with a group that does feral cat capture and release?" I assumed Raeleen would be well aware of all the local animal groups, since she was vice president of LARN. Some dedicated volunteers work for several animal rescue groups at a time.

"No, just her. Something's off about this, though, because the coworker said Raeleen was hinting about starting her own animal rights group and being the CEO."

What? That didn't make sense. Why split from a successful group to start your own—especially with no money? Raeleen didn't have a dime.

"Did they remember anything else?"

"No such luck." Even before Luke continued, I felt his frustration. "Raeleen always had one scheme or another going, she told me. Half the time, the coworker didn't even listen."

———

Back in my apartment we talked about the three deaths and how my video had gone viral. In my email were two new proposals from lawyer J.D. and his psychic client giving me a twenty-four-hour deadline to accept their offer. It now came with a bonus.

"You don't think J.D. would kill Raeleen just to complete the wish, do you?"

"That sounds unlikely," Luke answered, "but I wouldn't rule anything out. I know the police are frustrated. The more time that goes by after a murder with no arrest, the less likely the killer will be caught."

I don't know why but my mind circled back to the wish. All I wanted to prove was the wish wasn't at the heart of this mess.

Luke spent a moment reading the YouTube viewer reviews. "Some of these comments are out to lunch. I don't know how law enforcement would deal with them. Here's one person who swears they heard the devil speak in the background."

The devil? "That's one I must have missed. What did old Satan say?"

"Die."

———————

It was déjà vu all over again when Chief Garcia made an appearance at my apartment, this one preceded by a text from Luke and definitely not official. Cindy, my receptionist and his sister-in-law, rode shotgun.

Thanks to Cindy's presence, the chief was on his best behavior.

Four of us now sat around my kitchen table swilling tea and munching on baked goods. We'd cued up the video for the chief to see, only to find he had his own copy, thanks to Cindy.

"First of all, let me say that I don't believe in all this supernatural nonsense, but there are a lot of people who do."

"More than you think," Cindy said.

"What I believe," he continued "is that a criminal may be using your wish to justify the murder of one or more of our victims."

I couldn't believe what he was saying.

"So far Devin's alibi is holding up. Oh, and your friend Ashley is no longer a suspect. She turned over a video from her barn camera, which showed Raeleen sneaking in wearing the same coat she was killed in. The hay fragments, partial DNA evidence—it all was passive, picked up in the barn when she was snooping around."

"Did Rae steal anything?"

He hesitated for a moment before telling us. "We have her on the barn camera taking pictures of certain documents. The phone footage is being analyzed, as well as the contents of her desk at LARN."

"The plot thickens," said Cindy trying to lighten the mood.

"That means we're back to square one." Our police chief did not sound happy.

"Maybe all three deaths are murders," Luke proposed. "Or two out of three. Definitely one is."

The chief scratched his head. "I certainly think any of those scenarios are possible, but my office has its hands tied. Between the FBI and our friends in Kingston, we've been squeezed out. We know for sure someone murdered Raeleen. A ghost didn't pop up and shoot her. As for Eloise and Frank, with no evidence to the contrary, it's hard to prove their deaths weren't accidents. All evidence indicates that. Of course, when a member of the public starts asking questions…"

"Like Babs did," I added.

"Then we have to take another look." Something was bothering Chief Garcia, a stickler for detail. We soon learned what. "That New York City pathologist should've factored in weather conditions up here before he published his opinion. A sudden wind gust would account for his findings. Those things can knock you off your feet."

"Tell them what you told me," Cindy told her brother-in-law.

Decidedly uncomfortable, he said, "Speaking off the

record, I wouldn't be opposed to some fact-gathering by other interested parties."

I spoke up. "What if Luke and I and Cindy try one last time to find connections between Raeleen, Eloise, and Frank? Unofficially, of course."

"Anything you find out would be appreciated. There's no way I can justify my officers pursing a murder investigation into Frank's or Eloise's death with absolutely no evidence."

"Right away I can tell you one connection," Cindy said. "Raeleen hated Eloise for breeding bulldogs."

Luke added, "I can check for nuisance lawsuits in small claims court filed by Frank. He had a shotgun approach targeting multiple individuals or corporations or both."

That made me recall my conversation with Judy. "Frank had at least two lawsuits pending against Judy's Place. She wasn't the only one in town he was suing."

Chief Garcia cleared his throat. "To be completely transparent here, Frank also was suing me personally and the Oak Falls Police Department."

"Wait," I said. "Wouldn't that be a conflict of interest—you and your office investigating his death?"

"In retrospect, yes."

Luke spoke up. "Like I said, someone like Frank often filed multiple lawsuits in small claims court, where there are minimal legal fees. I'd like to know what specific case he had in front of the judge the morning of his death—the case he hired an outside lawyer for, instead of representing himself."

"That's something I do know," the chief said. "It was a weird one. He's suing some psychic who told him he didn't have long to live. He claimed psychological trauma. If he won, he intended to piggy-back that verdict into a whole slew of others to the tune of five hundred thousand dollars or more."

"Wow." Cindy obviously didn't know everything.

"Who was the defendant?" asked Luke.

"A woman named Delphina."

Since transparency now ruled, I had to confess everything, from going with Mari to Delphina for a reading, to the odd meeting with Athenina and her lawyer/agent J.D., along with their monetary propositions. The chief appeared nonplussed. Since he'd spent twenty-five years as a police officer, few things surprised him.

"Let me say," I began, "Delphina seems much too careful to make this kind of mistake with Frank. Maybe he misinterpreted what she said?"

"I believe she emailed him a copy of their session," Chief Garcia answered. "That's part of the evidence provided."

Luke returned with a fresh pot of tea and the last of the sweets he'd brought. "I'm afraid psychics, tarot card readers, and mediums all have disclaimers that their work is for entertainment purposes only." He poured Cindy and me fresh cups. "That's Law School 101, guys."

"Hey, one thing you're forgetting, Luke." The warm mist from the tea smelled of oranges.

"What's that?" He turned his attractively craggy face toward me.

"Delphina said Frank was going to die soon."

The chief turned to me, an idea brewing in his eyes.

"She was right."

Chapter Thirty-Eight

IF FRANK MARTINDALE'S DEATH WAS MURDER, IT WAS a very clever one. Because dependent on opiate pain-killers and alcohol, it wouldn't have taken much to push him over the edge. With a lot of free time I acted on something I should have done a long time ago. I decided to talk to Frank's nearest neighbor, the woman who adopted his cat, Teddy.

Ann-Marie Gilderman's family went all the way back to Dutch settlers who worked the land back in the 1700s. Those genes gave her clear blue eyes, a pleasant face, and a practical attitude. A sensible no-nonsense woman she'd been Frank's neighbor for twenty years. It soon became apparent to me that although she implied that she rarely saw him, the truth turned out to be far more complicated.

"He was a good neighbor," she told us. "Kept to himself."

That was the first nice thing anyone had said about Frank.

It seems they often shared conversations while taking out the trash, weed-whacking along their shared fence, or watching the antics of their cats. This widow knew Frank could be a little "slippery" about money, her late husband had warned her, but that never came up between them.

Not sure how to approach getting the dirt on Frank, I simply decided to tell her how his death upset me and all about my Christmas wish on YouTube.

"Of course you feel terrible," she agreed sympathetically as she poured me another cup of tea. "Who wouldn't? But I've lived long enough not to be surprised by anything anymore." She repositioned a book on the small table next to her. The inside of her home, painted in soft pastels and filled with plants, books, and artwork, felt calm and safe. We sat in a cupola with large windows on all sides, where geraniums and a Christmas cactus flowered in greedy abandon overlooking an icy garden.

I tiptoed around the next few questions about his many lawsuits.

"That's the way he got his jollies," Ann-Marie colorfully explained. "Frank sat around all year collecting disability payments for his on-the-job back injury. He had too much time on his hands. Too much time is the devil's playground."

"So, because of his situation he sued people or tricked them out of their money?"

"I don't think Frank thought of it like that," she explained, trying to put her thoughts into words. "To him it was a way to have fun. Frank liked to cause a bit of trouble, stir the pot up." A fond smile gentled her face.

As a target of Frank's and an example of stirring the pot, I didn't see how she calmly sat there and justified his actions. He needlessly and willfully hurt people.

When I questioned Ann-Marie about that aspect, she answered, "I'm not saying I agreed with Frank, only that I understand what drove him to it. He was an angry person, angry at his life but not willing to change it. Men need some kind of work to do each day. Frank had been a roofer and skilled carpenter. After his fall he wasn't able to lift his arms past his shoulders. Some days his back pain was so bad he'd sit in that chair all day—then other times you wouldn't know anything was wrong with him. He never knew what kind of day he faced until he got out of bed."

With her careful explanation I started to understand Frank Martindale a bit. "Chronic pain is very debilitating, both mentally and physically," I agreed.

"Very debilitating. Many a night I brought him a hot meal, so he didn't have to eat leftover pizza."

That might be the reason his front door was unlocked the night he died. After Pinky left, if Frank went back to his chair without locking the door, he wouldn't want to get up again. Then a simple miscalculation—too much whiskey and too many prescription pills—depressed his breathing and he died.

Simple and sad and all too common these days.

My other scenario about unknown killers sneaking into the house sounded far-fetched.

A few sunbeams fought through the clouds and shone into the room, making me forget for a moment the cold winter outside. How inviting this space was. I wondered how often Frank came over, or Ann-Marie visited him.

"By the way, Frank liked you, Dr. Turner. He thought you were an excellent veterinarian." Ann-Marie smiled and reached over to pet Teddy, who was curled up on the sofa next to another sleeping cat. "Please don't take his actions personally."

Anger flared in me then slowly died down. I was

about to tell her thank you when she added something even worse.

"You know, he only wanted a discount on his bill."

———

While Ann-Marie reminisced, I fumed.

"His favorite of all my recipes was prune-stuffed pork loin. I'd prepare it over at his place and we'd sit together and watch our programs. Once the dishes were done, I'd make him comfortable and help him take his medication."

"What do you mean," I asked, "help him take his medicine?"

My question seemed to annoy her. Ann-Marie's blue eyes shifted and her lips pinched in disapproval. "Frank found it hard to swallow large pills or capsules. I'd open them up and put them in his drink for him."

Astonished, I realized it was the perfect way to commit a murder.

"He couldn't do it himself?"

Wrinkles stood out around her lips, as if it hurt her to divulge any additional information. "His back and spine were damaged in the fall. Both shoulders and hands sometimes ached and tingled, depending on his activity level. On bad days he'd keep dropping his medication."

That might account for all the pills scattered around his recliner.

"Every night I picked up five or six pills and put them in the bowl next to this chair for later. We knew which was which by looking at them."

Every night? I looked more carefully at the woman sitting opposite me, attractive in a crisp white blouse and plaid skirt. Maybe the widow and the bachelor had a deeper relationship than they let on. Her white shirt gleamed in the sunlight. White enough to remind Pinky of an angel?

Ann-Marie paused. "Frank always predicted one day Dutch Schultz would make him rich. Guess he was wrong."

"What about Dutch Schultz?"

———

Half an hour later Ann-Marie and I still sat in her cupola plant room. I was getting a fast update about one of the biggest treasure hunts on the Eastern Seaboard—the millions of dollars' worth of gold coins, jewelry, money, or whatever the famous gangster Dutch Schultz hid somewhere outside of Phoenicia, New York, back in the 1930s.

"Phoenicia is right around the corner from here," I said.

She stared at me when I said the obvious.

"Frank told you he had a copy of the map?"

"So he said." Ann-Marie smoothed down her skirt with chapped hands. "But I took it as another one of his schemes. If he knew where the treasure was, he would have dug it up himself, believe me."

That seemed obvious. So Frank was running a treasure map scam. I wondered who fell for it? When I asked my hostess, she abruptly stood up.

"I have no idea." Ann-Marie firmly led me to the front door. "But there are plenty of suckers out there now, aren't there? Thank you, Doctor, for coming by."

———

Still in the driveway, I called Cindy from the truck and told her about Dutch Schultz. "What do you think?" Ann-Marie continued watching me from behind her parlor curtain. She didn't care that I saw her. My gut told me if I wasn't her veterinarian, this lady would have pulled out a shotgun and ordered me off her property.

My conversation with Ann-Marie tired me out. She radiated an unusual intensity, which I mentioned to Cindy.

"Strange lady" was her pithy comment.

"This whole Dutch Schultz thing sounds far-fetched, don't you think?" I backed the truck up and started back to the animal hospital.

"You might think so, but there are people digging up there near the Esopus River and outside Phoenicia all the time. It's a standing joke around these parts. Someone even made a television documentary about it."

As I got closer to my place, the trees lining the road were reduced to dark shadows blocking the weak winter sun. Ann-Marie had spun an intriguing tale. Was there really a treasure hidden in the Hudson Valley?

Might Frank have convinced someone too well? Enough to kill for it?

A treasure from the 1930s that involved gangsters,

deadly ambushes, and FBI car chases in the streets of New York City. It sounded so far-fetched I figured I'd call an impeccable source of knowledge, my Gramps.

Born and raised in the city, he was an amateur historian, especially knowledgeable of those very years. His father, my great-grandfather, had run an Irish pub in Brooklyn and during Prohibition dealt with the gangs that smuggled alcohol into the city. I wondered if he knew the story of Dutch Schultz and his buried millions.

"Of course I know about Dutch Schultz," he immediately answered when I finally got hold of him. "Vicious guy. You know, Dutch was a nickname—he was born Arthur Flegenheimer. Somebody been treasure-hunting up in Phoenicia?"

"How did you know that?" Often my Gramps astonished me.

"Katie, it's the only valuable thing Dutch left behind." After a deep breath, he continued. "That safe or iron box of his is supposed to be buried somewhere near you. But I doubt it's still there."

That confused me. "Everyone I talk to says the treasure has never been found."

He laughed and said, "There are also a million different stories about what happened to the map."

"My client, Frank Martindale, said he had the map."

"Him and a couple of hundred other people. It's more likely that the mob dug it up shortly after Dutch was murdered. They had to be pretty quiet about it. You may not realize it, but the IRS and the FBI were after Dutch for tax fraud. They wanted to confiscate whatever Dutch buried. Even back then, no one wanted to be targeted by the Feds."

"Well, that puts a damper on one motive for murder."

"What do you mean, Katie?"

When I told him about Frank and his Dutch Schultz map scam, Gramps chuckled.

"Glad to bring so much fun into your life," I said.

"Sorry, but a scam about Dutch's map...those have been around for years."

"Well, Frank had a bunch of irons in the fire, like nuisance lawsuits, trying to get discounts on bills and, of course, the map scam."

"Guys like him don't stop at one scam. He probably had a few running. You'd be surprised how many people fall for stunts like this. But, Katie, his luck might have run out."

"How so?"

"He's dead, isn't he? Maybe he scammed the wrong guy."

———

Gramps had a great idea, of course. I'd forgotten about Frank's victims—the people he'd sued or scammed. What if someone had a grudge against Frank and when he saw the YouTube video figured he could kill Frank and tie his death in to that? Eloise may not have been murdered. And Raeleen? Most likely her death had nothing to do with Eloise and Frank.

Back to square one. All these permutations were too much for my brain and did nothing to help solve Raeleen's murder.

Fighting off another headache, I sat in silence, my eyes closed. I visualized spider webs. Spun of almost transparent threads the net the spider creates grows larger and larger, ensnaring any that come too close—an indiscriminate trap. Each victim held by only a few interconnected silken threads. Were our three deaths random events, or did a hidden spider cleverly weave an intricate web for all the victims to share?

Luke touched base with me a half an hour later. "I didn't want to discuss it in front of the chief," he began, "but one of my professors is friends with Frank's longtime lawyer. Maybe I can get an introduction."

"That's wonderful. Meanwhile, Mari and I want to interview some of her dog-breeding friends."

"Want to be there when I talk to the lawyer? I thought I'd invite him out for a drink, and you can be my date. Make it casual, less like an interrogation." The last part of the sentence he said pretty fast.

"Pretend date, you mean?"

After a big sigh for my benefit, he agreed.

"Make it soon if you can. I've got spiders on the brain, and it's getting creepy."

Chapter Thirty-Nine

JUST AS WE WERE CLOSING THE NEXT DAY, I GOT A CALL from Luke.

"Remember me talking about getting together with Frank's main lawyer?"

"Yes."

"Can you meet us by seven?" He named a popular after-work place in town. Considering it was 6:15, I had a quick change and drive in front of me. At warp speed I showered, dressed, and jumped into the truck, arriving only five minutes late.

A cheerful rumble of voices enveloped me when I entered That Place, a new casual dining place in town. A sign announced Happy Hour weekdays from 5:30 to 7:30. Luke waved at me from a table close by.

Kissing me on the cheek, he pulled out a chair and made the introduction.

"Kate, this is Anthony Lorretti."

A somewhat attractive but morose man with glasses and a worried look shook our hands. "Sorry to ask this, but you don't have a lawsuit pending with Frank, do you?"

"No, not that I know of."

"Good," he said, taking a quick sip of his martini. "You'd be amazed at how many people he antagonized and sued over the last ten or fifteen years."

While looking over the menu, I stole a glance at

Anthony. In his late thirties, early forties, he had gray patches under his eyes that indicated lack of sleep or something weighing on him. "Were you close to the deceased?" I asked. Each time I spoke to a lawyer I sounded like an episode of *Law & Order*.

That made him grimace. I realized that the martini in front of him wasn't his first of the night. When he spoke, however, his words were carefully measured.

"Frank was my client several times over the last few years. Occasionally, he hired other lawyers when I was too busy to take on another case. We had a professional relationship. As with most lawyers, I try to keep my professional and personal lives separate."

A lot of words, but no real answer. He'd skillfully bypassed my question.

When the waiter reappeared, we all ordered, and Luke brought up the reason for this meeting.

"First, let me say that Professor Brackenberg thinks very highly of you."

A slight smile crossed his face. "That's very kind of him. I clerked for him for three years. He was a truly dedicated judge."

"There has been some talk that Frank's death was not an accident. What are your feelings about that?"

"There certainly were enough people around who wanted to kill him. I eventually found him too unpleasant to deal with."

Luke agreed. "Law enforcement has several concerns."

He nodded as though concern was anticipated. "I spoke to a detective about this twice, I believe. The day they found him I was in court talking to Sal Tragari, the lawyer representing him in a nuisance suit. Ironically, we were both complaining about Frank, especially since he owed me quite a bit of money from the last case. When he didn't show up for court, Sal and I suggested a wellness check to the judge citing concerns about his health."

Luke persisted. "What about his health?"

"I believe he told me he had high blood pressure and kidney issues." Another sip of martini must have jogged his memory because he added, "Oh, and back pain. That dated from his disability case. He took painkillers for his back. I often wonder if all the pills contributed to his aggressive personality. Possibly to his death, also."

That's what my opinion was too. I'd seen it for myself the day Mari and I discovered his body. Frank mixed opiate medications with alcohol and easily may have accidentally overdosed. I kept quiet about Ann-Marie Gilderman's disturbing habit of helping Frank swallow his pills.

We stopped for a moment when the waiter brought our food and another round of drinks to the men.

"Was there any merit to the case?"

"You're training to be a lawyer, Luke. You know the answer to that." Anthony sounded slightly exasperated. "If you are arguing a case before a judge, it must have merit."

From the look on both men's faces I assumed that was a legal term for cover your ass. I took pity on them and changed the subject. "You look tired," I said sympathetically, hoping he'd continue talking.

"I've had to put up with countless questions from Sal.

He's pissed I dumped Frank on him. The judge ordered him temporarily to oversee Frank's estate until it goes to probate and an executor can be appointed. To get even with me, Sal roped me in to search for a will."

"And?" Luke asked.

"An initial computer search was negative, so we went to his home. The place is a hoarder's paradise. One trip over there and I gave up. An impossible task. Poor Sal." The mirth that came with the last statement negated the words.

―――――

After getting all the info we could, we settled into dinner and the evening passed very pleasantly. Luke and Anthony traded stories about law school, and with his third martini, the mildly inebriated lawyer revealed the names of several people entangled in lawsuits with Frank, all of which would most likely be dismissed. I was surprised to hear Raeleen's and Devin's names.

"Another small claims court case having to do with a car repair."

"But Devin is the mechanic, not Raeleen," I told him.

"True. But Raeleen came along when Frank and Devin were arguing about the bill, and she and Frank… exchanged words. It drew a crowd before the police were called. Frank sued for defamation of character." He practically choked with laughter. "Defamation of character. What a joke." He downed the rest of his drink.

Remarkably, Anthony hadn't brought up my wish.

I wondered if this lawyer even knew about it or he was simply too involved with his own problems to care.

Luke signaled for the check. "Can I drop you off anywhere?" he asked Anthony, concerned about letting this lawyer drink and drive.

"Thanks, but I'm Ubering it tonight. That way I can relax and not find myself in court with a DUI. Boy would the ex-wife love that. Last time I'll get married without a prenuptial agreement, but her family insisted. You know my ex-mother-in-law is a witch. A real broom-toting witch."

Another reason for those gray patches and lack of sleep. Alcohol could numb pain only for so long—then it became another problem on your list.

We waited outside with him until his drive came, then helped him into the back seat.

"Thanks for getting me out of the crappy condo," he said, still remarkably coherent. "The ex took the house." Anthony pointed at Luke and gave him a big wink. "Don't forget, prenup," he yelled out the window as the car sped away.

———

Deep in thought, Luke walked me to the truck. "What do you think all that was about?"

"He wants you to get a prenup. Other than that, I have no idea," I joked. "Something is bothering that guy, and getting loaded with strangers isn't the answer. Looks like Frank spread a little chaos wherever he went. The question is, did he go to his maker because it was his time or did he get a little help?"

"I'm still up in the air," Luke admitted.

"Me too." I gave him a kiss. "Let's float around in the air together."

―――――――――

I'd checked the weather forecast before going to sleep. The weathermen predicted some snow overnight. Not much accumulation, maybe two inches or less. When I woke up, I was surprised to see that almost six inches lay on the ground. The updated forecast expected three more inches over the next twelve hours. Snookered by the snow, I wandered into my living room and texted Cindy.

Just before I hit Send, I noticed the roar of a powerful truck and the scrape of a plow, which meant Pinky was plowing us out. Plenty of time for a second cup of coffee.

Almost immediately, Cindy called me back.

"Well, this is an unpleasant surprise," she began. "I bet half the appointments are going to cancel."

I lifted the curtain and took a quick look out the window. "My side of the hospital is clear, and Pinky's heading for the front of the building." The snowplow's exhaust created a fog-like effect as it crisscrossed the lot, pushing snow against the property line. Drifts were starting to pile up again. "You know, these flakes are really coming down."

"That's because the forecast has changed again. I

swear, the meteorologists should look out the window sometime."

Cindy always complained about the weather reports, but this time I think she was right.

What sounded like someone yelling in the background faded after a door slammed. "School just closed, and now they're saying total accumulations of nine to fifteen inches. I'm stuck here until the hubby clears the driveway."

"Need me to do anything?" I asked. Appointments weren't supposed to start until nine, and it was only seven fifteen, but some people weren't fazed by bad weather. Despite the school closures and lousy driving conditions, I'd still pull on my scrubs and be ready to work.

It was as if Cindy read my mind. "I'm going to access today's appointments on my computer here and see if anyone wants to reschedule."

"Will you coordinate with Mari or do you want me to?"

"No, I'll call all the staff and juggle everyone's schedule. It mostly depends on who decides to keep their appointment. I'm going to try and make it a half day, for safety's sake."

"Totally agree."

"Now," she said cheerfully, "aren't we lucky you live right at the hospital?"

"Yeah," I answered, looking at my one-room converted garage apartment. "I'm ecstatic."

When you've got a whole day to kick back, your computer searches tend to veer off in bizarre directions, which is how I found myself reading about a disturbance in Kingston, nearly three years ago. Someone had fired a bullet through the window of a psychic, breaking the glass. No one was injured, and there were no witnesses.

The police asked anyone with any information to call the hotline.

The name of the psychic who rented the space was Delphina.

A picture accompanied the story, which showed the victim speaking to a police officer while a young woman in a flowing lavender dress leans against a car. Standing next to the younger woman, who looks like Athenina, his arm around her shoulders, is Anthony Lorretti, Frank's lawyer.

What?

Suspicion turned into fact. With more digging, I confirmed that Athenina had married Anthony at the tender age of nineteen, despite a twenty-year age difference. Is this the wife who took all his money? Who married him without a prenuptial in place? Whose ex-mother-in-law was a real witch?

Public records nailed down the same facts. Interesting that Frank Martindale was suing his lawyer's ex-mother-in-law, Delphina. Anthony lied to us. He didn't give the case to Sal; he couldn't take the case because of a conflict of interest. Money seemed to be tight for him after the divorce. I wondered what else he might be hiding. Did

Frank run his Dutch Schultz scam past his cash-poor attorney?

Another suspect and another coincidence.

This place was lousy with them.

———

A surprise waited in my email when I checked it during lunch, a quite pleasant surprise. Friends in Rhinebeck, a longtime married couple, announced they were pregnant. They were devoted to their Papillon dogs, and I knew they wanted to expand their family to include human babies. I replied with my congratulations and a promise to visit in the New Year.

My happiness for them reminded me that most of my friends and classmates were getting married, starting families, or pursing graduate degrees. It felt as though their lives were rolling along, while my life stayed stuck in neutral. That vague restlessness that had been part of this holiday season remained. I wondered if this wild-goose chase of an investigation was my attempt at keeping occupied so I didn't have to focus on important decisions I needed to make.

The many loose ends in this investigation mirrored the loose ends in my personal life. My two picks for boyfriends had been disastrous—Jeremy, a trust fund baby who couldn't be trusted, and Luke, who still had a thing for his ex. The job I poured my heart into was only temporary. I had no home, no car, and no big bank account. And this Christmas my only constant, Gramps, was pushing me to forgive my father and embrace his new family—the longest and most complicated loose end of them all.

Chapter Forty

BECAUSE OF THE SNOWSTORM WE'D CANCELED AN entire day of clinics yesterday, which meant today we'd be playing catch-up.

"This is going to be a hard one," Mari warned me before I saw the next client. I took a quick look at the history. A seven-year-old mixed-breed dog with a lump on its back.

Now a lump can mean anything from an abscess to a fatty tumor called a lipoma to a nasty form of cancer. I was hoping to tell this concerned owner some good news.

"Oh," my assistant added, "our new intern is here, and she says she knows you."

———

The dog's name was Sugar, and the name fit. Big brown eyes and a sweet doggy smile couldn't stop you from focusing on the gigantic hump on her back worthy of Quasimodo, the fictional hunchback of Notre Dame.

"Mari, can we get a weight?" I asked. Although she was a medium-sized dog, the mass on her back probably made up about a quarter of her total body weight. Her owner, Gerald Nelson, an elderly gentleman, looked and sounded distressed. I encouraged him to sit down and tell me Sugar's medical history.

"She was fine up until about a year ago," he told me. "This lump on her back was about the size of a plum, so I took her to our vet. They said to watch it, that it probably was benign. If I wanted it removed, they would do that, too."

So far so good, although I made a note of the lack of any biopsy.

"Then my wife got sick, and between taking her to the doctor's and chemotherapy, I didn't pay as much attention as I should have. Sugar's lump kept getting bigger and bigger, but she seemed fine. Eating and everything. But my wife went downhill."

I could only imagine how stressful that situation must have been and exhausting, both mentally and physically.

"When I lost my wife, I didn't want to lose our dog, too. But now...I know it's getting harder for her to walk with that thing on her back." His worried face stared at me, hoping I might have a miraculous answer.

I wish I did.

"Mari, let's watch her walk around the exam room."

Sugar did her best, but the weight of the mass put her off balance. Not to mention the strain it caused to her kidneys, heart, lungs, and joints.

"Mr. Nelson, I'd like to take an X-ray and run some blood tests before I suggest any surgery," I told him. "I should have some answers in about half an hour. Can you wait in reception? Cindy can get you a cup of tea or coffee, if you'd like."

Taking his arm, I shepherded him out to reception and handed him off to Cindy for safekeeping. Sometimes we had to keep an eye on our human clients as well as our animal patients.

In the treatment room, we took bloods and started running our preliminary tests, as well as preparing a sample for the regular laboratory. A quick X-ray on our digital machine gave me good news.

"Looks like no metastasis to the lungs, and the mass itself is very well defined." Mari nodded as she set up a slide of the needle biopsy I'd taken. Full of adipose or fat tissue, all signs were pointing to a fatty tumor of impressive size.

Oddly enough, early on in my career I'd assisted in the removal of a few large masses like this. One of our surgeons in Long Island had been board-certified, and I often worked with him on some unusual cases.

However, this time I was going to suggest we refer Sugar to a veterinary surgical team, about forty miles from us.

"I want you to do the surgery, Dr. Kate," Mr. Nelson said after I explained my treatment recommendation. "There's no way I can drive that far, and I trust you." Cindy had let me know the owner was on a fixed income and couldn't afford a large bill. He was too proud to talk about that.

————

Back in the treatment room, I explained my dilemma to Mari. But then a Christmas miracle walked through the door.

"Dr. Kate."

Strong hands grasped mine. Sure enough, this was my Juliet, one of the techs I had worked with on Long Island. "What are you doing up here?" I asked her.

"I'm in pre-vet," she explained. "Everyone said I should go to vet school, so here I am." Her big smile lit up the room, but it was her surgical skills I remembered. As a licensed veterinary technician with a surgical interest, she had assisted two board-certified surgeons five days a week for five years. If anyone could help me with our patient, she could.

Mari brought Sugar out to show her.

"Still have an active license?" I asked her.

"Yes. In fact, I work per diem during school holidays. My wife is a chef in Rhinebeck. She's the one who encouraged me to go back to school."

Sugar sat down, then slid to the floor to take the weight off her back legs. Juliet bent down to pet her. Her talented fingers palpated the mass, following the margins in a large circle.

Our eyes met.

"That's a pretty big one," she commented. "Maybe eight to ten pounds. Lipoma?"

"Yeah, about ninety-eight percent sure," I said.

"I've seen bigger, though. The largest one we removed was twenty-two pounds," she proudly announced. "Huge Labrador-Shepherd mix."

"Want to help me with this one?" I asked.

Her smile got bigger. "Cool."

It's always nice to be able to do something that changes a life for the better. After I spoke to Mr. Nelson, he agreed to leave Sugar with us so we could monitor her before the surgery. I still needed the lab to confirm her blood tests, and we had to prepare our surgical suite with the multiple surgical packs we'd require during this surgery. It wasn't so much the complexity of the procedure as maneuvering the chunk of fatty tissue and cauterizing all the blood vessels. Monitoring this middle-aged dog's fluids and electrolyte balance both during and after surgery was vital.

Unbeknownst to me, Juliet called in her markers. One of the board-certified surgeons she'd worked with, Keith, volunteered his time to us. As payment, Oak Falls Animal Hospital had to take him and his wife out to dinner. That's when I learned Juliet's wife was head chef in a rather famous restaurant.

Juliet never bragged about anything.

———

The look on Mr. Nelson's face when his Sugar walked to him the day after surgery lifted all our hearts. Free of the ungainly tumor, she had a spring in her step as well as almost one hundred stitches on her back. Suture removal certainly would be fun.

"Jingle Bells" began playing again over the sound system, and when Sugar woofed along, all of us joined in for a couple of woofs together.

———

At dinner, Keith Schraeder, our hero veterinary surgeon, regaled us all with multiple crazy surgery stories, the more gruesome and outlandish the better. Since nothing can rock the stomachs of workers in the veterinary field, we tackled our delicious food with gusto, warmed by the pleasure of a simple good deed. I'd invited Mari as my plus one, while Juliet's wife made an appearance at the table with a special dessert made just for us.

Stuffed to the max, I listened to the happy, excited voices around me.

"Juliet and Keith volunteered at a spay and neuter clinic in Mexico last spring," Keith's wife told us. "I work with quite a few groups who bring veterinary care to countries in need, so I helped coordinate with the local authorities and set up our surgical stations. Kate, you should join us."

Keith gave his wife a hug. "Lynn speaks fluent Spanish. We couldn't do it without her. "

"To Lynn." Juliet gave her a round of applause.

"I'm glad you called us, Juliet," Keith said. "The vascular pattern turned out to be quite unusual. Want to help me write it up for one of the journals?"

"Sure." Her broad smile mirrored Keith's grin.

"Spoiler. He would have done it even without the dinner," his wife revealed. "Now you know his secret. He's just an old softy."

In the glow of the candlelight, I stood up. "First, let me raise a toast to both our Christmas angels, Keith and Juliet. You made Mr. Nelson a very happy man today," I said. "In addition, let's celebrate Juliet's decision to take the plunge and go to vet school. You're going to make a great doctor."

We all raised our glasses. The crisp pings of glass touching glass made a celebratory sound.

In that moment of friendship and camaraderie I realized how much this murder investigation and the YouTube video scandal had taken out of me.

Someone had hijacked my life.

Enough was enough.

Chapter Forty-One

DRIVING BACK FROM A WEEKEND RUN TO THE STORE, I received a text from Ashley at Maple Grove Farms. Lobo had escaped through a loose gate. She'd alerted all her neighbors around her but wanted to know if I had any suggestions on how to get him back. I made a quick detour and told her I'd be there in ten minutes.

Mari rolled in a few minutes after me.

My plan was simple. Trap him with love.

Lobo loved Sweet Potato, the tranquil bay mare who was his preferred companion. Using her as bait, Mari and I planned to guide the mustang home.

"I saddled her up, but my knee still isn't flexible enough to ride," Ashley told me. "Besides, when he sees someone coming on horseback he goes on alert."

For most of his life people meant trouble. I understood how he felt. "Let's try a soft approach first. Once we've found him, Mari and I will walk both horses home."

I wanted to get started right away, so I tied my veterinary emergency backpack behind the saddle. A free-roaming horse up here faced all kinds of danger. Any large moving object might be mistaken for a bear or buck, and many folks shoot first and ask questions later.

The woods behind the farm were thick with broken underbrush, crisscrossed by old hiking and hunting trails. Not very appealing to a large horse. With brambles and downed tree limbs everywhere, I bet he'd stick to the edge of the woods, near the pasture line. We stuffed our jacket pockets with extra leads, halters, and a long lunge line, then walked Sweet Potato through the corral and out into the pasture. Securing her reins loosely over the Western-style saddle pommel, we led her by a lead rope clipped to her halter. A very gentle older horse, Sweet Potato nickered for treats. We decided to work that habit into our rescue plan.

We ventured in and out of the trees, the mare periodically nudging me with her muzzle. She could smell the horse goodies I carried, even stored in a ziplock bag. Somewhat familiar with the area, Mari weaved away from the field into cleared land deep in the woods.

"I can't see Ashley's place," I said after about a forty-minute walk.

Before we'd gotten off the main trail, I'd recognized the roof of the supermarket Raeleen had worked in poking up through the trees. Instead of moving closer to the road, we were moving away from it.

A flash of white ahead caught my eye. Whatever it was disappeared into the pines.

"Mari," I whispered. "I think he's just above us, moving parallel."

She casually scanned the tree line then agreed. "You're right. What do you want to do?"

We broke out of the trees and stood in a vast open

field. I needed to find a spot where we could trap him into holding still, calm enough to snap a lead rope on his halter, providing he hadn't scraped it off. After I explained my idea to Mari, she suggested we walk a little farther to where a cluster of apple trees created a small orchard, and a natural enclosed space.

"Where are we?" I asked her.

She glanced around. "I think it's an old abandoned homestead."

The dark woods encircled us. Without the mountains in view, my bearings were off.

"Well, let's divide and conquer. Once he comes to us, I'll handle Sweet Potato and you load Lobo up on treats. I bet he's hungry by now."

We leisurely strolled into the natural fruit-tree glade Mari had found. A few apples still clung forlornly to the leafless tree limbs. Sweet Potato saw them and nickered.

"That a girl," Mari said. "Tell him where the party is."

I almost laughed out loud envisioning the two horses having a frozen apple on a branch party. Still smiling, I was about to tell Mari when she held her finger up to her lips.

To my right Lobo slowly stepped into the cold sunlight.

———

It took some coaxing, but Lobo learned a valuable lesson. His barn and pasture were more comfortable than the icy woods. He tossed his blond mane and nuzzled Sweet

Potato, who seemed surprised to suddenly find him standing next to her. With a woven blue lead rope safely secured to his halter ring, we decided to circle back when Mari got a text.

"Oh, no. I've got to get home." Her voice sounded a little panicky.

"What's going on?"

"Lucy might be in labor. I left my friend Ted at the house with the dogs, and he says she's acting funny."

Although Mari had helped with many a dog whelping, it wasn't the same when it was your own dog.

"Take Sweet Potato and ride back," I told her. "Tell Ashley I'll follow with Lobo."

Mari had swung up and was already sitting in the saddle, scanning the horizon. "Okay. Want your backpack?"

"Sure."

She untied it and tossed it into my arms. "Have you got a cell signal?"

We had different service providers, and sometimes one phone worked better than the other. A quick look showed one bar. I held up one finger. "One bar. I'll be fine."

"I'm going to take a shortcut down by the road. Do you know your way back?"

"More or less," I said. "It's generally in that direction." I pointed off to the left. "I'm not going to take him near the road, though. He's spooked enough."

Sweet Potato whinnied in anticipation. With Mari on her back, she knew she was headed home.

"Okay. Keep the mountains above you and the road below you, and you'll be fine. There aren't many landmarks, I'm afraid. But most of the homes and the supermarket are near the road."

"Don't worry," I told her. "I'll call an Uber if I get lost."

She started to leave then stopped, puzzling Sweet Potato with the move. Her face backlit, she said, "I've got to tell you, Kate. Cindy told me not to but—it's important."

"What is it?"

"Devin's alibi for the night of Rae's murder, the mystery woman? It's Dina. He was with Luke's old girlfriend."

"Does Luke know?"

"I think so. But there's still two hours unaccounted for."

With that, Mari rode off, waving her hand.

It took a few minutes to process, but I realized the clues had been there all along.

And I bet Luke had suspected it too.

———

My plan of following our tracks back proved impossible. We ran into trouble pretty quickly after we moved from open field to forest.

The mustang constantly ducked his head to avoid the trees, but I noticed his sides were getting scraped up from low-hanging branches.

Trying to avoid being cut up by brambles and thorns, I decided to try a path that appeared to go in the right direction. Just large enough for one vehicle, it looked like an old logging trail. Overhead the sun broke out and warmed us up, a nice break from the damp, dark woods. Slush squished under my boots.

"Hey, can I help you?" a male voice called out from the clearing in front of me.

Lobo dug in and stood like a rock, ears flicking. Around the corner came a familiar face.

"What are you doing here?" I asked Devin. After giving Lobo a reassuring pat on the neck, I moved forward.

Raeleen's ex-boyfriend and Dina's current fellow fell in alongside me. "I'm draining the water pipes at my dad's hunting cabin. Usually it's winterized by now, but I haven't had much extra time to help him. How about yourself and your friend here?" Devin glanced at the horse then concentrated on me.

"Lobo made a break for it. We're heading back to his barn."

"A freedom run. I tried it, Lobo—it doesn't work." Glum for an instant, he shook it off and grinned.

Being the recipient of his high-powered smile and striking good looks, I could see how Greta and Raeleen and now Dina had fallen for him. He didn't really have to try. Women probably tripped over themselves to get his attention. Just looking great didn't do it for me anymore. I'd spent too much time mooning over those types in high school. Been there. Done that. Over it.

We kept on walking, happy not to be fighting with the forest. All I wanted was to keep going until safely back at the barn. And safely away from Devin.

He pulled the knit cap off that covered his thick, dark hair. "Is this the mustang from Maple Grove Farms? Raeleen showed me a picture of him. She wanted all mustangs to run free."

"That's the ultimate goal."

By now we were halfway across the clearing. A small cabin sat tucked into the woods, a beat-up old Land Rover parked in front. On the roof rack some duffel bags were secured with bungee cords, a tarp half covering them. "Packing up? Don't let us stop you."

He turned and noticed the tarp hanging loose.

"Yeah. I decided to take a little break. Too many memories there. Raeleen and me used to come up here and fool around after school." To my surprise he took a small bottle of whiskey out of his coat pocket and took a slug. "Want some? Keeps the cold away."

The sudden movement made Lobo halt. I felt his tension, muscles bunching up across his withers. I'd only seen good boy Devin up to now at the animal hospital and at his workplace. Now was I catching a glimpse of his flip side?

"No, thanks. I'm okay." The sun continued to come out from behind puffy clouds making it a glorious winter day. Picking a treat from my pocket, I calmed the wary horse.

"Hey," Devin said, excitedly. "Maybe you should rest him here for a bit, tie him up to the deck railing. We could go inside and fool around a little. You know—give the cabin a real send-off."

I almost laughed in his face. "Devin, that's not going to happen," I assured him.

"We don't have to do anything. I'd just like some

company. I hate being alone, you know. Look, a guy's got to try." With his eyes on both of us he added, "My buddies are avoiding me. They give me this funny look. Even my boss thinks I killed Rae for the money." He put his hand on Lobo's halter. "What about that famous wish you made? Feeling a little guilty yourself, Doc?"

This time I forced myself to smile. Devin was making me feel something, all right, but it wasn't guilt. He had me worried.

"Sorry, got to return a horse. See you," I told him and firmly moved Lobo in place behind me. The mustang danced a bit to the side then settled in as we made our way out of the clearing and continued on the logging road. Devin stood in front of his cabin, the sunlight glancing off the tin roof.

About ten minutes in we were moving through dense underbrush. The path had disappeared. Dodging branches, I slowed Lobo down. That uncomfortable encounter with Raeleen's ex disturbed me. I remembered too late the chief questioning the validity of this guy's alibi.

The forest loomed over us, around us and in all directions. Nothing on this trail seemed familiar.

A branch cracked and Lobo stopped again. I clucked my tongue, urging him forward. "Come on, boy. I'll get you out of this soon." It was slow going. The path at one time may have been maintained; however, it hadn't been kept up. Erosion had dislodged some large rocks in our way, causing a few detours. Problem was, I had no mountains or road to orient me. I checked my phone. No bars. No signal.

Another branch behind us snapped. Lobo's ears again twitched, eyes alert.

A dark figure wearing a knit cap appeared. "Sorry to frighten you," Devin said. "But this trail dead-ends. You should have turned off at the fork back there. If you want, I'll take you down toward the fields."

"I didn't see any turnoff," I told him.

"Musta missed it. Want me to show you?" This time when he reached for Lobo's halter, the horse jerked away from him.

"Let go of that halter," I ordered. "You're scaring him."

His hands opened in a conciliatory gesture. "Sorry. Sorry. I guess I've been celebrating a little too much. It's not every day you get a million bucks handed to you."

Over someone's dead body, I thought.

"Follow me and I'll lead you to the right trail. Then I'm going back to the cabin and sleep this off."

My instincts warned me to stay alert. What if he led us farther into the woods? I wished I'd taken my Swiss Army Knife out of my backpack or the pepper spray Gramps insisted I carry. Then again, wishes are what had gotten me here in the first place.

He plunged a bit ahead of us before holding both hands up to stop.

"Here it is."

In front of us I saw a path winding through the woods, the entrance partially hidden by a large oak. "Where exactly are we?" I asked him, still unsure if I should trust him. I maneuvered Lobo between us.

"It's either the Gilderman property or Rieven Acres,

I'm not sure. You can't tell till you get past here and out into the clearing. Some of these woods connect up weird."

"Okay. That doesn't help."

He pulled his knit cap off again and rubbed his hair back with a nervous gesture, black eyes glittering. With his body he blocked the trail. "Sorry about this, Doc," he said. "Rae shouldn't have told me about all that money."

Chapter Forty-Two

ONCE HE STARTED TALKING ABOUT RAELEEN AND HER untimely death, he couldn't stop. For the second time this month a man broke down and cried in front of me.

Devin pressed his face against Lobo's neck, the mustang still, sensing no threat. "What am I going to do without her? I'll just screw up like I always do. Already messed up." Eyes wet with tears, he turned away and stared out into the forest. Then he kissed the horse and rubbed his nose.

Now I saw why Raeleen loved him so much.

⸻

For the next ten minutes, Devin skillfully guided us until the main trail came into view. A lone pine soared high into the sky. Beyond it spread a vast flat field, which gradually sloped down toward the road. "Okay. This is it. Keep going straight out into the field. You'll see the road. Then turn left and walk parallel to the highway, and Maple Grove Farm is no more than a twenty-minute walk. You've got some stone walls to detour around, but it shouldn't be too bad."

Lobo and I felt the waning sunshine on our backs. Snow dripped off the nearby branches. That's when I noticed the big horse was favoring his left front hoof again, the same one I'd removed a stone from a few days ago.

"How close are we to the road?" I asked him.

"Maybe ten minutes. Something wrong with Lobo?"

"He's come up lame." I took out my phone. No bars and dead as a doornail.

"Can I use your phone, please?"

"Sure," he said. Devin reached into his pocket, then patted his jacket. "Left it at the cabin."

Lobo snorted and pawed the ground.

"Devin, do us a favor, please. Go back to the cabin and call Maple Grove Farm. Tell Ashley to have someone drive the horse trailer over and pick us up. Lobo and I will wait in the nearest driveway."

"No problem. We have four bars at the cabin. I'll call and then come back and keep you company if you want. Sun's going to be setting soon."

"Bring a couple of flashlights," I told him. "Will you be able to find us?"

"Sure. Straight down from landmark pine. Look for a lady and a horse." He turned toward the woods.

"Wait. Which way again?"

"Straight ahead. You'll hear the road." He pointed down the hill. "You know it won't be the same if these fields are sold off. City people are gobbling up everything. Some people just don't care."

As the coming sunset changed the sky to pink and gold above the dark blue mountains, I sympathized with him.

He waved goodbye before calling over his shoulder. "Hey, Doc. I'm not as big a jerk as you think I am."

———

While Lobo and I slowly started down the hill, I told the horse all my problems. He nodded sagely, periodically blowing warm breath into the cold air. Definitely on his way to being gentled, he trusted me.

I only trusted one person unconditionally, and that was Gramps. Maybe my New Year's resolution should be to trust a little more.

"What do you think, Lobo?"

If he knew the answer, he kept it to himself.

A stumble along the path made me glad I decided to trailer him back. Another five minutes walking and the outline of a roof sticking out of the trees became cause to celebrate. In the distance the faint sound of cars and trucks whooshing by confirmed we were nearing the road.

The smell of wood smoke as we passed some saplings meant civilization.

I slipped off my backpack and tied Lobo to a tree. Before the light faded, I wanted to see that hoof. Sure enough, a stone had wedged itself under his slightly loose horseshoe. I'd tell Ashley to get a farrier over as soon as possible. Meanwhile I used a trick with my trusty Swiss Army Knife, using the blunted side of the can opener and my fingernail to pop the stone out.

Faint trails of pink and gold briefly lit up the mountain before the sun made its final bow.

We continued on our way, a vast improvement in his gait. "Snow feels good on that I'll bet," I told the mustang as we approached the back of a house. I saw the faint outline of raised beds and someone in a heavy winter coat with a hood throwing trash into a metal barrel, flames and ash flying up with each new load. The flames worried Lobo who reacted by shying away. He backed up, knocking one of the plastic garbage bins on the ground.

"Easy boy," I said.

The man looked up, startled. "Get that horse off my property."

"Sorry. He's come up lame. Can we wait for our trailer in your driveway?"

Abruptly, he moved away from the fire. We recognized each other at the same time.

"Joe?" I asked. "Is that you?"

When he moved toward us, the motion detector light flickered on, casting a bright circle. Lobo turned his head away from the glare.

"Dr. Turner? I didn't know you had a horse."

The ashes from the fire lifted into the air as a breeze stirred. I moved Lobo back, away from the sparks, and tied him to a garden fencepost.

"Let me tamp that down. Not supposed to be windy tonight." He went back over to the fire and pressed a metal shovel down into the flames. "Trying to burn the stuff that's left."

Something glittered in the rubbish by Lobo's hoof. Instinctively, I bent down and picked it up. I recognized the gilt edges of a Christmas card and the gold collars on the cat and dog waiting for Santa Claus.

Then the light blinked out.

Joe's friendly voice said, "Don't worry. It comes back on in a minute."

Before he finished the sentence, the motion detector light shone again, too soon for me to hide the card from him.

"Sorry," I said, moving closer to Lobo. "He knocked over your trash. Can I help you pick it up?"

Our eyes met and he knew. Still affable, he offered an explanation. "Guess you recognized the Christmas card. Me and my fishing buddies mailed it to you for a joke. Sorry about that."

I pretended to believe him.

"Well, it wasn't funny. Just burn the darn thing, will you?" With my other hand I fished my dead phone out of my pocket and texted Luke. It didn't go through, but Joe didn't know that.

With a confident gesture, I handed him the card. "Maybe I should wait for the horse trailer somewhere else," I told him, my voice huffy with anger. Without looking I turned my back to him and headed for the woodpile, unzipping my backpack as I went, searching for the pepper spray.

The light turned off again. My boot banged into something hard. I reached my hand out to stop from falling.

"Ouch." I'd hit a log anchoring the tarp, slightly dislodging it. Another breeze caught the ragged plastic edge and lifted it up, scattering snow on the uncovered logs and all over my coat. That's when I knew. Joe had put a log in his mother's path and disabled the motion detector light. Pinky told the chief that Eloise was lying in the dark when he found her. When he got out of his truck to check her, the motion detector light didn't come on. He used his plowing headlights to chase away the darkness until the police arrived.

My anger rose picturing Eloise freezing in the night.

"You killed your own mother?" I screamed at him. Lobo reacted, his ears twitching.

"What are you talking about, Dr. Turner? Maybe you should come inside and sit down."

He made a move toward me.

I backed away. "I'll bet she was still alive after she fell. Down on the ground fighting for her life."

His chuckle chilled. "Yeah. The old bitch wouldn't cooperate and die. Made me wait out here for three hours till she finally shut up."

The son had killed his mother, while I would gladly have moved heaven and earth to see my mom once again.

The screen door that led to the sleeping porch rattled. Generations had slept there, seeking cooler air in the heat of the summer. The motive was there all the time. The house.

"Your mom knew you would sell this place as soon as she died, right, Joe?" His eyes narrowed. "She decided to change her will and donate it to the historical society. Babs was right."

His movements choppy, he paced back and forth in the snow. "Haven't got much time. Think. Think." Eyes darting back and forth, they suddenly stopped. He stared at Lobo.

"Go get the horse. Then lie down on the ground." He pulled out a gun and pointed it at my chest.

"Smart. Make them think the horse did it." I stood my ground. "Forget it. You'll have to shoot me. How will you explain that?"

He stared at me with a nasty grin. "I'll say I was aiming for the horse. Of course, that means I've got to shoot him, you know. To make it look good." His gun hand shifted toward Lobo."

"Is that what you did to Raeleen?" Slowly, I took a few steps back. I noticed Lobo nibbling away at his rope lead.

Joe followed me, keeping his distance. "Hey, I didn't expect her to be armed. I tried to jump her but she musta heard me. Turned around with a gun in her hand. We fought and it went off. It was an accident."

"You forget the shot to her head, Joe."

"Oops. My bad."

The overhead light blinked off again, and I made a dash toward the mustang.

"Good," he told me when it came back on. "Just where I want you."

Dead stalks poking up through the snow in the perennial garden Eloise had planted waved in the wind. No cars or trucks shone their headlights on the road behind us. I moved toward Lobo, now free from his lead.

"So how did you kill Frank?" I asked, stalling for time.

His eyes widened. "I didn't kill Frank. That's the beauty of it. After he died, mom called me up and said everyone was talking about your wish. She said she'd made an appointment with her lawyer to change her will, just in case she was next. That's when she mentioned donating the house and land." The veneer of affability cracked. "I'd get *NOTHING*. I hauled her around every Sunday for *NOTHING*? Listened to her yacking with her friends who kept boasting about their kids and their big cars and jobs. Like it made them better than me." Worked up, he revealed the narcissist hiding inside, who rationalized everything in terms of himself.

"You fooled me," I admitted. "You fooled me right up to the end."

"Shut up. Pretty soon I'll be out of here. That city fellow next door offered me a cash deal for way more than this place is worth. As is. Signing the papers tomorrow, then it's off to Belize." He gestured with the gun for me to move. "Sorry you won't be around to join me." Flames licked the edges of the burning trash barrel, their sparks reflecting off the barrel of Rae's gun.

It wasn't a fair fight.

Joe had a gun and a good sixty or seventy pounds on me.

I had a knapsack and a lame horse.

Like I said, it wasn't a fair fight. I planned to beat the crap out of him and wrap him up like a Christmas present.

Chapter Forty-Three

THE WIND SWIRLED AND THE FLAMES DANCED, RIBbons of fire twirling in different directions.

"Keep moving," Joe ordered, gesturing toward Lobo, who stared back at him. The horse's dilated pupils turned his blue eyes black.

Slowly, I did as I was told, head down, pretending to obey. My real goal was to get into a position to kick the gun out of his hand.

"If I had more time, you and me—"

My foot crunched his hand in mid-sentence. The gun dropped and he yowled, bent fingers cradling his right arm. I followed up with a kick to the groin, but he surprised me and grabbed my foot.

I flung myself backward, pulling him along, hands and fingers dug deep into his coat.

The landing knocked the wind out of me. Now on top, Joe grabbed me by the shoulders and started pounding my head into the ground.

My ears rang, and shards of ice cut my skin. Despite his weight I rolled back and forth trying to dislodge him, but he stuck like a bug. He grinned like a demon as he kept me pinned. So I went for his eyes.

Do it fast, my instructor had said. As my thumbs found their mark, he screamed and let go. I scrambled away, searching for Raeleen's gun. I found it mixed in with the debris, the crumbled Christmas card nearby.

Lobo stood still, his lead rope chewed in half, no longer tied up. Nothing was holding him back. Instead he snorted and dug his injured hoof into the ground, head tossing back and forth.

Joe's cries changed to moans, his breathing ragged. "My chest hurts. Give me your hand."

He lay on the ground, face twisted in pain. Something that psychic, Delphina, had said rumbled in my memory: "Remember to take the hand of your enemy."

"Please," he pleaded, his face turning red, a small smear of blood in the corner of one eye. "Can't catch my breath."

Keeping the gun in my right hand, I reached down with my left. "Onto your knees, and stay there."

If he was going to try something, he'd do it now. One knee hit the ground before he lunged at me.

Anticipating his move, I let go, prepared to shoot if I had to. That's when a horse head leaned over and clamped his teeth on Joe's back. Lobo jerked him sideways by his coat and pushed him into a raised bed of rose canes.

Howling in pain, his face contorted in anger, Joe struggled to his feet. Lobo swung his massive head flat against Joe's skull like a golf club hitting a ball and got a hole in one.

———

Duct tape from my backpack did a good job of wrapping up this killer. Lobo whinnied, his eyes focused on the trees above. In the distance a flashlight moved steadily closer, the beam moving up and down as Devin strode toward us.

I used his phone to call 911. Joe was lucky he couldn't move. I had to stop Devin from throwing him into the flames with the rest of the garbage.

The murders had been solved.

My fourth wish had come true.

Chapter Forty-Four

CHIEF GARCIA AND THE FBI GANG WERE QUICK TO take Joe Rieven into custody. The proximity of the arrest date to Christmas definitely sped things along.

My statement and time at the police station went by just as quickly. It seems that surrounded by an audience Joe started spilling his guts and even implicated himself in the long-ago death of his younger sibling. With a confession, the murder weapon, and his fingerprints all putting him in the vicinity of the supermarket the night of Raeleen's death, law enforcement felt optimistic on at least one conviction.

Of course, this meant the original wish didn't work. Soon after Joe's arrest I received an email from lawyer J. D. Dowd, revoking the unsigned contract for my story, and wishing me a very merry holiday season.

I didn't bother mentioning Delphina's prophetic words to anyone.

With Joe's confession, Pinky's customers scrambled to get him back. Bearing no hard feelings toward any of them, he agreed. But Pinky surprised Cindy by shyly accepting her Christmas dinner invitation and asking if he could bring Beth Orstead along.

Lobo seemed invigorated by our little adventure and let Ashley slip a halter on him and groom him with no fuss at all.

By chance a second cousin of Frank Martindale's was

found, not in California, but in High Falls, just down the road. A farmer, he was delighted to inherit anything.

Disgusted with Dina's lies, Luke kicked her out of his house and dumped her at her mother's place. Then he changed all the locks.

Mari's dog, Lucy, didn't whelp that day. She and her friends considered it a good dry run.

And Devin—well, Devin surprised us. Massive publicity after the arrest focused on the boyfriend, unjustly accused. Being photogenic didn't hurt either. Devin announced that he would split his insurance money three ways, between himself, Raeleen's family, and LARN, the animal rights group. That's what Raeleen would have wanted, he said. Next, he broke up with both Dina and Greta and went back to work repairing cars at Mr. Fix-it's.

Of course, he couldn't escape fame, now that he had become an internet sensation. Thanks to all the publicity and hunky photographs, Devin received offers of marriage on a daily basis. Because of his generosity to LARN, a famous actress, very active in the ethical treatment of animals movement, invited him to walk the Hollywood red carpet with her—all expenses paid.

No dummy, Devin accepted, he said, because Raeleen would have loved it.

———

On Christmas Eve I woke up early. The forecast was clear with snow later that day. Gramps was expecting me any time today. He had reservations at our favorite neighborhood restaurant, a short walk or cab ride from his place. Then, the following morning, we'd both brave the gauntlet and drive over to my father's home out on Long Island. We planned to be there no later than two with Christmas dinner around three o'clock. If all went well, we would stay the night.

Being a partner in a surgical practice had obviously been good to my dad.

With the whole day ahead of me, I took a long shower and did all those things I'd put off—polished my nails, blow-dried my hair, and generally prepared myself for intense scrutiny.

Nervous energy aside, I'd hung all my clothes on hangers in zippered garment bags fresh from the dry cleaner, to avoid any animal hair issues. My boots were polished, and the presents wrapped. Buddy was going to board with Mari and her dogs for the few days I'd be gone. Since the animal hospital was closed for Christmas, any clients in need of care were being sent to the emergency clinic. Cindy would be handling the hospital email, coordinating medicine refills, and answering non-medical questions. I'd be handling the veterinary part through text or email.

As I worked my way through today's emails and notes, I happily checked each one off the list. Cindy and I conferred on one issue and I was done.

"Isn't it getting late?" she asked.

"I'm leaving in a few minutes. Have a wonderful Christmas."

"You too. Safe travels and don't worry! Things will go great."

Confident and proud of myself for pulling everything together, I took out the garbage and unplugged the toaster. As I crossed the final item off my checklist, the phone rang.

"Mari, I was just going to call you," I said. "Can I drop Buddy off?"

"Ahh, I've got a slight problem."

———

Turns out that Lucy, Mari's pregnant Rottweiller, did decide to have her puppies early. We'd already ultrasounded her and knew she had seven pups. She'd delivered her first puppy four hours ago, and now there were six healthy puppies. Only one to go. Rottweillers are big dogs with big heads, but they usually whelp without issues. After two hours with no baby, my assistant started to worry.

"Go," she said to me. "You're supposed to have left by now. Gramps is waiting for you."

"I'm not going to leave until I'm sure Lucy is okay," I told her. "Can you bring the whole gang over here?"

"Be there in twenty minutes."

———

Nineteen and a half minutes later, Mari pulled up in front of the hospital. I had carefully taken my traveling clothes off and put on a pair of scrubs. Mari brought Lucy in while I carried a basket full of puppies.

"Don't worry, Lucy. Your babies are right here." A

first-time mother, this anxious Rottie mommy let out a nervous whimper.

I secured the babies under a nice heat lamp set on low, and then we brought Lucy into X-ray. I wanted to make sure I knew where this last pup was and if it was viable before I gave her the oxytocin to stimulate contractions. While we waited for the digital X-ray to develop, I put some lubricant on her belly and ultrasounded her. Sure enough, there was a little forearm moving.

We got her off the table and set her up in a double cage, puppies squirming next to her. With Lucy distracted, I took a quick blood sample to check her chemistries, especially the electrolytes and kidney function.

A chime alerted me to someone at the front door. When I opened it, Luke lifted me up in the air and kissed me.

"Nice surprise," I told him, the cold seeping through my lightweight scrubs.

"I thought you'd left, but I saw your truck. Let's go inside. You're shivering."

He closed the door and started to ask me a million questions, but I interrupted. "Ob-gyn emergency."

For an almost-lawyer, he caught on quick. "Mari and the puppies?"

"Got it in one."

———

Because of a few amorous stops along the way, it took a little longer than normal to reach the treatment room.

Mari sat with Lucy murmuring good thoughts. "Hey, Luke, welcome to puppyland."

"Let's try a little oxytocin," I told Mari. "If we can't persuade this puppy to hurry up, we're looking at a C-section, which we all want to avoid if at all possible."

"You and me both."

"And Lucy makes three."

"Count me in," Luke added. "No C-section, please."

Every pregnant animal is different. Some pop their babies out, and some deliveries stretch over several hours. I usually told my clients to call if more than two hours went by between puppies.

We were up to three and a half hours.

"Mari, if we need to do a C-section, I'm not letting you assist." This was a judgment call, but I didn't want anyone to assist on the surgery of someone they loved. "I texted Juliet before you got here, and she volunteered to come in and help me. She's a great surgical nurse. Lucy will be in good hands."

Luke made himself useful by brewing some coffee.

The expectant mother lay comfortably on her side, nursing and licking the puppies. The oxytocin didn't seem to have any effect on her. The drug usually stimulates contractions and helps move the babies into the birth canal from the uterine horns where they develop.

Mari looked worried. "I don't want anything to happen to her or the puppy. This is going to be her first and last litter. Most of the puppies are going to family members." She shifted her weight and moved into a lotus position on the floor.

"Take a deep breath, Grandma," I advised. "Massage Lucy's back from neck to tail in a downward stroke. I'm going to clean her up a bit, and then we'll try another dose of oxytocin. Keep the puppies nursing if you can. That ought to help, too."

Calculating her dose by body weight, I drew up the syringe, then took a moment to text Juliet to stand by. We would know soon if a C-section was necessary.

I got down next to Mari, gave her a hug, and administered the injection. We passed the time by checking each puppy's umbilical cord and noting the sex and weight. Luke wrote everything down for us. So far there were three boys and two girls.

"Any guesses? Girl or boy?" Luke said, trying to ease the tension.

"No idea."

Mari appeared calm, but her eyes said worried.

"I say girl."

She looked at me. "Why do you think that?"

"Because, she's already running late."

We both laughed, which was the purpose of my lame sexist joke. All of a sudden, Lucy stood up, puppies cascading off her shiny brown fur. She circled once, turned, and licked herself.

"Scoop the puppies up, Luke, and put them in the basket. I believe we're getting some contractions." As he carefully moved the little ones, some let out tiny squeaks, which made poor Lucy more agitated. When she sat down, she began shredding the newspaper at the bottom of the cage.

All good news. Lucy circled once then back again.

With Mari crooning words of encouragement, the dog whined, and slowly puppy feet appeared, then retreated, only to slide out in one last push. I reached down with my gloved hands and let Lucy lick her baby until it started wiggling and blowing bubbles on its own. To help things along, I cut the cord and cleared the airway. The lungs' ability to transition from a liquid environment to air was always remarkable to me.

"It's a girl," I said, handing the puppy to Mari. "Told you."

"Meet Turner. I'm naming her after you. Merry Christmas."

She passed Turner to me. I looked down at the new beautiful life in my hands.

Lucy curled up with her puppies, periodically licking them, a happy mommy dog expression on her face. Carefully, I positioned our last pup adjacent to a teat just vacated by a sibling, and she latched on immediately.

I looked up at the clock and noticed the time.

Luke came over and put his hand on my shoulder. "Didn't want to bother you, but it's started snowing."

So much for all my plans.

Mari checked her phone. "Weather report says it's snowing now with accumulations of three or four inches but will be clear by the morning. I'm sorry you missed your Christmas Eve dinner with Gramps. What are you going to do?"

Luke sat down next to us. "If it's okay with Dr. Kate here, I've got that covered."

"I bet you do," Mari said.

Mr. Cat looked down with disdain on all of us humans and dogs from his perch on high.

Chapter Forty-Five

Sunrise woke me up. Luke lay sleeping in the bed, hair tousled, curled up like a little kid.

"Merry Christmas," I whispered.

I took my time dressing, surprised at my nervousness. The room felt quiet without Buddy, who'd gone home with Mari, Lucy, and the puppies last night. A little yogurt and a spoonful of oatmeal was all I could manage. A scribbled note to Luke lay on the kitchen table. Throwing an emergency granola bar in my purse, I took a look around, then wheeled my overnight case out to the truck.

Pinky, bless him, had made sure the parking lot was clear and my windshield was clean—except for the Merry Xmas scrawled on the driver's side window with a happy face. Few cars braved the road so early. It didn't take long to get to the New York Thruway entrance at Kingston.

Luke and I had finally had that heart-to-heart talk we both put off for so long. The kind of talk that decides things for good.

He had a long road in front of him between attending school, passing the bar, interning, and joining a law firm. My options were open after my contract with Oak Falls Animal Hospital was up. I'd been putting off planning my future, undecided about almost everything. Did we dare commit to each other, given all the uncertainty in both our lives?

We decided to try.

I stuck to the speed limit and made good time. There weren't many travelers on Christmas Day. The old F-150 truck came equipped with a CD player, so I'd brought along a bunch of my favorites from college days. Many a time I drove back and forth from Gramps's brownstone in Brooklyn to the dorm in Ithaca, singing at the top of my lungs. I realized I never sang like that anymore.

With the familiar first notes sounding, I raised my voice and sang until my body relaxed. The Thruway was a familiar friend, the exits well known. I programmed my father's address into my phone's GPS. Since I was driving in from upstate, and Gramps was coming from Brooklyn, we'd arranged to meet at my dad's place in the Hamptons.

Time flew by, and I deliberately flew along with it until I turned onto the Long Island Expressway. Once there, I ejected my CD and rode in silence, counting down the miles to my exit.

My stomach started churning as I exited at the nearest gas station and called my Gramps.

"Hi, Katie. Are you almost here?" His warm, rough voice always calmed the storms.

"Yes. Probably fifteen minutes away. I'm just filling up the truck."

His voice lowered. "It wasn't as bad as I thought it would be. How are you doing?"

"Fine," I lied. "Love you, Gramps. See you soon."

My battered old F-150 looked out of place parked between the Mercedes and the Lexus, but I didn't care. As I put on the parking brake, my phone began to ding with text messages, as one by one my work family wished me a very Merry Christmas.

A line of dark green shrubs lined the walkway of my father's home.

The polished wooden door was hung with a real wreath that smelled of pine cones and cinnamon sticks. I looked for a doorbell, but all I found was a brass door knocker in the shape of a horse's head. It made a hard rapping sound against the thick oak.

I heard laughing and feet running. The door abruptly swung open, and a familiar face looked up at me.

"Hi. Are you Kate?" asked an eleven-year-old boy.

The timber of his voice, the set of his eyes... I glimpsed tiny hints of my brother Jimmy peeking out at me through this boy...my half brother. Behind him stood a girl with straight blond hair and serious blue eyes.

I looked like my father.

So did she.

They were my family.

The children stared at the stranger on their doorstep.

"Hi. I'm Kate," I said, as they rushed me and tugged at my presents. "But you can call me Katie."

Epilogue

LOBO LOOKED OUT OVER HIS HERD. NOT MADE UP OF his mother and sister and brothers, but his herd, nevertheless. The now familiar mountains rose behind him, blue in the afternoon light. He'd climbed them and run free again through the snowy fields.

And decided to come home.

Acknowledgments

Time passes so quickly. I can hardly believe this is the fifth Kate Turner book. A big thank-you to all my readers for making it possible. I'd like to acknowledge my critique group, the Sheridan Street Irregulars—Betty Webb, Sharon Magee, Art Kerns, Sonja Stone, and Charles Pyeatte—for their invaluable suggestions. I'm grateful to Barbara Peters for her thoughtful edits and insights into the storyline.

My inspiration for this book was meeting a few wild horses from the Salt River Reservation in Arizona who regularly came to visit our mare. We're lucky to have the Salt River Wild Horse Management Group watching out for their welfare.

So many people go into the production of a book. Here's a shout-out to Beth Deveny, Diane DiBiase, Anna Michels, and all my friends at Sourcebooks.

Finally, my husband, Jon, deserves a medal for being supportive and understanding as I walked around the house muttering about murder.

American wild horses represent a vision of freedom as they gallop across the desert, plains, and fields, but their reality is quite different. With their habitats shrinking and their population rising, responsible management is necessary for them to live their lives as Nature planned. Our lives are enriched by their lives. I urge you to support them and other wildlife—from bees to whales—in any way you can, because we are the most tenacious predator of them all.

About the Author

A practicing veterinarian for more than twenty years, Eileen Brady lives in Arizona with her husband, two daughters, and an assortment of furry friends.